the library
IN EAST AYRSHIRE

East Ayrshire
COUNCIL

Please return item by last date shown,
or contact library to renew

The Carpenter's Children

MAGGIE BENNETT

First published in Great Britain in 2009 by
Allison & Busby Limited
13 Charlotte Mews
London W1T 4EJ
www.allisonandbusby.com

A CIP catalogue record for this book is available from
the British Library.

10 9 8 7 6 5 4 3 2 1

13-ISBN 978-0-7490-7989-5

Typeset in 12/16 pt Adobe Garamond Pro by
Allison & Busby Ltd

The paper used for this Allison & Busby publication
has been produced from trees that have been legally sourced
from well-managed and credibly certified forests.

PEFC
PEFC/16-33-111
CATG-PEFC-052
www.pefc.org

Printed and bound in Great Britain by
MPG Books Ltd, Bodmin, Cornwall

Born in Hampshire, MAGGIE BENNETT worked as a nurse and midwife until her retirement in 1991. Having been an avid reader and scribbler since childhood, she first began to approach her writing seriously after her husband's death in 1983. She enjoyed modest success with articles and short stories before the publication of a medical romance in 1992, which won that year's RNA New Writers' Award, and she wrote six more before turning to mainstream fiction in 1996. Maggie has two grown-up daughters and a grandson, and lives in Suffolk.

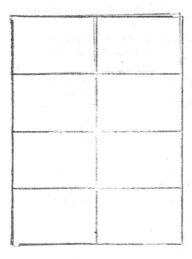

Dedicated to my
dear grandson,
Owen James Hayes.

Chapter One

1904

It was time to get ready for church, and Mrs Munday was bustling around the children, glancing frequently at the clock on the mantelpiece.

'Ernest! Do stop mooning around and do up Grace's buttons for her – and keep still for your brother, Grace. Aren't you wearing your hat with the brown silk bow, Isabel? It matches your frock better than the straw one with the daisies – oh, all right then, as it's a nice sunny morning.'

She called up the stairs to her husband, 'Tom? Don't forget to put a clean white handkerchief in your top pocket.'

Thomas Munday shouted back, 'Yes, Vi – soon as I've got my trousers on!'

'What? D'you mean to say you haven't… Oh, go away with you, Tom, and stop your nonsense,' she scolded as he came downstairs grinning. 'It's bad enough trying to get the children looking decent for church – you're the worst of the lot!' But her voice softened as she spoke, for the couple understood each other well after thirteen years of marriage. Tom knew how much she liked to impress their neighbours in Pretoria Road when the five of them walked to St Peter's on Sunday mornings.

She stabbed a long pin through her wide-brimmed hat, pinning it deftly to the knot of hair on the top of her head and they left the house, a typically happy family picture, or so Violet Munday liked to think they appeared.

St Peter's was the ancient parish church of North Camp, named for a Roman settlement which had once occupied the site on the Hampshire-Surrey border and pre-dated the nearby town of Everham. Once within its thick stone walls, Mrs Munday took note of who else was there. Silver-haired Canon Harrington would be in the vestry preparing to take the service, and there was Lady Neville of Hassett Manor, with her younger son, Cedric, and her unmarried daughter, Miss Neville, sitting in their usual front pew. Sir Arnold Neville and the elder son were in the diplomatic service, currently attached to the Viceroy of India. Looking around, Mrs Munday noted the Birds with their younger son, Ted, the same age as Ernest, and the daughter, Phyllis, one of Isabel's friends. The elder boy, Tim, must have gone out with his cycling club, she thought, but Ted still had to obey his parents. Mr Bird was a tailor, though called himself a gentlemen's outfitter, and was also a churchwarden. Then there were the Lansdownes who owned and ran a dairy with a shop attached; they collected milk from local farmers and distributed it either in bottles or straight from the churn into the customer's jug. Their daughter Rosie was another of Isabel's classmates at Miss Daniells' school. And over there were the Goddards who ran Thomas and Gibson's haberdashery for old Miss Gibson, with their daughter Betty and son Sidney. There was no sign of the Coopers, which was hardly surprising, considering that woman's notoriety as a drunkard, though Mrs Munday told herself not to be uncharitable, but to bask in the satisfaction of being the only family here, apart from the professionals, who were not shopkeepers. Her Thomas was a self-employed carpenter, always in demand for the high quality of his workmanship; he had even been called in by the churchwardens to inspect and advise about the woodworm in one of the choir stalls at St Peter's, with the result that he had been entrusted with removing all the infected wood and replacing it with sound, seasoned oak. That meant of course that he had had to copy the decorative carving of the other choir stalls so that it matched them. Canon Harrington had given him high praise, and said it was impossible to tell the new from the medieval.

That's what distinguishes Tom from any jobbing carpenter, thought his wife, for he had served his seven years' apprenticeship and was a master of his craft; even so, he was still looked upon as a tradesman, socially inferior to the clergy and the doctor. Violet Munday wondered if ten-year-old Ernest would follow his father's craft or go in for something of a more official nature, a junior clerk in a bank or solicitors' office; both would offer him the prospect of eventually passing the relevant examinations to become at least an assistant bank manager or junior partner in a legal firm. He was a quiet, thoughtful boy who needed to put himself forward more, thought his mother fondly; in September he would start as a pupil at Everham Council School, four miles away from North Camp, and five-year-old Grace would begin her schooling at Miss Daniells' Infants attached to St Peter's Church, where Isabel was now in the third form, a pretty girl with her father's blue eyes and straight brown hair hanging in a single plait down her back. It was Violet's dream that Isabel would one day become a teacher; meanwhile she frowned and shook her head at dark-eyed little Grace who was trying to attract her father's attention. Grace would do well at school, her mother was sure of it, and perhaps Miss Daniells would be able to curb that temper of hers; Grace could be very naughty when she failed to get her own way.

Morning worship proceeded and they stood, sat or knelt according to the liturgy. During the third hymn a collection was taken and Canon Harrington, in his white surplice and embroidered stole, climbed with some difficulty into the pulpit. His sermon was largely addressed to the children in the congregation, and Mrs Munday's thoughts were soon interrupted by a tiresome whispering, rustling and fidgeting among those very children, most disrespectful to the good old canon, she thought, although admittedly he was inclined to ramble, and Mrs Munday herself had lost the thread of his discourse. This would not do, she told herself, and straightened her back in the pew with her hands in her lap, to concentrate on the sermon and encourage Isabel and Grace to do likewise. There were some parishioners who argued that it would be better if Sunday School was held concurrently with Morning Worship instead of at the Jubilee Institute on Sunday afternoons, for which Isabel and little Grace would have to get dressed up again after their midday roast dinner, while Ernest would join the boys at the Bible study group held at the home of Mr and Mrs Woodman who were very 'evangelical'.

Thomas Munday glanced at Ernest who, though sitting still, was clearly not listening to the canon. That boy's a dreamer, thought his father, and should have been sent to the council school a year ago; it was high time he left that dame school and walked the four miles each way to Everham. It had been Violet's idea to send the children to Miss Daniells for the first five years because of its convenience and good reputation. Half a crown a week was not unreasonable and Tom Munday thought it ideal for the girls, but Ernest needed the discipline of rubbing along with older children. Tom had tried to teach him the basics of working with wood, but he doubted that the boy would follow the trade of his father and grandfather. Too booky!

He turned his attention to the sermon. Poor old Harrington was becoming as forgetful as he was deaf, and really wasn't fit to continue as priest-in-charge at St Peter's, but he had been the incumbent for as long as anybody in North Camp could remember, while curates had come and gone. Tom Munday had been doing some carpentry at the rectory, making two separate commodes disguised as ornamental cabinets for the canon and Mrs Harrington. She, poor old soul, had lapsed into senility, and in Tom's opinion the old man was going the same way. What on earth was he saying now?

'I'm sure that all you good children know how fortunate you are to be living in Great Britain,' boomed the canon. 'Our country stands at the head of the greatest empire the world has ever known, and our beloved king and queen, anointed by God to rule over it, have every right to expect our complete allegiance.'

Our beloved King Edward thinks more about horse racing and chasing pretty women by what I've heard, thought Tom Munday with a faint grin as he listened.

'And just as we must show loyalty and obedience to those set in authority over us, so must you good children show the same respect to your parents,' went on the canon. 'For example, I'm sure that you always stand up when your father or mother come into a room where you are idly sitting.'

Isabel Munday caught her father's smile. '*We* don't, do we, Daddy?' she whispered, and was immediately shushed by her mother. Even so, a ripple of surprised amusement passed over the congregation, and Tom grinned back at his eight-year-old daughter. How sweet his little girls looked in their wide hats and white pinafores over their Sunday frocks; Grace was already a dark-eyed charmer, and Tom remembered with pride how they'd all gone to St Peter's for a special service on the day of Queen Victoria's funeral three years ago, just as her subjects all over the country had done. Everybody had been expected to wear black, but Grace had been less than two years old, and Violet had settled for pale mauve dresses for both girls. Tom thought they had stood out from the black-clad gloom and bitterly cold weather like a pair of pretty spring crocuses. What a time of national mourning that had been, and it had nearly been followed by another royal funeral, for the new king had almost died of appendicitis and his coronation had had to be postponed for two months.

Canon Harrington was now leaning over the side of the pulpit and shaking a forefinger at the front pews, which included Lady Neville and her son and daughter.

'I call upon you all – all you subjects of our king and emperor, all of you in our overseas dominions and colonies – I call upon you all – call you one and all – all of you, all, all— '

And with this incoherent exhortation, the canon slumped over the side of the pulpit, his face contorted, his eyes staring, mouth gaping.

A gasp rose from the congregation and many rose to their feet.

'A doctor! Is there a doctor here?' called churchwarden Mr Bird. 'Dr Stringer – is he here?'

The local general practitioner came forward hastily, and with the help of some adult choristers lifted the inert, unwieldy body and set it down on the carpeted chancel floor.

Mrs Munday prodded her husband's side. 'You'd better go up and see if there's anything you can do,' she said, thoroughly shaken by the canon's dramatic collapse in front of his parishioners.

'I reckon there's enough o' them up there,' he replied quickly. 'No, you take the children home and I'll follow when they've decided what to do with him. They could use Lady Neville's carriage to take him over to the rectory, it's only across the way.'

'Ought we all to join together in a prayer for the poor canon?' she asked rather helplessly.

'That depends on whether anybody's willing to stand up and lead the rest, and I can't see Bird doing that, can you? Oh look, there's old Woodman, he'll take charge of any praying to be done, but they'd better get the poor old chap out o' the church first. Go on, Violet, take the children home, there's nothing here for them to see.'

Tom Munday rarely gave an order, but when he did, his wife and children invariably obeyed.

The year was passing and it had been a beautiful summer. September came in with continued warm sunshine, and Mrs Munday said it was a continuation of August except for the days getting shorter. Walking to school along country lanes with berried hedgerows on each side and by footpaths through the fields, Ernest Munday thought September's mellow glow quite different from the blaze of high summer. Whatever the season, it was always Ernest's favourite until the next one followed, but this September was different, for it marked a great change in his life. He had reluctantly said goodbye to Miss Daniells and must now make his way to Everham and back each day, to join his class of ten- and eleven-year-old boys and girls. Most of them had come up from Everham Infants, a separate but adjoining building, to the Big School, as it was known, where the minimum leaving age was fourteen, though the headmaster Mr Chisman encouraged the brighter pupils to stay another year if they were not needed to start earning to augment their families' incomes. Here Ernest mixed with a variety of children who lived in and around Everham, villages like North and South Camp and Hassett. Everham boasted two churches, Anglican and Methodist, and a whole high street of shops. It also had a hospital with twenty beds where local general practitioners carried out minor operations and delivered a few babies from mothers who had been sent in with complications. A handful of medical cases, mostly elderly, with failing hearts or inoperable growths, languished in the rest of the beds, though if nothing more could be done for them their relatives were expected to care for them at home, to make room for new admissions.

The stark brick walls of Everham Council School loomed above Ernest as he joined the others going through the boys' entrance and down the corridor to their cloakroom. He had at first expected to walk to school with Tim and Ted Bird, but they had spent only two years at Miss Daniells' before joining the infants' school at Everham. Ted, the younger and the same age as Ernest, was now also a beginner at the Big School, but was one of a group of boys he had already got to know, and Ernest preferred to walk alone than to be constantly teased by Ted's mates. Likewise Sidney Goddard avoided Ernest in case he got ridiculed by association, though Betty Goddard and Isabel were friends, and in another two years would follow their brothers to the council school.

'Hey, look who's here, it's our friend Fuzzy!' shouted a boy, for Ernest's curly hair had earned him the nickname.

'Yeah,' grinned another. 'Ol' clever clogs Munday goes to pray on Sunday – oh, haven't you *met* Miss Daniells' *pet?*'

Ernest ignored the jeers, for to answer back would lead to further confrontation, and to cry would be a disaster; he hung his cap on its hook and went to join the whole school in the assembly hall. Mr Chisman led them in Our Father, then read a few prayers for the school, the nation and the British Empire; they sang a hymn, accompanied on the piano by a lady teacher, and then were dismissed to their various classes where boys and girls studied arithmetic, English grammar, history and geography together in the mornings, and after their packed lunches they separated, the girls to cookery and needlework lessons, the boys to do woodwork, at which Ernest was expected to excel, but regularly failed to do so; then there was what Mr Chisman called 'sport', which meant cricket in the summer and football in the winter, both played on the same uneven field of flattened grass which was inclined to develop potholes in bad weather. Singing, drawing and play-reading, usually an expurgated work of Shakespeare, each had one weekly hour in the timetable, and at four o'clock the bell rang to signal the end of lessons for the day.

Ernest's steps on his homeward journey were more eager than in the morning, and his heart correspondingly lighter at having left Everham Council School behind for sixteen hours.

For he loathed it.

North Camp Church of England Infants' School had been opened in the mid-1880s by Canon Harrington who felt that the younger children of the area should have an alternative to the free education available at Everham Council School. He and interested residents petitioned the bishop and the church commissioners for a school to be attached to St Peter's with the canon as governor; the request was granted, the building was completed, and a suitable lady teacher was installed. It was said that Miss Daniells had been engaged to a young man who'd died of a fever in the West Indies, but this was never confirmed; she was a local farmer's daughter with the responsibility of elderly parents who would need looking after at some future time, and she had set about her duties with single-minded enthusiasm, and over the past decade she had built up a good reputation for 'Miss Daniells' School', as it was generally known by the parents who willingly paid the weekly half-crown.

September brought a new influx of pupils whose fifth birthday fell in the present year, and they included little Grace Munday, trotting in with her sister Isabel, her wide eyes taking in the big room with its raised platform at one end, on which Miss Daniells sat at a wide desk. An upright piano stood at one side of the platform, and a tall cupboard on the other; in the centre of the hall stood a coke-burning stove with a black flue that went up through the ceiling, and a circular fireguard around it.

There were four rows of desks, large or small according to the size of the occupant, with the little ones at the front and the older ones behind them. At the back the nine- to twelve-year-olds sat at two trestle tables, girls at one and boys at the other.

Isabel took her seat halfway back, and Grace stood up in front with two other new ones, a weeping boy and a scared-looking girl; even at five Grace knew the value of contrast, and smiled sweetly at the curious eyes fixed upon her.

'And this little girl is Grace Munday,' announced Miss Daniells, 'the sister of Isabel and their brother Ernest who has now left us for the council school, so we lose one Munday and gain another. Welcome, Grace! You may take a seat in the front row just there.'

Grace marched to her very own desk with satisfaction, soon to be joined on either side by the other two newcomers, somewhat emboldened by her example. Her education was about to begin, and she was eager to show what she could do.

Miss Daniells sat down at the piano to play the opening hymn.

Jesus loves me, this I know,
For the Bible tells me so –
Little ones to Him belong,
They are weak, but He is strong!
Yes, Jesus loves me! Yes, Jesus loves me! Yes, Jesus loves me!
The Bible tells me so!' chorused the children for three more verses. Miss Daniells then said a prayer for all the children at the school, and those who had left; she prayed also for their families, asking that they might always follow Jesus and put their trust in Him at all times.

'And now, Lord, we pray for dear Canon Harrington, founder of our school, laid low by a stroke and unable to rise from his bed. We pray also for his wife Mrs Harrington, that they both may find comfort in knowing that Thou carest for them in their affliction, O Thou who didst heal the sick who came to Thee. And Lord, we ask Thy blessing on the Reverend Mr Saville who has come to care for the parish of St Peter's. Grant unto him wisdom and strength, and always to put his trust in Thee.'

'Amen,' answered the children, and then recited the Lord's Prayer; thus began the day's lessons, with only Miss Daniells to teach them all. She was pleasantly surprised to discover that little Grace Munday knew her alphabet and could string a few three-letter words together, as well as write her own name clearly. As the youngest of three she had been able to learn from her brother and sister, especially Isabel who loved playing at being a teacher, with Grace and two reluctant cats as her pupils.

At playtime Isabel came to her sister's side with a paper packet containing two cheese sandwiches and two apples. She introduced Grace to other third-year girls and to her friend Mary Cooper, a pale girl whose hair hung loose instead of being tied back, and whose pinafore had an egg stain on it. Isabel took out a comb and a length of blue ribbon from her pocket to smooth Mary's hair back into a single plait hanging down her back.

A grinning boy approached them as they sat on a bench seat in the playground.

' 'Allo, you little girls! Wonder 'ow ol' Ernie's gettin' on at the council school, eh? If 'e's tellin' 'em 'ow 'e's been saved by ol' Mr Woodman, they won't 'alf give 'im a thrashin'!'

Isabel stuck her nose in the air and went on talking to Mary, refusing to be drawn; Grace, however, stared hard at the boy.

'I know who *you* are, you're the boy my daddy caught stealing apples from our tree. You're a *thief*, and ought to go to prison!'

The boy stared back at her and was about to deny the charge indignantly, but several children had gathered round and were laughing at the accusation. He knew he would be in trouble if he raised a hand against any girl, let alone this little new one, so he contented himself by sticking out his tongue as far as it would go, and sauntering away, making derogatory remarks about 'them daft Mundays'.

At half past three Miss Daniells ended the day's lessons with another hymn and the Lord's Prayer; she smiled upon them as they trooped out, but then sat down wearily and laid her head upon the desk. More and more she wondered how long she would be able to continue to teach these dear children without any help; at present she knew of no local girl of school-leaving age with the necessary requirements to be an assistant teacher, but trusted that the Lord would send one in His own due time.

A knot of girls stood at the gate of the Mundays' garden, still full of summer flowers. Phyllis Bird and Betty Goddard could hardly part from little Grace who bestowed her winsome smiles on them both, while Isabel stood waiting to go indoors. Then they saw Mary Cooper running up Pretoria Road towards them.

'I can't find my mum anywhere,' she said anxiously. 'And Dad must be out on a job somewhere. Can I come in with you, Isabel, just until Dad comes home? Your mum won't mind, will she?'

This was difficult. Isabel knew that her mother disapproved of the Coopers, for some mysterious reason that was only whispered about. When she hesitated she saw Mary's eyes fill with tears, and she looked at the other two girls. Betty shook her head, but Phyllis rolled her eyes and shrugged.

'You can come home with me, Mary. Just until your mum and dad turn up,' she said. 'Come on, my mother'll be wondering where I've got to!'

Isabel gave her a grateful nod, and led Grace round through the side gate to the back garden; but before they reached the kitchen door, they saw a sight that stopped them in their tracks.

A red-faced woman with loose, untidy hair was groping at

the door of Tom Munday's tool shed, called by his wife the holy of holies, and always kept locked.

'They've shut the door,' muttered the woman, turning round and catching sight of the two girls. She lurched against the tool shed, and put out a hand to steady herself, almost falling over. She gave a loud hiccup.

'Whoops! Sorry, little girls, but your lav's locked up, an' I can't hold it in – I'll have to go here among the cabbages,' she said in a slurred voice that filled Isabel with a nameless revulsion, and to their horror she began to pull her skirt up, fumbling with her petticoat.

'Whoops, can't get me drawers down, an' it won't wait – whoops!' she giggled, squatting down and urinating copiously. 'Tha's better – can't get me drawers down, gotta wet 'em!'

When she'd finished and tried to rise to her feet she toppled over backwards and lay full-length in the cabbage patch, her skirts pulled up and showing her soaked underwear. She closed her eyes and passed into semi-consciousness.

Isabel tugged at her sister's hand. 'Come on, Grace, let's go in and find Mum – quick!'

In through the back door they went, and Isabel called through the house.

'Mum, where are you? Come quickly, Mary's mum's in our back garden!'

Violet Munday came hurrying from the front parlour.

'Heavens above, Isabel, what are you shouting about?'

Grace spoke up excitedly. 'There's a lady been weeing in our garden and it went all over her clothes – and now she's gone to sleep with her head on a cabbage!'

'Good gracious! Merciful heavens!' cried Mrs Munday. 'You stay indoors, you two, and I'll see what's going on.'

When she found Mrs Cooper lying dead-drunk in the cabbage patch, snoring heavily, she gave a horrified exclamation and hurried back indoors, her face pale with shock.

'Go and fetch your father, Isabel, he's working at the rectory. Tell him to come home at once – *at once*, do you hear?'

Off went Isabel, and Mrs Munday told Grace to stop asking questions, while muttering under her breath, 'Of all the...what a disgrace...never seen anything like it...oh, my God!'

When Tom appeared, out of breath and alarmed, his wife told him firmly that he must find Cooper at once, and tell him to remove his drunken wife from their garden.

'She was trying to get into your tool shed, Tom, must've thought it was a lavatory – oh, what a degrading sight for our two little girls to see!'

Tom Munday went out to investigate, and came back looking grave.

'Thank heaven it's nothing worse, Vi, I thought one o' the children had been hurt. Can you give me a hand with her?'

'What? Certainly not, I couldn't touch the creature,' his wife replied with a shudder, leaving Tom to rack his brains as to what he should do without causing a public fuss. Eddie Cooper was a house painter, and Tom had no idea where he was working that day. Could he ask Bird to help him move the woman? No, Bird wouldn't want to leave his shop, and was likely to be shocked, churchwarden or not. Goddard? He could leave his wife in charge of the haberdashery, but she was such a tittle-tattler. Lansdowne? Yes, he'd ask old Bert Lansdowne who'd be finished in the dairy, and could bring his milk cart round.

'Isabel, go and ask Rosie Lansdowne's dad to come round

here, will you? And don't say anything to anybody else, d'you hear me?'

Off went Isabel again, and Mrs Munday locked the front and back doors to keep Grace in the house and to prevent that dreadful creature from reeling round trying to get in.

As soon as Bert Lansdowne heard the message he got out his horse and cart and came round to the Mundays'. When he saw the state of Eddie Cooper's wife, he whistled, nodded and buckled down to the job.

'You take her head an' shoulders, Tom, an' I'll take the bottom half,' he said, and together they lifted her up and carried her through the side gate to the front. 'She's shit an' all,' he remarked. 'Nobody about, come on, let's get the sleeping beauty on to the cart.'

When this was done, Bert asked about Mary Cooper. 'We mustn't let the poor kid see her like this, Tom. Is she with your missus?'

Tom had gathered from Isabel that Mary had gone home with Phyllis Bird.

'Good, we'll tell Mrs Bird to keep her until poor old Eddie can call for her.' Bert glanced at the lifeless form in his cart, and shook his head.

'You hear about drunken husbands, but it's the other way round here, ain't it?'

The two of them got on the cart, took Mrs Cooper home and carried her round to the unlocked back door, where they laid her on the kitchen floor.

'Thanks a lot, Bert. You get on home now, and tell the Birds that Eddie'll call for Mary later. I'll wait for him here,' said Tom, who was in fact quite shaken by the situation, feeling embarrassed on Eddie Cooper's behalf when the man came home and found an almost apologetic Tom Munday waiting for him. Tom heated some water in a large pan while Eddie undressed his wife, washed her and put a clean nightgown on her. Together the two men carried her upstairs and laid her in the matrimonial bed.

Tom then went to fetch Mary from the Birds' home in Rectory Road, telling them there had been a slight accident, nothing to worry about; and when he eventually got home he forestalled his wife's righteous indignation.

'Just let's be thankful we're not in that tragic case, Vi. If I was Eddie I don't know how I'd cope. The poor devil blames himself.'

'Blames *himself*? Why on earth should he think that?' asked Mrs Munday, none too pleased by the suggestion that Tom could be Eddie, which was like comparing herself with Eddie's wife.

'Yes, he blames himself, though it was more the fault o' that fool of a doctor when she had Mary,' said Tom, deeply saddened by what Eddie had told him. 'You remember how she had a very bad time, and was in bed for weeks afterwards, couldn't feed the baby and her mother had to come over to look after them – it was a rotten time, after looking forward to the baby.'

'Yes, I remember, but she got over it, didn't she? She's not the only woman to have a bad time birthing, and at least she didn't lose her life, like that poor girl over at Hassett last year,' replied Violet. 'And when I had Ernest, you may recall that—'

'But you got over it, an' had two more children, an' she couldn't have any more, that's why there's only Mary. Eddie says she went into a melancholy state, couldn't do anything at all, so Eddie called that doctor back to her. He advised her to take a glass of brandy each night, to make her sleep and cheer her up. So Eddie did what he said, an' it got to be a habit. She couldn't break out of it, no matter how hard she tried. He says she does her best to keep it under control, but sometimes it gets the better of her, an' she takes to the bottle again. Sleeps it off indoors, mostly, but today was bad.' Tom shook his head and repeated, 'Yeah, today was pretty bad.'

'Well, you've certainly done everything a friend and neighbour could do,' said Mrs Munday.

'Yeah – but he could've done with a bit o' help from a woman, Vi. It was pretty embarrassing, to say the least, 'cause *I* couldn't very well help him clean the poor woman up.'

There was a short silence, then Mrs Munday said in a somewhat subdued tone, 'Well, if ever Mary needs somewhere to go, I'd be willing to have her round here.'

'That's good o' you, Vi,' he replied gravely. 'None of us know when we might be in need of a friend – and that woman needs a friend now, if anybody does.'

Violet did not attempt to answer, feeling herself rebuked.

Up in the bedroom shared by the girls, Isabel was becoming irritated by Grace's persistent questions about the strange and very rude lady in their garden. Why was she trying to get into Daddy's shed? And why did she wee in the cabbage patch? And why was Mummy so angry about her?

'Oh, go to sleep, Grace, I'm tired,' snapped Isabel. Their mother had told them not to talk about what had happened, and to forget all about it. Yet Isabel sensed that she would never forget the sight of Mary Cooper's mother who, Isabel now realised, had been drunk – which was something that only happened with men, or so Isabel had thought until now. Something of her mother's shock and disgust had been passed on to her, and she knew that she would be haunted by Mary's mother, like a grotesque picture in her memory that would never quite go away. And what she would remember above all was the lost, bewildered look in the woman's eyes.

On returning from school Ernest at once realised that something bad had happened, something that the girls had been ordered not to talk about. If he knew his little sister Grace, she would find an opportunity to whisper it to him sooner or later, whether he wanted to know it or not. There were many other matters on Ernest's mind, and lying in his bed that night he recalled the unthinking cruelty of his classmates, and how he was learning to endure their sometimes obscene taunts by keeping quiet; he was getting better at meeting ridicule with a bland silence that hid his inward distaste.

But not on Sunday afternoons. Ah, not at Mr Woodman's Bible study group for boys. Though one of its youngest members, Ernest's opinion was often invited, and he could freely share his thoughts on the matters under discussion: the dictates of conscience and the path of duty; God's judgement, and also His mercy, His constant love and forgiveness – all the things Ernest had to keep to himself at school. He was especially devoted to Paul Woodman, the elder son, aged about eighteen and intending to train for ordination. Paul's conversation was precious to Ernest, for he could tell him almost anything without being made to look foolish; the jeers and taunts of the boys at Everham Council School were mere pinpricks when placed against the thoughtful, courteous words of Paul Woodman.

With his mentor's face in mind, Ernest smiled and drifted peacefully to sleep.

Chapter Two

1911

'Old Mr Cox hasn't been in for his money today, Miss Munday. Have you seen him at all?'

'No, Mr Teasdale, nor his daughter,' answered Isabel, looking up briefly from counting stamps.

'And he wasn't in with the others yesterday, though he's usually outside waiting for me to open up on pension days!'

And the other old people aren't far behind, thought Isabel, for the ten shilling weekly pension introduced two years ago was an enormous help to the elderly and their relatives. She closed the folder of unsold stamps. 'Shall I make a cup of tea, Mr Teasdale? It's nearly four o'clock.'

'That would be very nice, Miss Munday, thank you.' He shot her a look of fatherly concern. 'You're rather pale today, if I may say so, Miss Munday. Are you not feeling so well?'

'Yes…I mean no, I'm quite well, thank you, Mr Teasdale,' she answered, not quite truthfully, for she had developed a cramp-like pain at the bottom of her tummy – her mother disliked the word belly – and felt slightly sick. A cup of tea might do her good, she thought, and set about putting the kettle on to boil in the little kitchenette behind the office. The door pinged as a lady customer came in, and Mr Teasdale put on his usual polite smile to attend to her.

While she waited for the tea to brew, Isabel sat down on the hard wooden chair, feeling peculiar in a way she could not understand. She wished she was at home; Mr Teasdale was a pleasant enough man who always addressed her properly as Miss Munday, but he was still a man, and Isabel felt the need for a woman's reassurance. As she sat there, she was suddenly and alarmingly aware that something was happening: she was leaking! She jumped to her feet and hurried out to the lavatory which, like the Mundays' own, had to be entered from outside. Something felt wet and warm between her legs, and she pulled up her long skirt and petticoat; when she took down her drawers, she nearly fainted with shock at seeing the blood on them, and…oh, heavens, it had leaked through to her skirt while she'd sat on the chair. In utter dismay she realised that this must be the start of her *periods*, which her mother had never mentioned to her, but Betty Goddard and Phyllis Bird had whispered about their own experiences, so Isabel was not entirely unprepared for this first visitation. Whatever was she to do? She must go home at once, but how to explain to Mr Teasdale?

Pulling up her soiled clothes with trembling hands, she smoothed down her skirt and returned to the post office.

'Mr Teasdale, I'm sorry, but—' she began, thankful at least that there were no customers in at present.

'Why, Miss Munday, whatever is the matter?'

'I shall have to go home straight away, Mr Teasdale. I-I…' And poor Isabel burst into tears in her shame and humiliation; she dared not turn round because of the stain on the back of her skirt.

This put the postmaster in a dilemma. He felt fairly sure of the reason for his young assistant's distress, and that this was an emergency. The only thing he could do was to take her home at once, but he could not leave the post office unattended, and there was no available female he could call upon to escort Miss Munday. He had a telephone, but nobody else in the village had one apart from the doctor and the vicar.

Isabel had left Everham Council School at Easter. Miss Daniells looked forward to having her as a pupil teacher, but not until she was fifteen. It was Mrs Munday who had obtained the place for her as post office assistant, though Mrs Goddard had offered her work in the haberdashery.

'I'm not having a daughter of mine working as a shop girl, ordered around by the likes of Mrs Goddard!' Violet Munday had declared. 'Nor is she going into domestic service.' The post office was a good compromise, though Mrs Munday could have wished that there had been a postmistress instead of Mr Teasdale.

'Still, he's a respectable married man, and won't stand for any nonsense from customers,' she told her husband, 'and she'll learn how to deal with people and improve her arithmetic.'

In fact Isabel had found life behind the post office counter far less interesting than school. Only the postmaster could deal with the business side, sorting out the letters that arrived on the early train with the newspapers, to be distributed over a wide rural area by the postman and newsboy. On certain days there were magazines and comics to be displayed, and boiled sweets and liquorice sticks were sold from large glass jars. Isabel was entrusted with these sales, though as the place was primarily a post office she was counted as an assistant rather than a salesgirl.

But now Mr Teasdale was in a quandary, with no prospect of assistance. Unless...

The door pinged, and Mrs Cooper came in, wearing her habitual anxious expression. She looked from Mr Teasdale to his tearful assistant, and having noted that she was sober, he turned to her for help in his predicament.

'Mrs Cooper, may I ask you a favour on behalf of my...of Miss Munday? She's...er...not feeling well, and needs to be taken home to her mother. Will you...could you possibly go with her, Mrs Cooper? She really needs a woman's help,' he finished lamely, spreading out his hands in a helpless gesture.

Mrs Cooper stared at them both with her washed-out blue eyes, and something like a smile softened her worried face.

''Course I will, Mr Teasdale, if she don't mind. D'you want me to come home with you, Isabel dear?'

'Yes, please, Mrs Cooper,' sniffed Isabel, wondering how she could hide the stain on her skirt. 'I'll get my hat and gloves. I'm sorry, Mr Teasdale.'

'That's quite all right, Miss Munday. Don't come in tomorrow if you don't feel up to it. Thank you so much, Mrs Cooper,' he added to the lady who had not even been served.

Outside in the street, Isabel sobbed out her trouble. Mrs Cooper listened sympathetically.

'And I think the back of my skirt is—'

Mrs Cooper discreetly looked, and took off her own long black jacket. 'Here, dear, put this round you, so's people won't see. It's all right, I'm warm enough without it, it's a nice May day.'

Isabel accepted gratefully, but when they arrived at number 47 Pretoria Road, Mrs Cooper said she would not come in. Isabel took off the jacket and handed it back. All of which was observed from the parlour window, and Mrs Munday then appeared at the front door like an avenging angel.

'Isabel, come in at once! *At once,* do you hear me?'

Isabel obeyed, and Mrs Cooper went on her way, glad to know that she had been of some use for once, and little Isabel Munday had been so grateful, even though her mother had ordered her indoors with unspoken disapproval. Where could she go now? Back to the post office for the stamps Eddie wanted for his invoices? Yes, that's what she would do; she didn't want to go back to an empty house, now that Mary was working for Mrs Yeomans at the farm, and didn't get home until six or later, and Eddie never knew how long a job was going to take, so might be early or late. Joy Cooper dreaded being alone in the house, fighting off the craving that gripped her like a physical ache, making her groan out loud and long for some distraction – anything to keep her from going to her secret hoard in the loft, the hoard which Eddie didn't know about; he would have had a fit to see her climbing the loft ladder. Just to know that it was *there* helped her through the day, but sometimes the urge to take a tot of brandy was uncontrollable, and she'd promise herself that it would only be one little tot. *No!* She dared not go home, but retraced her steps to the post office.

'Most kind of you, Mrs Cooper. I'm sure Miss Munday's mother appreciated your care for her daughter,' smiled Mr Teasdale. 'Now, what was it you came in for?'

Having purchased the stamps, Joy Cooper forced a smile, and engaged the postmaster in conversation – anything to delay going home to an empty house and the temptation in the loft. Mr Teasdale was always happy to exchange a word or two with his customers when not under the pressure of work, as on pension mornings. The thought led him to mention Mr Cox's absence this week.

'Oh, I see – and you're wondering if he's all right, Mr Teasdale? Hasn't his daughter been in?'

He shook his head. 'Not a sign of either of them, Mrs Cooper.'

'Would you like me to call on him to see if anything's the matter?' she asked, grasping at anything that would take up a bit more of her time.

'Why, yes, if you'd be so good, Mrs Cooper, and I'm sure he'd be glad to see you,' said the postmaster, who had been wondering if he should check on Mr Cox. 'I expect there's some perfectly good reason for him staying away.'

'Very well, Mr Teasdale, I'll go round there and let you know if there's any sort of trouble,' she promised.

But by the following morning all of North Camp knew that old Mr Cox had suffered a stroke, and had lain on his kitchen floor all day. His daughter Mrs Blake found him at five o'clock, having spent the day shopping in Everham with her sister. When Joy Cooper arrived she found that the old man had regained consciousness, but was unable to speak or use his right arm and leg. Mrs Blake was hysterically accusing herself of not having checked on her father that morning, and Mrs Cooper calmed her as well as she could, saying that she would go at once to Dr Stringer. Mr Cox was taken to Everham Hospital where after three weeks he had recovered sufficiently to be allowed home under the care of Mrs Blake, helped by the district nurse and Mrs Cooper who promised to look in on him every day, privately thanking God that Mr Cox's misfortune had turned out to be her salvation.

'How *very* unfortunate that this should come on while you were at the post office!' exclaimed Mrs Munday in a tone of mixed annoyance and self-reproach. '*So* embarrassing for you, dear, with only Mr Teasdale there. I'm very sorry that it's happened this way.'

She had made Isabel strip off her clothes and put on a wool dressing gown. The stained garments were soaking in a pail of cold water, and a white-faced Isabel sat with a folded linen square between her legs, secured by safety pins to a narrow cotton belt; so now she knew what wearing a diaper felt like.

'But it was lucky that Mrs Cooper was there to bring me home and lend me her long jacket, Mum,' she pointed out. 'I don't know how I'd have got home else, with that awful bloodstain at the back.'

'Yes, well, it was unfortunate,' repeated her mother with a frown. 'And...er...I suppose you knew where the blood came from...comes from, Isabel? You do understand that this is your first monthly period, and it means that your body is ready – it means you're a woman now,' she added awkwardly, annoyed with herself for blushing.

'Yes, Mrs Cooper told me that on the way home, and said that when it comes again next month I'll be prepared for it, with a diaper and safety pins.'

'I'm sure there was no need at all for Mrs Cooper to talk to you in such a way, Isabel – that's *my* duty, not hers, and of course I'll see that you're prepared for it next time,' said Mrs Munday, ignoring the fact that Isabel had been entirely unprepared. 'I didn't think you'd start so soon. I...er...I suppose other girls at school talk about it sometimes, don't they?'

'Yes, Betty Goddard and Phyllis Bird have already started, and they're more or less the same age as me,' replied Isabel. 'Betty's mum told her about it before, and made sure she had a…a diaper with her for when it started.'

'Yes, well, we won't go into details, it's not a very nice subject to talk about, and in any case I think it's up to your teachers to warn you girls about it – I mean the lady teachers of course,' said Mrs Munday, not noticing the inconsistency of this assertion. 'Now then, dear, you're going to rest on your bed, and I'll bring you a nice cup of tea. You look a bit pale.'

Violet Munday felt thoroughly put out, and tried to justify herself in her own mind. After all, *her* mother had never told her anything, and she'd learnt from two older sisters about their various bodily changes. And she didn't blame her mother because – well, she'd found out how difficult it was to talk about periods and things, it was too personal, and she'd never shared her memories of her own courtship with her daughters. After all, it was nothing to do with them.

And yet… Violet's eyes softened as she turned back the years to that long-ago summer at Hassett Manor, where she had been an eighteen-year-old housemaid and Tom, a year younger, was starting his seven-year apprenticeship with his own father, old Fred Munday, who still did jobbing carpentry and gardening in Hassett, carrying his worn toolbag from place to place. She remembered how Tom had come into the kitchen and asked for a drink of water for his father and himself – and the cook had nodded in the direction of the new maid. Tom later told her that he never forgot his first sight of the rosy-cheeked girl with curly hair and dark eyes that had smiled shyly into his – which was why he'd gone back again and again to ask for more water; it was a very hot day, and he and his dad were thirsty, he'd told her. That had been back in 1884, and the attraction had been mutual. Seven years later, when Tom's apprenticeship was done, he had saved enough, with his father's help, to put down payment on a tiny cottage for himself and his new wife Violet Terry. In those days young couples had expected to wait until they could afford to set up house – although Violet did not let her memory dwell too long on certain moments in those seven long years when she had walked out with her young man in the woods around Hassett Manor, and their longing for fulfilment had sometimes been almost unbearable. She remembered how he had slipped his hand inside her blouse and felt her nipples, sending a thrill like lightning throughout her whole body, and she had become aware of the hardness through his trousers, and heard his sharp intake of breath – and their kisses! It was just as well that she'd had to be in by nine o'clock on her one free half-day each week. But it was all a long time ago, and was a secret never to be spoken of, just as her present lawful union with Tom Munday was a very private matter, and nothing to do with her daughters.

She wondered about Ernest; had Tom said anything to him about growing up? For seven months now they had worked together as master and apprentice, and she supposed that Tom must have had some sort of man-to-man talk with his son when a suitable opportunity arose.

Ernest was wondering how much longer he could go on pretending that he wanted to follow his father's trade as a carpenter and joiner, whether self-employed like Tom or with a builder's firm such as Harry Hutchinson's, who employed a bricklayer, carpenter, plasterer and painter, and towed his sacks of sand and cement on a trailer attached to his Ford Model T, the wonder of North Camp. Tom Munday had advised his son to choose the latter course, because he was clearly never going to be up to his father's standard of craftsmanship, and the boy felt this; he suspected that Dad did not even like to see his precious tools being used, or rather misused in Ernest's uncertain hands. Tom Munday's toolbag was his trademark, and he carried it with pride; it was cut from leather instead of the usual strong calico, and when opened it was in the form of a circle with pockets for the various kinds and sizes of tools, the hammers and chisels, bradawls and screwdrivers. It folded in half and was tied with sturdy tapes, with leather carrying handles. Larger tools like planes were kept in a separate bag, as were the saws, their teeth protected by narrow wooden shields into which the blades slotted; everything was cleaned and polished to shining perfection. The tool shed was Tom's own creation, built from elm, its roof sealed with pitch and its window kept as sparkling as those of the house. Shelves lined the walls, holding tins of paint, creosote and varnish; brushes were graded according to size, and cleaned with white spirit. There were small wooden boxes with a variety of nails and screws, and a locked cupboard where he kept his paperwork, the invoices and receipts; here too were his carpenter's pencils, rulers, tape measures, set squares and compasses. Nobody was allowed in the tool shed, which was kept locked; Mrs Munday called it the holy of holies, and Ernest never felt comfortable in it. He dreamt of books and of writing poetry – which he did, secretly in his room, and sometimes in his head while working, to the detriment of his concentration.

'Ernest! What the devil are you dreaming about now?' his father would ask with increasing exasperation as the months went by and Ernest seemed as slow to learn as when he'd begun. Worst of all, he showed no pleasure in woodwork, no keenness to improve.

Violet Munday sensed the lack of camaraderie that ought to

exist between father and son, and renewed her suggestion that Ernest should be sent to the commercial college at Guildford to learn basic office skills that would stand him in good stead as a junior clerk with a legal firm or bank. At first Tom had disagreed with her, but now that Ernest was almost eighteen and was clearly never going to be a practical man, he began to wonder if she was right. What he dreaded most was to hear his son spoken of disparagingly, as not being up to his dad's standard, not a chip off the old block; Tom thought he would feel the shame of it perhaps more than his son. But commercial college would have to be paid for, and the boy would need to get lodgings in Guildford, a good fifteen miles away, and there was as yet no regular railway service from North Camp. Ernest would have to cycle to Everham Station to board the Guildford train, and Tom pointed this out to Violet who disliked the idea of her boy living in lodgings.

She frowned. 'He's very young, Tom.'

'Good heavens, there are boys of eleven or twelve working in mills up north where every penny counts for families living in poverty, they've got no choice. What that boy needs is to start fending for himself and learning a bit of independence.'

And to get away from your mollycoddling, he added to himself. Much as he loved his only son, he occasionally felt like giving him a boot up the backside, and it would be good for him to get out from under the too comfortable parental roof.

And so it was decided. Mrs Munday made an appointment for Ernest to attend an interview with the superintendent of the college, and she accompanied him. They learnt that Ernest would be enrolled as a student for a one-year course in business studies, commencing in September. He would become proficient at typing and Pitman's shorthand, bookkeeping and accountancy, together with basic French and German. It was pointed out that male students were outnumbered three to one by their female counterparts, but the numbers evened out in the more advanced subjects. Mrs Munday had no criticism to make about this, and her husband thought it a definite advantage, for Ernest was not a good mixer; Tom had become aware of the opposite sex at an earlier age than Ernest, and a year later had set his eyes on pretty Violet Terry; it was high time for Ernest to wake up and start to use his eyes and ears.

The college bursar, having taken the enrolment fee, recommended a Mrs Green who took student lodgers, and on leaving the college they went to call on her.

'She seems a clean, respectable sort of woman,' Mrs Munday reported to Tom. 'She only takes young gentlemen, and I made arrangements with her for Ernest to take up residence when the new term begins. I told her he'd be coming home at weekends.'

'Mm. Do him a world o' good to stay in Guildford, Vi.'

'There's something I'd like to mention, Tom,' she went on, sitting at her dressing table, brushing her long hair. 'Have you had a word with Ernest, I mean about…well, the things he ought to know about growing up? Isabel had rather a shock when her first, er, period came on, and I don't want that to happen with Grace – well, she'll find out from Isabel, of course, with them sharing the same room. But what about Ernest? Have you spoken to him at all?'

'Mm. Boys don't have periods, do they?' he said with a flicker of amusement that irritated her.

'Don't be tiresome, Tom. You know perfectly well what I mean. Ernest is old enough to…er—'

'To clap his eyes on a pretty girl, you mean, like I did, remember?' He grinned as he pulled back the eiderdown for her to get in beside him.

'No, I'm quite serious, Tom. It's your *duty* to speak to your son, and warn him about the...the ways of the world, especially if he's going into lodgings, the temptations that await him, like—'

'Like meeting a saucy little minx with bold black eyes and a come-hither look?'

'Oh, you're impossible! No, take your hand away. Will you just answer my question, Tom Munday, whether you've had a talk with Ernest or not?'

'Violet, my love, I did try when he was in his last year at school, but we didn't get very far. He went as red as a beetroot, and said he'd never joined any of the other boys when they, er, played around.' It was Tom's turn to feel awkward.

'Played around? What, like football or something?'

'No, Vi, I'm sorry to say that some boys have a habit of playing with themselves – and each other – in the school lavs, you know, erecting their cocks for the...just to be rude. I'm sorry, but that's what some o' them get up to on the quiet, and Ernest said he'd never had anything to do with such, er, immature fellows. And that was as far as I got, I'm afraid.'

After an initial gasp of disbelief, his wife was too shocked to answer, and to Tom's relief she plumped her two pillows, turned over and went to sleep.

But poor Mrs Munday was in for another and worse shock. The following day she took Grace aside in the front parlour, intending to have a private talk. Her youngest child was now a high-spirited eleven-year-old who loved looking in the mirror at her pretty little face.

'Sit down, dear, and listen to me carefully. I expect you've noticed that Isabel has started her periods – that's something that happens to all girls when they become women. Do you know what I mean, Grace?'

'Oh, Mum, I knew all about *those* before Isabel started hers,' answered naughty Grace in a matter-of-fact tone. 'It shows she's ready to have a baby.'

'Oh, my goodness, not yet!' exclaimed her mother, taken aback by her younger daughter's knowledge. 'We'll talk about babies later, when you're older. We'll just talk about periods this morning, and what happens when the, er, flow of blood occurs.'

'But Mum, we all know that it's when the womb gets ready to catch an egg on its way down, and if it doesn't grow into a baby, it comes out with the blood, and that's a period,' said Grace with deliberate casualness, knowing that her mother would be horrified. 'And some o' the big girls told us what makes an egg grow into a baby,' she added slyly, with a sideways look at her mother to see how this was received.

Violet Munday's jaw had literally dropped. 'Who told you this? Tell me at once!' she ordered.

'Oh, Mum, the big girls talk about it all the time, and we *all* know how it's done!' protested Grace, rather alarmed at her mother's reaction, for Mrs Munday had turned quite white as she continued her questioning.

'But which of them told *you*, Grace, things you're not nearly ready to know yet. Who was it told you?'

'There was a crowd o' them stood at the back o' the girls' cloakrooms, and we could hear what they were saying,' replied Grace, beginning to wish that she had not spoken so boldly.

'Which girl in particular did you hear it from? I insist upon knowing, and won't let you leave this room until you tell me!'

Now Grace had no wish to get any of her fellow pupils in the first year at Everham Council School into trouble, so she hit on the idea of naming the girls in Isabel's year, those who had left the school now and were working.

'Well, there was, er...' Grace thought of making up a name, but was awed by the fury in her mother's eyes. If she said Betty Goddard or Phyllis Bird or Rosie Lansdowne, Mrs Munday would go straight to their mothers. She thought quickly. 'Well, there was, er, let me see, there was Mary Cooper, I *think*, yes, I think she might've been one o' them,' she said. Nobody went to the Coopers' home, and people only asked Mary round to visit them because they were sorry for her.

'*Mary Cooper*? The girl I've tried to befriend and asked to tea, and made an effort to treat her the same as any girl from a respectable home? And is this the thanks I get, filthy talk that no young girl should hear? Wait till I see her parents, I'll give them a piece of my mind!'

'Oh, *please*, Mum, don't get her into trouble!' begged Grace, now very much regretting that she had mentioned Mary's name. 'She wasn't the only one – oh, *please*, Mummy, I don't think it was her, it was another girl, some girl whose name I've forgotten!' She said *Mummy* to make herself sound younger, the little girl who had usually been able to get her own way with either parent.

But Violet Munday had heard enough, and dismissed Grace to her piano practice. Not even hearing about the goings-on of adolescent boys had shocked and upset her as much as this; she could hardly bring herself to tell Tom what she had heard from their little Grace – and when she did, he was not as angry as she thought he ought to be.

'Stands to reason, girls talk between themselves about that sort o' thing, Vi. Boys may mess about with themselves, but girls are more for talking. It just shows it's best to start early, telling them the truth.'

This failed to impress Mrs Munday who made it her business to speak to mothers of girls who had been in Mary's year, to warn them about her, even though these girls had now left school. Bert Lansdowne and his wife thought it a big fuss over nothing much, and continued to be friendly towards Mary, now in service to Mrs Yeomans at Yeomans' farm. And Isabel surprised her parents by standing up stoutly for her old school friend.

'It's not her fault that her mother drinks, and anyway, look how kind Mrs Cooper was to me when I had to come home from the post office—' She stopped speaking at the recollection of that shameful episode, and Tom Munday nodded.

'That's right, my girl, the day old Cox had a stroke in his kitchen, and Mrs Cooper went for Dr Stringer. That was two good deeds in one day, poor woman.'

'Poor Eddie, that's what *I* say,' sniffed Mrs Munday, 'and I won't have that girl round here again.'

'There's no need to, now that she works for Mrs Yeomans all day,' muttered Isabel; the friends had inevitably drifted apart now that their schooldays were over.

As for Grace, she had learnt her lesson, and kept quiet at home, though at school she continued to instruct her awestruck classmates in the mysteries of human reproduction.

On the twenty-second of June there was great excitement and rejoicing all over the country when the new King George V was crowned in Westminster Abbey with his beautiful Queen

Mary at his side. Special services were held in thousands of churches, and towns and villages were bedecked in flags and bunting to celebrate the momentous event. Many years ago the Princess May, as the Queen had formerly been known, had been engaged to George's elder brother Albert, the Duke of Clarence who had suddenly and tragically died quite young, so George, being the next in line to the throne, had inherited both the crown and the princess; but this was ancient history, and the royal pair, now in their forties and married for seventeen years, had raised a family of five sons and a daughter. Their photographs showed them as regal and upright, a picture of devotion and domestic harmony.

'They're a proper example of what family life should be,' said Mrs Munday approvingly, and the rest of the country must have thought the same, judging by the crowds who stood outside the abbey while the three-hour coronation ceremony was taking place, and who cheered the king and queen as they progressed along the route in the state carriage, as handsome as their portraits.

At St Peter's a special thanksgiving service was held at the same time as the coronation, followed by a picnic organised by the vicar's wife Mrs Saville, held on the vicarage lawn. Lady Neville drove over from Hassett Hall with Miss Neville, a pale, thin young woman who was seldom seen in public, and gave an opening speech in which she reminded her hearers of the honour they shared as subjects of Great Britain, presiding over a worldwide empire, in which her husband Sir Arnold and their son played their role, assisting the Viceroy of India in his duties as the king's representative.

'Our king and queen will lead us forward into a time of even greater prosperity,' she said, and Tom Munday silently nodded;

he and Eddie Cooper had attended a meeting in Everham Town Hall where their Member of Parliament had given a public lecture on the tremendous industrial advances made in the previous century, and how the social ill effects of that upheaval were now passing, while the advantages of mass production were becoming enjoyed by all, to the advantage of nation and Empire. Lady Neville seemed to be entirely in agreement, and her speech was greeted with enthusiastic applause.

Practically all of North Camp came to the picnic, and families took their places on the grass or at trestle tables, to be waited on by Mrs Saville's team of helpers, recruited from the Mothers' Union. Older children sat at a separate long table, with the new curate, Mr Storey, in charge, assisted by young ladies who had willingly volunteered their services. These included Isabel, looking a picture in her summery dress and wide-brimmed straw hat, her glossy red-brown hair pinned up beneath it, with a few tendrils escaping at the nape of her neck.

'She's a proper little lady,' thought Tom Munday, suddenly surprised at how much older she looked. Mr Storey, suitably attired in clerical black, gave her a briefly admiring smile as he handed her a tray of egg sandwiches to pass down the table. Isabel thought him very handsome, and wondered what it would be like to be a clergyman's wife. Now that she had become a woman, her thoughts sometimes strayed to marriage and having babies; life in a vicarage must be ideally happy! She caught Mr Storey's eye again over the laden table, and blushed furiously at the thought that sprung unbidden to her mind; she quickly lowered her eyes and turned away, little realising that Mark Storey had noted pretty Miss Munday from the post office. He thought how refreshingly shy and modest she was, compared to some of the young ladies who eyed him boldly and the ministry, though he had changed his allegiance from the Church of England to the Methodist form of worship. His parents, taken aback at first, had soon followed suit, which meant that they now had to walk all the way to South Camp each Sunday to attend the rather nondescript building with its corrugated iron roof, where the preacher weekly exhorted his largely impoverished flock of menial workers to turn away from sin and be saved, celebrating their conversion with hearty, ecstatic hymnsinging which gave rise to some local complaints about the noise.

The evangelical tone of the Bible study group remained much the same as it had always been, and Ernest, now one of the older members, was sometimes asked by Mr Woodman to lead the younger boys in prayer. He also found himself thoroughly enjoying the Saturday explorations of the all-male cycling club, pedalling out to Guildford and the Hog's Back, and to Hindhead and the Devil's Punch Bowl. The sun and the wind on his face were exhilarating, as was the sheer physical exertion when they had to pedal uphill, and Ernest would overtake half of his puffing companions, some of whom had been scornful classmates at Everham Council School.

'Are you looking forward to leaving home and going to that commercial college, Ernest?' Isabel asked him one evening towards the end of August.

'I think I am,' he replied with a smile. 'It'll be good to know that I'm training to do the sort of work I know I could do well.'

'You mean like being manager of some big firm?'

'Perhaps one day,' he said, though he privately saw himself as a chief librarian who also wrote and published poetry.

'But you'd have to start off as a junior in some poky little office, wouldn't you?' Grace chimed in, having heard

whispered to each other behind their hands, which he foun
most disconcerting. He wondered how long he could expec
to remain curate at St Peter's; since Canon Harrington's death,
the Rev. Mr Saville had become vicar, and had been given the
newly ordained Mark Storey as his assistant, a young unmarried
man who occupied a room in the vicarage and joined the family
for meals. It was an exciting life in the Lord's service, as Mark
saw it, and he hoped he would not be moved to another parish
for at least the next two years.

'What d'you think of Mr Storey, Isabel?' whispered Grace,
having noticed the glance that had passed between the curate
and her sister.

'Nothing at all,' replied Isabel, frowning at Grace's saucy
manner.

'He's very handsome, isn't he?' observed Grace unabashed,
but Isabel turned away to pour out cups of tea, wincing in
case Mr Storey might have overheard Grace's nonsense; what a
disaster it would be!

And yet... She had noticed Phyllis Bird smiling at Ernest
when he and Ted Bird set out with the Everham Cycling Club;
Ernest of all people, her brother! The two lads pedalled off with
the club every Saturday, but Mrs Munday would not allow her
son to join them on Sundays.

'If the Birds are willing to let their sons desert their
church, that's up to them, though I'm surprised at Mr Bird, a
churchwarden,' she declared. 'But of course, my Ernest wouldn't
want to miss going to church with his family.'

And it seemed she was right, for Ernest continued to attend
St Peter's without protest, and he also remained a member of
Mr Woodman's Bible study group on Sunday afternoons. Paul
Woodman was now at Bristol in his final year of training for

their parents discussing his future prospects.

'I'll be quite happy to work my way up!'

'D'you think you'll miss us *lots?*' persisted Grace.

'Yes, but I'll be home at weekends, so Saturdays and Sundays will be the same as now,' he answered, smiling, and Isabel wondered if he was thinking about Phyllis Bird.

'I want to get away from North Camp just as soon as I'm old enough,' said Grace with a pout. 'It's a *boring* place, and nothing ever happens unless you count church fêtes and picnics.' She wrinkled her nose at the mention of these tame entertainments. 'Everything's always the same here from one week's end to another.'

But in this she was mistaken. Two days later old Mr Cox died in his sleep, leaving Mrs Cooper with nobody to call on and care for every day. She enquired in vain for some useful work, looking after some other old person or housebound invalid, anything to get her out of the empty house during the day, and keep her mind off the temptation up in the loft. She even offered her services free of charge.

'That's where she's making a mistake,' said the North Camp gossips. 'People don't appreciate anything they don't have to pay for, and with *her* reputation...' Heads were shaken and knowing looks exchanged.

Until they were shocked into silence. For in the end Joy Cooper could not hold out against her enemy, and one afternoon she climbed the rickety ladder up into the loft, grabbing at the brandy bottle and drinking straight out of it. Within the next hour she had got on a bus to Everham which put her down at the railway station. She bought a platform ticket and waited for the express train for Southampton, due to come hurtling through before three o'clock; the brandy helped her to perform her last desperate act, and she threw herself in front of it.

At the coroner's inquest the train driver said that he'd had to make an instant decision whether to brake the train at full speed, putting at risk the passengers in the carriages behind him, or go straight ahead and then slow to a stop, having run over the woman on the line. The coroner agreed that he had been wise to choose the latter course.

The head shaking turned to gasps of horror on hearing the dreadful news, and Mrs Munday was not the only one to shed tears; in fact more of Joy Cooper's neighbours turned out to mourn at her funeral than had ever shown her friendship in life. Eddie Cooper and Mary stood beside the grave while Mr Saville read the Burial Service from the prayer book, and after her body had been committed to earth, Eddie turned round to shake the hands of Bert Lansdowne and Tom Munday. Mary kissed Isabel and told her not to cry, and then the bereaved husband and daughter abruptly left the churchyard, cutting short the tentative expressions of sympathy.

Violet Munday was unusually quiet and thoughtful as she walked home.

Chapter Three

1912

Just what is that boy going to do with his life?

Ernest was uncomfortably aware of his father's unspoken question, though Tom Munday had not recently broached the subject with him. The final term at the commercial college would be starting after Easter, and the question of employment at the end of it loomed large; fellow students like Ernest's friend Jim Quayle were applying for posts and going for interviews. Mrs Munday had always believed that Ernest would be in demand with his new qualifications, confirmed by a certificate of proficiency in basic business skills, but looking ahead to the end of that last term, there were not any obvious openings in the Guildford area for newly trained clerks. When Brights department store advertised for an assistant floor manager, the post had been quickly filled, and in any case Mrs Munday hoped for something better for her son. The college superintendent frequently told students that the best opportunities were in London, but country-loving Ernest had no wish to rent a room in the sprawling capital, and besides, he wanted to keep up his membership of both the Bible study group and the cycling club, though his weekends at home had curtailed any chance of a social life in Guildford. Jim Quayle, who also lodged at Mrs Green's, had introduced Ernest to tennis which they practised on weekday evenings, and after a while Jim had invited two enthusiastic girls from the college to join them in mixed doubles. It soon became apparent that Jim had a fancy for one of the girls, and began to court her seriously; but when no similar attraction developed between Ernest and the other girl, the foursome had broken up, amicably enough, but leaving Ernest with a puzzling sense of loss. He and Jim had shared a lot in common, or so he'd thought, but this appeared to be the parting of their ways.

For Isabel Munday life was more certain and much brighter. At fifteen she was leaving the post office to become Miss Daniells' teaching assistant at the start of the summer term, and there she would remain for the next two years, before enrolling at a teachers' training college. A sweet-faced girl with a genuine love of children, her parents regarded her with pride: Tom with quiet satisfaction, his wife far more volubly, irritating the parents of other North Camp girls. Betty Goddard helped her father to keep the accounts at Thomas and Gibson's, and was referred to as his secretary by her mother, and as a shopgirl by Mrs Munday. Phyllis Bird took over Isabel's place in the post office, and Rosie Lansdowne assisted in her father's dairy, with a view to enrolling as a nursing cadet at Everham Hospital the following year. Mary Cooper had moved into the Yeomans' farmhouse to assist Mrs Yeomans who had surprised herself by having another baby at forty, and so needed more help in the house, especially at haymaking and harvesting, when hired labourers clumped into the stone-floored kitchen for bread, cheese and beer. And Eddie Cooper had astounded North Camp by marrying again, his new bride being Annie the barmaid at the Tradesmen's Arms, a lady of about thirty who expertly drew pints for others but was herself teetotal. It soon became known that Mary and her stepmother did not get on, and this was borne out when the second Mrs Cooper produced a baby son, but Mary stayed on at the farm to help Mrs Yeomans with her new baby, also a boy. The older Yeomans children, two girls and a boy, were all working; the boy, now twenty, was his father's right-hand man.

Tom Munday was getting more demands on his skill than he could reasonably deal with, so took on another apprentice school-leaver who showed more aptitude for carpentry than Ernest ever had. Tom and Eddie agreed that times were good and getting better for working men as wages rose and prices fell; Lady Neville's confident prediction, and that of the MP, seemed to be justified, that Great Britain was surely marching forward to ever greater prosperity.

And then suddenly in mid April came news of a terrible disaster, the shock-waves from which reverberated around the world. The great new passenger liner *Titanic* of the White Star line, alleged to be unsinkable, struck an iceberg in mid Atlantic on her maiden voyage from Southampton to New York, and had sunk with the loss of fifteen hundred lives. The news cast a shadow over every conversation, and there were those who asked why God should allow such loss of life on so great a scale. Mr Saville preached a sermon pointing out to his congregation that the liner's wealthy passengers had been enjoying every luxury, drinking, dancing and playing cards when sudden death and destruction had come upon them, and he counselled his hearers to trust in the Lord's justice, and give thanks for the survival of some seven hundred souls, rescued from the freezing cold sea by the liner *Carpathia*. It should give them all pause for thought, he warned, to review and perhaps renew their lives.

Tom Munday, listening to this, was not so certain about the theology of it; but he felt a nameless unease, something he could not put into words, a sense of the precariousness of human life, in spite of the wealth and prosperity of the age. He agreed that the tragedy had shaken them all out of their complacency, for if the unsinkable *Titanic* had proved unable to withstand an iceberg, who knew what other disasters awaited a generation that increasingly put its faith in scientific advance?

Isabel had similar thoughts when Miss Daniells led the school in prayer, impressing on them the need to live good Christian lives, and not to follow the ways of this world, which to her meant modesty in dress and behaviour, especially on the part of young women who played tennis and golf, even on the Lord's day.

'I simply don't know what the world's coming to, Miss Munday,' she sighed, though she commended Isabel's brother Ernest for putting his church before cycling on the Sabbath. If only all families would follow the example of the Mundays, she said, how much better life would be for the whole nation.

But just one week into the new term, the exemplary Mundays were called upon to face a humiliating blow. What they had dismissed as Grace's self-will and naughtiness was now a real cause for concern – to the extent that Mr Chisman the headmaster had summoned her parents to his private office where he informed them that their thirteen-year-old daughter's behaviour would soon result in expulsion unless she changed her ways as a persistent troublemaker. The Mundays stood together before Mr Chisman's desk as if they were the culprits, and begged for Grace to be given another chance.

'It is only because I know you as respectable and caring

parents that I have not taken this step before,' he told them gravely. 'I had hoped that she would improve as she grew older, but this has not been the case. Cheating in the weekly class tests and copying other pupils' homework is one thing, but using foul language – which I know she won't have learnt at home – and attacking her classmates with fists and nails is something that cannot go on. Other parents have complained of injuries inflicted by her on girls and boys alike. And I'm sorry to say that Grace has the ability to turn into an angel of light when challenged, and will break down in tears, pleading that she had only been defending a younger child who was being bullied.'

'She's told us about an incident like that, Mr Chisman, and I can assure you that she has often stood up to bullying, both in school and out of it,' said Mrs Munday, anxious to defend her daughter.

'That may be so, Mrs Munday, but I have to tell you that she is thoroughly disruptive in class,' said Mr Chisman. 'She has a regrettable tendency to stir up trouble and then disappear from the scene, leaving others to take the blame. I'm sorry, but this cannot be allowed to continue.'

He frowned and turned to address Tom Munday. 'I am prepared, more for your sakes than hers, to overlook her behaviour on this occasion, but there will not be another reprieve. Do I make myself clear, Mr Munday?'

Tom nodded and murmured his thanks, but the ignominy of the situation reduced his wife to tears; Tom looked very grave as they left the school.

'We've spoilt her, Violet. We've let her wrap us around her little finger, and it hasn't done her any good – quite the opposite.'

'Heavens, Tom, she's only thirteen, a child as yet, and it's probably just a phase she's going through. We just need to be a little bit firmer with her, let her see how upset we are, and I'm sure she'll take it to heart and make up her mind to be good in future,' said Mrs Munday, wiping her eyes.

'If it isn't already too late,' muttered Tom, half under his breath. He blamed himself entirely for his blindness and lack of firmness with his wife as well as his daughter. It's up to me, he thought, to see that things would be different from now on.

At Miss Daniells' school Isabel blossomed. Seated at a small table near to Miss Daniells' desk, she was adored by the children, especially the five-year-olds who were her particular responsibility. She showed them how to form letters and numerals on their slates, allowing for their mixed abilities; from seven onwards the children had exercise books supplied by the parish council, but reusable slates were more economical for the little ones' scribbles. Her duties extended to their physical needs, and she took them to the lavatory, wiped runny noses and sticky hands, and was always there to pacify and encourage. She could play the piano when required, freeing Miss Daniells to stand in front of the whole school to teach a new song or chorus and explain the scriptural message it conveyed, made simple and tuneful for little voices. Miss Daniells was delighted with the benefits Isabel brought to the school and to herself, for she now felt far less tired. She praised Miss Munday to the Reverend Mr Saville on his regular visits to the school as chairman of the parish council and school governor; Miss Daniells assured him that her young assistant was worth every penny of the seven shillings and sixpence she was paid weekly.

And there were the days when the vicar had other duties and responsibilities, and sent his curate Mr Storey in his place.

Isabel blushed as she answered this visitor's courteous questions about her duties with the little ones, and was rewarded by his smiling approval. He would then take time to go among her small pupils, praising whatever they'd scrawled on their slates and commending their teacher. To Isabel he was the epitome of all that a good clergyman should be, and it was impossible *not* to imagine falling in love with such an excellent young man, some ten years older than herself. She was thankful that he could not know how her heart fluttered when he came to the school, though she was unable to hide her blushes and hoped he put them down to shyness. As long as he remained unaware of her feelings, she thought, there was no great harm in indulging in her half-acknowledged dreams.

How little she suspected Mark Storey's own thoughts, and his dilemma over this beautiful young girl! He had been used to dropping in at the post office with letters to hand in or collect for the vicarage, and exchanging a smile and perhaps a casual remark about the weather with her. On the day he went in and noticed that she was no longer there, he was utterly dismayed, supposing that she had left North Camp to take up a new job; but on learning from Mr Teasdale that she was now a pupil-teacher at the church school, he gladly looked forward to many more opportunities to see and speak with her again: to feast his eyes upon her unspoilt beauty.

For Mark Storey was in love, and had been ever since he had first seen her. And now his thoughts turned to the serious possibility of marrying her in another two or three years' time. Girls married at eighteen, and he reasoned that if he had been appointed to a living by then, there would be a house available; and even if not, there might still be a house for a married curate, a home to which he could take her as a bride if she accepted him and her parents approved. But if he was moved from North Camp before then, another man might step in and claim her. For him she was everything that could be desired in a clergyman's wife: a devout Christian, a dutiful daughter and good with children – ideal in every way except for the matter of her age. Mark's thoughts circled round and round, without coming to any resolution.

Then came a visit from the bishop of the Winchester diocese to Everham and its surrounding villages, North and South Camp and Hassett. His lordship was a pleasantly jovial man, outwardly uncritical, though neither Mr Saville nor his wife forgot for one moment that this was an inspection. Mark did not expect the great man to have much to say to a humble curate, but to his surprise he was taken aside during an informal tea at the vicarage, and asked to accompany his lordship on a walk in the garden, or rather the grounds, for this was where fêtes and parish picnics were held. After a few questions about his curacy, the bishop surprised Mark by asking with a fatherly smile if there was any young lady in the parish that he particularly admired.

'Such as a sensible, industrious young woman, Storey, not necessarily a beauty, but amiable and likely to make a good wife for a clergyman – somebody who would discreetly support you in your parish work, never causing embarrassment by injudicious talk. Tell me in confidence, have you met anybody who might suit?'

Mark Storey was speechless, and for one mad moment imagined himself answering, Yes, indeed, my lord, I am desperately in love with a girl of barely sixteen, and dream of her by day and night. She's the daughter of a local tradesman, and is the sweetest, most beautiful girl I've ever seen. I'm willing to wait until she's older, but please don't send me away from North Camp, my lord, because if another man came and took her from me, I don't think that I could…well, I'd join the China Inland Mission and leave this country for ever.

But of course he said nothing of the sort, and the bishop interpreted his silence as meaning that he had in fact got a suitable young woman in mind.

'No great hurry, of course, Storey, but think over what I've said. A bachelor vicar can find himself in an awkward, even scandalous situation, there being many young ladies in every parish who are drawn to the cloth – and a few older ones, too,' he added with a smile. 'A good clergyman needs a good wife to look after him, that's what I say to all you newly ordained men. Anyway, if there *is* a young lady in your sights, Storey, I won't move you for the time being, though I don't usually keep single curates in one place for longer than two years, because you need to widen your experience of parish life. What do you say, Storey?'

Mark took a deep breath. 'Thank you, my lord, I-I'd prefer to stay in North Camp for a while longer if you will allow me.'

'Good! Then I take it that you've answered my question,' the bishop answered kindly. 'Mr Saville speaks very highly of you, and if there were any, er, obstacles in your path, I know that you could safely confide in him. Right, my boy, let's get back to sampling Mrs Saville's delicious scones!'

Ernest's last term at college was clouded with growing anxiety about his future. Since disappointing his father's hopes that they would work together as partners, he had taken a good deal of money from that father, with no foreseeable prospect of paying it back. He searched the local and county newspapers in vain for a suitable opening, and began to think that he might, after all, have to go to London to find work, which would mean finding lodgings there, as Ted Bird had done. Ted had become a junior assistant with an exclusive London tailoring establishment patronised by the nobility, and in the course of time he would return to Birds' Gentlemen's Outfitters in North Camp, to be his father's successor. Thinking about Ted led Ernest's thoughts to Phyllis Bird, now working in the post office in place of Isabel, and quite unmistakably smiling in Ernest's direction. It was she who had told him about the tennis courts, newly built beyond the North Camp cricket pavilion, and the jolly young people who gathered to play tennis in the long, light evenings.

'It's such a beautiful summer,' she said, looking up at him shyly, having learnt from Isabel that he played tennis at Guildford. 'It seems a pity not to take advantage of it while you're at home at the weekend. We're a very friendly crowd, and you'll know most of them – Cedric Neville's home from Cambridge, and he came over from Hassett one evening last week with another fellow from his college, to play a couple of games. Why don't you give it a try?'

She was a pleasant girl, and their families knew each other well. There was no good reason to refuse, and Ernest accordingly accompanied her to the courts one Saturday evening, where his skill surprised everyone, Phyllis included. He had walked her back to her home in the twilight, and parted with her on the doorstep with smiles and thanks for a delightful evening. She was a nice girl, he thought, from a family much like his own, and a few more evenings on the courts might well lead to a good-night kiss, though the idea alarmed him, having had no previous experience, and if he was honest with himself, no real inclination to kiss Phyllis Bird. In the end he decided that the cycling club held more appeal for him than the mixed membership of the tennis set, and in any case the pressing need to find himself suitable employment drove other thoughts from his mind.

Mr Chisman's interview with her parents had thoroughly shaken Grace Munday, and their severity with her was worse than she'd expected, especially from her father who was not to be won over by tears and protests to 'dear Daddy' that she had never meant any harm, and had been sadly misunderstood by her class teacher Miss Forster who had never treated her fairly.

'Stop that whining, my girl, and think yourself lucky you weren't expelled!' he said sharply, and she drew back, her dark eyes wide; tears began to flow again, but Tom Munday hardened his heart, and told her that she had shamed her whole family, especially her mother who had been deeply distressed. He demanded her promise that in the time remaining to her at school she would endeavour to be a credit to her parents, and not a disgrace. She had sobbed bitterly, and promised not to cause any more trouble at school, 'no matter how unkindly they treat me, Daddy!' – but inwardly she made up her mind that if Ernest *did* go to London, she would join him there, just as soon as her fourteenth birthday freed her from that rotten school. She'd get a job in a music hall, and progress from the chorus to being a star turn like the beautiful, daring Marie Lloyd; she too would become famous and wear elegant, expensive outfits – and she'd visit North Camp and Everham to show herself off, and all the girls would envy her. Oh, yes, Miss Grace Munday would show old man Chisman and that bitch Miss Forster how mistaken they'd been about her!

But meanwhile she kept her pretty little nose down and her eyes lowered; right now she needed to get back into her parents' good books.

Tom learnt that the Mundays were not the only family to have problems with a daughter. As he talked with Eddie Cooper over a pint at the Tradesmen's Arms, he heard the latest about Mary, now living at Yeomans' farm, so her father rarely saw her. When the farmer had asked him to repaint the dairy throughout, he had eagerly accepted, and put Yeomans at the top of his order list, thinking it would give him a good opportunity to see and speak to his daughter.

'But I wasn't so pleased, Tom, when I went into the kitchen and found her, all smiles and rosy cheeks, in the middle of half a dozen clodhoppin' farm-hands, in for their bread and cheese. "Mornin', Mary," I said, lookin' pretty straight at her, and she started tryin' to explain, said that Mrs Yeomans was busy with the baby cutting his teeth or somesuch, and she was takin' her place in the kitchen. They found their manners when they heard her call me Dad, but I made up my mind to have a word with her, soon as they'd gone back to the fields.'

'And did you get a chance to speak to her, Eddie?' asked Tom.

'More than enough,' came the terse reply. 'When I went back mid afternoon I found her laughin' and gigglin' with that oaf Dick Yeomans – you know, the son – and he was ticklin' her with his great hands and tryin' to kiss her, if you please!'

'The devil he was! I'd've given him a clout, Eddie! What did you do?'

'It's not that easy, Tom,' said Eddie with a sigh. 'Mrs Yeomans has been good to Mary, and given her a better home than she's ever had before, but the girl's never crossed our threshold since Annie had the baby. I couldn't very well go for that lout in his own kitchen, so I just grabbed hold o' Mary, and said, "Here, that's enough o' that, my girl" – and told him to take his dirty paws off her, or I'd be lettin' his father know. He turns round and says somethin' about who the hell are you, this isn't your house – but when he sees I'm her dad he looks a bit sheepish. Mary just looked down at the flagstones, and I felt that helpless, Tom, I didn't know what to say to her, so in the end I just told her that if she wanted me at any time, she knew where I was.'

'And what did she say to that, Eddie?' asked Tom, wondering how he would have reacted if it had been his daughter Isabel. Or Grace.

'She nodded and muttered something, and then said, "Excuse me, I can hear the baby crying" – and off she went.'

'Must be rotten for you, Eddie – put you in a bit of a spot, didn't it?' said Tom, knowing of the dislike between stepmother and daughter. Everybody knew that Mary had not once visited her little half-brother, and most felt sorry for Eddie who'd patiently endured years of worry with his first wife, and yet had looked after his daughter as well as he could.

'They just don't get on, Tom, Annie and Mary, and that's the top an' bottom of it,' said Eddie, shaking his head. 'Means I worry over Mary and that damned Yeomans boy, and there's nothin' I can do to look out for her. Been through a lot together, Mary an' me.'

Tom Munday looked at him with real pity, but had no useful advice to offer. 'So will you have a word with Yeomans?'

'Yeah, but I'll have to go carefully. Don't want a quarrel, and Mary losin' her job. There's nowhere else for her to go,' answered Eddie flatly.

'Just a quiet word with him, then, that should do the trick,' said Tom, trying to sound encouraging. 'You could ask him to speak to his wife about it – she'd be the best one to look after Mary.'

'You won't say a word, will you, Tom? Not to your missus?'

''Course I won't,' Tom assured him, adding to himself, especially not to the missus. Poor old Eddie, stuck between two women who couldn't get on, and a daughter facing temptations that could ultimately ruin her life; he, Tom Munday, could only be thankful that he had no such anxieties.

That was until he walked into the parlour one afternoon when Violet was out visiting Mrs Bird, and stopped in his tracks at what he saw. Grace was parading in front of the mirror, wearing her mother's best hat trimmed with silk roses and an ostrich feather; she gestured with Isabel's parasol and winked as she sang to an imaginary audience.

'If I show my shape just a little bit –
Just a little bit, not too much of it –
If I show my shape just a *little* bit,
It's the little bit the boys admire!'

The song was cut short as Grace became aware of her father's reflection in the mirror, standing behind her. She spun round to face him, her dark eyes pleading.

'I just found this copy o' Marie Lloyd's songs, Daddy, and thought I'd try to sing—'

'Hand me that rubbish at once, my girl,' he ordered sternly, taking up the sheaf of music that lay on a bookshelf. 'And get those clothes o' your mother's back into her wardrobe straight away, before she gets in.'

'Yes, Daddy, o' course, Daddy, I'm sorry, I was only trying to…' Grace began, putting down the parasol and taking off the hat in preparation for another angry reprimand and no doubt punishment from her father.

But Tom Munday did not feel equal to a confrontation just then, and having confiscated the Marie Lloyd songbook, he dismissed Grace without another word. He decided against telling Violet, it would only kick up a further rumpus. But he wondered, like Miss Daniells, what the world was coming to.

On the fourth Sunday of each month, the morning service at St Peter's was followed by the sacrament of Holy Communion to those members of the congregation who wished to receive it. Mrs Munday decided that it was a good time for the whole family to partake of it, Grace having been confirmed at Easter; both she and Ernest might obtain benefit from it, their mother thought. Accordingly they all stayed behind and moved up to the altar rail where they knelt with about a score of others while the Rev. Mr Saville recited the prayer of consecration, and the bread and wine having been blessed as representing Christ's body and blood, he moved along the line of communicants, administering a small cube of bread into the cupped hands of each, uttering the traditional words over them. He was followed by Mr Storey, holding the chalice from which each communicant took a sip of wine. Ernest said his 'Amen' with fervour, for his thoughts were in such a turmoil of anxiety that he did not notice the slight disturbance when the curate moved on to Isabel who knelt next to him. His college days were over, and he was qualified and unemployed. What was he to do? His mother was now advising him to take any job on offer, no matter how menial, while waiting for something better to come up. For instance, Mr Graves needed somebody to keep a watchful eye on his coal yard, and deal with the orders that came in to his grimy little office. Ernest shuddered, but now was no time to be choosy; he would go and see Mr Graves tomorrow.

Meanwhile it was a hot August day, and after the usual Sunday roast dinner, Ernest walked to the Bible study group at Mr Woodman's. Should he ask them to pray for him at some point? To pray that he might be shown the path he was to take, both now and in the future?

When the Reverend Paul Woodman opened the door to him, Ernest felt his heart leap at the sight of his mentor, the young man for whom he'd felt such gratitude and affection as a boy. He knew that Paul, now in his late twenties, was an ordained Methodist minister, and that he had married; could there still be the old special understanding between them?

'Ernest!' cried Paul, taking his hand and shaking it warmly. 'How good to see you! I'm visiting my parents – it's my mother's birthday, so I've come over with Rachael and our little daughter. You must meet them. But how are you, old chap? And what are you doing now?'

Before Ernest could answer, Mr Woodman came into the hall. 'Come in, Ernest, come in!' he beamed. 'We shall be holding our study group this afternoon as usual, but with the pleasure of having Paul with us. It will be just like old times!'

But not quite, thought Ernest, putting on a cordial expression and saying how happy he was to meet Rachael, a dark-haired young woman who greeted him with sharply observant eyes. A little girl of about two clung to her mother's skirts and hid her face in their folds when Ernest awkwardly bent over to speak to her.

'Rachael is not from a Christian family, but praise be to God, she has accepted Christ as her Saviour,' said Paul, looking tenderly at her. 'Lucy has been baptised in the faith, and we pray constantly that Mr and Mrs Schelling and Rachael's brothers and sisters be brought to the foot of the Cross in the course of time.'

Ernest nodded, wondering if Rachael was a Roman Catholic; but no, they called themselves Christians, even though sadly misguided.

'You may possibly meet some of them soon, Ernest, because Rachael's uncle and another relative—'

'His sister's son, Aaron,' Rachael put in.

'That's right, her uncle and his nephew, they've left London and have come to start up a business in Everham,' continued Paul. 'They've been working for an insurance firm in the city, but Mr Schelling feels that the time has come for him to start his own business. He's bought up the old bakehouse at the end of the high street, and is having it turned into an office. They'll deal with house and fire insurance, and expect to do quite well with the farmers.'

'They'll be known as Schelling and Pascoe,' said Rachael with a little nod.

'Yes, and all they need now is staff – reliable trained staff with good accountancy skills and some knowledge of German, if that's possible, as Mr Pascoe has recently come over from Germany and isn't very fluent in English yet,' explained Paul. 'Father says it's asking rather a lot in a place like Everham, but Mr Schelling will offer a very good salary to the right— er, I say, Ernest old chap, are you all right? Your jaw has dropped nearly to the floor!'

Ernest nodded but could not trust himself to speak, so full was he of incredulous amazement. He had come to Mr Woodman's Bible study group that afternoon with the intention of asking for prayer that he might be shown the way forward in his life and work. And it seemed that his prayer had been answered, even before it had been offered up.

Having administered the chalice to Ernest, Mr Storey turned next to the beautiful young girl who had so captured his heart. His hands had begun to shake as he held the cup and the square of white linen used to wipe the rim between each partaker. A priest is instructed to look straight into the eyes of the communicant as he murmurs the time-honoured exhortation, but Mark's throat was suddenly constricted and speech deserted him. Not only his hands shook, but he trembled from head to foot, almost spilling the wine, as he stood before the girl who filled his waking thoughts and haunted his dreams; only he – and he presumed God – knew of the times when he had given way to unlawful thoughts of her, and now here she knelt before him in all her purity and innocence. He could not look into those clear blue eyes; his head bowed over the chalice and he feared he was about to disgrace himself and his office in front of her and her family and everybody present. Mr Saville was looking at him in frowning concern: what could he do? Oh, merciful God, what was he to do?

Then Isabel Munday lifted her head, a sweet smile on her lips as she held out her hands to take hold of the chalice; and he found himself answering her in the words he had been saying to each communicant.

'The blood of our Lord Jesus Christ which was shed for thee, preserve thy body and soul unto everlasting life...'

She took the chalice between her hands, and their fingers briefly touched.

'Amen,' she replied, and he passed on to Grace who had not

missed a moment of this little scene acted out beside her.

On the way home Mrs Munday remarked that the curate had not looked well.

'Did you see how he stood there as if he didn't know where he was? I thought he was going to faint,' she said. 'I wonder how Mrs Saville feeds him? He's out such a lot, I expect he gets warmed-up leftovers half the time.'

Grace smirked, but otherwise there was no reaction. Tom Munday had seen the curate's strange behaviour, and had drawn his own conclusions. He thought of Eddie Cooper's dilemma over Mary, how Eddie was unable to talk to her; it could be difficult for fathers of daughters, but his Isabel was a good, sensible girl, conscious of her parents' love for her, and likely to be much less of a worry than Grace.

After Sunday dinner had been cleared away and Ernest had left for the Bible study group, Isabel put on her flowery hat and said she was going to see Betty Goddard, which pleased her father; a good talk with a friend of her own age would probably be the best thing for her.

It wasn't a downright lie, but only half a one; Isabel knew that Betty was likely to be visiting her grandmother as she usually did on a Sunday afternoon, but she called at the Goddards just to make sure, and was thankful that nobody appeared to be at home. Oh, how she longed to get right away from everybody and walk as far as she could, alone with her own tumultuous thoughts – a mixture of hope, apprehension and sheer joy; for when Mr Storey had hesitated in front of her at the altar rail, and she had raised her face to him and smiled, holding out her hands for the chalice, some wordless message had passed between them, and she had at last acknowledged what was in her own heart. It was as if a jigsaw puzzle had finally fallen into place, and whereas before she had imagined what it must be like to be married to a clergyman, now she acknowledged the truth: she was in love with Mr Storey. She could tell nobody, certainly not her parents, for they would neither believe her nor approve; they would point out that she was only just sixteen, as if she didn't know.

She hurried out of the village and made her way down to the meadowlands on the near side of the Blackwater river, where a clump of trees stood on what was still common land. Here she could hug her secret to herself, and she twirled round and round, holding her hat by its white ribbon and laughing at herself.

And that was how Mark Storey came upon her, for he too was out walking on this late summer afternoon, alternately rejoicing for love of Isabel Munday and then accusing himself of weakness on account of it. He was thankful that Mr Saville had merely asked, 'Are you all right, Mark? You looked a bit pale during Communion.'

'I'm all right, thank you, Mr Saville. I just didn't sleep very well last night, that's all.'

'Yes, it's this heat. A good dinner will put you to rights. Would you care for a glass of sherry before we sit down?'

As soon as he could possibly excuse himself after the Sunday roast, Mark had put his straw boater on his head, and strode forth, deciding to make for the Blackwater meadows and lose himself among the trees. Yes! As long as nobody else knew of his secret, life could go on as usual, worshipping her from a distance. Or so he thought.

And then he saw her, like a vision conjured up from sheer longing. He stood stock-still at first, watching her until she caught sight of him and at once stopped twirling; she put her hat back on, and for a long moment they stared at each other.

Then he spoke. 'Isabel.'

It was only one word, her Christian name instead of *Miss Munday*. But it was enough. They began walking towards each other as if impelled by some force beyond themselves, and she held out her hands as she had held them out for the chalice that morning. He folded his arms around her, and she laid her head upon his shoulder. Released from its pins, her hair tumbled down over her shoulders; he thought he had never seen anything so breathtakingly beautiful. For a while there was silence, and then he spoke quietly and clearly.

'I may not declare myself to you, Isabel, so young as you are, not without your parents' knowledge. There would be a fearful scandal if…if…'

'Then we won't tell anybody, dear Mr Storey,' she replied, lifting her head and looking full into his face. 'Nobody but ourselves will know, and it will be a secret, won't it? And then…oh, *then* if you have to leave North Camp and be sent to another parish, we two would still *know*, wouldn't we?'

'Yes, my love, and I'll wait for you until you're eighteen, or older – I'll wait for you as long as I have to, Isabel.'

'And I'll wait too, dear Mr Storey!'

'Call me Mark, Isabel.'

'Mark,' she murmured, and then more clearly, 'Mark!'

Their first kiss was no less loving because it was gentle and chaste, but they both knew that a bridge had been crossed and there could be no going back.

'We'd better go back to the village, my love,' he said at length. 'I won't take your arm, much as I'd like to. In fact, it would be best if you walk on ahead, and I'll follow.' He felt that he had to be careful of her good name, and so with a last tremulous kiss, and enveloped in a mutual intensity of emotions, they returned separately to North Camp.

But they had been seen.

'I saw you lingering back along Bent Lane, with your young man following on behind,' announced Grace as soon as her sister had stepped over the threshhold. Isabel coloured and frowned.

'Don't be silly, Grace, Mr Storey is just a nice man who's very good at his – at his work,' she replied, though unable to hide her blushes and shining eyes, for it was not in her nature to deceive. Grace laughed.

'And the band played, "Believe it if you like!" Come off it, Izzy, he's crazy about you, anybody could see that in church this morning!'

Poor Isabel. Poor Mark Storey, a serious-minded man wanting to do the right and honourable thing, decided against secrecy after all, and confided in the Rev. Mr Saville that same evening, who passed it on to his astonished wife. The bishop was speedily informed, and before the end of September Mr Storey had been transferred to a parish in the East End of London. Isabel wept bitterly at his departure, confirming Tom Munday's suspicions that Storey's love for her was returned, and he could only commend the curate's honesty. Violet on the other hand was pained by what she saw as Isabel's deception of her parents, and the curate's perfidy.

'Don't be annoyed with them, Vi,' Tom counselled her gently. 'Just thank heaven that Isabel's a good girl, not one to bring shame on her family – which is more than can be said for some I could mention.'

Tom quietly let Isabel know that she and the Rev. Storey could correspond, not oftener than once a month, and that he must see all the letters that came and went. She vowed again that she would wait until she reached an age when she'd be considered old enough to become a clergyman's wife. Tom privately considered that one or other of them would grow tired of waiting. And there the matter had to rest.

At Schelling and Pascoe's smart new office in Everham High Street Ernest Munday was thankful beyond words that he had at last found his niche in life, for his employers were delighted with him. Mrs Munday had at first been shocked and sorry to hear that the Schelling family were *Jews*, but her son was so obviously happy with them and so highly commended by Mr Schelling that she ceased to mention it, especially to their neighbours in North Camp. After only a month Ernest was entrusted with charge of the office on Saturdays, the Jewish Sabbath, and conforming to national practice they closed on Sundays. Mr Schelling was a jovial, thick-set man with a wife and two daughters, and Rachael Woodman was the daughter of his brother. Mr Aaron Pascoe, the son of a Schelling sister, was a thoughtful young man who enjoyed discussing social and international issues with Ernest. He also hinted at unrest in Germany, which was why he had left his childhood home and come to England.

'Our race has always had to be ready to break camp and move on to other pastures,' he told Ernest with a smile and a shrug. 'We have to stand with our lamps lit and our loins girded, ready for an exodus.' He had eagerly accepted a junior partnership with his uncle who treated him like a son, having none of his own.

Getting to know and respect this Jewish family, Ernest sometimes felt puzzled. While they did not acknowledge Jesus

Christ as their Saviour, but were still awaiting the coming of their true Messiah, they were strict in the observances of their religion, which made them no less considerate or good-humoured. Ernest felt no missionary zeal to preach the Gospel to them as if they were heathen, and had no wish to damage the cordial relationship he had with them. He wondered how they had reacted to Rachael's conversion to Christianity, and one day when talking with Aaron, he asked him tentatively about the matter.

'My aunt was very distressed about her daughter's marriage at first, and said she wouldn't attend the wedding in a Methodist church,' Aaron answered. 'But my uncle took the view that they must never disown Rachael, and I think Paul did a lot towards encouraging her to stay in touch with her parents, and well, being such an obviously decent fellow, they couldn't fail to like him. And then when Lucy was born - well, you know what women are like with babies – my aunt succumbed, and there was reconciliation of a sort. And of course Paul and Rachael live quite a distance away from the family.'

Hearing this, Ernest still wondered how Paul had persuaded Rachael to forsake the religion of her race; was it that she genuinely came to believe that Christ was her Saviour? Ernest concluded that she had, though a part of him suspected that she must have been passionately in love with Paul, and determined to marry him in defiance of parents and grandparents.

Just as he himself would have married Paul if either of them had been a woman.

Chapter Four

May, 1914

Tom Munday sat reading the monthly letter his daughter Isabel had written to the Rev. Mark Storey, the newly inducted vicar of St Barnabas' Church in the East London borough of Bethnal Green. Each month Tom felt more uncomfortable about this censorship of their letters. The one-time awkward, well-meaning curate now had charge of a rough, sometimes dangerous parish, and the shy girl dreaming of love in a vicarage had become a capable young woman of eighteen, as pretty as ever, and much loved and respected at Miss Daniells' school. And she remained as unwavering in her attachment to Mark Storey as his for her. They had served almost two years of enforced separation from each other, during which time they had not once met, for when Mark had invited Isabel and her parents to attend his induction earlier in the year, Tom had given way to his wife's insistence that they should decline. A complete separation decreed by a bishop should be strictly observed, she argued, though Tom was not as convinced as she was, and now regretted their decision. For one thing, it would have given Isabel an opportunity to compare the relatively rural life of North Camp with the poverty and hardship of an East London parish, a life that she might be required to share in due time.

Tom sighed, and reread the letter, imagining what she might have written if her words had been for Mark's eyes only.

I was interested in all that you said about the Settlement that has been such a help to the young people, and the football team for the boys. You describe it all so vividly that I feel myself actually there, and I only wish that I were. It has been so long.

(That means 'I long to see you and share your life,' thought Tom.)

Life at school goes on as usual, the children are happy and learn well on the whole. I often think of the poor, ragged little souls that you tell me about who have no chance to learn to read and write. They come to mind when I am teaching my little ones to say their ABC, and my heart goes out to them. It seems so long since you used to come on school inspections for Mr Saville.

('How I should love to teach your poor, bare-footed urchins, and welcome your inspections to see what progress I have made! Your smiles and commendations would be all the reward I needed.')

Mr Saville preached a very solemn sermon last Sunday about the unrest in Europe, and he obviously doesn't admire the kaiser, though our late King Edward VII was his cousin, and they seemed to be friendly. My father agrees that this trouble in the Balkans could be a threat to peace in that part of the world, and may spread to Germany and Austria. The newspapers contradict each other, and I find it all quite bewildering. Here we have lovely spring weather, and when I get time to walk in the Blackwater meadows, thoughts of war seem very far away. The trees look so beautiful in their new green foliage, and yesterday I heard a cuckoo calling. That place holds happy memories.

('I felt as if I were walking again with you in that place where we first declared our love. If only we could be together again, I wouldn't be bothered by these rumours from abroad, whatever Mr Saville says.')

Tom Munday folded the letter and put it in its envelope, ready for posting. And at that moment he made up his mind to discontinue this censorship of their letters. His daughter and Mark Storey had proved the enduring nature of their love, and had earned the right to privacy. It had been two years, for heaven's sake, and as far as Tom Munday was concerned, the couple could meet and make plans for their future.

Stepaside was a high-class tea room in Everham, known for its excellent home-made cakes and atmosphere of quiet refinement; it was situated conveniently for lady shoppers, and Lady Neville always took refreshments there when she came to Everham on business or shopping. It was run by a Mrs Brangton and her daughter Miss Brangton, and when an advertisement appeared in the *Everham News* for a suitable young lady to work as a waitress and assist in the kitchen at Stepaside, Grace Munday saw it and begged her father to let her apply, even though she had not yet had her fifteenth birthday, and was still a pupil at the council school. When approached Mr Chisman made no objection, and Grace, overjoyed at the prospect of escape from boring lessons and spiteful teachers, attended an interview with Mrs Brangton, where her pretty manners and dimpled smiles won her the place. Overnight she turned into Miss Munday, a young lady dressed in a long black skirt and high-necked white blouse, who earned her own living and travelled daily on the horse-drawn omnibus between North Camp and Everham. Her parents had mixed feelings at first, but she settled well, and her obvious happiness reassured them.

Stepaside opened at midday, but behind its genteel frontage the morning activity in the kitchen was intense. Miss Munday arrived at eight, donned an overall and tied a triangular white square around her head, to assist both ladies in their tasks. Miss Brangton baked the cottage loaves which went into the oven at nine, having been 'proved' and rekneaded since the dough was made at seven. Mrs Brangton made the cakes of all kinds – fruit, chocolate, coffee and walnut (a great favourite), and sponges plain and flavoured, halved and filled with buttercream. While she wielded her wooden spoon and poured the mixtures into baking tins, Miss Brangton sliced vegetables for soup, simmering them with ham or beef bones, and Miss Munday had to assist both ladies who frequently needed her at the same time. At half past eleven she sat down to a delicious bowl of freshly made soup and a slice of home-baked bread, still warm from the oven, and at five to twelve she put on a frilly white apron with a matching cap, ready for her duties as waitress, in which she was joined and supervised by Miss Brangton. A stout woman called Mrs Hodge arrived to do the washing up; she stayed in the kitchen, while Mrs Brangton disappeared into an inner sanctum to do her accounts, issuing forth from time to time to greet her customers and exchange a word here and there – as if she hadn't been working her socks off all the morning, thought Miss Munday admiringly.

Lunches consisted of the delectable soup and bread, with the addition or alternative of something on toast – poached or scrambled egg, cheese or grilled tomatoes. Miss Brangton prepared these, and kept two big kettles on the boil for tea. Lunches continued until two o'clock when there was a lull before teas began at three and continued until half past five. This was the busiest time, when the afternoon shoppers arrived for their usual treat, tea at Stepaside. Miss Munday welcomed all the ladies and the occasional gentleman, usually a husband, with smiling deference, taking their orders and dealing with each one promptly. She loved it.

But one afternoon there was a difficulty. Mrs Bentley-Foulkes, a very elegant lady and regular patron, arrived with a female companion and demanded her usual table beneath the window. Miss Munday took their order, tea for two and lemon cake. When she brought the tray with two generous slices of lemon cake, Mrs Bentley-Foulkes regarded it with a frown.

'I ordered a teacake, toasted and buttered,' she said. 'Mrs Whittington ordered the cake. Please change it.'

'But madam, you ordered lemon cake for both of you – didn't she, Mrs...er...' protested Miss Munday, turning to the other lady for confirmation.

'Don't you answer back at *me*, my girl,' retorted Mrs Bentley-Foulkes in indignation. 'Take that slice of cake away *at once*, and bring me what I ordered.'

'I'll change it for you, madam, but you definitely ordered cake,' insisted Miss Munday, quickly removing the offending slice and returning with a teacake, hastily toasted by Miss Brangton; she set it down without a word.

When Mrs Brangton emerged from her office to speak to her customers, she returned looking very grave, and beckoned to Miss Munday.

'I'm appalled to hear that you were insolent to one of my most valued customers, Miss Munday,' she said. 'You will have to go and apologise to Mrs Bentley-Foulkes at once.'

'But she distinctly asked for lemon cake in the first place, and then said she hadn't, Mrs Brangton!' protested Miss Munday, reddening. 'She was in the wrong, and as good as called me a liar!'

'Hold your tongue, Miss Munday, and don't ever raise your voice to me again, or you will be dismissed without notice!' Mrs Brangton told her, also reddening. 'Stepaside has a reputation as a high-class tea room, where the customer is *always* right, and don't you ever forget that. Now go and apologise to Mrs Bentley-Foulkes and her companion – *at once*, Miss Munday!'

Grace Munday drew several deep breaths and adjusted her face to one of pained submission as she went over to the table and muttered, 'I'm very sorry, Mrs Bentley-Foulkes.' The lady nodded in frosty acceptance, and Miss Munday went to take an order from another table. It isn't easy to be subservient to one you regard as a stuck-up, overdressed Lady Muck, and a seed of rebellion was planted.

'Looks as if there could be civil war in Ireland over this Home Rule business,' said Ernest Munday, looking up from his newspaper.

'Hm!' grunted Aaron Pascoe, biting into his cold roast lamb sliced with unleavened bread. They were sitting at the wooden table in the yard at the back of Schelling and Pascoe's offices, taking advantage of the midday sunshine while keeping an ear open for the doorbell.

'All very well saying "Hm!" It could be a dangerous game if we have to send troops over there,' said Ernest reprovingly.

'My dear old chap, there could be far more dangerous games ahead if this trouble between Serbia and Austria goes on and develops into outright conflict,' said Aaron, looking so serious that Ernest glanced up sharply from his paper. He had never been able to take a real interest in events happening in a distant part of the world, and the Balkans, though not as far away as India or Africa, seemed particularly remote. Oddly, the great Dominions of the British Empire, Canada, Australia and New Zealand, seemed nearer because of their close historical links with Great Britain, while the United States of America, though independent for well over a hundred years, spoke the same language and could still be called cousins of their country of origin. Serbia and Croatia, Turkey and those eastern European countries with their incomprehensible languages and current stirrings and rumblings, held far less importance in Ernest's view than, say, an upheaval in a part of the Empire, such as India which had had its uprisings and rebellions, but which was now peacefully governed by the viceroy and a network of district commissioners like Sir Arnold Neville. Ernest thought back to the great durbar of 1911 when the king and queen had visited India and been proclaimed emperor and empress, among scenes of magnificence and rejoicing among their loyal subjects there. How could local squabbles in the far eastern end of Europe compare with such strength? And yet there was a warning note in his friend's unexpectedly solemn voice.

'Truly, Aaron, do you believe that there could be real danger from Serbia?'

'Certainly, if Germany gets involved, as Austria already has,' replied his friend in the German accent that Ernest found so engaging. 'I have written to my parents in Elberfeld to suggest that they come over with my younger brothers and sisters, and hope that my father will take heed.'

Aaron's father was English, though known as Herr Pascoe in Germany; his mother, a Schelling sister, enjoyed a comfortable life in Elberfeld, and wanted Aaron to return to what she called his home.

'Why? Do you mean for safety's sake?' asked Ernest incredulously. 'Surely that's being overcautious! Why not wait to see how things turn out? These rumblings may die down in another year or two.'

'Ah, Ernest my dear friend, you English can seldom see in front of your noses, and you have been caught unawares in history before now,' said Aaron, shaking his head but softening his words with a wry smile. Ernest caught his breath at the words, 'my dear friend', an unusual way for one young man to address another, and Ernest put it down to the warmer terms and phrases used by Europeans. And over the past two years, working together, cycling together over Surrey's open heaths and Hampshire's rounded hills, by farms and orchards, by ancient village churches, by river banks and stretches of open water like Frensham Pond where they had swum and then sat in the shade – they had become close friends. Ernest privately marvelled at the fact that they had been unwittingly brought together by Paul Woodman, simply because he had married a Jewess; they had another child now, a son they named David, and like his sister he had been baptised as a Christian in the Methodist tradition. Ernest no longer attended Mr Woodman's Bible study groups, for after attending church with his family on Sunday mornings, he was off on his bicycle with Aaron. This was the most beautiful summer he could remember, and the call of the open air had never been stronger than now, sharing it all with Aaron. A bond had grown between them that could only be broken by the marriage of one or the other, though this was never mentioned. Or rather, it had not yet been mentioned.

One Sunday afternoon, resting near St Catherine's Chapel, looking across to the Hog's Back, that great chalk ridge that rises between Farnham and Guildford, and gives a wide view of peaceful Surrey countryside, now shimmering in a heat haze, Aaron lay on his back, gazing up through the thick branches of a yew. Ernest produced a stone jar from his backpack, removed the cork and offered Aaron a gulp of water from its narrow neck.

'Mmm, that's good! Amazing how the stone keeps it cool – thanks.'

He passed the jar back to Ernest, and suddenly it seemed a right moment to broach the subject which Ernest had been turning over in his mind for some time, but which he had been half-afraid to mention to his friend. Now he could; now he must.

'Aaron, may I ask you a question?' He spoke quietly, but his heart beat fast.

'Hush, you're disturbing the silence of a perfect summer afternoon,' teased Aaron. 'Go on, then, ask your question, only I hope it isn't deeply philosophical.'

'It's simple enough. You're already twenty-four. Haven't you had any thoughts of, er, of getting married? If you don't mind me asking, Aaron.'

'Oho, have you got someone in mind for me? If so, I hope she's beautiful.' Aaron smiled and closed his eyes as if in delighted anticipation.

'Don't be ridiculous, I'm quite serious. Surely you must have had *some* ideas about marriage and family life? Isn't that an important part of your religion?'

'Ah, you sound like my mother. And there's the difficulty. You may have noticed that Jewish girls are not abundant in Everham and district. If I'd stayed in Elberfeld, I'd probably be a husband and father by now.'

'But suppose you met someone you liked in Everham – a

girl at the tennis club, for instance,' persisted Ernest, thinking of Phyllis Bird who had become something of a flirt, and was at present walking out with Will Hickory, whose parents owned the bakehouse in North Camp.

'You mean a Gentile girl? No, my friend, there was enough wailing and gnashing of teeth when Rachael married out and gave birth to two Christian children. To lose another, and a man, would be too much to inflict on the family.'

There was silence as a brightly coloured butterfly alighted on Aaron's arm, and he lay absolutely still so as not to disturb it. He gave a long sigh, and Ernest wondered whether it was one of contentment, or was asking him to stop his questions; he was reluctant to pursue the matter, yet felt he needed to know the answer. Aaron must have read his mind, because without dismissing the butterfly, he spoke again in an easy, matter-of-fact way.

'It will rest with my mother – that is, if she and Father take my advice and return to England. In her absence my uncle Schelling will no doubt be instructed to write to a rabbi at a synagogue – in London, probably, where there's a thriving Jewish quarter, and ask him to look out for a suitable young woman who is desperate to meet a country-loving, bicycling junior partner in an insurance firm. And then we'll take it from there. Does that answer your question, Ernest old chap?'

'Yes, I see. Thank you, Aaron.'

The butterfly flew away, and the subject was closed. Ernest was more or less satisfied, for there seemed to be no early likelihood of losing his friend to marriage. Not in the foreseeable future, anyway.

While Ernest sat in thought, Aaron had his own private deliberations. Dear old Ernest! At twenty he had little knowledge of the world, and was clearly totally inexperienced. Bless him, he was so tentative, so cautious, so *English*! It was typical of him to talk of marriage rather than of women in general, their relationship to men – their bodies, their soft breasts, their mysterious, exciting caves where a man might enter and cry out aloud with pleasure. It wasn't that Aaron had much personal knowledge of these natural processes, especially since he had come to Everham, but he took it for granted that one day he would indeed marry a pleasing Jewish woman, one he would find for himself or have found for him; what, after all, would it matter?

By which it might be assumed that in spite of his superior knowledge, Aaron Pascoe had never truly been in love.

'Isabel's off to London next week,' Tom Munday told Eddie Cooper over their Friday night pint at the Tradesmen's Arms.

'Oh, ah?' Eddie waited to hear more. Just about all of North Camp knew of the young curate's banishment to a London parish two years ago, and there were those who said it served him right for carrying on with a sixteen-year-old girl. He had not been seen or heard of since, and the affair was thought to be over. Eddie, however, had known of the censored correspondence, and lately Tom had confided to him that he had told Isabel she was now free to visit the Rev. Mark Storey in his East London parish. Mark had written to her and to Tom in happy acknowledgement, and an arrangement was made for her to go up at half-term, from next Friday to Monday. A married couple in Mark's congregation had agreed to give Miss Munday lodging in their home, and he had paid them in advance.

Tom relayed this information to Eddie who nodded his head in approval.

'Yeah, if they both feel the same after all this time, I reckon they deserve to see each other again,' he said. 'Girls are getting married at her age. And after all, he's a clergyman, and she's older now. Good girl, your Isabel.'

Tom Munday smiled, and returned a complimentary remark about Eddie's daughter.

'Mrs Yeomans thinks the world o' your Mary, I hear – the way she helps her with the baby and cooks meals for them all.'

'Yeah, she's good with little Billy, same age as our Freddie, goin' on for two. Never comes to see us, though, not on birthdays or Christmas or anything. I drop in at Yeomans' farm now and then, to see her and have a word with her, so at least I know she's being looked after, like.'

'No trouble with young Dick these days, then?'

'Not a thing since I had a word with old Yeomans, and he must've told his wife. They don't want any trouble, either, so Dick has to behave himself. He'll be taking over the farm one o' these days, and they don't want him to marry for a year or two. Mind you, he could do worse than my Mary.'

'Yeah,' responded Tom thoughtfully. 'We none of us know what the future holds for any of our children – and I reckon there's not a lot we can do for them as they get older and go their own ways.'

'Your Ernest's still at home, isn't he?'

'Yes, his mother's happy to go on cooking and washing for him,' answered Tom with a shrug. 'He pays her, of course – well, he can afford to, he's got a good job with that insurance firm.'

'Jews, aren't they?'

'Yes, but that doesn't make any difference. They keep to their religion and Ernest keeps to his, and apart from that you'd think he was one of the family. No hanging round pubs and chasing after girls for our Ernest!'

'Good,' said Eddie who'd heard that Ernest Munday and the junior partner in Schelling and Pascoe were as thick as thieves.

The train had passed through Clapham Junction and Vauxhall, and the tracks were converging as it approached the terminus. Isabel's heart beat a little faster as she glimpsed the Thames with Big Ben and the Houses of Parliament on the other side. London! In minutes she would be at Waterloo, where Mark Storey had said he would await her at the ticket barrier.

'I'll come up with you, Isabel,' her father had said, but she had refused his offer. She was grown-up now, and wanted no witnesses to her meeting with her intended husband. Things just might be awkward, for there were undoubtedly uncertainties; their declaration of love had taken place on one afternoon, a time span of less than two hours, to be weighed against a separation of two years, and Mark might be disappointed in this older Isabel. How would he greet her?

The moment had arrived. Isabel took hold of her suitcase and stepped down from the carriage. She was a long way from the ticket barrier; would he be there?

'*Isabel!*' He was here on the platform, only a few yards away! She looked up at a dark-suited figure with a clerical collar, older than she remembered, partly due to his having grown sideboards, but there were the beginnings of deep grooves from his nose to the corners of his mouth, giving him a sterner appearance, and there were lines around his eyes; yet Isabel saw only the love in those remembered grey eyes, the incredulous joy. He was still the Mark she had known so briefly, and with whom she had exchanged a couple of dozen bland letters, passed through her father's hands.

As for the Reverend Mark Storey, he was transfixed. The young girl he had loved almost from first sight was now an even more beautiful young woman in her wide, flower-decked hat, silk blouse and tailored skirt; what would she think of him? How must he appear to her now?

He was soon left in no doubt of her unchanged heart. She had set down her suitcase and was walking towards him, holding out her gloved hands.

'*Mark!*' He prepared to take her hands in his, but she slid naturally into his arms, closely enfolded against his heart, her face uplifted to his, inviting his kiss on her mouth. Her hat came adrift from its pins and fell to the platform, where it was picked up by a woman who handed it back to her with a reproachful look: such goings-on in public, and with a man of the cloth!

'Let me take your case, Isabel – there's a cab waiting outside,' he said a little breathlessly as she replaced her hat on her tumbling hair. He took her arm to lead her through the barrier and across the wide, thronging concourse of the station.

'How I've lived and longed for this moment, Isabel. I can't believe that it's really true – that it's *you* again at last!'

She looked up at him with shining eyes. 'But it *is* true, Mark, I'm here and so happy to be with you again!'

The open horse-drawn cab took them quite a long way, at first through scenes that Isabel knew from a day visit with a group from St Peter's Church, the landmarks of history and the heart of the city. They passed through wide streets with huge shops, theatres and restaurants which Isabel found rather overwhelming; this was the London her sister dreamt of, she thought, the bright lights and the glamour that Grace was determined to be part of one day. They journeyed up Ludgate Hill and passed under the great dome of St Paul's Cathedral, at which Isabel looked up in awe, which made Mark smile.

'You'll find St Barnabas' Church a little less imposing, my Isabel.'

'I shall prefer it,' she answered contentedly.

East of St Paul's the shops gave way to housing, and the neighbourhoods became noticeably shabbier; soon they came to narrower streets with tightly-packed terraced houses opening directly on to the pavement, and backing against another row of similar dwellings separated by narrow communal yards, across some of which lines of washing were hung. Women stood talking outside small butchers' and grocers' shops, and a group of children, some with no shoes, gathered round a lamp post, yelling up at two boys who had climbed it. There were a number of public houses, some with a jug and bottle door, and Isabel knew that premises with the three balls sign were pawnshops.

'This is my parish, Isabel,' said Mark quietly. 'I came here as curate, and now I'm its vicar. It's a long way from North Camp and St Peter's, and I shall quite understand if you do not want to make your home here. One day I'll be transferred to another parish, but that may not be for—'

'Hush, Mark,' she interrupted, holding up her gloved hand. 'You've told me so much about this place in your letters, and haven't I told you how much I've longed to share it with you, and help serve these people as you do? I want to be where you are, Mark, haven't I written that often enough?'

He could only nod and squeeze her hand, for he could not trust himself to speak. She pointed to a church spire a couple of streets away.

'Is that St Barnabas' over there?' she asked.

'Yes, that's my church and this is Old Nichol Street, sometimes called Old Nick's Street, not without reason,' he said with a shrug. 'Go on a little further, driver, into Ainsworth Road, and it's number thirty-seven – and oh, there's Mrs Clements at her door, bless her, waiting for us!'

Number thirty-seven was one of a long terraced row, with gleaming windows and a well-scrubbed white doorstep. Mrs Clements was a neatly dressed woman of about fifty, in a black blouse and skirt, her greying hair drawn back into a bun on the crown of her head, fastened with two large tortoiseshell pins. Her eyes softened at the sight of Mark, but she looked questioningly at Isabel, as if wondering whether to shake her hand or curtsey.

'Here she is, Mrs Clements – Miss Isabel Munday who is visiting our parish for the weekend,' said Mark with easy familiarity as he helped Isabel down with her suitcase. 'Mrs Clements is the mainstay of St Barnabas', Isabel, a lady I can always rely on in difficult times!'

'Good afternoon, Miss Munday, very pleased to meet yer,' said the reliable lady in an unmistakable London accent. She held out her hand. 'It'll be till Monday afternoon, then?'

Isabel nodded and smiled. 'Yes, I'll be staying until then. It's a pleasure to meet you, Mrs Clements.'

'Well, ye'd better come in. I've put the kettle on, and the front room's ready.'

'I'll take Miss Munday's case up to her room, shall I?' asked Mark.

'Certainly not, Mr Storey! Clements'll carry that up for her,' replied the lady, clearly shocked at the very idea of him entering the bedroom of a female guest. She led them both into a small, rather overfurnished front parlour, and Mark smiled at this sign of respect; front parlours were only used on very special occasions.

To Isabel the room felt cold and unlived-in. She sat down on an armchair and accepted a cup of tea from Mrs Clements.

'What time d'yer want yer tea, Miss Munday?'

The term *tea* was also used in the Munday household to denote the evening meal, and Isabel hesitated; Mark broke in to explain what he had planned.

'When Miss Munday's seen her room and has settled in, I'd like to show her over the church, Mrs Clements.'

'What, before she's had her tea, Mr Storey?'

'Yes, please, if it won't inconvenience you.'

'Right, when she's ready I'll bring her over.'

Isabel was about to say that she could make her own way to the church, but Mark silently placed a finger over his mouth. When Isabel had drunk her tea, seen her room and freshened up at the wash bowl on a marble-topped stand, Mrs Clements put on a hat and jacket and escorted her over to the small, soot-bricked vicarage. She rapped on the brass knocker, and when a smiling Mark appeared to take Isabel over to the church, Mrs Clements followed them; while he pointed out objects of interest to Isabel, Mrs Clements sat herself down in a pew at the back. When the couple reached the altar rail and were out of earshot, Mark whispered an explanation.

'She's a good-hearted, hard-working soul, Isabel, and as concerned for my reputation as she is for yours,' he said with a smile.

Isabel smiled back, but uncomprehendingly. 'How do you mean, Mark?'

'Anybody who saw us coming into an empty church will have seen our chaperone, too.'

'Oh, Mark! Does this mean that she'll come with us everywhere?'

'No, my love, not everywhere, only in the church if there's no service on, and certainly in the vicarage. Don't be hard on her, Isabel, I care about your reputation, too, and I don't want you talked about!'

Isabel nodded and said that she understood, but privately she felt that Mrs Clements combined admiration of the Rev. Mr Storey with a suspicion, even a vague disapproval, of this chit of a girl who was so obviously after him.

So the sooner they were married, the better.

'Grace seems to have found her niche at Stepaside,' remarked Tom Munday.

'Yes, for the time being – I mean, while she's so young,' replied his wife who had opposed the idea of Grace leaving school early to get work as a waitress, no matter how genteel the place. At least it wasn't in North Camp where every move would be watched.

'She's got a good woman to teach her and keep an eye on her there, Vi, that's what I'm pleased about.'

'Mrs Brangton? Yes, and Miss Brangton, too – it sounds as if they both like her,' said Violet. 'It'll be good training for her.'

'In more ways than one,' replied Tom. 'You can see that it suits her, by the way she dresses and behaves – she's a changed girl. I said it would do her good.'

'Let's just hope it continues,' said his wife with a sniff. She hadn't much liked being overridden, and didn't want to show too much enthusiasm. It was bad enough for Isabel to go gallivanting off to London for a weekend with that curate, for so Mrs Munday still regarded Mr Storey. Thank heaven for Ernest, doing so well at Schelling and Pascoe, and content to live at home, though she knew that Tom vaguely disapproved, instead of being thankful for a good, hard-working, home-loving son.

As for Grace, the episode with Mrs Bentley-Foulkes still rankled, and she had begun to feel a little bored with the refinement of Stepaside, the rarefied atmosphere of high-class tea rooms presided over by a lady of quality who swanned among her guests, just as if she had not been cake-making all the morning. Grace liked earning a small wage of her own, and she told herself that it didn't cost anything to bow and scrape, but Stepaside was not the only place to eat in Everham. The Railway Hotel did brisk business with the dinner trade or, as it was beginning to be called, *lunch*, served from midday to businessmen, commercial travellers and representatives of firms – and more recently, the military and naval personnel travelling between London and Southampton. These clients needed more than soup and little bits and pieces on toast, and when Grace heard roars of male laughter from the hotel restaurant, her curiosity was aroused; she wondered how much could be earned by a waitress serving steak-and-kidney pies and mutton chops to its patrons – men who would give her a second look and might even exchange pleasantries with her, not to mention the tips pressed into her hand. There was only one way to find out: by going to see the manager as soon as she left Stepaside at closing time, even if it meant missing her bus.

With a thumping heart she entered the Railway Hotel by the front door which opened into a narrow lobby. A middle-aged man in shirtsleeves and smoking a cigarette stood talking to a younger man.

'Mr Coggins won't want to be disturbed at this time o'day,' he told Grace when she asked if she might speak to the manager. 'What's it about?'

Grace knew that a firm approach would be preferable to the shyness she felt.

'I'm enquiring about any vacancies for staff to serve lunches,' she said boldly.

'We don't need no extra kitchen staff,' the man replied with a discouraging shake of his head, and for a moment Grace's hopes were dashed. She was not going to be put off by this man, however.

'Well, perhaps my name could be put down as a possible future waitress,' she volunteered, raising her voice, and at that moment Mr Coggins called from his office.

'Who is it, Tubby?'

'Only a slip of a girl askin' about a job servin' lunches,' the man called back.

'How old?'

'I'm sixteen, sir!' cried Grace, adding a year to her age.

'Fetch her in, Tubby, and let's have a look.'

Grace didn't need Tubby to fetch her anywhere, but stepped smartly to the half-open door where Mr Coggins sat at a desk, a glass at his elbow. He looked her up and down.

'We've only just taken on that lad from the Union, CC,' said Tubby irritably.

'Yeah, but this is a girl. Any experience, missie?' asked Mr Coggins.

'Yes, sir, I'm at present employed by Mrs Brangton at Stepaside.'

'Oho, so you know your manners. Well, I'm sorry, Miss…er, what was the name?'

'Miss Munday, sir.'

'Sorry, Miss Munday, but I don't need any new staff right now.'

'But Mr Coggins—'

'Right, you 'eard what Mr Coggins said, so off yer go,' said Tubby nastily, but Mr Coggins held up his hand.

'Wait a minute, there might be a job for her later on, Tubby, and not so far off, neither,' he said in a low tone but perfectly audible to Grace.

''Ow'd yer make that out, CC?'

'We could get a lot busier if there's any, er, trouble,' said Mr Coggins cryptically. 'All right, Miss Munday, you can go back to your posh Mrs Brangton, and I'll know where you are if I need more staff, right?'

To which Grace could only smile, nod and say politely, 'Thank you very much, Mr Coggins. Good evening.'

And ignoring Tubby, she walked out of the Railway Hotel with her head held as high as if she had not received a disappointment.

July, 1914

It was Saturday, the first in July. Aaron and his uncle had taken the train to London, to observe the Sabbath at their family's synagogue, and Ernest was in charge of the office, with a new girl at the typewriter. Windows were open to let in what breeze there was, and there was very little business: a couple of inquiries about farm and shop insurance, and a client paying his premium in cash, coins carefully saved in a money box; there being no bank in North Camp other than the post office, the firm was used to dealing with cash payments delivered by hand. Ernest had time, therefore, to indulge his secret passion undisturbed except for the occasional ping of the doorbell.

He opened his exercise book of blank lined pages, and dipped his pen in the inkpot. His head was full of images, and as he tried to capture them on paper, they turned themselves into sentences, and fresh pictures came to his mind. He wrote of *eternal sounds of summer* and *the silent tread of dusk upon these hills*. The landscape that he loved was his subject, and he saw himself as a rural poet in the tradition of John Clare and Thomas Gray; but now a new theme was emerging, and whether he walked by ancient pathways through the woods or lingered beside a familiar stream, he found that his lines were leading in a direction he had not planned, yet which seemed so right and natural.

Beneath the deep, dark shadow of the yew, you lie with limbs outstretched, he wrote, and *In softly shifting clouds a face appears to me and me alone.*

In blaze of noon, in coolness after rain, your steps return again, and yet again.

Again, again, again. Ernest's half-formed sentences took shape as four-lined verses with a rhyming couplet at the end of each, a refrain, a moment shared and recalled: *And each fair vista speaks to me of you.* He crossed out *you* and wrote *thee.* His pen flew across the pages, writing a poem. A love poem.

Ernest put down his pen and closed his eyes, for these innocent verses revealed to him that at twenty his restless heart had found a focus. He smiled. Undeclared and unreturned his love might be, yet it filled his heart and life, raising him up to walk with kings and gods.

'Ernest, old chap! There's a rare crop of rumours going around London about this business in Sarajevo!'

'Where?' Ernest was taken off guard by Aaron's sudden appearance in the office, shortly before it was due to close.

'Sarajevo, it's in Serbia – this unfortunate Archduke Franz Ferdinand!'

'Who?'

'You know, the one who was shot dead in the street last Sunday – they're saying that it'll trigger off the most enormous political explosion – it could even lead to war!'

'But *why?*' asked Ernest in bewilderment. 'What has this man's murder got to do with *us,* Aaron?'

And in all the time that lay ahead, Ernest never found a satisfactory answer to his question.

Chapter Five

July–August, 1914

Nobody could remember a more glorious summer. Front and back doors stood open, and everybody wanted to be outside; as soon as the children came out of school, they ran off to play on the common or down by the Blackwater which was so low that even children could wade across it, and punts that drifted too near the banks got stuck in the mud. Cricket pitches and tennis courts echoed to the sound of bat and racquet against ball, and the cheers that rose from the onlookers sitting in the shade. It was a time of sunbathing and swimming, picnics and trips to the seaside.

Yet a shadow was gathering over Europe, and the talk in the Tradesmen's Arms echoed its menace.

'What d'you make of it, Eddie?' asked Tom Munday. 'They're holding a special service in St Peter's on Sunday, to pray for peace – that things'll settle down and the old kaiser'll stop banging the drums o' war.'

'I can't see it coming to anything, myself,' replied Cooper. 'Don't know what it's got to do with us, anyway.'

'I'm not so sure,' said Tom, frowning. 'Ernest's friend Aaron Pascoe is doing his best to persuade his parents to leave

Germany and come over here. His father's English, but the mother's German, a sister of old Mr Schelling that Ernest works for. They've got a very nice place out there, and I don't suppose they fancy leaving it all and coming to live with her Jewish relatives in London.'

'You can hardly blame them! Why does their son want them to?'

'Ernest says that if there was a war, they'd be on the wrong side, wouldn't they? That's reason enough!'

'Get away with you, Tom, things aren't that bad. And your Ernest always was a worrier!' Eddie smiled as he drained his glass. 'Havin' another?'

'No, thanks. And don't be so sure. The British Regular Army's being mobilised, and young Cedric Neville has gone to join his unit in the Territorials. Before we know where we are, they'll be calling up the young, single men – and that could mean Ernest and young Pascoe. It's all right for you, Eddie, your little lad's only a tiddler.'

Eddie thought a change of subject was called for. 'How's that daughter o' yours getting on? The one that's moving to London to be near her curate?'

'Storey's a vicar now, with his own church, and they're both determined to be married, whatever his bishop says,' answered Tom with a half-smile, for he sympathised with the couple. 'He's coming to stay a couple o' days with us next week, and I won't be saying no to them, Eddie. Violet's against it, of course, and says Isabel's much too young. I think she's worried that the girl could have a couple o' kids before she's twenty-one – before she's had any life of her own. But if it's what they want, God knows they've waited long enough, and I won't stand in their way.'

Eddie nodded. 'I think you're right, Tom. If my Mary had the chance of a decent man like him, I'd give 'em my blessing, though so far she's been happy enough with the Yeomanses, in fact they're more like parents to her than I am.'

'I'll tell you what, Eddie, I'd be a jolly sight more worried about my Grace if she hadn't got this nice little job at Mrs Brangton's, a sensible woman who keeps an eye on her. You never saw such a change in a girl, and it's a big relief to her mother and me, I can tell you!'

While the threat of war drew closer, Grace Munday had never had so much fun in her life as now. When Mr Coggins's summons came to her at Stepaside, she at once pulled off her frilly apron and cap, and tossed them into Mrs Brangton's office.

'Sorry, Mrs B, but I've got better things to do!' she called out happily. 'Say good-bye to Mrs Bentley-Foulkes for me!' And she literally ran all the way from the high-class tea rooms to the Railway Hotel, where her expectations were fully justified. On every hand there were smiles and complimentary words for the pretty young girl tripping daintily between the tables crowded with officers off to their regiments, sailors going to rejoin their ships, and men on their way to enlist. The fact that she did not report her change of employer to her parents was simply to avoid an unnecessary rumpus, and she intended to wait for an opportune moment. A spirit of adventure filled the air, and Grace soon learnt that a large number of the Railway Hotel's new clientele was actually hoping for war and the chance to play their part in it.

Neither Ernest Munday nor Aaron Pascoe felt any desire to respond to all the excited talk of a call to arms. Aaron's fears for his parents and their younger children in Elberfeld had dominated every other issue, and having discussed the matter with his uncle, the whole Schelling family, supported by their rabbi in London, had brought all their influence to bear on Aaron's father, Victor Pascoe, to persuade him to bring his family over to England and settle with the strong second-generation Jewish community in Tamarind Street, Whitechapel.

'My mother's very reluctant to leave the home they have in Elberfeld and cram themselves in with her London relations,' Aaron told Ernest, 'but with the situation as it is now in Germany, my father had no choice but to insist. They're arriving sometime next week, and my uncle's giving me time off to meet them at Southampton and then travel with them to Tamarind Street. I shall be so thankful to see them safely installed with my Schelling grandparents.'

'And I'll be thankful to know your mind's at rest,' Ernest answered fervently, for his friend's strained and anxious eyes troubled him. 'Just so long as you don't decide to stay in London with them!'

Aaron laughed briefly. 'No fear of that, they're much too ambitious for me to take over Schelling and Pascoe at some future time! Come on, Ernest, let's go and have lunch at the Railway Hotel today, and see what news we can pick up at first hand. I'm tired of newspaper conjecture, and if men are enlisting at the rate the papers say, I'd like to meet a few of them and hear what they're saying.'

'Yes, ask them if they really want to go abroad to fight and kill other young fellows like themselves,' said Ernest with a shiver. 'Leaving home, parents, families, friends, everything they hold dear.'

'But it's to defend those very things, old chap, don't you see, that's what's firing them all to join up – come on, let's go and see what we can find out!'

On entering the restaurant, the first thing Ernest saw was his sister Grace serving at the tables, and she saw him. She came straight over.

'I'm going to tell Dad today, Ernest, really I am,' she pleaded. 'Mr Coggins, he's the manager, simply *begged* me to come in and give a hand, they've got that busy! I can be so much more *useful* here than in that other silly little…that quiet little place.'

She glanced at Aaron, and saw him smiling at her brother's discomfiture. 'Honestly, Mr Pascoe, I have to work *much* harder here, and Ernest knows how tired I am when I get home from work,' she said with a beguiling look. 'Please, you *must* ask him to keep it to himself for the time being – our parents are so dreadfully strict!'

Ernest regarded her gravely. 'I won't tell on you, Grace,' he began, but cut short her smiles as she clasped her hands together in gratitude. 'I'll give you the opportunity to tell them yourself. This evening. Yes, Grace, they'll be hurt because you should have told them earlier, but if you tell them that you're sincerely sorry, I'll put in a good word for you.'

Grace's smile faded, to be replaced by penitence. 'All right, Ernest, as long as you let me tell them myself first, and I'll say how very, very sorry I am.' She turned to Aaron with a wink that her brother could not see. 'And now, gentlemen, may I take your order?'

When she reached home that evening, artful Grace did not confess immediately to her mother, who she knew would be shocked and furious, but waited until her father came in, hot and tired after a day spent building a new chicken house at Yeomans' farm. Grace waited until he had finished his supper, then gently tugged at his sleeve and, looking up demurely, whispered, 'Will you come out in the garden, Daddy? I want to tell you something.'

Tom was at once alerted by being called *Daddy* instead of *Dad*, and her air of a worried little girl expecting blame. He gave her a reassuring smile as they went outside, thinking there may have been some trouble with a customer at Stepaside. But when he understood that Grace had been working for the last two weeks at the Railway Hotel without mentioning the fact, let alone asking her parents' permission, he was truly stunned, and she saw that she was not going to get off lightly.

'It was worrying me, Daddy, because I *knew* I ought to tell you and Mum, but the longer I left it the harder it got – and then today I knew I couldn't go on deceiving you any longer.' She burst into tears.

'Well, I must give you credit for owning up at last, Grace, though your mother will be very upset about the way you've deceived us.'

'I know, Daddy, I know, and I'm so very, very sorry!' she sobbed, tears pouring down her cheeks. 'Will you tell her for me, Daddy?'

'No, Grace, you'll have to tell her yourself, and I hope you'll feel thoroughly ashamed for causing her such a shock. I'll have a word with her afterwards, but you must go indoors *now*, this very minute, and ask her to come to the parlour with you, to tell her privately.'

Violet Munday was indeed horrified, not least because all their North Camp neighbours had been told of Grace's favoured position at Stepaside; heaven only knew what they would say about the Railway Hotel, if they didn't know already, and how they would laugh! Yet after a long talk between herself and Tom that night, it was decided that Grace might as well continue to work for Mr Coggins, seeing that she seemed to be settled there, and there being no chance of her returning to Stepaside. Violet had no choice but to agree, but she felt hemmed in by trouble on all sides: the Reverend Mark Storey was coming to stay for two days, from the Tuesday until the Thursday of the last week in July, and he had made it quite clear that his purpose was to discuss his marriage to their daughter Isabel.

'He's not sleeping *here*, not under *this* roof!' declared Violet. 'It would be most improper, and heaven knows what people would say.'

Tom did not attempt to override, for he felt sure that the young clergyman would be more at ease sleeping at another house, away from Mrs Munday's cold disapproval.

'There are plenty o' kind-hearted people in North Camp who'll be glad to put him up for a couple o' nights, and I'll write to tell him we haven't got a spare room,' he answered, even though Ernest had volunteered to give up his own room to Mark and stay with the Schellings, where the anxiety over Aaron's family was growing by the day, and Ernest was affected by it on his friend's behalf.

But the Mundays were in for a surprise. At church that Sunday the Rev. Mr Saville stopped them as they filed out and said that he and his wife were looking forward to having Mark to stay with them.

'He'll be back in his old room, and we only wish that he could stay longer,' he said. 'The problem will be that so many of our parishioners will want to see him again and speak with him – and of course he will be otherwise *engaged*, won't he?' He smiled at his own little pun.

Isabel was delighted and Violet astonished by this change of attitude since the banishment of the lovesick curate. It gave North Camp a clear message that Mr Storey had earned his right to marry pretty, popular Miss Munday, and that a local wedding was in the offing. It was also a signal to Violet Munday that she too would need to change her viewpoint and look kindly on her future son-in-law; it was much better to receive congratulations than condolences.

So Mark received a very cordial welcome when Isabel led him into the front parlour to meet her parents, who were at once impressed by his older appearance and confident air. There's a man who's chosen his path in life and is following it, thought Tom Munday, giving him a warm handshake, and Violet graciously offered him her hand. When Ernest and Grace arrived home from their places of work in Everham, they too greeted him with undisguised pleasure, and when Mrs Munday and Isabel announced that dinner was ready, the whole family sat down to a roast leg of mutton with vegetables from the garden, and Mark said grace on behalf of them all.

The conversation flowed fairly easily at first, and Tom admired Mark's enthusiasm for his work, the genuine concern he felt for his parishioners, churchgoers and non-churchgoers alike.

'Mr and Mrs Clements send their love to you, Isabel, and asked me to say that you'll always be welcome in their house,' he said, for Isabel had entirely won over Mr Clements and almost won over his wife during her recent short stay.

'I shan't need their hospitality for much longer, will I, Mark?' she said, looking up at him with shining eyes, then turning to her parents, she told them of their proposed plans.

'We shall be married here at St Peter's, and Mark and I want it to be a quiet wedding,' she said. 'And we think that the middle of October would be a good time, so that I shall be there to help Mark at Christmas.'

There was a gasp, and the Mundays looked at each other in shocked surprise.

'*October?*' Violet could not hide her dismay. 'So soon? Don't you think you should wait another year or two, until Isabel's at least twenty, and…and all this talk of war is over?' She glanced at her husband for his support, but Tom had already guessed his daughter's intentions, and nodded at Mark to hear what he had to say.

'I can understand how you feel, Mrs Munday,' began Mark courteously, 'and your views are shared by my own parents to some extent, but it's partly *because* of the uncertainties of the times that Isabel and I want to make a firm commitment to each other *now*, rather than later. None of us know what the outcome will be, but the signs are not hopeful, and—'

'Mark and I know each other's minds, and we've waited long enough,' cut in Isabel, her voice firm and clear. 'And until our wedding, I'm going to stay at the home of Mr and Mrs Clements—'

'Oh, no, Isabel, *no!*' cried Violet Munday. 'You can't leave your home so soon, you must stay with us for Christmas – shouldn't she, Tom?'

Tom had also suffered a pang at the news of his daughter's imminent departure from home, but he could only offer her his blessing, because she was as determined as Mark, and no amount of persuasion would change her mind.

'I want to get to know as much about Mark's parish as I can,' she told them, 'and then when I go into St Barnabas'

Church as his wife, I won't be a stranger to them. You must try to understand, Mum and Dad, it won't make any difference between us, I'll always love you as much as I do now.' Her voice faltered a little, and Tom reached out his hand to touch hers across the table.

'We know, Isabel, we know, and your mother and I wish you well. I think you're probably doing the right thing.'

Ernest felt that a few words were required of him, and smiled at his sister.

'I...we shall miss you, Isabel, but knowing that you're with Mark, we shan't mind as much...as if...' He could say no more, and for some reason his thoughts flew to Aaron; he looked down at his plate to hide his eyes, suddenly full of tears.

'And *I* shall be bridesmaid!' exclaimed Grace, clapping her hands together and beaming round the table.

The visit passed quickly, and all too soon, it seemed to Mark, it was time for him to leave North Camp; he and Isabel had not had much time alone together, but she was to come to Bethnal Green at the end of August, to stay with Mr and Mrs Clements.

'But what about Miss Daniells and the children who need you at the school?' asked her mother. 'Surely you're not going to leave them in the lurch?'

'No, Mum, this is the opportunity Phyllis Bird has been waiting for,' replied Isabel with a smile. '*She'll* be taking my place in September, and she won't be sorry to leave the Post Office, I can tell you!'

At some time before the wedding Mark planned to take Isabel to visit his elderly parents in Gloucestershire. Isabel knew that his father was a retired clergyman, and that his parents had their reservations at his marrying such a young girl, though they were prepared to give him their blessing.

When he returned to the vicarage on the Thursday evening, she walked with him as far as the thick, curving beech hedge, where they stopped just inside the gate, unseen from the house. He at once folded her in his arms.

'Dearest Isabel, I am afraid that there may be war ahead, but God's given me the greatest blessing a man can possess, so I don't need to fear the future,' he whispered, his lips against her hair.

'I-I just hope that your parents will accept me,' she whispered back.

'When I take you to see them, my love, they won't have any more doubts, they'll just marvel that such a wonderful girl could have chosen *me!*'

The sweetness of their kisses said more than any words, and Mark at last drew away from her, and said she must go back; he could not trust himself further.

When Ernest arrived at the office of Schelling and Pascoe on the Thursday morning, Aaron had departed for Southampton, and thoughts of him and his returning family filled Ernest's head; no news came through that day, though the newspapers were full of alarming stories, including that the British Fleet was preparing to go to sea; there was nothing about a ship docking passengers at Southampton. At noon on the Friday the telephone rang in Mr Schelling's office, and Ernest sat stock-still and with bated breath, waiting for the news it brought, if any.

'That was Aaron, and he says they have arrived!' shouted Mr Schelling, and Ernest exhaled a long sigh of relief. The rest of the day was spent wondering if the Pascoes had managed to get a train to London, for the railways were in a state of chaos, with long delays and cancellations. When the office closed that evening, there had been no further news, and Ernest was loath to leave Mr and Mrs Schelling who were clearly very worried.

'You will take charge of the office tomorrow as usual, Mr Munday,' said Mr Schelling, 'and if there is no more news overnight I shall travel up to Waterloo by whatever train is running, to see if they've arrived at Tamarind Street or not.'

'Of course, sir,' Ernest assured him, though he felt helpless to be of any real use or comfort, and spent a sleepless night, tossing and turning, trying to pray for the safety of Aaron's family – his parents Victor and Eva Pascoe, their son, Jonathan, and the girls Greta and Devora; he felt that he knew them personally, having heard Aaron constantly talking about them during the last month. His parents heard him groan out loud at one point in the night, and Violet wanted to get up and go to him.

'He's fretting over Isabel, that's what it is,' she said when Tom advised her to stay where she was, and not to embarrass their son. '*I* noticed how upset he was when Isabel said she was leaving home so soon, even if the rest of you didn't. I understand only too well how he's feeling.'

Ernest cycled away early after a breakfast of tea and toast, and arrived at the office to find that Mr Schelling had already left for London. There followed another day of waiting and wondering, while rumours circulated and Mrs Schelling reported that Everham shops were becoming depleted by a rush to lay in stores of provisions. Mid-day came with no news, and it was nearly four o'clock when suddenly Aaron burst through the door and flung his arms around Ernest in an emotional embrace. Mr Schelling followed close behind him, his voice shaking but triumphant.

'They're safe in London!' he announced breathlessly, hugging his wife. 'I've seen my sister Eva, poor soul, she blames herself for the delay – but they got here, and Aaron took them to London – we've come from Tamarind Street!'

Ernest was conscious only of Aaron's arms around him, Aaron's tears against his face; he yearned over his friend, longing to hold him close, but resisting, for he knew that Aaron's emotion sprang from concern for his family and relief at their safe arrival. And besides, the presence of the Schellings restrained the dictates of his heart.

'So they got here safely, Aaron,' he whispered. 'And...and how are they?'

Aaron withdrew himself from Ernest's passive embrace, and raised haggard eyes. 'They...they looked pathetic, Ernest, utterly exhausted – there were lots of them, refugees, some of them with nowhere to go when they got off the ship,' he said brokenly. 'Women and babies, just in the clothes they stood up in – and my poor mother's face, she blames herself – oh, it's horrible, Ernest, there's going to be war, and you and I are going to have to fight in it!'

For Ernest that Saturday afternoon marked the beginning of the war, though it was not until midnight on the Tuesday that Britain officially declared war on Germany, and the Foreign Secretary, Sir Edward Grey, uttered his solemn prediction:

'The lamps are going out all over Europe; we shall not see them lit again in our lifetime.'

Chapter Six

August–October, 1914

The wave of patriotic enthusiasm was almost palpable, like a crackle in the air. Rumour had given way to certainty, and it was as if the British lion had suddenly awakened with a roar, stirred by the threat to liberty. *Rule, Britannia*! was sung in theatres and music halls, on football pitches and at any open-air gathering where Britons felt the need to declare that they *never, never, never shall be slaves.*

And Britannia was not short of heroes ready to defend her shores. Recruiting offices were opened in every town, and long queues of excited young men, some scarcely more than boys, formed up to be enlisted in the British Army or Navy, and it was known that the British Expeditionary Force had been despatched to France to assist in holding back the German invasion. Everham swarmed with new soldiers, mostly without their khaki uniforms, and some armed with their own weapons: rifles and revolvers used for shooting rabbits and pheasants, now brought out, oiled and fired into the air for practice. They drilled on school playgrounds, cricket pitches and wherever there was a piece of level waste ground. Brass bands assembled and rehearsed to lead the columns of new recruits, and townspeople turned out to wave Union Jacks and cheer as they marched through the streets of Everham with hardly a foot out of step.

The Bird brothers, Tim and Ted, were among the first volunteers, while Dick Yeomans hung back, as did Sidney Goddard. Cedric Neville was already with the Territorials, and expecting to be sent to join the BEF any day soon. At first Tom Munday said nothing to Ernest about enlisting, knowing that his son hated all forms of killing, including that legalised by warfare. Violet Munday dreaded the very idea of her son facing mortal danger, and insisted on believing the editorials of those newspapers that predicted that it would all be over by Christmas.

'Let's hope that turns out to be right, Eddie,' Tom told the friend in whom he confided his deepest fears. 'The boys are under a lot o' pressure to join up – I mean look at all these posters with old Kitchener pointing his great finger straight at you. It's bound to have an effect, making out they're cowards if they don't join in.'

The posters did indeed have their effect on Ernest and Aaron, who discussed the matter openly and honestly, coming to the conclusion that there was no need for them to join the army at this point, for there were surely more than enough men who had already done so; and Ernest reported this to his father.

'Aaron and I are opposed to killing our fellow men, Dad, be they Germans or any other nation. And we're not afraid of the charge of cowardice.'

Tom said that he understood and supported his son, though inwardly he breathed a sigh of *Thank God*, and passed on the reassurance to Violet. He was in fact more troubled by the departure of Isabel for Bethnal Green. Having planned to go at the end of August, the declaration of war had made her more anxious to be near Mark, and despite her mother's protests and sighs, she left for London midway through August. Tom encouraged her and praised her decision, though partly to cover his own distress at losing a daughter who would never again return to live at home, because home had become another place, the place where Mark Storey lived and worked. Tom and Violet accompanied their daughter to Everham Station in a horse-drawn cab, as the omnibus had no room for her travelling trunk.

'Goodbye, dearest Dad and Mum. Thanks for coming to see me off,' she said with a bright smile, and Tom tried to force a smile in return, to counteract Violet's copious tears. Only when Isabel's train had completely disappeared from sight did he allow himself to put his arm around his wife to comfort her.

'We haven't lost her, Vi, she's got a good man to look after her now, just as we've done. We've still got Grace at home, and Ernest is absolutely dead set against joining up,' he added cheerfully, though his own heart was heavy with a sense of loss, for inwardly he too longed to keep Isabel at home for another year or two. She was so young to be getting married, too young to be wrenched from her family and condemned to early motherhood and the cares it would bring. But Tom Munday kept these thoughts to himself as being unhelpful and not likely to do anybody any good.

Grace had to run for the omnibus to North Camp, and called out to the driver to wait for her, which he did, though with disapproval.

'This is the third time ye've kept us waitin', an' I won't wait for yer again,' he grumbled as, breathless and dishevelled, Grace climbed up to the dozen passengers' seats behind the driver. He cracked his whip, and the horse ambled forward, pulling its too heavy load.

'Sorry, busy at work, thanks for waiting!' she panted, taking one of the two remaining seats. Her apology was wasted on the driver who had called in at the Railway Hotel for a half pint of ale, where he had seen this young miss exchanging a lingering kiss with an army officer in a corner alcove of the public bar. Asking for trouble, the flighty little hussy, and he shouted out in the hearing of all the passengers:

'Ye'd've been in Queer Street if I'd gorn without yer, there ain't another bus to North Camp for an hour, and I ain't goin' to wait around for yer again!'

Grace considered it beneath her dignity to reply, and sat watching the passing hedgerows, laden with autumnal berries. If she'd missed the bus, she'd have walked home – and perhaps that charming lieutenant would have been pleased to walk with her... Grace smiled to herself as she recalled the open admiration on his handsome face. His name was Nick, and he was soon to be sent to France to show the Jerries what a mistake they'd made in taking on the British. And he'd only asked her for one little kiss, the memory of which made Grace shiver with delight and a thrilling sense of her own power. Would Nick be at the Railway Hotel tomorrow, looking for her again? Life was so exciting these days, and romantic! She would ask Dad for a bicycle to travel to Everham and back each day, as Ernest did, thumbing her nose at old Miseryguts and his boneshaker omnibus as she pedalled past!

Tom Munday was not so keen on the idea of her cycling four miles each way, six days a week. 'Winter's coming on, and the evenings are getting darker, Grace. There are some lonely places you'll have to pass, and some strange characters about.'

'But Daddy, I don't like telling Mr Coggins that I've got to leave when the restaurant's busy, just to catch that old omnibus! Cycling will actually be *quicker* for me, and there are several others who do it every day, so I shan't be on my own, and think of the fares I'll save! In fact I could cycle in with Ernest every day, and return with him, likely as not!'

'But Ernest sometimes doesn't get home till quite late, when they've had a busy day,' her father objected. 'You couldn't be expected to wait an extra hour – I mean, what would you do with yourself?'

'Work an extra hour at the Railway,' said Grace with a smile. *Dear* old Dad, so kind and caring, and such a worrier! She had no intention of cycling home with her brother every evening, though Ernest might be useful as a messenger sometimes, to tell their parents that she was working a little later. She had no wish to lose all her admirers to that cheeky blonde barmaid Madge Fraser, and could always say that Mr Coggins had personally asked her to stay for longer, on double pay. She knew he thought her an asset to the Railway Hotel, much to the chagrin of that miserable Tubby, but both she and Madge were under strict orders not to meet any of the patrons out of hours. The girls could be as provocative as they liked when working but, as their boss, he said he could not be responsible for what they did outside.

In the end Tom Munday gave in and allowed Grace to cycle to and from work, though Violet thought it would be much too tiring for her.

The train journey down from London to Cheltenham seemed endless, and from there Isabel and Mark had to take a slow omnibus to the little village of Instone, from where they walked to the pretty, hidden-away cottage where the Reverend Richard Storey and his wife lived in seclusion. The sight of the peaceful countryside, the fat cows grazing in the autumn sunshine and the lanes like green tunnels with the trees meeting overhead, made it difficult to believe that England was at war; and to enter the Storeys' home was to travel back in time, with oil lamps and candles as the only lighting, and every piece of furniture an antique. The old couple received Isabel cordially, and said how much they hoped that Mark would soon be transferred to an easier parish than St Barnabas'. Mrs Storey poured tea for them from a silver tea service, and they ate bread and butter spread with home-made jam, supplied by the Storeys' daughter, Mrs Reynolds, who'd married a farmer, and lived near Hook in Hampshire. After tea, Isabel sat talking with Mrs Storey while her husband took Mark on a tour of the garden. She would have been surprised to hear their conversation.

Old Mr Storey took an envelope out of his pocket, addressed simply to the Rev. Storey, Instone, Glos. He drew out a letter and handed it to his son. It was from Tom Munday, and Mark hesitated to read it.

'Go on, Mark, he asks me to have a word with you about your marital union with Isabel, and I must say that I'm in complete agreement with him,' his father said gently. 'You should take care not to give her a child for at least a year, not until she is well experienced as a clergyman's wife, and not until this dreadful war is over. If you will pardon two old men for advising you on this matter, Mark, and if you could give me your word that you will take heed of what we say, your mother and I would be much reassured, and happy to attend your wedding to this very young girl.'

Mark was surprised at the depth of feeling showed by his father, and gave his word that Isabel would not be made a mother too soon; but inwardly he knew that he would have to pray for self-restraint, for he longed above all things to hold Isabel in his arms and make her his lawful wedded wife.

On the twenty-third of August came reports of a battle fought at the Belgian town of Mons, and at first there was rejoicing and flag-waving; but after a day or two the news came through that the Allies had been defeated and forced to retire. Only after more than a week had passed did the death toll become known: the British losses were reckoned to be about five thousand men.

'My God, five thousand,' Ernest said, looking across at Aaron's newspaper as they sat at their desks in the office. '*Five thousand.* And it wasn't even a victory.'

'We may yet be called up, Ernest,' replied Aaron sombrely. 'And called on to give our lives.'

'No. *No*, Aaron. I shall *never* agree to go anywhere to kill my fellow men,' said Ernest, his words like a groan of pain.

'My poor friend, you may have to.' Aaron spoke very quietly, and Ernest made no answer, but sat with his head between his hands.

Life at the Clements' was reassuringly the same, and Isabel's welcome much warmer than on the first occasion. Mrs Clements took a great interest in dear Mr Storey's wife-to-be, and when Isabel said she would be working as a teacher, starting at the beginning of the autumn term, she was very happy to advise her.

'Mr Storey'll get you into St Barnabas' Church School,' she said. 'It's much nicer than the one in Barnett Street, run by the London School Board, that's an *awful* place, and the children don't attend half the time, 'cause the mothers keep 'em at home to mind the babies – and there's always plenty o' *those* round here, ten or twelve kids to a family. I knew one o' the teachers, nice girl, but she ended up with a nervous breakdown and laryngitis from shoutin' at the dirty little rascals, and the girls were as bad as the boys, she said. That's what comes o' free education, I reckon, nobody puts a value on it. Now at St Barnabas' they pay a shillin' a week, and the two ladies who run it are reg'lars at St Barnabas', mornin's and evenin's every Sunday. They'll be glad o' your help. Miss Munday!'

Which was why Isabel told Mark that she would like to apply to Barnett Street School as a teacher for the younger pupils there, for which she was well experienced.

'But it's in the roughest area of the parish,' he told her, 'and not many of my congregation send their children there!'

'Dearest Mark, I've come here to be the wife of the Reverend Mr Storey, and to live among the people my husband serves, churchgoers or not,' she replied, smiling. 'You've told me about Barnett Street in your letters, and how you've got a football team going for the boys – well, *I* shall see what I can do for the girls!'

Her application was well timed, and she was accepted at once.

'It's only fair to tell you, Miss Munday, that we fight a constant battle with poverty here,' said the headmistress, 'and all the social evils that go with it – drink, debt and poor health – so we have difficulties with behaviour: some children learn bad language at home, and flaunt it here at school. I *do* occasionally use the cane as a last resort, but we try to instil Christian principles by example and patience. I hope that you have plenty of patience, Miss Munday!'

Isabel found the first week very challenging, and as different from Miss Daniells' school as it was possible to be. The new intake of five-year-olds was a mixed bag of the noisy and mute, the defiant and timid, the well-scrubbed and the smelly. A quarter of them were barefooted, and another quarter had ill-fitting and much-repaired boots, while their clothing similarly reflected parental care or lack of it.

At first they were in awe of her, but as she encouraged them to talk about themselves, they began to open up and sometimes told her quite extraordinary things, like the little boy who cheerfully informed her that 'Me mum 'ad a baby in 'er bed last night, miss, and it wasn't 'alf a bloody mess! The nurse shoo'd us all away, an' we ain't 'ad no breakfuss!'

There had been campaigns and parliamentary debates for and against the provision of school meals over the past two decades, and Barnett Street School had reached a compromise, by which a bowl of soup with bread and cheese was offered for one penny unless the parents applied for exemption; the headmistress tended to turn a blind eye to children who could not produce their penny, and no child was denied the midday refreshment. Isabel was able to go to the kitchen and beg at least a slice of bread and butter for the breakfastless.

Miss Munday quickly became an object of interest to her little pupils who saw her as a beautiful lady who spoke kindly to them and listened to their stories; in return they gave her their attention, and made varying progress with learning to read and write, and doing simple sums of addition and subtraction. In spite of Mrs Clements' predictions, Isabel told her fiancé that children were the same everywhere, and her pupils were at heart no different from the ones she'd taught at Miss Daniells' church school in North Camp. And she loved them.

❧

Ernest knelt beside his parents and Grace in church and tried to pray; it was the first Sunday in September, and there would be no cycling that afternoon with Aaron who had gone to visit his parents and family in London. Ernest knew that he should be praying for peace in Europe and for Aaron's family, and yet he found himself asking that Aaron might not decide to leave Everham and join them. He knew that Mrs Pascoe and the children were miserably homesick for Elberfeld, but Mr Victor Pascoe had gone out determined to find employment, and found it in a small Jewish family tailoring establishment where the hours were long and the standard of work was high.

'I am learning how to be a tailor instead of a man of business,' Pascoe had told his son. 'It isn't easy, but a man must live and feed his dependents.'

Since Aaron had confided this to Ernest, the fear of losing his friend was constantly on Ernest's mind, and he was thankful that Mr Schelling urged Aaron to stay in Everham rather than swell the already crowded conditions in Tamarind Street; but was it right for a Christian to pray that he might not lose his Jewish friend, for purely selfish reasons? Surely there was no harm in praying for the Pascoes and their children, now starting at a new and unfamiliar London Board school.

While these thoughts troubled Ernest's mind, his sister Grace peeped through her fingers at Philip Saville, the vicar's sixteen-year-old son who, having been educated at a public school and therefore out of sight during term time, had suddenly turned from a freckled schoolboy into a handsome, golden-haired youth as tall as his father. Grace wondered idly if he had kissed a girl yet, and her mouth curved in a satisfied little smile as she remembered Nick's kisses when they met at the Everham crossroads on her way home. She stood her bicycle up against the ancient oak tree there, and took her place beside it for ten delicious minutes or more to enjoy Nick's kisses and his increasingly bold hands – she almost gasped aloud at the memory, but checked herself in time. Oh, what would she do after he was sent to France?

Beside her Tom Munday echoed Mr Saville's prayers for peace. The news of a battle on the river Marne sounded confused and indecisive, though it seemed that this time the Germans were in retreat; but the shock of Mons lingered in the minds of the public, and Tom Munday was becoming less sure of an early victory as the days went by. A hundred thousand men had enlisted to fight for their king and country, yet the recruitment campaign went on, and Lord Kitchener was demanding a hundred thousand more, which surely meant that he must be expecting a longer war than had been predicted. Suppose, just suppose that Ernest was persuaded – or compelled – to join the army and be sent to France to halt the German invasion, and suppose…but no, Tom could not allow such hideous thoughts space in his brain. He simply commended his wife and three children to the Lord's care.

Violet Munday also prayed for peace in the world, especially in Europe. How tiresome this war was, just as Isabel was about to be married, the first of her circle of friends! Their neighbours would stare at her clergyman bridegroom, whose father was also a man of the cloth, and as the bride's mother, Violet would reflect her share of the glory. *But…* Violet had been truly shocked on her one visit to Bethnal Green and Mark's East End parish. What a dirty, disreputable place for her daughter to live in, with people like that rattletrap Mrs Clements whom Violet had disliked on sight. The mean streets, the pubs and pawnshops – and that ugly school building where Isabel taught, though the girl insisted that she loved her work – had upset Violet and brought back her earlier doubts; now her chief hope was that Mark would soon be transferred to a more respectable parish. Old Mr Storey seemed to think it likely, though he'd gently reminded her and Tom that Christ came into the world to save sinners, and that Mark must answer that call. Mrs Munday had agreed, but was glad the wedding was to be held here at St Peter's, so nobody need see where Isabel was going.

On Sundays the bar of the Railway Hotel opened at three in the afternoon, with the man known as Tubby in charge; Charlie Coggins did a little under-the-counter selling of pies and pasties, as the restaurant had to be closed all day. The undersized young man who usually assisted at the bar was allowed Sundays off, and with the surge of uniformed men seeking refreshment, Tubby resented the extra work involved.

'Pity young Ratty can't come in an' lend a hand, CC,' he grumbled to the boss who had come to help serve at the bar.

'The poor lad's got to have some time off, same as the girls,' replied Coggins, giving out two pints of bitter with a pork pie. 'They work jolly hard, do Madge and Grace, and keep the place cheerful!'

'Huh! They certainly do their job well, when it comes to keeping the lads entertained,' returned Tubby spitefully. ''Specially that one from North Camp – I s'pose you know she meets 'em after hours?'

'Does she? Are you sure o' that, Tubby? Have you caught her at it?'

'Don't need to, I 'ear 'er layin' 'er plans – "see yer by the usual tree", that sort o' thing. And mark my words, when she gets knocked up, it'll be your fault, my fault, anybody's fault 'cept 'ers. Ye're too trustin', CC.'

'And *you'd* better watch your mouth, Tupman, with ears open all around,' answered the boss sharply, distancing himself by giving the man his proper name, which infuriated the barman.

'Couple o' sluts,' he muttered under his breath, wiping a glass so vigorously that it broke in his hand and cut his thumb. 'Bugger!' he said aloud, to the amusement of the young servicemen waiting for their drinks; they were new faces, for Grace's lieutenant Nick had been sent to France.

Charlie Coggins privately decided to have a quiet talk with the two girls at some time during the coming week, but he suspected his barman of jealousy rather than true moral indignation.

The October wedding more than fulfilled Mrs Munday's expectations, and gave North Camp a midweek treat to take their minds off the war for one afternoon. The sky was clear, and a mild autumnal sun shone down on Isabel in her virginal bridal gown and veil, accompanied by her sister Grace in pink, clutching a garden posy of Michaelmas daisies and bestowing her merry glances on all and sundry.

St Peter's Church was well filled, and Violet Munday's heart swelled with pride when the bride arrived with her father in Lady Neville's own carriage, lent for the occasion by that beneficent lady who arrived at the church with her daughter a full quarter of an hour early, and then despatched the carriage to 47 Pretoria Road. Tom Munday had done some intricate woodwork in the drawing room of Hassett Manor, and this was his reward. Mrs Goddard would never be able to match *that* when Betty married, thought Mrs Munday, giving her neighbours a condescending nod. On the groom's side of the aisle sat Mark's parents and his sister Mrs Reynolds with her husband and four children; they had offered the couple the use of the bailiff's cottage on their farmland for a two-night stay after the wedding, and this had been gratefully accepted.

The service opened with the Twenty-third Psalm, and when the time came for Mr Saville to ask, 'Who giveth this woman to be married to this man?' Tom Munday, who had held his daughter's arm tightly on their walk up the aisle, now led her forward to stand beside Mark Storey in his black cassock and surplice, an ordained priest in the Church of England. Both bride and groom made their vows clearly in the silence that fell upon the packed congregation, and as Mrs Munday wiped away a tear, Tom felt a tremor go through him, a moment of apprehension, almost of fear, for the future of this beautiful woman who was his daughter, leaving her parents' home for whatever her husband could provide for her.

When the couple had been legally joined in matrimony, and signed the parish register, their radiant faces as they progressed down the aisle were a measure of reassurance to Tom. To the strains of Mendelssohn's 'Wedding March' they looked upon a sea of faces, all beaming goodwill towards them, from Lady Neville to Mary Cooper who sat with Mrs Yeomans on the groom's side of the church, the bride's side being filled to overflowing. Mr and Mrs Eddie Cooper and their little boy sat at some distance from Mary, with the Birds, Lansdownes and Goddards, and Miss Daniells was given a place of honour beside the gentry. Ernest, dressed in a well-cut grey suit made by Mr Bird, was grateful for Aaron's presence at this Christian ceremony; Mr and Mrs Schelling had sent their polite regrets, but a pleasant surprise awaited Ernest when Mr and Mrs

Woodman entered with their son the Rev. Paul Woodman and his wife, daughter and young baby, all the way from Bristol. There were smiles and handshakes, and Ernest reflected on his past devotion to Paul which had led him eventually to Aaron, and was happy to see the two of them talking in a friendly way.

A family group photograph was taken by a professional man from Everham, and the wedding reception was held at the Jubilee Hall, North Camp's recognition of Queen Victoria's Diamond Jubilee in 1897; it was used for assemblies of all kinds: weddings, funerals, parties and public meetings, though as church property it was not hired out for dances, only such dancing as might end a private party like this. A substantial cold buffet was laid out, at its centre a two-tier cake made by Mrs Munday and decorated by Mrs Lansdowne with edible white roses made from icing sugar and inedible silver leaves arranged round a silver horseshoe. Isabel and Mark were assured that this was North Camp's wedding of the year, and their parents were congratulated, though Mr and Mrs Storey senior were gazed upon with a certain amount of awe. Grace stood at the centre of a group of young people that included handsome young Philip Saville, clearly impressed by her looks and pretty manners. (And now that Nick had gone to fight for his country, where was the harm in a little innocent flirtation?) Tom noticed that Eddie Cooper had left his wife and son for a few minutes' talk with Mary and Mrs Yeomans, and hoped that it might be the start of a reconciliation.

When it was time for the bride's father to give a speech, Tom's was brief but straight from his heart, referring to the 'precious treasure' that he and his wife had today given in marriage to a worthy husband. When his voice began to shake a little, he sat down abruptly to loud applause. The bridegroom's speech fully echoed this sentiment, and Mark said that the Lord had blessed him indeed. Making reference to the two-year separation required of Isabel and himself, he said that it had only served to deepen and strengthen their love, culminating in this day of days. There were enthusiastic nods of agreement and more applause.

At five o'clock the newly-weds left for their brief honeymoon, travelling with the Reynolds family in their open carriage. Taking leave of their daughter, Mr and Mrs Munday kissed her, and Tom silently echoed the words of the psalm sung at their wedding: *Thy loving kindness and mercy shall follow me all the days of my life.* Let it be so for them, O Lord, let it be so!

Daylight was fading on their arrival at the farm, situated between Hook and Dogmersfield in the quiet Hampshire countryside. The cottage usually occupied by the farm bailiff and his wife was a quarter of a mile from the farmhouse, and Sylvia Reynolds unlocked it for her brother and sister-in-law.

'There's a fire laid ready to be lit, and the bed's aired,' she told them. 'There's bread, milk, butter, bacon and eggs in the larder for your breakfast, and you can come up to the house any time you like,' she said with kindly tact.

'Good old Sylvia, she knows we want to be left alone!' said Mark, smiling.

'Yes, alone together at last, dearest Mark!' Isabel exclaimed, throwing her arms around his neck. 'Husband and wife!'

He held her close, and kissed her forehead. 'Dear wife, your happiness is everything to me. Your father gave me a charge, to…to care for you as he has done, and to make you happy.'

She laid her head on his shoulder. 'Dearest Mark, I'll be

happy as long as we're together – you need have no doubts about it, you solemn old thing!' She smiled up into his worried eyes. 'Let's have supper – bread and butter will be fine, and I'll light the fire and get a kettle on the hob. After that, we'll be ready for – well, it's been a long day, and...' Somehow she could not bring herself to utter the word *bed*, though she longed to lie in his arms and yield herself to him completely.

And Mark knew that it could not be. He knew her to be a virgin, like himself, and that she might not expect their marriage to be consummated on this first night, but sooner or later she would wonder why he did not possess her fully as his wife. She was so innocent and trusting, and he could not bear to lose even a part of that trust; he thought of her father and the practical counsel his own father had given him, but was fearful of upsetting or offending her. He tried to pray for guidance, but it didn't seem a proper subject for prayer, and the words wouldn't form in his head.

And yet his plea was answered, above all that he could hope for or imagine.

They agreed that they didn't want any supper other than a cup of tea, and took to the large, downy feather bed in which the bailiff and his wife usually slept. Mark caught his breath at the sight of her lying there in her white nightgown, her hair spread out on the pillow. He wore a new nightshirt, one of three that his mother had made for him, with the unusual feature of a good-sized pocket. With the nightshirts had come the gift of a dozen large white handkerchiefs, one of which now resided in the pocket.

He lay down beside her and put his left arm under her shoulders; she snuggled close to him, and with his right hand he stroked her body, marvelling at the beauty of her firm breasts under the cotton nightgown, the softness of her belly, the curve of her hips, thighs, knees, feet...

'Oh, Mark, I love you.' Words from the Song of Solomon came to her mind:

His left hand is under my head, and his right hand doth embrace me.

He felt himself becoming aroused; his heartbeat drummed in his ears, and his breathing quickened, though he checked himself from making any sound. She gave a little moan, and closing her eyes, she slowly began to pull up the nightgown, higher and higher until he could lay his hand on the soft fuzz of hair between her thighs and that secret place where no man had ever been. She too felt her heart racing, and caught her breath; she made no attempt to remove his hand, but spread out her legs and gave his forefinger entry, sighing as she felt it move inside her. There was one sharp stab of pain which made her gasp momentarily, but it was quickly overcome by an overwhelming sensation of pleasure as he put a second finger inside. She felt it as exquisite beyond description, this special bond between Mark and herself, between a wife and her husband.

My beloved put in his hand by the hole of the door... I rose up to open to my beloved.

She writhed from side to side as a wave of pleasure swept over her, followed by another and another – and then a climax that tingled and shivered throughout her whole body; she found that she was sobbing, but whether crying or laughing she could hardly tell. And then Mark was kissing her, thanking her, murmuring words of love as their shared passion gradually subsided. After a few minutes she gave a long, contented sigh and drifted into sweet, deep sleep. She did not see Mark attending to himself with the handkerchief, or know of the relief which swept over him – for it had been a beautiful shared experience, untroubled by the possibility of conception, for which he knew he would be censured by his father, her parents and most of all by himself. She was safe from his lust, and if it meant another two years to wait for parenthood, so be it. And so he slept beside her, having breathed a heartfelt prayer of thanks.

Grace Munday was feeling distinctly out of sorts. She had received one postcard from Nick at what they were calling 'the front', which had told her very little about where he was or how he was, just that he was looking forward to seeing her again, but no indication of when that would be. Her work at the Railway Hotel continued to be demanding, and worst of all, Mr Coggins had summoned her into his office to ask if she had met any of their patrons, especially those in the armed forces, out of working hours. At first she had firmly denied it, but he looked unconvinced.

'I've told you already, Miss Munday, that I can't be responsible for your safety if you're foolish enough to meet anybody outside. If anything untoward happened – and I'm sure you know what I mean – the Railway Hotel and its staff would bear the brunt of the blame, myself in particular. So I'm asking you again, have you met that lieutenant, what was his name, Nick somebody – or any other o' the military who come in here?'

Grace burst into tears, and fished out a handkerchief to hold to her eyes.

'It's true that I met him once or twice, but he's an officer and a gentleman, Mr Coggins!' she sobbed. 'And now he's gone to fight for his country, and I miss him so much!'

The sight of her tears moved Mr Coggins, who coughed and told her not to cry.

'Only just don't let it happen again, Miss Munday – Grace – because if I hear of it, you'll be dismissed without notice, do you understand?'

Full of apologies and promises, Grace persuaded Mr Coggins that he could rest assured it would not happen again. He told her to run along, and encouraged her to hope that Nick would come home safe and sound. She thanked him and left the office determined to find out which snake in the grass had been telling tales about her. It must be that sly blonde bitch Madge Fraser who was jealous because Nick hadn't looked at her. Yes, that would be it – and everybody knew Madge was carrying on with a sergeant from South Camp who'd already got a child by a housemaid at Hassett Manor. Wait till I get her alone, thought Grace, I'll have her guts for garters!

But Madge soon answered her back in no uncertain terms. 'Don't start getting' on at me, Grace Munday, I've already 'ad a dressin' down from the boss. 'E says I'll be sacked on the spot if 'e 'ears I bin meetin' Sergeant Samms again!'

'What, you as well?' Grace stared back at her, open-mouthed. 'Where did you meet him?'

'On that bit o' waste ground be'ind the 'Ippodrome.'

'Did anybody see you?'

'Nobody who'd bother about it. That boy Coggins got from the Union, 'e might've seen us, but 'e wouldn't say nothin' –'ardly ever opens 'is mouth.'

'What, young Ratty? Did *he* see you? Good heavens, Madge, that horrible Tubby's obviously been using the snivelling little beggar to spy on us! I can see it all now, Tubby's never liked me.'

'So there's nothin' we can do, Grace – he's got us over a barrel, ain't 'e?'

'Don't worry, Madge, I'll find a way to stop his tricks.' Grace's dark eyes narrowed. 'Only you'd better not have any more hanky-panky behind the Hippodrome if you want to keep your job.'

Madge grimaced. 'No fear, not with '*im* on me tail.'

'Tell you what, Madge, let's both do ourselves up this evening, as if we were going out to meet somebody – and we'll meet *each other* behind the Hippodrome, say at half past six.'

'But what good will that do?'

'Just an idea. Meet me there at half past six, right? I'll come a different way.'

And it was as Grace had suspected: when she met Madge at the specified time and place, she saw a small figure lurking in the shadows of the Hippodrome's stage door, quite clearly on the lookout.

'There he is, the little weasel – Ratty! Watch me, Madge!'

She strode towards the boy and grabbed him by the collar. 'Why, if it isn't our little friend Ratty! Have you come to meet Madge, by any chance?'

'No, miss, I ain't!' he muttered, vainly wriggling in her grasp, for she now seized his bony shoulder. 'Lemme go, I ain't done nothin'!'

'Oh, yes, and where will you go, Ratty? Back to the Railway Hotel?'

'Yeah,' answered poor Ratty, for it was his only home since leaving the Union, as the Everham workhouse was called.

Grace took a long shot. 'Tell me, Ratty, how much does Mr Tupman give you for spying on us?'

''Alf a crown,' he gasped, falling into the trap.

Grace loosened her grip on his shoulder. 'Well, I doubt if he'll give you half a crown when you go back and tell him who we met tonight. Go on, be off with you!'

'Poor little bugger,' she remarked to Madge as he took to his heels. 'He'll more likely get a clip on the ear from old Lardyface.'

'My, ye're a sly one, Grace,' said Madge admiringly. 'Tubby won't 'alf be mad when 'e 'ears we know what 'e's up to. 'E won't send Ratty to spy on us again!'

'No, and he'll be scared stiff that we'll report him to CC,' said Grace with a grin. 'We've got *him* over a barrel this time!'

When Grace went into work the next morning, Madge was at the bar assisting Tubby whose face showed a mix of aggression and puzzlement. There was no Ratty to wash glasses and wipe tables.

'Good morning, Mr Tupman!' said Grace cheerfully. 'Where's Ratty?'

'He's not here,' said Madge with a significant look.

'Little bastard's upped an' run off,' muttered Tupman sourly. 'No great loss.'

'D'you mean he didn't come back last night?' asked Grace, and Madge shook her head. ''E's just disappeared,' she said in an undertone.

Grace began to feel anxious. The boy had looked so terrified when she'd let him go. Where had he gone, if not to the Railway Hotel, the only home he knew? Had he slept out in the open on a cold October night? Or... Grace suddenly pictured the dark Bridgewater river as it flowed through Everham, and fear clutched at her heart.

'I'm going to speak to CC, Madge,' she said in a low voice.

'What? Yer can't do that, Grace! Everything 'ud come out, an' we'd be in Queer Street,' whispered Madge. 'Ratty ain't our, er, resp...respiration, is 'e?'

'Responsibility,' Grace corrected her. 'But maybe he *is*, Madge. We were the last to see him...' Her voice faded, unable to utter the word *alive*. 'It's no good, Madge, I'm going to own up,' she said, and to the barmaid's alarm, she went straight to Mr Coggins's office. He frowned at her.

'Well, what is it, Grace? I'm busy.'

'It's about Ratty, Mr Coggins.'

At once he was all attention. 'D'you mean you might know where he is? Nobody else has any idea.'

'Have you spoken to Mr Tupman, sir?'

'Yes, and *he* doesn't know anything. Why d'you ask?'

Grace took a deep breath and recounted the events of the previous evening, which meant she had to tell of Madge's meetings with Sergeant Samms.

'Are you actually saying that Tupman was paying that boy to spy on you both?' asked Coggins incredulously.

'Yes, half a crown, Mr Coggins.'

'Are you sure of this, Grace? Ask Madge Fraser to come to my office at once.' When Madge's story matched Grace's in every detail, Coggins reached out to his telephone. 'Get me Everham Police Station,' he told the operator.

They heard that Ratty had returned to the Union where he had spent a loveless childhood; Coggins was called to see him there, and noted how the boy cowered with fear at the thought of facing Tupman again. Coggins assured him gruffly, but not unkindly, that there would be no need for that, and took him back to the Railway Hotel where he was sent up to his bed while Tupman was interviewed. Grace and Madge exchanged significant looks at the shouts and obscenities from behind the closed doors of Coggins's office, and saw the man leave, sacked and disgraced. And vowing to get his own back on the snivelling little bastard and the two sluts who had brought about his undoing.

Coggins said no more to Grace or Madge, and another barman was found; Ratty, from henceforward to be called Rob, was allowed to stay, and from then on he worshipped Grace and Madge with dog-like devotion. And he began to smile.

The evenings were drawing in, and it was getting dark at six o'clock when, after a busy day, Grace mounted her bicycle to pedal the four miles from Everham to North Camp. Tom had fixed a battery-driven light to the handlebars, and a thin beam showed Grace the way ahead. As always she felt a pang when she reached the crossroads and the oak where she and Nick... There had been no further postcards from him, and the lists of dead and wounded grew longer each week.

What happened next took less than ten minutes. A dark figure leapt out from behind the oak and Grace felt two rough arms around her body, hauling her from her bicycle which fell over in the road. She was thrown to the ground and a hand was clamped over her mouth so brutally that she bit her own tongue. Her assailant's other hand tugged at her skirt, pulling it up over her hips, and grabbing at her drawers and suspenders.

I'm going to be raped, she thought, and struggled fiercely: her hands clawed at the wrist of the hand over her mouth, but it only clamped down harder, so that she could scarcely breathe. Grace did not lack courage, and terror sent a wave of strength through her frame; she kicked furiously with her legs as her stockings and underwear were ripped from her, but her kicks met only the air, cold upon her exposed flesh. She could see a faint glint of two eyes in the darkness, but his face was covered with something black. A bolt of pain tore through her as he brutally handled the soft, tender flesh, and a knuckled fist punched between her thighs. A finger was brutally thrust inside her, followed by another, then a third pitiless finger violated the place where no man had been. The pain was excruciating, and Grace could not utter a word, let alone scream.

The man had indeed intended to rape this girl he loathed and yet lusted after, but found it impossible to perform the act upon a fully conscious and fiercely resistant woman; to knock her senseless would spoil the satisfaction for him, so to assault her violently with his free hand was the most he could do to take his revenge. He did not speak, but panted and grunted his wordless fury.

Grace felt her strength failing for lack of air, and as she weakened, he removed his hand from her mouth and the other from between her legs. He stood up and gave her a savage kick, then turned and left her lying on the ground, bruised and bleeding.

Eventually she managed to sit up and then, painfully, to stand. Her mouth was bleeding, and a trickle of blood coursed down her legs. Leaving her tattered underwear, she pulled down her skirt and with an effort bent down to pick up the bicycle. Wheeling it and leaning on it like a crutch, she limped along the dark and winding lane, not meeting another soul, or seeing so much as a rabbit or a hedgehog scurrying across her path. Half a mile from North Camp she saw a flickering light ahead, which turned out to be a lantern held by her father; her brother Ernest came towards her on his bicycle, calling out her name. He dismounted, and shouted back to her father who began to run; and a minute later she collapsed into their supporting arms.

The man was never found. By the time the police were alerted he was on his way to London to enlist in the army, and besides, Grace had no way of proving his identity, not having seen his face or heard his voice.

Chapter Seven

1915

A new year was beginning, and Tom Munday was thankful that Christmas was out of the way. Far from being 'over by Christmas', the news from the front continued to worsen, and the whole nation was shocked by the mounting death toll. Tom knew that Ernest was deeply troubled, plagued by conflicting thoughts, and though he never spoke of his feelings at home, Tom rightly guessed that Aaron Pascoe was confidant and confessor to his son, sharing their mutual unease at the exhortations to join up and defend their country, knowing their detestation of killing – and yes, their natural fear of facing danger and death. Tom's heart ached for his son, but he said nothing, knowing that the two friends would have to solve their problems in their own time and in their own way. He neither encouraged nor discouraged Ernest to 'join up', although Violet scarcely let a week go by without begging their son to be sensible and stay at home and in employment with Schelling and Pascoe, with good prospects.

And then of course there was that dreadful business about Grace, which had left both her parents shocked and distraught. Tom had simultaneously sent for Dr Stringer and for the local police after he and Ernest had carried her upstairs to her room. The doctor had examined her in her mother's presence, and seen the bruising and swelling of her female parts; he had asked her a number of searching questions, and finally gave his opinion that she *might* have been raped, though from her own confused and tearful description of what had happened, it was more likely that her assailant, holding one hand over her mouth while she kicked and struggled, had brutally violated her with his other hand, not actually raping her. The police officer's questions failed to gain more information, as Grace repeated that she had neither seen her attacker's face nor heard his voice, so was unable to identify him. Later the police questioned her employer Mr Coggins who told them that Miss Munday had always been a good worker; when questioned about the other staff, he named Tupman as having being recently sacked for bullying the young pot boy. The man's present whereabouts were unknown, he told them, though he had spoken of joining the army. Coggins avoided any criticism of his two young female staff members, having no wish to create a scandal around the Railway Hotel.

And there the trail had ended, and because the Mundays had told nobody else about it and no proceedings could be taken against an unknown person, the incident was mercifully kept out of the *Everham News*, much to Violet's relief.

Tom, however, was unsatisfied, and knowing his daughter Grace, suspected that she was hiding something. *Had* she in fact known the man who attacked her, and arranged to meet him at that particular corner by the oak tree? Tom could not bring himself to ask her, for that would be to accuse her of lying, but the man must have had *some* motive for committing such a crime – and *had* she been actually raped? When Violet, weeping with relief, told him that Grace's monthly period had returned as usual, Tom closed his eyes and thanked God. They had kept her at home with them for the rest of the year, but now she was clamouring to get back to work to earn some money. When she mentioned the Railway Hotel, Tom put his foot down and absolutely forbade it.

'You're never going back there, my girl. I blame myself for allowing it in the first place. There's to be no more serving of drink to men in a public house – not for any daughter of mine!'

Grace knew that he meant it, and resentfully waited for an opportunity to strike out for freedom again. She'd had a wretched Christmas, with nothing more exciting to do than attend St Peter's with her parents and Ernest; she had no idea whether Nick was alive or dead, or had completely forgotten about her. Madge Fraser had promised to keep any postcards that arrived at the Railway Hotel for her, but Grace had heard no more; she longed to see Madge and exchange cheeky jokes with her instead of moping around at home, where she grew sulkier each day.

From Ernest and Grace the carpenter's thoughts turned to his precious Isabel, whose absence from the Christmas dinner table had left a great emptiness. Tom had to remind Violet that Isabel could hardly leave Mark to conduct the Christmas services without his wife at his side to help him with all the extra duties involved at the festive season. Isabel's letters were full of enthusiasm for her parish work and Barnett Street School, where she had organised a nativity play. She wrote of Mark's unfailing kindness and the happiness of their marriage, to her father's great relief, but even so, he missed her more than he could express.

❦

'I can't send Annie to school, missus,' said Mrs Plumm defiantly. 'I need 'er 'ere at 'ome, wiv four little'uns to look after, and *'im* laid up, coughin' 'is 'ead orf! Besides, she ain't got no decent boots.'

The vicar's wife nodded sympathetically, and the woman continued, ''Sall very well for that Miss Wotsername sayin' she should be learnin' 'ow to add up sums – my Annie already knows 'ow to make a little go a bit further. Miss Whosit ain't got seven mouths to feed, an' nor 'ave *you,* missus.'

Isabel smiled. 'That's quite true, Mrs Plumm – and looking at your family here, I can see you do a very good job with so many difficulties.'

She looked round the room at the pale little faces; the two eldest recognised her as the nice lady who taught the 'little'uns' at school, but wondered what she was doing coming into their home and asking their mum questions.

Isabel was getting used to the squalor of the slum dwellings around Old Nichol Street, and was sadly aware that she could do very little to relieve the miserable conditions of the poor, especially on cold, dark January days when the windows had to be kept shut to avoid losing what little heat there was from a small, smoky coal fire. This place had the familiar smell of poverty, a mixture of dirt, grease, damp walls, and today being Monday, wet clothes hanging on a rope across the room. Isabel had taken it upon herself to visit the homes of pupils, though at first she met with suspicion: the Rev. Mr Storey had a seat on the Board of Guardians which dealt with parish relief, and they thought she might be spying on them to see if they really needed the 'outdoor relief' of a basic weekly ration of bread and a small allowance to help pay the rent. This was eagerly accepted, but 'indoor relief' meant the Union, or workhouse, which was definitely not. *That* was the notorious last refuge of the old, sick and unwanted, the bastard children, the feeble-minded, the crippled. Mrs Plumm's thoughts must have led her to this subject, for she raised her voice and glared at the visitor.

'We ain't goin' to no Union, missus! I'd starve afore I let me fam'ly be broke up an' sent in there – it'd be the death of 'em!'

'Oh, no, no, *no*, Mrs Plumm, that's not my idea at all. I'll let my husband know about your difficulties, and he'll try – I know he'll *try* to ask the Guardians for a little more, er, money.'

'Thanks, missus, though I can't see that tight-fisted lot givin' anythin' more to an 'ungry family. They wouldn't give nothin' to poor Ethel Taylor, 'cos 'er 'usband drinks an' wallops 'em reg'lar, it ain't their fault but they gets blamed for it. An' I'm supposed to manage on six shillin's a week for rent an' everythin' else.'

'I'll tell Mr Storey about Mrs Taylor too, Mrs Plumm. I can't promise anything, because there are some, er, unsympathetic minds on the Board.'

'Tight-fisted buggers the lot of 'em,' agreed Mrs Plumm with a grimace, ''cept for your 'usband, o' course – everybody likes '*im* – but thanks all the same.'

Isabel's face was grave as she walked home to the vicarage; it was already dark, and Mark had left a note to say he'd been called to a sickbed, and didn't know when he'd be back. Isabel sighed. Even on Christmas Day he had been sent for as soon as the morning service was over, and had been two hours late for his dinner. Mrs Clements had come fussing over, and to Isabel's annoyance she'd told Mark that his young wife looked very tired, and warned him not to overwork her.

'Mrs Clements means well, I know, Mark, but she's no right to interfere between us!'

'As if anybody or anything could come between us, Isabel,' he'd replied, putting his arms around her from behind, and nuzzling his lips against her neck. 'Oh, my dearest, the difference you've made to my life and my work! – but don't mind Mrs Clements, she's kept house for me these two years and more, so why don't you make her happy by letting her go on doing it, while you teach and do your parish visiting? You're such an asset to me, Isabel. Women feel that they can open up to you more than to a man, and everybody likes you – loves you! But Mrs Clements is quite right, dear, you *do* look tired, and that's my fault.' He raised his head and turned her round in his arms so as to look into her eyes. 'And this hateful war looks like going on for longer than we thought at first. When it's over, and you're a year or two older, we can make other plans for our future, can't we?'

The last sentence was whispered very softly, and Isabel knew that he meant having children. Dear Mark, how good he was! She thought of the harassed women she saw in the parish, worn out with childbearing before they were thirty, and losing many of them to infectious diseases like measles and whooping cough – and the dreaded diphtheria which almost always killed its victims. How different it was for her, thanks to Mark's carefulness and self-restraint. She now understood how he prevented a too-early pregnancy by using his fingers to penetrate her and a handkerchief to attend to himself. His love-making never failed to make her happy, but she could not be sure if he too was satisfied. She didn't ask him, because she knew he'd say yes, of course he was. How blessed she was in being adored by such a man! She would not have changed places with the queen.

And yes, she would ask Mrs Clements to go on looking

after the vicarage as well as the church, where that good lady polished the brasses, dusted the pulpit and lectern and laundered the altar cloths and surplices, all for the love of God and the Reverend Mr Storey!

By New Year, Grace had reached breaking point, and begged to be allowed to get a job, any job locally, shop girl or housemaid, anything but being cooped up at home.

'Dad, I'm completely well, and I simply *must* find work again! I want to do my bit for the war effort!' she wailed, using a current slogan to emphasise her patriotic zeal, and Tom realised that life at home must be boring for a girl of her nature. And then he had an idea: he had recently been repairing skirting boards for Lady Neville, and noticed that Hassett Manor had lost menservants to the army, like the gardener and a young stable hand, leaving the female staff to take over their work where possible. A housemaid had left to marry a young man going out to join the troops at the front, and Lady Neville had little hope of replacing her missing staff. Tom Munday saw a possibility.

'Look here, Grace, you're not yet sixteen, but maybe you could help out at Hassett Manor for a while. Lady Neville'd be glad to have you.' *And* you'd be looked after and supervised, he thought, by a sensible woman. The only remaining man on the staff was an ancient butler that Lady Neville kept on out of the goodness of her heart. Grace would surely be safe there.

Seeing that there was no alternative, Grace shrugged and agreed to accompany her mother to an interview with the lady everybody respected, and by mid January she had become a general housemaid and kitchen assistant, resident at Hassett Manor but allowed to go home on Saturday afternoons, returning on Sunday evenings.

It was certainly a change. The other staff consisted of stout Mrs Gann the cook, Flossie the other housemaid, old Mr Standish the butler and a worried-looking woman who came in to help with the heavy scrubbing and sweeping. Grace was not required to sleep in the attic, but shared a second-floor room with Flossie, a plump country girl who slowly and painstakingly read romantic stories, and frequently sighed for the absent Mr Cedric – "E's ever so nice, Grace, we don't 'alf miss 'im!'

Her lament reflected the general atmosphere of Hassett Manor, with Sir Arnold and young Mr Arnold Neville away in India, Cedric at the front, and only Miss Letitia and four regular servants left. A few rooms had been closed and the furniture covered with sheets – like shrouds, thought Olivia Neville with a shudder. Shocked by the long lists of dead and wounded, she visited not only the homes in mourning, but also those with a family member at the front, such as Mr and Mrs Bird, both of whose sons were away. She shared with them her own fears for Cedric, and encouraged them to be hopeful. Partly to ease her own loneliness, she made an effort to draw closer to her remaining servants, and in response to Flossie's oft-repeated sigh of 'It ain't 'alf quiet 'ere now', her ladyship invited them to join her and Miss Letitia in the drawing room after dinner each evening. Accordingly, Mrs Gann, Mr Standish, Flossie and Grace sat in a half-circle, facing the mother and daughter.

'It's important that we all keep our spirits up,' she told them. 'Miss Letitia is happy to play the piano for us, so perhaps some of us would like to sing to her accompaniment. If any of you volunteer, I'm sure the rest of us would enjoy it.'

Her ladyship and Miss Letitia led the way with a duet, 'Where E'er You Walk', and Grace had to bite her lips to stop the urge to giggle. After a while she joined in the singing of 'Love's Old Sweet Song', and 'Home, Sweet Home'. Lady Neville complimented her on her clear soprano voice, and asked what else she would like to sing. 'It's a Long Way to Tipperary' was thought to be more suitable as a marching song than for a musical evening, and Grace knew better than to suggest any of Marie Lloyd's ditties; she chose 'A Wand'ring Minstrel, I' from Mr WS Gilbert's largely unsuitable repertoire, but felt her talents to be wasted on this audience, though Flossie was quite overawed and breathed, 'I say, Grace, you ain't 'alf clever!'

It was a far cry from the saucy exchanges at the Railway Hotel.

The turn of the year was overshadowed, as Christmas had been, by the lack of progress of the British and French against the Germans, who seemed to be better equipped for warfare, and January brought a new terror to the population at home: the Zeppelins, great balloon-like airships that crossed the Channel and dropped explosive bombs on towns, killing indiscriminately wherever they landed. The east coast was the first to be attacked, and this gave a boost to the recruitment drive; Ernest and Aaron were once more faced by their consciences, the fact that they were not fighting for their king and country. A pacifist society had been formed, the No-Conscription Fellowship, which opposed the killing of fellow men of whatever nation, and its members were known as 'conscientious objectors'. Ernest wanted to join the movement, but Aaron held back.

'I'll only join the NCF if conscription's made compulsory, Ernest. There's no need to become voluntary targets for abuse and ridicule while it's still a matter of personal decision. Besides, think how it would reflect on our families, especially yours – your parents and sisters, if you were pointed out as a conscientious objector! You might as well wear a placard with 'coward' round your neck. No, my friend, let's wait a while and see how these Zeppelin raids go.'

And after a few weeks with no further Zeppelin attacks, Ernest agreed. It possibly meant that the Germans were getting ready to negotiate for peace, said Aaron – but Ernest shared his father's view that the January raid had been an attempt to scare the nation with a foretaste of what was to come: warfare in the air. Tom Munday saw it as a sign that the English Channel was no longer the effective barrier against enemy attacks, as it had been from time immemorial.

Suddenly, on a windy day in March, Hassett Manor was thrown into a turmoil of excitement and a certain amount of dread. The news came through that Cedric had been wounded and sent back to England. He was in London's Charing Cross Hospital, one of the clearing stations where injuries were assessed and the patient sent to another hospital or to his home; and Cedric was considered fit to travel by train to Everham. He was coming home!

Lady Neville went to meet him at Everham station in her carriage, with old Mr Standish acting as coachman, ready to take Cedric on the last lap of his journey. Grace and Flossie eagerly joined in the general welcome to the wounded hero who was pale, thinner, and looked very tired, though he managed a smile and a handshake for them all, and embraced his sister. His right arm was in a sling, and Dr Stringer was sent for to inspect the deep flesh wound on his shoulder and change the dressing. He was ordered to bed for at least three days, and a light, nourishing diet was prepared for him by Mrs Gann. On the fourth day his mother asked if he would like to join in the regular music entertainment held in the drawing room, and he came in to sit between his mother and sister.

'Oooh, yer can see 'e ain't 'alf glad to be 'ome, poor Mr Cedric!' said Flossie, but it was Grace who caught his eye and smiled demurely, which he acknowledged with a wink. This was more like it! She gave a pretty rendering of 'Sweet Lass of Richmond Hill', and to her great satisfaction he joined in her next song, 'Barb'ra Allan', taking the bass part and holding out his left hand to her and then to Letitia the pianist as the small company applauded. Things were definitely looking up at Hassett Manor!

Overjoyed as she was to have her son home, Olivia Neville was willing to indulge him in a little harmless flirtation with the Munday girl. She sensed that Cedric had changed; as his wound healed, he was slow to regain strength. He was nervous and wary, called out in his sleep and was unable to hold a conversation for any length of time. He would sit staring into space, and when his mother gently tried to question him, he would tense up and seem unable to speak, his face an expressionless mask with eyes that looked beyond the four walls of the room. Sometimes he raised his left arm to his face and turned his head away, as if to blot out what he saw. He was at his best during the 'entertainment hour' each evening, and introduced some jollier songs, such as when Grace stood up and lamented:

'There was I, waiting at the church…',

wiping her eyes and boo-hooing until Cedric came in at the end with:

'Can't get away to marry you today,
My wife won't let me!'

'Oooh, yer don't 'alf sing together well!' sighed Flossie. 'I don't 'alf wish I could sing.'

When Lady Neville suggested inviting former friends of Cedric's to join the musical evenings, he firmly shook his head.

'I'm not ready to meet other people, Mother. I can't put up with their stupid questions. You people at home have got no idea – no idea at all. Only the chaps who went through it can possibly...' His voice faded into silence.

When she realised that he could not talk of the war and what horrors he had seen and heard, Lady Neville made an important decision: she would open Hassett Manor as a convalescent home for wounded officers. No sooner was the idea born than she began to act upon it: the War Office was informed that Hassett Manor could take a dozen men, dust sheets were removed from the closed rooms, and Tom Munday was summoned to make some modifications to the house. Local people were asked to donate or lend single beds, and North Camp rose to the occasion with offers of help: two nurses, Miss Payne and Miss Beaty, were sent from Everham Hospital to assist with caring for the injured men, and several women offered to come in daily to help with the cleaning, cooking and washing of bedlinen.

Grace was in her element, pushing furniture around and making up beds to receive the new arrivals from clearing stations. By the end of March all the beds were occupied, and from a melancholy silence the manor was transformed into a hive of activity and animated voices.

'It ain't 'alf noisy 'ere now,' remarked Flossie, 'but I like it, don't you?'

Grace was at first directed to housework and assisting Mrs Gann in the kitchen, but she found frequent reasons to visit one or other of the three rooms which had become wards, with four men in each. Lady Neville ordered her sharply back to her own domain, but it was soon obvious that the pretty young girl had a beneficial effect on the men – as one of them remarked, she was 'just what the doctor ordered'. These men were convalescent, so although there were a few remaining bandages, sticks and crutches, they were in fairly good general health, and less reticent than Cedric at speaking of their experiences at the front, though mainly to each other. Cedric found that he could go among these men who'd shared his own experiences, and talk freely with them; it was like a brotherhood which bound them together in a way not understood by their families and friends at home.

Grace was therefore the first of the Mundays to hear, or rather overhear, at first hand of the horror of the trenches, frequently half-full of freezing water, the constant noise of shelling and machine gun fire, the rats, the lice, the all-pervading mud – and a memory of one man's brother hanging dead on a barbed wire fence bordering on No Man's Land, the gap between the two opposing sides where to walk was to invite the fatal bullet. The latest terror had been poisonous gas released from canisters in the enemy trenches, attacking eyes, throats and lungs.

Grace took these stories home on her free Sundays, and this was how Ernest Munday came to hear them, passing on his knowledge to Aaron. It was no incentive to enlist and go the same way, yet Ernest's mind became more troubled every day, and he imagined that every neighbour, every client and everybody he met was pointing an accusing finger in his direction.

'*I'm not ready to die!*' he almost shouted at Aaron one evening after the office had closed, and his friend had no answer except to repeat that they should continue to wait. But he held out his arms to Ernest and held him in a silent embrace so close that they could hear each other's hearts beating.

The end of April brought news of a big Allied offensive against Turkey, which for some obscure historical reason had joined the conflict on the side of Germany. It became known that several divisions of troops, augmented by Australian and New Zealand forces, were to make a series of landings along the Gallipoli Peninsula from the straits of the Dardanelles, and force the Turks back to Istanbul.

'Sounds warmer and drier than the trenches in France,' commented Aaron, as once again the question of military service came up, but it was not until the seventh of May that the die was cast, with the sinking of the Cunard liner *Lusitania* by a German submarine just off the west coast of Ireland, with a loss of more than a thousand lives. This appalling incident gave rise to a further recruitment drive, and there was another consequence of the tragedy: a surge of anti-German feeling spreading like a fever, notably in London's East End, and anybody with a German-sounding name was likely to have their homes attacked, likewise their shops and offices.

Aaron looked sombre as he and Ernest arrived in the office one morning in the following week, and sat down at their desks. That fateful morning, as Ernest was to remember it.

'It's been terrible,' Aaron confided. 'My own family's windows in Tamarind Street have been smashed, and they've been subjected to threats and abuse. That family tailoring business where my father worked has been attacked and looted. They've lost their three sewing machines, and that was their livelihood.'

'Oh, my God. And your mother and the children?' Ernest tentatively asked.

'The name of Pascoe has saved them from direct harm, though my father was treated as badly as his employers. And we've all decided that my mother and the two girls should leave Tamarind Street and come to stay with us at Everham, so they're arriving on Friday. My father and Jonathan are staying in London.'

'Heavens, your uncle's house will be crowded! Does it mean you'll have to give up your bed?'

Aaron did not answer at first, but looked his friend straight in the eyes; Ernest felt a shiver go down his spine.

'Soon I shan't be needing a room,' said Aaron quietly. 'This business of the *Lusitania*...'

'Yes?' Ernest prompted, though he already knew what he was about to hear.

'I'm going to enlist, Ernest. I've got to. Since the *Lusitania*, I can't go on dodging the issue, I've got to go.'

He spoke with conviction, and their eyes met. 'I've got to go,' he repeated.

'I can't let you go,' replied Ernest with equal conviction. 'Not without me.'

'My dear chap, you don't have to join up just because I do, and I wouldn't dream of asking you. You must make your own decision, speak to your father, ask yourself if you really need to risk your life—'

'Don't talk to me as if I were a child, Aaron,' interrupted Ernest, almost sternly. 'Can't you see, can't you understand that you're dearer to me than my life? Where you go, I must follow, so we'll go to the recruiting office in Everham and enlist together.'

There was a short silence, and Aaron passed a hand over his eyes.

'Ernest, we've never actually spoken of...of this before, but of course I've known about how you feel. I'm the same, except that...well, you know how the law stands on this, and society in general. I don't want you to enlist just to be near me. And in any case we'd probably be separated.'

'If we get separated and ordered to different divisions, I shall at least be with you in spirit, knowing that we're in the same war together, and you'll know that I'm not skulking around at home as a conscientious objector. No, Aaron, don't say any more, if you're prepared to fight and kill men in the name of freedom, then so am I.'

Ernest's face was so grim that Aaron smiled. 'So, if I cannot get rid of you, my friend, I shall have to enlist with you and go out to fight together. Thank you.'

'And thank *you*, Aaron,' Ernest said solemnly. 'I couldn't bear to be left behind.'

Seeing that they were in the office of Schelling and Pascoe, where at any moment they might be interrupted, they continued to sit at their desks as if their conversation had been mere trivia.

It was what Tom Munday had been expecting, but it still filled him with dismay. He hardly knew what to say to his son.

'It's not going to be easy telling your mother.'

'I know, Dad, and that's why I'm leaving that to you. I'm sorry.'

'All right, son, it's better coming from me. And it's not only her that'll worry, you know that.'

'I do know, Dad. It was because of the *Lusitania* that we finally made up our minds.'

'We? You mean you and young Pascoe?' Tom's voice was sharp.

'Yes, Dad, we've thought the same all along, and we're of one mind.'

'Which one o' you spoke first? One o' you must've led the other.'

'No, we've always been of one mind. And neither of us would want to leave the other behind,' Ernest told him steadily. 'In a way I feel a sort of relief.'

'Because your mother would hit the roof if she thought you'd followed after him,' Tom said bluntly.

'There's no need for Mum to think that, Dad. At least she'll be able to look Mr and Mrs Bird in the face.' He smiled. 'She'll have her ladyship coming round to visit! Mum'll appreciate that, I know.'

'Huh!' was the only response. Even a visit from Lady Neville would hardly compensate Violet Munday if Ernest was at the front – or fighting the Turks at Gallipoli, either way facing death or serious injury.

That same afternoon, when Ernest and Aaron walked along Everham High Street on their way to the recruitment office, a well-dressed young woman approached them boldly.

'And what might you two healthy young fellows be doing here, taking your ease at a time like this?' she demanded melodramatically. 'Why aren't you defending your country? Shame on you!' Opening her handbag, she took out two large white goose feathers and handed them to Ernest and Aaron. Ernest bemusedly took the feather she offered, but Aaron waved her aside.

'You should think twice or three times before you make public accusations, madam,' he told her, and snatching the white feather out of Ernest's hand, he threw it on the ground. 'Come, my friend, let's get our business done!'

Though Aaron's tone was contemptuous, Ernest was silently thankful that the white feather of cowardice had come too late to accuse him; it was something he'd been dreading.

Violet Munday went chalk-white, then red as she burst into angry tears.

'It's young Pascoe, that damned Jew, who's put him up to this!' she sobbed. '*I* could see how the poor boy was worrying, and now here he is, my own gentle, sensitive boy going to fight in a senseless war that nobody wants, except for that wicked old kaiser, damn and blast him! Curse him!'

Yet even Violet could sense that Ernest's mind was set, and no amount of persuasion or protest would change it. It was Tom who had to bear the brunt of her tears and reproaches, and he let it wash over him, not mentioning his own fear.

Grace was unexpectedly upset at her brother's change of mind, and somewhat regretted repeating the graphic accounts of trench warfare she'd heard at the manor. Her work among the injured had brought the war into focus for her, and she now saw it as cruel rather than glorious; and now that her own brother was being inexorably drawn into it, she felt its dark shadow spreading over all their lives.

'Oh, Ernest, I hope you'll be sent to the Dardanelles rather than those dreadful trenches of France,' she said, clinging to her brother's arm.

But slowly the news came through that the Gallipoli landings had been an utter fiasco, with heavy loss of life among British, Australian and New Zealand troops. The Turks had proved stronger and better prepared than expected, and were on their own familiar hot, dry terrain. It was said later that more Allied lives were lost to dysentery than to enemy action.

Chapter Eight

August, 1915

Late August sunshine slanted across the kitchen wall as Mr and Mrs Munday sat down to a 'high tea' of cold boiled bacon, bread, butter and seed cake.

'Very nice, Mother,' said Tom, carving them each a slice. 'You can always tell Yeomans' bacon from any other, his pigs are properly looked after.'

'Don't call me "Mother", you know I don't like it. And I haven't put the mustard pot out,' she said, getting up and going to the cupboard. 'I'd better mix some fresh.'

Tom sighed. Her reaction was fairly typical these days, he thought, no matter how hard he tried to sound more cheerful than he felt.

'Little did we know this time last year that all the children would be leaving us,' she said as she sat down again, and Tom nodded, knowing that it was Ernest she missed most, her son who was in Turkey with a second landing of troops on the Gallipoli Peninsula, four months after the costly April fiasco, from which lessons had been learnt, so they said. Tom was at a loss to know how to encourage her. At fifty Violet was still a handsome woman, though the anxieties of the past year had etched a network of fine lines around her eyes, and her mouth drooped when in repose.

'Ah, but Isabel's a happily married woman, and our naughty little Grace is doing good work at the manor,' he reminded her. 'We mustn't forget that, Vi.'

'Not such good work in bringing home horrid stories from that place,' she answered sharply. 'If it hadn't been for her repeating every far-fetched tale she heard, for Ernest to pass on to Pascoe, he might still be here with us now!'

'He'd been turning it over in his mind for some time now, Vi. Sooner or later he… they'd have decided to go.'

'There I must disagree with you. My boy was put under pressure by that Jew Pascoe, and don't try to tell me otherwise. Not an hour of any day goes by without me remembering Ernest and praying for his safety,' she said, pouring out tea for them both, and refilling the pot with hot water. 'First we had to see him off to Aldershot, and then after less than a month he boarded that troopship at Southampton, and I haven't had a quiet moment since.'

Tom reflected that he found 47 Pretoria Road much *too* quiet without their son and daughters, but refrained from saying so; it was his duty to hide his own natural fears for his son, because she needed his help to bear her burdens.

Grace Munday, now sixteen, was feeling aggrieved. She had been banned from the three wards, all because that spiteful cat Nurse Payne had gone tittle-tattling to Lady Neville.

'She says I spend too much time talking to those poor men,' she grumbled to Flossie. 'Anybody with half a heart can see that they need cheering up, and where's the harm in having a bit of a joke? Or singing them a song?'

'Yeah, they don't 'alf say nice things about yer, Grace,' said Flossie, whose only contact with the men was at mealtimes, when she helped with serving and clearing away; Grace had been forbidden even to do that.

'She's got a downer on me just because she's past thirty and with a face to turn milk sour,' Grace continued bitterly. 'Fancy telling Lady Neville that I'm a shameless flirt! I could tell her ladyship was trying not to laugh, even while she was telling me off. I bet old Payne-in-the-backside wishes somebody would flirt with *her*!'

Flossie giggled, but thought Grace should keep out of Nurse Payne's way for a while. 'I wouldn't 'alf miss yer if yer was sent away. It's bad enough sayin' goodbye to Mister Cedric again.'

Cedric's wound had healed, and he had been discharged by the army surgeon as fit for duty. Not to the blood-soaked fields of France, but to join the reinforcements sent for a second strike at the Turks at Gallipoli, the first invasion having failed. Grace wondered if he would come across her brother and Mr Pascoe on the warm shores of the Dardanelles. She sighed, having heard no more of Nick, swallowed up among the thousands facing death at the front.

September, 1915

Isabel's thoughts were also of her brother, from whom she received little news; her parents wrote to pass on the scanty information they heard. Turkey seemed such a long way off, and she had never even heard of the Gallipoli Peninsula. Her life at Bethnal Green and the parish of St Barnabas' was full; every day brought news of some new hardship among the crowded slums, and a fair number of the young men had gone to enlist in preference to working locally for a pittance which would have to mingle with the family income. Isabel discovered that when sons went off to join the armed forces to fight a war, poor families suffered just as much anxiety and heartbreak as the better-off.

The September evenings were drawing in, and curtains were being closed as Isabel made her way back to the vicarage. Some curtains consisted only of sacks or sheets of newspaper, and Isabel pictured the cheerless scenes behind many of them.

As she had expected, Mark was out, and the thought came to her that a baby of her own would make a big difference to her life – but then of course she would not be able to teach or visit in the parish, not unless she was willing to expose her baby to all sorts of infections. No doubt Mrs Clements would gladly offer her services as a baby-minder, but what was the use of such idle dreaming? Mark had decreed that there must be no babies until after the war, and by then she might be many years older...

After making tea and toast, Isabel sat down with a copy of *The Woman's Book*, given to her by her mother, and full of advice on household management, cookery and home nursing, including the care of babies and young children. Feeling tired, her eyelids began to droop, and the book fell to the floor. Presently she was awakened by a strange, pulsating, humming sound which grew louder and louder, until suddenly there was an enormous explosion that shook the ground. Outside people began to run to and fro, their excited voices raised in amazement and fear. The front door opened, and Mark rushed in, calling out, 'Isabel! Isabel dear, are you here?'

She rose to greet him, and he clasped her in his arms and held her while another ear-splitting explosion occurred, and a man's voice was heard calling out.

'Get back indoors, everybody! It's one o' them bloody airships – get inside!'

'It's a Zeppelin!' screamed a woman. 'We're all going to be killed!'

In fact forty people were killed and many more injured by the first Zeppelin raid on London, and the damage caused by the bombs dropped between Tower Bridge and Euston was considerable. People looked up as searchlights illumined the dark sky, catching the airship in crossed beams. A crackle of artillery fire caused its crew to turn it round, dropping their last bomb near Liverpool Street Station, blowing an omnibus to pieces. A huge fire broke out in a warehouse which smoked and smouldered for days. The terror of the Zeppelins had recommenced, and London was the chief target; its citizens gazed in horror at burning buildings and the havoc caused by damaged gas and water pipes.

Isabel's parents demanded that she should return to the safety of North Camp forthwith in the face of such danger, and Mark reluctantly agreed, saying that he had no right to keep her in Bethnal Green. But Isabel Storey had her own ideas about where her duties lay, and she absolutely refused to go.

'We were forced apart for two years, Mark,' she said, 'and we are never going to be parted again.' She thanked her parents for their concern, but told them she was staying in London, like the king and queen.

'Now I shall have a daughter to worry about as well as a son,' wailed Violet Munday. 'And heaven only knows where he is and what's happening to him, we never hear any news – oh, Ernest, Ernest my poor boy!'

ↄ

Nine-year-old Devora Pascoe's world had been turned upside down, and there was no one but her sister Greta, three years older, to whom she could turn in her bewilderment. Her mother worked in the Everham offices of Schelling and Pascoe, trying to take the place of both her son Aaron and his friend Ernest; she always seemed tired and cross these days, and could not speak of her son without emotion. The two sisters knew that they should be grateful to their Aunt Ruth and Uncle Abel Schelling for taking them in, but this house was dark and old-fashioned compared to the lovely home they'd left behind in Elberfeld and might not ever see again.

Both girls had been sent to Everham Council School, but Greta was in a higher class than Devora, and they were struggling to speak English more fluently – and to understand their teachers who sometimes spoke too quickly for Devora to follow, so that she fell behind on subjects like history and geography; arithmetic was the same as in German, but written down in a confusingly different way. They were excluded from scripture lessons and the daily school assemblies because of their religion, and were the only Jews in the school. There was no synagogue in Everham, but once a month they accompanied their mother, uncle and aunt to London where they could celebrate the Sabbath with their father and brother Jonathan who still lived in Tamarind Street. And London had now become a dangerous place where horrible Zeppelins came through the air in the night and dropped bombs that killed and injured people and destroyed buildings.

And worst of all, their much older brother Aaron had been sent far away with the army, and they'd had no news of him; he might even be dead, and they dared not even speak his name to their mother, or her face would harden and angry tears came to her eyes.

'How should *I* know where he is or how he is? *I* never sent him away! And speak in *English,* Devora, we don't want to be mistaken for Germans and sent to an internment camp! If you don't use it, you'll never learn anything. You're in *England* now!'

Yes, they were in England, strangers in a strange land, like their Israelite ancestors – *Jews*!

When half-term was reached, their Aunt Ruth had an idea.

'You know that Aaron had a very close friend called Ernest Munday who worked here with him and went with him to fight the Turks? Ernest was a good, serious young man, and his parents must be missing him as much as your mother misses – as we *all* miss Aaron. I know where the Mundays live in North Camp, so shall we go and visit them on Friday afternoon?'

The girls agreed, and accordingly they boarded the horse-drawn omnibus with their aunt; she made her way to Pretoria Road and stopped at Number 47. A woman came to the door in answer to her knock, and stared at them blankly.

'Good afternoon, Mrs Munday. I'm Mrs Schelling, and these two young ladies are Aaron Pascoe's young sisters, Greta and—'

'Good God, is there news? Have you heard from – from Aaron?' demanded Ernest's mother, wide-eyed. 'Does he speak of Ernest? Tell me, for God's sake!'

'No, Mrs Munday, we haven't heard from them, but—'

'Then why are you here? What have you come for? What do you want?'

'Only to meet you, Mrs Munday, and share our – our thoughts with you. Can't we comfort each other in our distress?' begged Mrs Schelling, recognising the suffering behind this woman's ungracious response. 'May we come in and talk with you for a little while?'

'Talk to *you*? When it was Aaron Pascoe who took my son

to… Why should I…? Oh, go away!' Violet Munday started to close the door, but suddenly she sagged against the door-frame, her face chalk-white. Mrs Schelling stepped forward quickly and caught hold of her.

'She's going to faint, Greta – help me with her. Go and find a chair, Devora.'

Mrs Munday found herself lolling on a chair in the little entrance hall, supported by a strange woman she didn't know. 'What's happened? Why are you here?' she moaned weakly.

Mrs Schelling was at a loss as to what to say, but the thought occurred to Devora that this woman was like her mother, both sad and angry at the same time. She forgot all about correctness, the discretion that Jews were taught to observe when dealing with Gentiles, and stepped forward, putting her arms around the woman and speaking softly in her ear.

'Don't send us away, Mrs Munday. We only wanted to meet you because you're Ernest's mother, and we're unhappy too, about Aaron and his best friend.'

Violet Munday focused on the little girl's anxious face, and tears filled her eyes. Mrs Schelling and Greta stared in surprise as Devora's embrace was clumsily returned, and Mrs Munday muttered something unintelligible through her tears.

'Don't cry, Mrs Munday,' said Devora, touching her face gently. 'We've all got to be brave, so we mustn't cry.'

And in that moment Violet's bitterness against Aaron and his family began to melt, for it was impossible to hold a grievance against this child. She released Devora and stood up rather unsteadily, but in command of herself.

'I suppose I'd better put the kettle on,' she said, avoiding Mrs Schelling's eyes. 'Do you, er, drink tea?'

So when Tom came home in mid afternoon for a tool he needed from the shed, he found the visitors still there, drinking tea and praising Violet's apple pie.

How can we write home? he silently asked himself. What could we tell our families about the voyage in the overcrowded troopship with the poor, terrified horses, and the constant threat of German submarines? How could we describe the landing in darkness at Suvla Bay, and the stench that came to meet us before we went ashore and has filled our nostrils and throats ever since, from the thousands of bodies left after the failed April invasion? How might we tell them that our regimental headquarters is a dugout covered with corrugated iron, doing duty as meeting room, mess room and restroom, approached by a maze of curving trenches? That our adjutant, stick-thin and with a week's growth of beard, practically sleepwalked out of the dugout to greet us and tell us we were badly needed? How can we write of the scorching heat, the flies, the never-ending boom of gunfire? And the warning sign of hoof marks and footprints four inches deep, baked hard in the clay until the autumn rains come again?

No, I can't write any of that. I haven't the materials or the opportunity to use them, and if I had, I still couldn't tell them the most important fact of all – that through all this my beloved friend is with me, sharing the torments and making them bearable. We don't say much in this place, but we've never needed words; we know that our love is what renews our strength and failing courage.

O Lord, be merciful, and let us not be parted! Don't let one of us be lost to the other, but grant that we may survive together or die together. Amen.

October, 1915

Eddie Cooper saw little of Tom Munday these days. Tom's conscience kept him at home with Violet in the evenings, though he missed his occasional hour in the Tradesmen's Arms, and sharing his thoughts with Eddie; it was the only time when he could honestly speak his mind, and Eddie was the only one who could hear him with sympathy but without alarm. Eddie had his own problems, both past and present, but he had not got a son facing death in the war. Tom had to hide his own fears from Violet, and appear more certain than he actually was of their son's eventual return, safe and sound. Perhaps Violet Munday subconsciously realised this when she made the unexpected suggestion that they ask Eddie and Annie Cooper with little Freddie over for tea on the following Sunday afternoon.

'Grace won't be coming this weekend, Lady Neville's asked her to change to another day, so we might as well have some company,' she said.

'That's very good of you, Vi,' said Tom, as pleased as he was surprised. 'Be nice to see old Eddie again, he's always been a good friend.'

'As you've been to him,' she said. 'I've got nothing against Annie Cooper, even if she *was* a barmaid at the Tradesmen's…' Violet hesitated for a moment, remembering Grace at the Railway Hotel '…and any wife would be better than his first one, though we mustn't be uncharitable now the poor woman's been at rest for… how long is it? Must be five years, because little Freddie's three.'

'It's a nice idea, and…er, couldn't we maybe ask his daughter

Mary as well?' ventured Tom. 'Give her a chance to meet her father and Annie on neutral ground – it'd mean a lot to old Eddie if they could be reconciled. It's ridiculous, the way this break has gone on for year after year. D'you think it'd be a good idea, Vi?'

Violet had become less judgemental after making peace with Aaron's family, and agreed to ask Mary Cooper, but thought she should be warned that her father and unacknowledged stepmother would also be present.

Tom thought it over for a minute, and then said, 'Let's tell her that Eddie'll be here, but not to mention Annie and the kid. When she sees them close to, she may see sense as well, and Freddie's such a smiley little fellow, I reckon she won't be able to hold out against *him*, whatever grudge she's got against Annie. I'll drop in at the farm one day next week to ask her. Thanks again, Vi,' he added, and planted a kiss on her cheek, an affectionate little gesture that gave them both a lift of the heart.

But his visit to Yeomans' farm drew a blank, and he returned to report that he had not even seen Mary who was working outside.

'Mrs Yeomans said she misses Mary's help in the house, because she's needed just about every hour of the day on the farm,' he said ruefully. 'Rounding up the cows and helping Dick with milking, seeing to the pigs, setting the horses to the plough – the girl must be whacked out. Since old Yeomans lost his farmhands to the army, he's had to manage with her and Dick, all the hours God made. Anyway, I left a message for her about Sunday, but Mrs Yeomans said she doubts it, *she* hardly catches sight o' Mary these days.'

Mrs Munday shrugged. 'It sounds to me as if Mary's just

making an excuse. It's too bad of her; after all Eddie went through with her mother, you'd think she'd be glad to see her father happy again. Anyway, nobody can say we haven't tried. Is there anybody else we can ask? The Birds? Their boys are—'

But Tom needed to have some time to talk with Eddie, and didn't want a third man intruding. 'What about Miss Daniells? She was a very good teacher to them.'

Violet agreed, thinking that if she and Annie Cooper turned out to have little in common, the schoolmistress's presence would make things easier.

And so it proved. The scones, home-made jam and fruit cake were highly praised, and little Freddie toddled from one to another, happy to be the centre of attention. When the ladies settled down to a freshly brewed pot of tea, Tom asked Eddie to come outside to look at the garden, not that there was much to see on a chilly late autumn afternoon with fallen leaves lying everywhere. They took refuge in the tool shed where they shook their heads over the scarcity of work.

'There aren't many jobs goin' these days, Tom. People are leavin' their paintin' and decoratin' till after the war.'

'Same here,' replied Tom. 'And I see old Harry Hutchinson has lost his bricklayer and carpenter. I reckon he'd take us on like a shot, but I can't say I'd fancy working for him, would you?'

'Nor any other builder,' agreed Eddie. 'Harry'll be in the same stalemate as us, people aren't looking for new house-building while this show's on, and Lord knows when it'll be over.' He glanced quickly at Tom as he spoke, remembering that there had been no word from Ernest. The newspapers were guarded in their reports of the war in Turkey, but it was becoming clear that the second strike on the Gallipoli Peninsula was no more successful than the first. The weather was said to be hampering the movement of troops, with storms and heavy rain.

Tom nodded, having followed Eddie's train of thought. 'We're not the only family desperate for news and at the same time dreading it,' he said sombrely. 'Lady Neville's going through it, too, with her son Cedric out there, and not a word from him since the day he embarked.'

'An' there's goin' to be a lot more sent out afore long, Tom. This National Register's got the names of *all* men between eighteen and forty-one, and now they've got to sign on and say that they're willin' to join up if asked. I see the king has added his two pennyworth, askin' for more recruits from men of all classes, single ones first, unless they're in reserved occupations, like coal minin' or in one o' these factories turnin' out guns an' shells an' whatnot.'

'What would you call a reserved occupation, Eddie? I mean, what about clergymen? And the farmers, surely we need them to provide food. How d'you think Dick Yeomans'll get out of it? I hear he slogs from dawn to dusk, seven days a week.'

This touched a nerve, as Tom had expected it might. Eddie frowned. 'That's right, he does, and so does my Mary. She's out in all weathers, seein' to the livestock an' any other job ol' Yeomans can find for her. And o' course she's always side by side with young Dick, so they're bound to get close. I see her as a farmer's wife, Tom, an' a damn' good one – not that it makes any difference what *I* think.'

Tom smiled, remembering Eddie's earlier indignation over the farmer's son's behaviour. 'Well, I just hope that Dick's occupation turns out to be reserved. I wouldn't wish the Yeomanses to go through what Violet and I…'

He stopped speaking as his throat constricted and his eyes filled with tears.

'Oh, Eddie, if I'd only appreciated my boy's good points, instead o' criticising him all the time! And now I'd give my right arm to see him home again, and…oh, Eddie, I have to pretend to Violet that I'm sure he's all right, but it wears me out, hiding my fear and dread from my wife! God help the pair of us if…'

Eddie Cooper had put a hand on Tom's shoulder, and now his arm encircled his friend. 'All right, Tom, all right, you don't have to pretend to me,' he said quietly. 'All right, ol' man, let it out. You know I'd never tell a soul.'

And so Tom Munday leant on his friend's shoulder, and experienced a kind of relief in so doing.

Some twenty minutes later, as the October dusk began to fall, the two men returned to the house through the kitchen door, where Tom dipped a dishcloth in cold water and dabbed at his face, standing in front of the shaving mirror.

'That's better! Now practise a grin,' said Eddie, deliberately adopting a light-hearted tone. 'The women won't notice a thing.'

'Where on earth have you two been?' demanded Violet Munday as they re-entered the parlour. 'What do you think of them, Annie? Men accuse *us* of chattering, but when *they* get together, they have twice as much to say!'

'They call it putting the world to rights,' agreed Mrs Cooper, smiling down at little Freddie who had climbed up onto her lap. Miss Daniells also smiled at the child, but said nothing; something about the men's subdued manner suggested to her that their conversation had amounted to a good deal more than lofty male pronouncements on the state of the world.

That night Tom Munday put his arms around his wife and whispered, 'Thank you.'

'What for?' she asked.

'For asking those four to tea with us. It meant a lot to me.'

'I can't think why,' she answered with mock reproach. 'You spent half your time outside with Eddie Cooper.'

At the farm the lamps were lit, and little Billy had been put to bed by his mother, who then joined her husband at supper in the kitchen, after which they retired early to bed, both having got colds. Bread and cheese and half a pigeon pie were left on the kitchen table, covered with a cloth. It was past nine o'clock when Dick and Mary came in, tired after attending the farrowing of a sow and putting the eight piglets to take their first feed from their mother. They hung up their jackets on a row of hooks in the scullery, and left their boots there. When they saw the repast on the table, Dick decided to open a celebratory bottle of apple cider from the pantry.

Mary Cooper, pretty and plump, stood with her back to the last glowing embers in the range oven, and watched as Dick drew the cork from the bottle which foamed all over his hand; he hastily poured it into two mugs from the dresser.

'Another long day, Mary.'

'But a good one, Dick.'

And then for the first time they melted into each other's arms, as naturally as breathing, their tiredness forgotten; their supper would have to wait.

December, 1915

Rain, rain, torrential rain; nothing and nowhere was dry. Trenches overflowed, washing dead bodies over the parapet and opening shallow graves; No Man's Land was awash with mud and blood and worse. Horses' hooves and men's boots sank inches deep as they moved. Lieutenant Neville wondered how long it would be before what remained of his company were all gone; with no clean water and nothing to eat but biscuits, tinned bully beef and tinned apricot jam with no bread to spread it on, it was no wonder that they were succumbing to agonising dysentery and the freezing cold, more likely to kill them than enemy fire.

After twenty-five days on the line, a record for what it was worth, Neville had fifteen men left out of a company of fifty, and in poor shape, wet and shivering. The MO had died in the night, poor devil, and his body had been dragged out of the latrines with that of another unconscious man lying in his own stinking excrement. Neville thought he vaguely knew the man from North Camp, and ordered that he be carried down to the beach and put on a lighter to take him out to the hospital ship anchored in Suvla Bay. 'He's a goner for sure,' the escort had commented. 'They won't want *him* on their ship in that state.'

Neville shivered. Thank God he still had Lance Corporal Pascoe who could be relied upon to do whatever was needed, whether digging deeper trenches, patrolling the front line, grabbing an hour's so-called rest or trying to sort out a fair ration from the depleted stores for each man who could still tolerate food. Pascoe would have to take charge if he, Neville, were struck down. God in heaven, what a waste...what a shambles it had all been, from the ill-fated landing on the Peninsula back in April, when huge numbers of Australian and New Zealand forces had gone ashore at Gaba Tepe, further down the coast, to create a diversion from the British invasion, and later to link up and together push the Turks back to Constantinople. That had been the plan, and it had sounded feasible; but nobody had reckoned the Turks to be such ferocious warriors, with the added advantage of fighting on their own terrain; nobody had foreseen the administrative bungling, the lack of liaison, the shortage of ammunition; the Dominion troops had eventually taken the hill at Gaba Tepe, but their numbers had been decimated, so it could hardly be called a victory. The second landing in August had met with no better success, and conditions were made even worse by the abominable weather; even the Turks had been flooded out.

A messenger appeared at Neville's side, with an envelope from the battle headquarters. Neville took it, opened it and stared at the single page; at first he could hardly take in what it conveyed, which was that all Allied personnel were to be withdrawn from the Peninsula, and that those at Suvla Bay, his own company, would be evacuated on the night of December 18th, only three days away; those at Helles would go in early January. Neville momentarily closed his eyes, then wrote a brief note for the messenger to take back, to say the message had been received.

'Look at this, Pascoe,' he said to the pale, mud-spattered figure who had just come into the dugout. 'They say we're to retreat, so whoever's still breathing and standing up on the day appointed will take himself down to the beach and get on the lighter to the hospital ship.'

'I hear you, sir,' was all that the lance corporal replied. Since his best mate had been dismissed as a goner, his dreams of escaping from this place had become just that – dreams. And not likely to come true.

'I'll assign you to a rearguard action, Pascoe, with a couple of others to be decided. I'll lead the rest of the men down, and see them onto the lighter, then wait for you and the others, to see you all safely on board.'

'There'll be a fair bit of farewell shelling from Johnny Turk, sir.'

'We'll have nothing to lose, Pascoe.'

Just hope I'll live to see it, thought the lance corporal, as an ominous pain stabbed him in the belly.

It was later observed that the Gallipoli fiasco, which had caused such disastrous loss of life to both British and Dominion troops, achieved an evacuation with almost no losses, though there were a number of deaths on the hospital ship and at the military hospital on Malta to which the sick and injured had been taken.

Pascoe stirred as he awoke, but did not open his eyes. He wanted to go on sleeping in this wonderfully comfortable bed, so dry and warm. He began to be aware of the sounds around him: the coughs, snuffles and grunts, the rattle of trolleys and clatter of bowls and basins; he could hear women's voices speaking in low tones. The strong smell of carbolic disinfectant was a sweet, clean scent compared to the stench of a battlefield, and he gratefully breathed deeply as he drifted in and out of sleep...

'Pascoe!' whispered an eager voice. 'I say, Pascoe old chap, it's good to see you here! How're the old guts – any better?'

Pascoe opened his eyes slowly and looked at this young man who had been his latest company commander. 'Lieutenant Neville,' he whispered. 'W-where?'

'Where? We've landed up in hospital on Malta, old chap, and I wouldn't change it for the Ritz. Can I get you anything? Water? Cigarette? They let you smoke in here.'

Pascoe's eyes were now wide open. 'Corporal M-Munday,'

he muttered. 'Can you tell me anything? Is he dead from dysentery, like the MO?'

'No, he's been very bad with dysentery and dehydration, but he's here, in another ward. He—'

'Let me see him. Let me go to him, sir.' Pascoe struggled to sit up.

'You can't see him just yet, old chap. It's been a close-run thing, and he's not out of the woods yet. You'll have to wait till—'

But Pascoe had already thrust one leg out of bed, and now heaved out the other to stand beside it on the cold tiled floor, swaying slightly. 'Let me lean on your arm, sir, and take me to him. If he's alive, I must see him.'

Neville was about to tell him not to be a fool, when an orderly came over to see what the fuss was about. Neville tried to apologise, but the orderly saw Pascoe's desperation and reckoned that to bend the rules might be the best course. He went to find a wheelchair, but changed his mind and came back with a stretcher trolley.

'This could get me into trouble, old son, but if it calms you down... Would you care to push the stretcher, Lieutenant? D'you know where Munday is?'

'I'll find him,' said Neville, and obediently trundled Pascoe out of the ward and down a long corridor to another ward. It was quieter than the one they had left: men lay silently in their beds, weakened by the ravages of gastro-enteritis. Pascoe's glance darted round the ward, alighting on an emaciated figure whose body hardly showed beneath the bedclothes. His eyes were closed, and his face was ghostly pale.

'There he is – that's him over there,' said Pascoe, pointing to the man. The trolley drew up alongside the bed.

'Be careful, Pascoe – don't alarm him,' warned Neville, and Pascoe nodded.

He stretched out a hand and lightly laid a forefinger on the man's forehead.

'Ernest,' he said softly. 'It's me, Aaron. It's all right, we're in hospital, we're together again, Ernest. We're alive.'

Ernest Munday turned his head slowly and fixed hollow eyes on the face of his friend. A smile of pure joy lit up his face. His prayer had been answered after all.

Chapter Nine

April, 1916

'I'm tellin' yer, it's a jolly good life, Grace! – and right up your street, ye'd be top o' the bill in no time!' enthused Madge Fraser, on a visit to her sister in Everham. Sunday was her day off, as it was for Grace Munday who had cycled over to see her, having told her parents that she would be unable to attend church with them and Ernest because she was meeting a friend.

'Do we know this girl?' her mother had asked sharply. 'What's her name?'

'Marjorie Fraser, Mum, we met while she lived in Everham.'

'Fraser?' repeated her father. 'Wasn't she the other girl at the Railway Hotel?'

'Yes, Dad, but she's moved to London now, and works as a chambermaid at the Ritz Hotel,' replied Grace, not quite meeting the eyes of either parent. 'She's visiting her sister this weekend, and asked if I'd like to go over. And seeing that I've got Sunday off, I said I would. You don't mind, do you?'

Neither parent looked pleased, but they reluctantly agreed to forego the pleasure of her company this Sunday.

'As long as *you* don't go tootling off to London at a time like this, my girl. Your mother and I have enough worry over Isabel living in constant danger from those Zeppelins.'

'And make sure you call in and see your brother on the way back,' added her mother. 'He's out with Aaron just now, and he's very upset that Aaron's going back to the fighting next month, in France this time.'

'Oh, poor Ernest! Poor both!' exclaimed Grace in genuine concern. 'D'you think Ernest'll ever have to go back, after he's been so ill?'

'He's regaining strength day by day,' began Tom Munday, but his wife broke in. 'I'm *sure* that Ernest won't *ever* be called back into the army!' she said emphatically. 'Not after all he's been through. The very idea! He was at death's door.'

Tom said nothing, but wished that he could be as sure. 'Enjoy your day with your friend, my girl, and call in on your way back.'

Grace pedalled off, a slightly guilty smile on her face as she reflected on what an old darling her father was. At least she'd told the truth about visiting Madge, even if she'd fibbed a little over Madge's new life in London: she was not a chambermaid, but a chorus girl at Dolly's, one of the new licensed music halls that had sprung up in London since the war began, as if to cock a snook at the Zeppelins.

'A couple o' girls share lodgin's with me, but we could make room for one more little'un!' Madge continued gaily. 'It's the best life I've ever 'ad, Grace! The ol' Railway 'Otel was nothin' compared to this – London's *full* o' soldiers on leave, wantin' to forget about the war till they 'as to go back to it. They just *flock* in to see the show, twice nightly an' a good chance o' bein' invited out arterwards – there's these 'ere night clubs all over the place, champagne flowin' like water. An' fellers to dance wiv – an' they all got money to chuck around – I tell yer, Grace, I never 'ad as much fun before – *and* no ol' Tubby Tupman to spoil it!'

'It sounds good, Madge,' said Grace, 'and I'd be tempted to come and join you, only…well, I've got a good life at Hassett Manor, looking after the wounded as they recover, you see. It makes me feel that I'm doing my bit for the war effort.'

Madge gave her a broad wink. 'Believe me, Grace, so am I!'

Grace smiled and shook her head. It wasn't only that she enjoyed her work at Hassett Manor; she knew her parents would hit the roof if she were to go to live in London at seventeen, to take on a way of life that Madge talked of so invitingly. Perhaps in another year or two…

When he was judged to be on the road to recovery, Ernest had been shipped home in February with other men who had survived the Gallipoli landings, and was overjoyed to see England again. His appearance shocked his parents, and Grace thought he looked worse than some of the admissions to Hassett Manor. His reunion with Aaron had to be somewhat restrained in company, but their hand clasp and the look in their eyes conveyed their thoughts as well as any embrace. Their happiness was short-lived, however; Aaron had orders to return to active service in May, and he would soon be followed by Dick Yeomans, called up under the new Military Service Act of January that year, as a single man not in a reserved occupation. Farmer Yeomans protested in vain, and Mary Cooper was heartbroken, for by now their mutual attachment was common knowledge, and Dick was in favour of a quick, quiet wedding before he went for training at Aldershot. His parents had disagreed, however, thinking him too young to make such a commitment in a hurry; but when he marched away to war,

Mary wore a silver engagement ring, and carried a promise that they would be wed when he came home. Meanwhile two land army girls had been sent to assist on the farm, and both the farmer and Mary had their work cut out, she told her father, to train and supervise them in the daily rigours of life on the land.

'The poor girl's upset, o'course,' said Eddie worriedly. 'It sounds as if there's goin' to be one hell of a battle when the British and French charge at the Jerries eye-to-eye. Dick Yeomans'll be takin' his chance along of all the others, and God help us all if...I don't 'old with farmers bein' called up, Tom. They're more use at 'ome than out there, riskin' their lives.'

Tom found this difficult to answer. He and Eddie had in a way changed places, now that Ernest was at home and Eddie's probable son-in-law was away.

'Did you hear about the Goddard boy, what's his name, Sidney?' he asked. 'Got called up but didn't pass his medical, seems he can't see without spectacles. He seems a pretty fit bloke otherwise.'

'Yeah.' Eddie nodded. 'I s'pose they'll draft him into some reserved occupation, so he could end up in one of these munition factories, turnin' out guns an' whatnot. In which case he'll stand a better chance o' comin' home than Dick Yeomans,' he added bitterly.

'Old Goddard'll miss him, though. He's not been so well lately, and they've been looking to Sidney to take over the shop if – er...' Tom sighed. 'Seems to be trouble everywhere you look. Young Neville's gone back, and his poor mother keeps herself going with Hassett Hospital, as they call it.'

'What about her husband and the elder son? Still out in India, aren't they?'

'Yes, Sir Arnold's even more of a bigwig out there, recruiting local native chaps to join in the fun. And young Arnold, I don't know what he's up to, but you can bet they'll be stuck out there as long as the war's on. The whole world's changing, Eddie. Not many able-bodied young men left around.' Tom's mouth tightened, remembering Ernest's return from Gallipoli, thin and gaunt – and the first question he'd asked, 'Is Aaron home?' And now young Pascoe was to go back to active service on the Western Front. To face death. And for what? It just didn't make sense.

May, 1916

Young Mrs Storey was much in demand at Barnett Street School, and even more in the parish of St Barnabas. The lives of the poor, which had always been hard, now seemed gloomier and shabbier than ever, and she listened to tale after tale of hardship and heartbreak. The news of a son killed in the trenches caused as much grief in an overcrowded tenement block as in a neat suburban avenue, and they all feared the dreaded telegram with its message of 'killed' or 'missing', which usually meant the same thing. 'Wounded' just *might* mean that the soldier would eventually return, minus a limb or two, and perhaps horribly scarred. Isabel's own anxiety for her brother Ernest had drawn her closer to these people, and they looked to her for comfort and reassurance.

'Ye'd better be careful, Mrs Storey,' warned Mrs Clements. 'Some o' these women expect too much o' yer. Ye're too soft-hearted, and they take advantage.'

Isabel smiled a little wearily. In fact she was quite well aware of those who tried to play on her sympathies, and she was as gently firm with them as she was generous to the more deserving. She could not offer money, but she could advise them about 'Outdoor Relief' and how to apply for it to the Board of Guardians, sometimes putting in a word to the Rev. Mr Storey.

'And as for that *disgusting* drunken woman Tanner, shoutin' and hollerin' in the street, shakin' her fist and behavin' worse'n an animal, ye'd do better to keep away from the likes o' her,' continued Mrs Clements. 'It's a scandal, in front o' children an' all!'

Isabel sighed. She had alarmed even her husband by the way she had shown kindness to poor Mrs Tanner, linking arms with her and guiding her to her dismal home, where she'd brewed a pot of tea. She had called again the next day, and listened to the woman's wretched story.

'I got nuffin' left, missus, nuffin'. I was brought up in an' 'ome, never knew muvver or farver, an' when I was sixteen I got work scrubbin' floors an' doin' them sort o' jobs…an' then I met Alf Tanner, an' we took to each other straight away, so we got married, and I was expectin' a baby an' was as 'appy as a woman could be… Oh, missus, we was that 'appy, I fought I was in 'eaven.'

Mrs Tanner collapsed in sobs, and Isabel put her arms around her. There seemed to be nothing to say, and she waited until the woman was able to continue.

'Go on, my dear. What happened?'

'My poor Alf was killed when one o' them airships came down in flames an' landed on top o' the factory where 'e was workin' nights. I couldn't believe it at first, an' the shock was so bad I lost the baby. In the 'ome we was told that God loves us an' takes care of us, but 'E ain't done nuffin' for me, missus, an' the only time I get away from meself is when I 'as a drop o' gin.

I can't understand it, missus, I ain't been a bad woman, I never 'ad any man but Alf, but now I got nuffin'. Nuffin'!'

Isabel's heart ached with pity. How could she tell such a woman to put her trust in God rather than turn to drink for a few brief hours of oblivion? She did not even try, but held her close and rocked her gently. The memory of Mary Cooper's mother came back to her, the lost look in her eyes, the tragedy of her life and death.

'What's your Christian name, my dear?' she asked.

'Sally, an' I ain't no Christian, missus.'

'Well, Sally, rcmcmbcr how Alf loved you, and try to be brave for his sake, and live as he'd have wished you to,' Isabel said softly. 'He'd want you to look after yourself properly, and keep occupied – I mean keep busy. There's a new clothing factory opened on the Commercial Road, and they need women to stitch khaki uniforms for the soldiers. Why don't you apply for a job there? I'll help you to write a letter, and if they offer you work, take it and do it as well as you can – and earn yourself some money!'

Sally sniffed and wiped her eyes. 'I'll try, missus. It's good o' yer, missus.'

That evening Isabel told Mark of her encounter with Sally Tanner, and how she hoped that Sally would regain her self-respect in paid employment.

'Poor soul, she's lost everything that made her life worth living,' she said. 'Having a job to go to each day will give her self-discipline, and she'll meet other women. She promised me that she'd try.'

Mark was not entirely in agreement. 'But Isabel dear, suppose she can't give up the drink, and loses her job because of it, she'd be in a worse case than she is now, with a sense of failure added to loss, and likely to become dependent on you if you allow her.' Mark frowned, for he did not relish the idea of his wife associating openly with drunks and hangers-on. 'If you could restore her faith, get her to pray and put herself in God's hands…'

'Oh, Mark, she thinks that God has let her down, and who can blame her? Perhaps if she could learn to put her trust in *me*, and not want to let *me* down, she'd make the effort, seeing that I haven't condemned her, as others have.' Isabel spoke seriously, seeing the look of surprise on her husband's face. 'Surely we can only teach the love of God by *showing* it, as Jesus showed it to tax collectors and poor women who were…well, harlots.'

Mark drew her close and kissed her. 'You are an angel, Isabel, and I don't deserve you. These people of ours learn more from you than they learn from me.'

'And I've learnt from *them*, Mark, and I'm still learning,' she answered.

For Isabel knew that she was not an angel; she knew that Sally Tanner had lost the love of her life, while she, Isabel, still had hers, living and breathing and loving.

Tom Munday felt as if he were the repository of too many secrets, by which he meant the things he couldn't share with his wife, who needed to be shielded rather than confided in. At forty-nine Tom was only eight years ahead of the age limit for having to go to war, following the second Military Service Act, which now included married men between the ages of eighteen to forty-one. It would bring yet more heartbreak into homes as husbands and fathers were drawn away from their dependents, for the attitude to the war had changed from enthusiastic patriotism and adventure to shock and grief at the death toll so far in the conflict. Whereas in 1914 there had been long queues at recruiting offices, now there were men who openly declared themselves unwilling to make 'the supreme sacrifice' for king and country. Some went further, and the members of the No Conscription Fellowship increased. These 'conscientious objectors', also called conchies, cowards, slackers and any number of epithets, were howled at and spat upon, their meetings were broken up with jeers and throwing of rotten eggs; hauled up before military tribunals, they were thrown into comfortless prison cells where they were often beaten and half-starved.

'It requires a different sort of courage, Dad, to stand up and say you're a pacifist in time of war,' Ernest had said after seeing Aaron off to France. '*I'd* have been a conscientious objector if it hadn't been for Aaron who decided to go to war against our country's enemy. I couldn't let him go alone.'

It was then that Tom began to realise the depth of the relationship between the two young men, which he could not condemn, but had of course to keep to himself.

'And when they tell me I'm fit for duty again, I'll have to go, Dad.'

And it will be up to me to comfort your mother, thought Tom, to bear with her grief and rage, as if I wasn't suffering just as much.

As the sunny days passed, Ernest's health improved rapidly, but Tom secretly wished that his son might remain a pale, anaemic invalid; it would only be a matter of time before he followed Aaron to the battlefields. William Hickory said goodbye to his sweetheart Phyllis Bird, and went to join her brothers Tim and Ted who had been early volunteers; and the Rev. Mr Saville and his wife had to say goodbye to their

handsome, golden-haired son, Philip, now eighteen. Sidney
Goddard was reluctant to go out of doors or face the customers
who came in to buy haberdashery from his father's shop,
tactlessly remarking that all the best men were now in the army.
And Eddie Cooper told Tom how his daughter Mary had wept
when she saw Dick Yeomans off on his train.

'He'll be home for Christmas, as like as not,' Eddie had told
her, but she had gone on weeping, refusing to be comforted.

June, 1916

Lady Neville had gone to visit a bereaved family some distance
away on the other side of South Camp. She drove herself in the
one-horse two-seater gig, waving aside old Mr Standish's offer
to drive, as she needed to concentrate her mind on her sad task,
and what she could say to a couple who had lost a son.

'You'll serve me best by staying here,' she told him, noting
his crestfallen look. 'Nurse Payne has the day off, and Miss
Letitia is in her room with another of her headaches, so I'm
having to leave the manor in the charge of Miss Munday and
Flossie. Mrs Gann will leave as soon as suppers are cleared away,
so I'll be very grateful to know that you're here to keep an eye
on things.'

The old butler brightened as she had known he would, at
being given this responsibility. 'Trust me, your ladyship, I'll
take care o' them all.'

She nodded and smiled. All the present patients were
recovering, and only one amputee was still confined to bed.
She trusted Grace Munday who had been re-instated as ward
domestic assistant, much to Nurse Payne's indignation,
especially when the men addressed the saucy young hussy as

'Nurse'. Lady Neville had taken on Grace largely for her father's sake, but she had grown to like the girl for her cheerfulness and initiative, and the fact that the men found her amusing.

It had been a beautiful day, and after supper most of the men had gathered in the spacious conservatory at the back of Hassett Manor. It was known as the salon, and was furnished with comfortable basket chairs and a couple of tables. An upright piano stood at one end, flanked by potted palms, and one of the patients sat idly tinkling out tunes while the rest played cards, read, talked or sat looking out at the rose garden, drinking in the peace of the evening, contrasted with the scenes they had recently experienced. Old Mr Standish sat on a garden bench smoking his pipe, and the aroma of his tobacco smoke mingled with the scent of roses rising on the still air and drifting into the salon through the open windows and casement doors. The men were dressed in the uniform of the wounded, blue tunics and red ties; some needed crutches or sticks to aid their walking, and Grace was chatting with the one still confined to bed; it was he who gave her the idea of having a sing-song around the piano, and she called Flossie to help her move the man's bed out to join the other men in the salon.

'No, no, we don't need any help,' she said when a couple of patients offered to push the bed along on its casters. 'Pansy Potter, the strong man's daughter, that's me!'

'Now, then, let's see what songs we've got!' she said, riffling through the sheet music kept in the piano stool and on top of the instrument, looking for something rather livelier than the songs that had been acceptable at Lady Neville's musical evenings. 'Hm – practically all of Gilbert and Sullivan's and *Sentimental Songs for the Family... Old Favourites...* ooh, and what's this? *The Music Hall, a Selection of Songs Made Popular*

by Miss Marie Lloyd – hooray! We'll have a go at some of those.'
She looked up and raised her voice. 'Gather round, everybody,
give our pianist another glass of Adam's ale, and who's going to
start us off? We all know "Daisy, Daisy, Give Me Your Answer,
Do!"'

The men sang it with gusto, and Grace then gave them
'There Was I, Waiting at the Church', with all the men roaring
out 'My wife won't let me!' at the end.

'Coo, yer don't 'alf sing a treat, Grace,' marvelled Flossie,
round-eyed.

'So what about you, Flossie? What can you give us?'

'I know 'London Bridge Is Falling Down',' offered Flossie,
but Grace stopped her. 'We don't want reminding of the
Zeppelins, thank you – does anybody know a "round",
something we can divide up into parts?'

'Three Blind Mice' was suggested and duly sung in four
parts, and an Irishman felt encouraged to stand up and sing a
solo.

'So I'll wait for the wild rose that's waitin' for me

Where the mountains of Mourne sweep down to the sea!'

At the end of this soulful rendering, Grace ostentatiously
pulled a handkerchief out of her overall pocket and dabbed her
eyes in an excess of pretended emotion; when she'd recovered,
she led the company in 'Oranges and Lemons', sung in two
parts, one behind the other, a bit of a fiasco that ended in
laughter. Flushed with pleasure at the men's enjoyment, she
asked the pianist to look up the Marie Lloyd songbook, and
told Flossie to go and fetch a wide-brimmed hat from the row
of hooks in the kitchen corridor.

'And a parasol if you can find one,' she called after the girl,
though Flossie could only find a navy-blue velour hat that Mrs

Gann wore during the winter, and the nearest thing to a parasol was a large, dark-coloured umbrella.

'They'll just have to do, it's up to me to make the best of them,' said Grace with a rueful grin. 'At your convenience, Mr Piano-man!'

As he struck the opening chord, she climbed up on to one of the tables, the hat at a jaunty angle, the umbrella/parasol unfurled and twirling round her head as she gave a robust impersonation of the great music hall diva.

'If I show my shape just a little bit,
Just a little bit, not too much of it –
If I show my shape just a little bit,
It's the little bit the boys admire!'

Whistles, cheers, laughter and delighted applause greeted this, a heady mixture that Grace found intoxicating. She opened and closed the umbrella, pirouetting on the table, her hips swaying as she belted out the song again, with many winks and suggestive glances from her dark eyes.

'Watch that table, Grace, it ain't 'alf wobbly!' warned Flossie, and three of the men got up to hold it steady while Grace cavorted above them in reckless abandon. All eyes were fixed on her – which is why nobody noticed Nurse Payne creeping quietly into the salon, drawn by the sound of 'shameless goings-on', as she was later to describe the scene to Lady Neville. At the same moment Miss Letitia Neville left her room to investigate the noise which was keeping her awake; she descended the stairs and stood behind Nurse Payne, a pale figure with tragic eyes. Grace carried on singing and dancing, unaware that retribution was about to fall on her. Flossie was the first to see Nurse Payne, and froze: the men followed her gaze and made frantic signals to Grace who eventually turned and saw, not outrage but grim triumph on the face of her adversary.

'*You*, madam, will go straight to Lady Neville as soon as she returns,' promised Nurse Payne with relish, and Miss Letitia, who had no wish to take part in a 'scene', disappeared upstairs again.

Old Mr Standish, awakened from his doze by 'the sound of revelry,' as he called it, appeared at the open casement door and gaped at the suddenly curtailed entertainment. However would he explain this to her ladyship, who had entrusted him with the care of the manor?

Lady Neville was late returning from the grief-stricken family, and told Nurse Payne firmly that any breach of discipline would be dealt with in the morning, which meant that Grace had the night hours to speculate on her fate, which did not make for peaceful sleep.

Lady Neville spoke with her daughter over their shared breakfast about the events of the previous evening, and at ten o'clock she sat at her desk in the improvised office she used to conduct all matters relating to Hassett Manor as a convalescent home for war wounded. She sent first for Nurse Payne and heard her story, then dismissed her and sent for Flossie, then Mr Standish and the patient who had played the piano. Finally she sent for Grace Munday.

'I'm very surprised indeed to hear what happened last night, Grace, and it is your parents I'm most sorry for,' she said gravely. 'You've already been warned once about foolish and undignified conduct, yet as soon as my back was turned, you've let yourself down again. It's such a pity, because you have many good qualities, but I cannot allow a valuable trained nurse like Miss Payne to be offended a second time, and she would be if

I allowed you to stay. You will therefore pack your belongings and tidy your room, and leave by midday on Friday.'

'But Lady Neville, I only wanted to cheer up the patients, and they really did enjoy themselves, and they'll tell you so!' protested Grace, close to tears. Whatever would she say to her father?

'I understand that your motives were good, but my dear girl, your behaviour was foolish in the extreme,' said her ladyship, not unkindly. 'If you were a few years older, I could imagine you entertaining servicemen at bona fide concerts, for you certainly have talent. I have no choice but to dismiss you from Hassett Manor, but...no, don't cry, Grace, but listen carefully to some good advice. I think you should train as a nurse, but as you're only seventeen, I suggest you apply to the matron of Everham General Hospital to work as a nursing cadet for a year. I happen to know her, and will put in a good word for you – I won't send you away without a reference. I shall be very sorry to part with you, but oh! Grace Munday, you'll have to learn to control that wayward, wilful streak in your nature, or it will land you in real trouble one day, and it won't only be yourself that will be shamed, it will be your whole family. I will write to your parents about my recommendations. You may go now.'

'But Lady Neville—' Grace began, but the lady held up her hand.

'This interview is ended. You may go.'

And out Grace went, smarting with anger against Nurse Payne and what she saw as injustice on the part of Lady Neville.

The post arrived while the vicar and his wife were at breakfast in the kitchen, and Isabel eagerly went to pick up the three envelopes on the doormat.

'One from Mum,' she said, setting it down beside her bowl of porridge. 'And one from your dad, there – and one from – let me see…' She sliced open the envelope. 'Oh, it's from my old friend Mary Cooper! There must be a good reason for her to write.' She sat down and read the letter between spoonfuls of porridge.

'Poor Mary! She and Dick Yeomans are engaged, but he's been conscripted and sent off to France. What a dreadful shame – and so has Philip Saville the vicar's son – I wouldn't have thought him old enough, but he's just eighteen, she says, and goes on to say there are hardly any young men left in North Camp, only Sidney Goddard because of his short sight. She says she wishes Dick had short sight, too – oh, Mark, she sounds heartbroken. I must write to her today.' She glanced at the clock. 'Another cup of tea, dear, before we go?'

'Er…no, thank you, Isabel.' He too looked at the clock. 'I'd better be off, the Board of Guardians meets this morning, and I need to have my ammunition ready.' He rose from the table.

'But aren't you going to read your letter from your dad?'

'Not just now, dear, later, when I've got a chance to look at it properly. Goodbye, my love – don't let them work you too hard at that school –'bye!'

And with a brief farewell kiss he was gone, the letter from the Rev. Richard Storey tucked away in an inside pocket. Isabel thought he seemed preoccupied, but reminded herself that he always had a lot on his mind, things he shared with her and things he didn't, like the confidential circumstances of his parishioners, by reason of his office as a priest in holy orders. She looked forward to the evening when they could sit down and share the news in their letters. Meanwhile she perused the one from her mother, and learnt of the latest events in

Grace's life; Isabel frowned as she read it. It was too bad of her thoughtless younger sister to get herself dismissed from Hassett Manor, subjecting her parents to yet more gossip. It seemed that she had now started working as a cadet nurse at Everham General Hospital, thanks to the kindness of Lady Neville. And that wasn't all, for Mrs Munday worried constantly about Ernest, now sufficiently recovered to assist both his father and Eddie Cooper in their respective trades as the need arose. Work was getting scarcer as people postponed the jobs that needed doing until after the war.

'You can imagine my mixed feelings, Isabel, when I see your brother looking healthier and feeling stronger every day. Your dad and I can't speak of our deepest fears for him, and this is yet another burden to bear. We've never had secrets from each other before, yet I'm afraid to ask him what he really thinks. Oh, for an end to this wicked, wasteful war!'

Isabel folded the two depressing letters into their envelopes and placed them in the rack on the parlour table. They would hardly make for happy reading when shared with Mark.

'And what was in your dad's letter, Mark?' she asked that evening as they sat down to supper.

'Oh, nothing much, dear – ecclesiastical stuff, mainly.'

'Well, come on, then, let's hear it!'

'I've gone and left it in the vestry or somewhere, would you believe – not that there was much in it, as I said. My father likes to argue over issues of the day, relating them to his faith, questions of right and wrong, that sort of thing – cerebral rather than practical!'

Her eyes were fixed on his face as he tucked into his supper of bacon ribs with cabbage and boiled potatoes, avoiding her eyes.

'What about your mother?' he asked. 'What did she say in *her* letter?'

Isabel put down her knife and fork, and fixed her eyes steadily on her husband until he had to look up and repeat his question: 'What did she say in her letter?'

'We've always told each other the truth, Mark,' Isabel answered solemnly. 'My mother's worried about Ernest, in case he has to go back to the fighting, and my sister Grace has been dismissed from Hassett Manor for bad behaviour, though she's now a nursing cadet at Everham General. Now, tell me what your father wrote.'

He sat back in his chair and closed his eyes, silently praying for a few moments while she waited for him to speak.

'My father and I have been thinking about this latest Military Service Act,' he said at last. 'And whether it can be right for a man to leave his family and go to fight in a war he doesn't properly understand, to kill other men like himself for some political ideology – or for whatever reason. Is it ever justifiable, and what should a man do? Your brother Ernest thought this over for a long time, and came down on the side of king and country, as he has proved in that Gallipoli fiasco. But what should *I* do, Isabel? Tell me what *you* think I should do.'

She replied without hesitation. 'Oh, Mark, my dear, good, foolish husband, why haven't you told me this before? I've known that you had something on your mind, and why couldn't you *tell* me? You're like my father, unable to confide in my mother about his fears for Ernest. Now, listen! A man like you, a clergyman whose life is dedicated to God, can *never* go out and kill his fellow men – and besides, it's against your nature. You couldn't do it.'

'Ah, but dearest Isabel, I wouldn't go with the intention of killing, though I'd wear a soldier's uniform. I'd be an army chaplain.'

Isabel went pale; a suffocating sensation of fear seized her, but she resisted it; she had learnt from her experiences at St Barnabas' to be strong; she had toughened, and was no longer a shy young bride, though she trembled as she spoke.

'Then you'll have to do what you believe God wants you to do, Mark,' she said. 'I mustn't kneel to you, begging you not to go. W-what does your father say?'

'He'd already advised me to write to the bishop of the diocese,' he answered bleakly.

'And have you?'

'Yes. It seems that I have a choice, to stay here or join the army as a chaplain. He says he can only give me guidance, and the final decision must be mine.'

'And who'd do your work here, in an underprivileged parish in desperate need of a wise spiritual leader?' asked Isabel, chalk-white.

'It's been suggested that my father could come here and take over.'

'But that's ridiculous – impossible! Your father's old and retired, and your mother's much too frail!' cried Isabel, feeling as if she was in the grip of a nightmare, and must wake up at any minute.

'My father is willing to come out of retirement – he won't be the only one to do so – and my mother would go and stay with Sylvia and her family.'

'Good God! You've thought all this out between yourselves, but without a word to me. Oh, Mark, how could you leave me out?' There was deep reproach in her voice, and he got up from his chair and went to her side, putting his arms around her shoulders and kissing her cheek.

'I didn't want you to be worried until I'd come to a decision, Isabel. There was no point in upsetting you until there was something definite to tell you, either way.'

'And can you tell me now?' she demanded in a voice made strange and unfamiliar by fear.

'Up until this day – this minute, Isabel, I hadn't anything to tell you for certain, either way,' he replied. 'But now I have.'

'And?'

'And I must go, dearest.'

She gave a long, drawn-out moan, and he gathered her up in his arms and carried her into the parlour where they sat together on the settee, her head on his shoulder. There seemed to be nothing more to say; words were hollow and empty.

Chapter Ten

July, 1916

The all-out Allied attack on the German trenches in the Somme valley on July 1ˢᵗ was at first reported as a success, with heavy enemy casualties. It was only when the long lists of Allied casualties began to take up whole pages in national newspapers that the truth began to filter through to a horrified nation; *The Times* had to print additional pages to record the numbers of men killed, missing and wounded, and they ran into tens of thousands.

Looking back later on that sunny summer, Tom Munday always shuddered. His mind reeled away from the daily news of young lives lost, and terrible as it was to contemplate such a national disaster, it was when the dreaded telegrams brought news of deaths of local boys that the shock truly hit home. Among those killed on that first day of the Battle of the Somme were Dick Yeomans and Ted Bird, the younger of the two brothers who had been among the first to enlist. Dick had been conscripted for less than two months when his parents received the news that they would never see him again, and they had to break the news to Mary Cooper. The devastation at the farm was only equalled by the grief at Birds' Outfitters; the shop was closed for a week while Ted's parents mourned for him, and

Phyllis's grief for her brother was compounded by her fears for William Hickory. Miss Daniells advised her to take some time off work until things were more settled at home, but Phyllis felt that she needed to get away from the grief-stricken house of mourning, so continued her teaching of the youngest pupils, hiding her sadness as she unfolded to them the mysteries of the alphabet and names of numbers.

On Sundays St Peter's usual congregation was augmented by a few who now turned to the church for a word of spiritual comfort in their deep distress. The Reverend Mr Saville found it difficult to offer consolation, for he and his wife lived in daily fear for their son Philip, but this very fact brought him closer to his sorrowing flock, and they forgave him for talking about a Christian's duty to trust in the Lord at all times, when any day might bring him the news that would test his faith to the uttermost.

While there was unity among the bereaved and those fearing they would become so, there was little tolerance for those with no son at the front, and sometimes active hostility towards families who still had a son at home and not in uniform. Sidney Goddard was a case in point, saved by his short sight – his good luck, as some said, in failing his medical examination for the army. He became an object of scorn by patrons of Goddard's haberdashery shop, and some women refused to enter while he was there. Children on their way home from school would shout, 'Old Specky Four-Eyes!' if they met him in the street, and his mother found herself shunned by Mrs Bird and Mrs Munday. Tom thought this unfair, but did not take his wife to task over it as he might have done in other circumstances, for the day was fast approaching when they would have to part with Ernest again. He had quite recovered from the enteritis which had struck him down in Gallipoli, and had put on weight; the army doctor at

Everham had therefore passed him as fit to recommence active service, and a date in mid August was confirmed by a terse communication from the War Office, which also noted his request to be sent if possible to the same battalion as Lieutenant Pascoe, both men being now warrant officers.

Violet Munday broke down and wept, and Tom suggested that Ernest had better take himself off for an hour or two, until she was calmer.

'I can deal with her better than you can, son,' he said, having grown used to hiding his own fears, and not wanting Ernest to be upset by his mother's tears. 'Er…could you cycle into Everham and get me a couple o' sheets o' sandpaper from the hardware store? And some linseed oil while you're there?'

''Course I can, Dad.' Ernest gave a little smile to himself, for he knew that his father was giving him an opportunity to visit the Pascoes at Everham, to see Aaron's mother and his two young sisters. Their mutual love for Aaron had drawn Ernest close to them, especially to Devora who most reminded him of her brother. They greeted him warmly, and made him sit in the Schellings' garden to tell them of his coming departure and his chances of being in the same company as Aaron; Mrs Schelling brought out lemonade in a large glass jug, and handed round home-baked biscuits.

As he lounged in a garden chair Devora laid her innocent head upon his shoulder and confided that she would pray every day for him and Aaron fighting in this war together. He whispered his thanks, closing his eyes and knowing that this would be a golden memory to take back with him to Aaron at the front and whatever horrors awaited them in that valley of death.

☙

'Haven't you finished the bedpan round yet, Munday?' asked the staff nurse. 'The doctors will be here soon.'

'Sorry, but Miss Clandon's been sat there for ages, and can't go,' replied Grace. 'The rest o' them have finished, and had wash bowls.'

The staff nurse frowned. 'Well, take Miss Clandon's bedpan away, and let her try later – and be quick about it, I've just seen Dr Lupton arriving.'

Grace rolled up her eyes and went to the red-faced old lady who was sitting astride an enamel bedpan and straining hard.

'Nearly there, Nurse,' she panted.

'But the doctors are coming in, Miss Clandon, and I'll have to take it away and let you try later,' said Grace, knowing that there would be a fuss. And there was.

'You can't take it away *now*, Nurse, I've nearly done!' Miss Clandon's loud protest echoed round the now quiet ward. 'Another couple of minutes'll do the trick!'

The other women in Princess Alexandra Ward looked at each other, some smiling, others muttering about the cruelty of bullying an old lady. Grace was inclined to agree with them, and went to fetch two wooden-framed screens from a corner, pulling them along on their casters. She arranged them round Miss Clandon's bed just as the ward sister came in with Dr Lupton, junior partner to Dr Stringer. All the patients in Everham General Hospital were under the care of their own general practitioners who sometimes called in a specialist. Grace fervently hoped that this doctor had not come to see Miss Clandon, and watched as he and Sister stopped at another patient's bed and studied her temperature chart.

'Nurse Munday, fetch the screens,' ordered Sister, and Grace pulled forward another pair of screens. Dr Lupton spent a few minutes with his patient, and then moved on to another.

'Screens, Nurse!' hissed the sister, and Grace hurried to transfer the screens from the first patient's bed. At that moment Miss Clandon called out triumphantly.

'I've done it, Nurse! You can take it away now, and bring me some paper,' she said with satisfaction. 'Sorry about the horrid smell.'

Grace went to remove the bedpan and take it to the sluice room, where she emptied it and returned with a roll of coarse paper. She left the screens round while the old lady wiped herself, and Sister raised furious eyebrows and gave her a look that plainly said, *I'll speak to you later.* The other women in the ward watched the little drama with amusement, and one of them winked at Grace who grinned back at her, then hastily composed her face to total blankness.

It was very different here at Everham General after the easy informality of Hassett Manor with its twelve convalescent servicemen. The hospital was a solid Victorian building with forty beds divided into fifteen on Prince Edward Ward for men, and twenty-five for women on Princess Alexandra; children were put into Alexandra, including boys up to the age of twelve. As a cadet nurse, Grace did the daily sweeping of the floor, damp-dusting the bedside lockers and scraping the casters of beds and screens. She emptied bedpans down the sluice, rinsed them and replaced them on wooden shelves. Her only nursing duties were bedpan rounds followed by washing bowls. She helped make empty beds, turning the horsehair mattresses and arranging the three pillows allotted to each patient. If a woman asked her for anything other than a bedpan, such as pain relief or a change of dressing, she had to call a staff nurse or one of the probationers in training to deal with it.

'My name's Bedpan Annie,' she would explain, but when some of the patients jokingly called her by this name, she was eyed with disfavour by her seniors who thought her frivolous, which did not worry her as long as the patients liked her. Due to her long and irregular hours of work she needed to be resident, and slept in a small, bare room on the third floor; a necessary arrangement that suited Grace, preferring it to the mounting tension at home as Ernest's departure drew near.

'You'll find Isabel an invaluable help to you, Dad,' said Mark Storey, 'just as she's always been to me. She seems to be able to bring light into the darkest places, and women especially turn to her for comfort. She's an angel.'

Father and son were seated on a bench in the small back garden of St Barnabas' vicarage, where a dusty privet hedge screened them from view. The sound of children's sharp little cockney voices could be heard from the street where they were playing, and an angry shout from a man with a cart ordering them out of his way; barking dogs and women calling from front doors added to the background noises of the warm summer evening, and the two men spoke in lowered tones.

'I shan't demand too much of her,' replied the Reverend Richard Storey who in his seventies had volunteered to come out of retirement and deputise for his son at St Barnabas'. 'She's got so many duties, teaching at that school and parish visiting, whereas most clergy wives only have the church and the vicarage to care for – and run the Mothers' Union, of course.'

'Ah, we are very fortunate in having Mrs Clements to do those duties,' said Mark with a smile. 'The church is *her* domain, polishing the brasses, doing the flowers, if there are any, and laundering the altar linen and surplices. And she

comes in almost daily to cook and clean for us, in fact she's
a treasure, and all she requires is to be regularly told so. She's
inclined to gossip a bit, in fact if you want anything to be
known in the parish, you've only to tell Mrs Clements and it'll
be all round in no time, but if there's any trouble between her
and other parishioners, Isabel's the best one to deal with any
differences.' Mark paused, noting how frail his father looked,
and yet how firm of purpose. 'I can't tell you how grateful I
am...we are to you, Dad, leaving Instone and coming here –
and being separated from my mother.'

'Your mother will be well looked after at Sylvia's, son, and I
came here in answer to a clear call from God,' replied the old
man firmly. 'I'd been turning the matter over in my mind and
conscience for some time, wondering what His will was for me
at this time of national crisis, and when your letter came to tell
us that you were joining up as an army chaplain, everything fell
into place and I could see my duty clear before me – just as
you do, Mark. Your mother is in total agreement, and willingly
commits us both to God's care. I shall do what I can for the
souls of this parish, with His divine help. Let us bow our heads
for a moment, Mark, and pray for our country and your part in
its defence.'

The two men duly lowered their heads and the father
commended the whole family into God's care and protection;
as Mark added his fervent *Amen*, Isabel called to them that
supper was ready.

Isabel looked pale and was rather silent as she served her
husband and father-in-law with a stew made from neck of
mutton and root vegetables with the addition of a little pearl
barley 'as the Irish do, to make it go further,' she said with
a little smile. Bread-and-butter pudding followed – 'it's

margarine, actually,' – and when they had finished old Mr Storey tactfully withdrew to his room, saying that he needed to spend some time in prayer. In fact he felt tired out.

'We shan't be late to bed, shall we, my love?' said Mark when they had finished the washing-up and the table was laid for breakfast. Isabel took her husband's hand and followed him up the stairs to their room and the bed awaiting them. They opened the window on to the fading light; a brilliant sunset lit the western sky.

Lying side by side, Mark spoke with a certain hesitation. 'I haven't any words, Isabel, only that I love you and I'll think of you and pray for you every day we're apart.'

'And so shall I, Mark,' she replied, and flinging her arms around him, she whispered, 'Love me, Mark! Love me now, tonight, always!'

At once he felt his defences were broken, and he took her at her word, seizing her and throwing his body over hers. 'You want me to, Isabel, and by God, I *will*.'

He pulled up her nightgown, something he usually left her to do when she felt ready, and clasped her in his arms so tightly that she gasped for breath; instead of waiting for her to open her thighs to him, he roughly forced the weight of his body between them, and instead of touching her secret place with a questing forefinger and gradually bringing her up to a peak of pleasure, he thrust his rigid member inside her, hard and harder still, flattening her down upon the bed. She gave a little gasp of discomfort, but he seemed not to hear.

'Isabel, I'm here, I'm here with you – I'm here within you!' he groaned with a kind of desperation. There was no tenderness, none of the consideration he had always hitherto shown her; never before had he used her in such a *brutal* way, if such a word could be applied to her gentle, serious-minded husband, a clergyman of the Church. She was overpowered, unable to move or resist, utterly helpless. It made her remember stories she had heard from women of the parish whose drunken husbands had forced themselves upon their wives; they had confided in her as a married woman who would understand the meaning of the word *rape*, and this night she felt that it was happening to *her*. She had not sufficient breath to cry out, and her attempts to push him away were ineffectual; she simply had to lie there until at length he gave another wordless groan and collapsed panting, his passion subsided. She was at last able to move away from under him, her flesh bruised and sore.

'Isabel – oh, Isabel.'

Shocked and bewildered, at first she had no words for him. He, her husband, the dedicated and highly respected vicar of St Barnabas' had forced her, just as a drunken brute might have done, or a soldier quenching his lust with a whore.

'Isabel, my love, forgive me. Forgive me, Isabel.'

What should she say? How could she reply?

Lying silent and still beside him, her eyes closed, she prayed earnestly for the right words; she reflected on his gentleness and courtesy over the past two years, patiently and self-effacingly denying himself his full conjugal rights throughout all this time, for her sake. *Until now.* And remembering this, she had her answer. She understood his anguish at leaving her to go and serve in a war from which he might not return, and his need to make love to her fully and properly before what might be their last farewell.

She turned to him and put her arms around his neck; she kissed him with an almost maternal tenderness, and gave him her whispered assurances that there was nothing to forgive.

August, 1916

'Yes, we saw Ernest off yesterday, and Isabel's husband went last Friday,' Tom Munday said bleakly. 'Makes you wonder how many more good men are going to be sent out there to be slaughtered.'

Eddie stared in some surprise. It wasn't like old Tom to speak in such an unhopeful way. The two of them were sitting in the dusty yard at the back of the Tradesmen's Arms on what would have been a perfect August evening had it not been for the tension and anxiety in the air. All over the country families waited for news and searched the casualty lists dreading to find a loved one's name.

'How's old Yeomans taking it?' asked Tom. 'I reckon your Mary won't be short o' work.'

Eddie Cooper shook his head. 'He's a broken man – aged ten years overnight. And my Mary has to put in a twelve-hour day, and keep them two land girls at it. She'll crock herself up, that's what she'll do. Looked exhausted when I went over to give 'em a hand with the haymakin' last weekend, seein' there's no casual labour to be had, they're all at the front. It's desperate – God knows how it'll end.' Eddie downed his glass of beer. 'Anyway, Tom, you'd better be gettin' back to that missus o' yours – she'll be lookin' out for you.'

'Not just yet. I'll take another five minutes before I go home and pretend to look on the bright side for her sake. I'm bloody worn out with it.'

Eddie gave him a sharp glance. 'Yeah?'

'Trouble is I can't speak the truth to Violet, Eddie. I have to hide behind a lot of comforting words, and I'm just about emptied out. My son's at the front, so's my son-in-law, Isabel's on her own in a rough East End parish, with Zeppelins flying overhead. And I have to grin like a fool and pretend not to be worried. Hah!'

Eddie's eyes showed his helpless sympathy as he tried to think of something encouraging to say. 'What about your girl Grace?' he asked. 'She's settled well enough at Everham General, hasn't she?'

'Yeah, she's a ward maid or somesuch. We don't see much of her because she has to live in. Just as well, really, home isn't very jolly these days.' He got up from the garden seat. 'So long, Eddie. Hope your Mary keeps going at Yeomans' farm.'

'I thought you were never coming home,' grumbled Violet Munday. 'You say you're short of work, but there's still time to gossip with Eddie Cooper down at that pub. I'd have thought you'd want to get home as soon as you can, knowing I'm on my own here.'

'Sorry, Vi,' he said, kissing her. 'Eddie was telling me what it's like on Yeomans' farm now that Dick's gone, and no labour to be had.'

'It's downright scandalous that a farmer's son's sent out to get killed while that white-livered milksop Sidney Goddard stands in that damned shop selling ribbon and buttons and stuff – and our son facing death—' She broke off, wringing her hands. 'You won't catch *me* going in there, and I'm not the only woman in North Camp to shun Goddard's haberdashery, I can tell you!'

Tom heard the hysterical edge to her voice, and gently put an arm around her shoulders.

'Sidney Goddard failed his medical on account of his poor sight, Vi,' he reminded her mildly. 'What do you think he ought to do, if not to look after his father's business?'

'Find some work that a proper man can do – go down a coal mine, go and quarry stone and break it up, drive a goods train and stoke up the furnace – *anything* as long as he hides his stupid face in shame!'

'Now, Vi, don't get yourself into a state, it won't make any difference to the war,' soothed Tom. 'As a matter of fact, I think I can find a job for young Goddard.'

'Why on earth should you bother yourself about *him* when you've got a son and a son-in-law risking their lives every hour of the day at the front? I'll never understand you, Tom Munday!'

'Come on, Vi, calm down, there's a good girl. We've got to go on being brave for Ernest's sake – and for Mark and Aaron and all of them out there.'

She burst into a storm of weeping. 'For God's sake, shut up about being brave! Dick Yeomans killed last month, and our son could be next – and if you only saw the misery of poor Ethel Bird, her son Ted gone, and Tim still out there – don't you *dare* talk about calming down and being brave – *shut up* and leave me alone!'

'All right, Vi, only don't forget I'm feeling it too. I'll get the supper—'

'Don't bother about supper for me, I can't eat anything. Just leave me alone.'

'I'll make a pot o' tea, then.' And do some watering, he thought to himself. The tomato plants were looking droopy, and life had to go on. An idea had come into his head, and tomorrow he'd have another word with Eddie and perhaps call on the Goddards. Desperate times call for unusual solutions.

⁓

Cadet Nurse Munday had fallen asleep after the alarm bell had gone off, woke with a start, leapt out of bed and dressed, grabbed a cup of stewed tea from the staff dining room and scuttled into Princess Alexandra ward where Matron was already taking morning prayers. It was going to be one of those days, Grace thought. She tiptoed towards the nurses standing around the sister's desk, heads bowed and ready to recite the Lord's Prayer in conclusion. Before Matron left to take prayers on Prince Albert ward, she eyed Nurse Munday with disapproval.

'Unpunctuality is slackness, Nurse. Don't make a habit of it.'

'Sorry, Matron,' muttered Grace with downcast eyes, and hurried into the ward kitchen where tea, porridge and bread and butter were waiting to be served to the patients, who included two children; one was a little girl of four who was to have a removal of tubercular glands of the neck that morning. Grace had a special smile for her and a word for Mrs Temple, a mother in her thirties who had undergone a mastectomy for breast cancer and was only slowly recovering.

'Poor little Tilly can't understand why she's not having any breakfast this morning, Mrs Temple, and thinks it's because she's been naughty – and old Mrs Stephens has to be fed her porridge, otherwise she just lays back and says her family have put her in the workhouse,' Grace said cheerfully. 'And there's two women asking for bedpans before the breakfast things are cleared away – just try and hang on for another two minutes, ladies!'

A staff nurse came hurrying in. 'There's an accident case on the way, a young girl who's broken her arm,' she said. 'And her mother's on the hospital management committee. Better get this ward tidy quickly – hurry up, Munday!'

A disturbance was heard at the entrance to the ward, and a haughty female voice raised above others. Matron returned, followed by the ward sister as the double doors swung open for a frightened looking girl of about sixteen in a wheelchair, accompanied by a very imperious lady with a huge, flower-decked hat.

'We shall want a private room for her,' this lady demanded, and Grace pricked up her ears. She knew that voice, and it held no pleasant memories for her.

The ward sister shook her head. 'I'm afraid there's no single room available at present, but Diana could go in a corner bed. Nurse Munday, get Miss Clandon's bed out of that corner, and move the empty bed into it. Come along, be quick! And fetch the screens to put round it.'

Grace looked sideways at Mrs Temple, and whispered, 'Delighted to oblige, I'm sure, if I could have another two pairs of hands,' and aloud she said, 'Right, Sister, I'm just finishing breakfasts and starting bedpans – be with you in a minute!'

A probationer nurse was summoned to assist with the bed-moving, and transferring the new patient from the wheelchair to the empty bed.

'*Do* be careful, my daughter has a broken arm,' said the girl's mother, and Grace rolled up her eyes. 'Oh, heck!' she muttered to Mrs Temple. 'It's Mrs Bentley-Foulkes, a fearful old hag. Watch out, this is going to be a right do-and-a-half!'

'Diana's GP has been sent for, and meanwhile she must stay absolutely still,' said Matron, and the sister nodded. 'Nurse Munday, bring a bedpan for Miss Bentley-Foulkes, we need to collect a specimen of urine for routine testing.'

Grace approached with a covered bedpan straight from the washer in the sluice, and attempted to help the girl to sit on it.

'Ow! That's hot, I can't sit on that!' protested the girl. 'It'll burn my bottom!'

'Oh, I'm very sorry, I'll go and cool it,' said Grace, whispering to Mrs Temple as she passed her bed, 'I'll fill it with ice cubes next time, your ladyship.'

'You're so entertaining, Nurse,' Mrs Temple whispered back, trying not to laugh. 'It's better than medicine when you're around. Only do be careful,' she added, nodding towards the corner bed.

It appeared that Diana Bentley-Foulkes had fallen off her bicycle as she set off for her voluntary work at the day nursery, and was in great pain with her left arm. When her GP arrived to examine her he announced that it was her left clavicle, or collarbone that had been broken, and that it would need to be manipulated into position under a general anaesthetic. Another GP, skilled in anaesthesia was duly sent for, and Mrs Bentley-Foulkes was told that her daughter was allowed nothing by mouth, not even water.

At this point the theatre trolley arrived to take little Tilly for her operation, and Grace made up her bed ready to receive her back. Screened off from the group gathered round Diana's bed, Grace could hear every word.

'Has that urine specimen been tested?'

'Er, no, Sister, Munday forgot to save it,' answered the probationer.

'Oh, how careless of her! It means we shall have to obtain another.'

'My daughter's not going to be able to produce any more if she's not allowed even a sip of water! Who *is* that wretched nurse? I seem to recall her face from somewhere. What's her name?'

'Munday, Mrs Bentley-Foulkes, she's a cadet nurse, fairly recently taken on.'

'I knew it! That's the one, Munday, she used to work as a waitress in a very high quality tea room, and got dismissed for insolence. Yes, now I remember Mrs Brangton telling me, she then went to work in a *public house*. A most unsuitable choice for a nurse, I must say – surely Matron must have asked for references? I'll have a word with her about it.'

Behind the screen, but in view of Mrs Temple, Grace made a rude gesture towards Mrs Bentley-Foulkes, putting her thumb to her nose. Mrs Temple stifled a giggle, and there was a sudden silence. The ward sister gave a cough and cleared her throat.

'I'll say this much for Munday, the patients seem to like her, and she keeps them entertained. In these days of so much sorrow and bereavement, that's quite important. As a matter of fact, Munday herself has a brother serving in France.'

'I don't see what that's got to do with it, Sister. A great many of us have a son or a brother in the armed services, and as for the patients, she's not here to entertain them but to *nurse*. I can just imagine a girl of that type, telling vulgar jokes and appealing to a certain class of person. Well, I shall see that Matron is informed about her past history, and then decide about her future here.'

A gasp went up from the patients who could see Grace listening, followed by a low murmur of protest. The sister realised that Cadet Nurse Munday was behind the screen and must have heard everything. Mrs Bentley-Foulkes also guessed the situation, and for once looked slightly embarrassed.

Grace Munday pulled back the screen and revealed herself standing by the little girl's bed. She stared very hard at Mrs Bentley-Foulkes, who flushed.

'I don't retract a single word of what I've said, miss, and I can only say that if the cap fits, wear it.'

'You think you're somebody, don't you, Mrs Bentley-Foulkes,' said Grace clearly and evenly, 'but you're nobody. Nobody but a stuck-up bitch – and I don't retract a word of *that*, either.' She turned to the astonished ward sister. 'I'd better leave now, hadn't I, Sister? Good morning – good morning and goodbye to you all.'

As she walked out of the ward, some of the patients called out, 'Good luck, Nurse! Good for you, Bedpan Annie!'

Grace's sister Isabel also experienced support and sympathy from those she served, and the work continued at St Barnabas' Church without young Mr Storey, led by old Mr Storey and his popular daughter-in-law. Each of them worried about the other, and they shared their worries over Mark, completing a short training at Aldershot before sailing for France and the continuing battles raging in the Somme valley. Mrs Clements fussed over them happily, and although looked upon as a busybody by many parishioners, proved herself to be a treasure; from her early resentment Isabel had come to feel real affection for her, and Mr Clements never once protested about his wife's frequent absences from home – some said because he didn't dare to, and others thought he must be thankful for a bit of peace and quiet with the old girl out of the house. She was determined not to be outdone in her care for the church, the vicarage and its occupants; she took on the leadership of the St Barnabas' branch of the Mothers' Union, a position traditionally held by the vicar's wife, though she put a lot of people's backs up by her bossy ways, and the membership fell, to Isabel's dismay. She confided in her father-in-law and asked him whether she should take over the Mothers' Union in addition to her school teaching and parish visiting; and after careful consideration he suggested that she take on the position of secretary to the MU, from where she would be a familiar face, keeping an eye on their activities and quietly influencing the leadership without appearing to interfere. This worked very well, as Mrs Clements was no writer, and being seen conferring with her secretary, the vicar's wife, no less, gave her even more prestige. Sally Tanner was not strictly eligible to join, not being a mother, but Isabel used her influence to enrol Sally as a member on the grounds that she had lost a child through miscarriage; and Sally gave her great satisfaction by doing well at the garment factory and keeping away from drink. 'If I'm tempted, Mrs Storey, I think of you, and know I mustn't let you down!'

Not many letters passed between Isabel and her parents; her father did not want to worry her with her mother's melancholy state over Ernest, though he felt obliged to let her know of Grace's latest scrape, trying to make light of it and his hope that his younger daughter would eventually find her niche in life, and stay in it.

When Grace Munday cycled home to North Camp to tell her parents that she was no longer a cadet nurse at Everham General, she was shocked by their chilly reception of the news. Her mother looked thin, pale and drawn, and hardly seemed interested in her daughter's confrontation with Mrs Bentley-Foulkes.

'I might have known you wouldn't last long there,' she said dully. 'You've been thrown out of that cafe and the Railway Hotel and Hassett Manor, and now this. Well, don't expect any fussing over from *me*, I've got worries enough over my son, facing death every day in those horrible trenches.' And she turned away from her errant daughter in a way that was worse than loud anger and accusation.

When Tom Munday came home to find Grace there with her story, he sighed heavily. 'You might have given a bit of thought to your mother, my girl. She's making herself ill with worry over your brother, and you might have thought about that before defying this woman. All I can suggest is that you go back to the hospital and apologise.'

'Oh, Dad, I *couldn't*! Not after what happened today, I couldn't possibly!' pleaded Grace, horrified at the mere thought of crawling to Mrs Bentley-Foulkes and saying she was *sorry* for what she'd said that morning. 'I just couldn't do it, Dad.'

'Look, if you ever thought about the trouble you've caused ever since you were at school, Grace, you'd put your pride in your pocket and go and see the matron, tell her you regret what you said and beg her to keep you on as a ward maid or whatever you are. Otherwise I don't know what you can do, apart from going to work in a munitions factory – they're always advertising for more girls, though the work's hard and not without its dangers. I'm sorry, Grace, but I can only say again, go back and see the matron.'

Grace's spirits were at a very low ebb when she cycled back to Everham in the afternoon, and presented herself at the door of Matron's office, bracing herself to apologise, and ready to face a serious reprimand.

But Matron turned out to be unexpectedly sympathetic. 'I'm very sorry about what has happened, Miss Munday, and the patients on Princess Alexandra ward will miss you, I know. I would have been prepared to give you another chance, but I'm afraid the damage has been done. Your defiance towards Mrs Bentley-Foulkes was so public, witnessed by the ward sister and staff, and of course the patients. It can't be hushed up, on the contrary, it's already a nine-day wonder, and you have alienated Mrs Bentley-Foulkes beyond apology. I'm truly sorry, but regretfully I can't keep you on.' She looked Grace in the eyes, and repeated, 'I can't keep you on, Miss Munday.'

There was nothing more to be said, except 'Thank you, Matron,' and Grace left the office and made her way up to her room. She took a large leather suitcase down from the top of the wardrobe, and packed her clothes and the few other belongings she had kept here; she counted the money in her purse: enough to pay for a one-way ticket to Waterloo Station, tip a porter and hire a cab to take her to the address that Madge Fraser had given her.

'A couple o' girls share lodgin's with me, but we could make room for one more little'un – it's the best life I've ever 'ad, Grace!'

'I'm on my way, Madge,' murmured Grace as she stood on Everham Station platform. 'Because it's certain nobody wants me *here*!'

Chapter Eleven

September, 1916

'I don't know which was worse, Annie, the Yeomanses or the Goddards,' said Eddie Cooper, sitting down wearily and taking the mug of tea from his wife's hand. She waited for him to continue.

'Ol' Yeomans is as surly as a man can be, and *she's* not interested in the farm and wants Mary indoors to help her with the house and little Billy – which is hard on Mary who's wanted just as much outdoors. And she looks awful, does my poor girl.'

Annie Cooper refrained from making any comment on her stepdaughter, having long given up trying to win over the girl. 'So, come on, what did they say to the idea?'

'He said he'd take on anybody who'd do a day's work, but he didn't want no young fool in a suit – them were his exact words. Mary told him it was worth a try, at least, but he didn't show much interest. Trouble was, Tom Munday was goin' to see the Goddards, but he's that frantic over Grace disappearin', and his missus pinin' away before his eyes, can't eat, can't sleep – he's at his wit's end, poor ol' Tom.'

'So you went and spoke to the Goddards yourself, then?' prompted Annie. 'How did Sidney take it? And Mr and Mrs?'

'Not too badly, considerin' they've been snubbed by all o' North Camp 'cause o' Sidney not bein' over there with the other lads. Ol' Goddard ain't been so well lately, she thinks he's got an ulcer, and they both look under the weather. Sounds as if the daughter Betty has taken over servin' in the shop.'

'Well, go on, then,' said Annie with interest. 'Did you see Sidney? He's the one to say yes or no. Which was it?'

'He's startin' work there first thing on Monday. Says he doesn't know how he'll take to it, but anything 'ud be better'n the cold-shoulderin' he's had from folks round here.' He sighed. 'The lad ain't got much gumption – looks like an owl, standin' there squintin' through them round spectacles.'

'Poor Sidney. I s'pose he's never had to get his hands dirty.'

'Well, he's goin' to get more'n his hands dirty lookin' after cows an' pigs. Makes me wonder if I ought not to have interfered – I'm not so sure whether this was a good idea o' Tom Munday's.'

'Don't be daft, Eddie. There's two possibilities, ain't there? Either he'll settle down to it or he won't. At least he'll be hidden away from all the jibes. By the way, have *you* got anythin' on this weekend?'

'Not really. I thought I'd go over and give 'em a hand on the farm again.'

Annie shrugged, guessing that he was worried over his daughter. 'That's good o' you, Eddie, seein' as I don't s'pose old Yeomans pays anythin' for your trouble.'

Eddie didn't answer, because she'd guessed right. Apart from providing a midday dinner, old Yeomans didn't pay him a penny.

❧

The days were drawing in, and the hay was cut, dried, collected and made into haystacks within the barn, old Yeomans' expertise aided by Sidney Goddard's efforts to heave the bales on top of each other and secure them with ropes. Dust and specks of straw flew around, getting under their clothes and making young Goddard itch all over as he tried to follow Yeomans' shouted orders; the man seemed to be in a permanently bad temper. The two land girls had tried to initiate him into the skills of 'udder-plucking' as they referred to milking, having themselves been instructed by Mary Cooper, and which Sidney found as difficult as it was unfamiliar. Pails were kicked over, spilling the precious milk, milking stools were overturned, sending Sidney sprawling, just as the cow raised her tail to rid herself of a steaming heap of dung. Caring for the pigs was relatively easy at this time of year; there were two sows in one sty, alternately giving birth to a litter of squeaking piglets, sired by a boar who lived in a separate sty and was as ill-tempered as the farmer; one sow at a time was allowed to keep company with him daily in the small apple orchard until it was obvious that he had done his duty by her. All the animals needed feeding, and their sties and sheds cleaned out regularly; both cow and pig manure were used as fertiliser to spread on the fields of turnips, mangolds and swedes used to provide winter feed for the cows, while the pigs lived on offal and kitchen scraps, with extra milk and whey for farrowing sows. There were no bulls on Yeomans' farm, and a business arrangement was made with a farm at Hassett where a huge and terrifying bull obligingly served the cows that were led to him.

Sidney Goddard was regularly cursed by old Yeomans, and teased by the land girls for his clumsy lack of expertise. By the end of each day he was too exhausted to do anything other than climb into his bed and sleep until woken by the dawn chorus and the lowing of the cows in their byre, waiting to be milked; but he no longer had to face the contempt of North Camp neighbours, being mercifully out of their sight.

After morning milking Mary served porridge and bread and cheese in the farm kitchen; she took a tray to Mrs Yeomans and little Billy; the boy saved his mother from giving way to helpless grief for Dick, and she fussed over him accordingly, though she failed to notice Mary's pallor and the dark circles under her eyes. She had no idea of the stomach-churning nausea that Mary felt when serving breakfast to old Yeomans, Sidney and the land girls, and it was only when the girl fainted and fell on the kitchen floor that Mrs Yeomans realised what Mary now knew for certain: that she was carrying Dick Yeomans' child, and was now over three months into her pregnancy.

Tom Munday occupied the usual family pew in St Peter's Church and followed the service of morning prayer, sitting to listen to the readings and the sermon, kneeling when prayers were offered up, and standing for the Gospel and the three or four hymns. He was alone, his three children far away from North Camp, and his wife unable and unwilling to accompany him: he had left her in bed after a disturbed night. In her dreams she invariably saw Ernest lying dead on the field of battle; the certainty of his death was fixed in her mind, and she was mourning for him already, before the dreaded telegram arrived, and would not be persuaded to believe otherwise.

Tom's thoughts were centred more on his daughter Grace, and he blamed himself bitterly for the unkind words he had spoken when she'd arrived home from Everham General on that fateful afternoon. Now he would give all he possessed to have her back again, but he had no idea of her whereabouts. He had written to the management of the Ritz Hotel in Piccadilly, asking if a chambermaid by the name of Grace Munday was employed there, and mentioned that she was a friend of Marjorie Fraser, known as Madge, also on their domestic staff. He enclosed a stamped, self-addressed envelope for a reply, and when it reappeared on the front door mat, he seized it and tore it open; his hopes were immediately dashed, for the brief typewritten letter informed him that neither of the two names he had mentioned had ever been on their staff in any capacity. He told Violet as gently as he could, but all her thoughts were fixed upon Ernest; and in church on this Sunday morning Tom prayed earnestly for his three children, Ernest in the trenches of France, Isabel in London without Mark to protect her, and Grace wherever she was and whatever she was doing. Tears came to her father's eyes when he remembered how he had rebuffed her plea for sympathy.

And on the following morning – oh, what joy, what thankfulness! – his prayers were at least partially answered, for there on the doormat was a picture postcard of Big Ben and the Houses of Parliament with a message from Grace to her parents. She was living in lodgings with Madge Fraser, she told them, and 'We've both got good jobs and there's no need to worry about me.' She sent them her love and promised to keep in touch, though she gave no address.

'She's alive and still cares about us, Violet,' he said. 'We must thank God for that much, and trust that she'll come back to us when she's ready. We'll have to be content with that.' He leant over his wife's chair to kiss her, but she drew away.

'*I'd* rejoice and be thankful if we could only hear from Ernest, but Grace has given us nothing but trouble. God knows what she's up to, a girl of seventeen adrift in London – I never liked the sound of that Madge, who's obviously a liar, because the Ritz Hotel has never heard of her.'

Violet Munday had lost all patience with her daughter Grace, but the following morning it was her turn to rejoice, for there on the mat lay a crumpled postcard from Ernest! Violet seized and kissed it, and they both eagerly read the message.

'My dear parents, I can't tell you where we are, but we are together and sharing everything, our thoughts, our parcels from home, our life-saving friendship. We send our love to both our families, and we are full of hope. Ernest and Aaron.'

Now Violet returned her husband's kisses, began to regain her appetite, knelt beside their bed at night to give thanks, and slept with the postcard under her pillow. She caught the bus to Everham and went to visit the Pascoes and old Mr and Mrs Schelling, taking them a fruit cake she had made and two jars of her own raspberry jam. Her former antipathy towards the family was forgotten.

'Ernest and Aaron share everything with each other,' she told them, 'so it's only right that we should share, too.'

It was like the lifting of a cloud, but Tom was wary of rejoicing too soon. The war was by no means over.

Eddie Cooper had long believed that the Yeomanses had taken Mary for granted, expecting her to work long hours in the house and on the farm, with hardly any time off and scarcely more than her bed and board in payment. Since the news of Dick's death the pressure on her had increased, and the addition of Sidney Goddard to the farm workers had not made life any easier for her, as far as Eddie could see. In the Yeomans' sorrow over the loss of their son, Mary's own grief had hardly been considered, and on those weekends when Eddie went to lend a hand, it irritated him to see his sad-faced daughter constantly at the beck and call of both husband and wife, without the spirit to answer them back or in any way to stand up for herself.

But on this particular Saturday morning when he met old Yeomans in the yard, the farmer gave him an oddly hesitant look, almost as if he felt embarrassed.

'Ye'd better step into the house and have a word with that girl o' yourn.'

'Why, what's up?' asked Eddie, alarmed. 'Is she ill? What's happened?'

'Ye'd better step in and speak to the missus,' replied old Yeomans, and disappeared behind the hay barn.

Eddie entered the kitchen by the back door, where to his amazement a red-eyed Mary was sitting by the oven in a wicker chair, and Mrs Yeomans was washing the breakfast bowls at the stone sink. *This* was something new, thought Eddie, and went straight to his daughter's side.

'What's up, Mary?' he asked, but it was Mrs Yeomans who answered.

'Your girl says she's expectin' Dick's baby.'

'Oh, my God – oh, Mary!' gasped Eddie, and took hold of both Mary's hands in his. 'You poor kid – why didn't you tell me? You'll have to come home now…'

'She's stayin' here, Cooper,' said Mrs Yeomans firmly. 'We've looked after her these five years or more, and now she's carryin' our grandchild and we're standin' by her – so here she stays.'

'But she's my daughter, and it's my grandchild, too!' cried Eddie.

'Didn't you hear me, Cooper? She's stayin' here.'

Throughout this exchange Mary had not spoken. Eddie now

turned to her, still holding her hands. 'Is this true, Mary?'

She nodded slowly, her eyes lowered. 'I'm sorry, Dad. I should've told you, but – the fact is they've given me a home here, and I can't very well leave now. And your wife won't want me.'

'Good heavens, Mary, if you'd only give Annie half a chance, she's always been willin' to…to be a mother to you.'

'She's not my mother.'

'Well, a friend, then. Come home with me, Mary.'

'No, Dad, not with your wife and son there.'

'That's enough from you, Eddie Cooper,' said Mrs Yeomans, turning round to face him squarely. 'She's stayin' here, and that's that. You can go any time you like.'

'You'd better go, Dad.'

'All right, Mary, I'll go, but you know where you can find me if you need me.' He leant over the chair and kissed her. 'My poor girl,' he murmured softly, then got himself out of the kitchen before he broke down. And I'll be damned if I ever do a day's work for old Yeomans again, he told himself, crossing the yard and making for the gate that led into the lane. It also led past the pigsties, and he caught sight of a young man raking out the dung and piling it on to a wheelbarrow; he had a bale of clean straw ready to replace it. He looked up and saw Eddie who hadn't recognised him in his filthy grey shirt and trousers.

''Morning, Mr Cooper!'

'Oh…er…Sidney, g'mornin'. How're you doin'? Looks like hard work.'

'It's hard going, but anything's better than having to face people in North Camp. Thanks for…er…suggesting it.'

'It was Tom Munday's idea, to be honest.' On an impulse Eddie stopped and crossed the path to speak quietly over the stone wall of the sty. 'Look here, Sidney, keep an eye on my daughter Mary, will you? And if they ain't treatin' her right, let me know. D'you understand?'

'Er…how exactly do you mean, Mr Cooper?' asked Sidney, scratching his head and realising too late that his hands were smeared with pig muck.

'I mean they've worked her like a bloody galley slave for years, an' now she needs to rest more – so keep an eye on her, will you?'

Sidney was surprised at Cooper's vehemence. 'Er…yes, I'll try.'

'Well, mind you do, then. Good mornin' to you.' And Eddie strode away abruptly, thinking what a booby the Goddards' son was.

When he got home, Annie asked why he hadn't stayed to 'lend a hand', as he'd intended.

'I don't feel inclined to go on slogging my guts out for 'em any longer – and I got somethin' to tell you, Annie.'

When Annie Cooper heard how things stood at the farm, she shrugged sympathetically. 'Poor Mary, she won't be the only girl left in trouble after a young fellow's marched off to war and got killed – but she's got the Yeomanses to look after her and their grandchild, so she's better off than most.'

'It's no good, Annie, I just can't stand them Yeomanses.'

His wife didn't answer; whatever Eddie thought of the Yeomanses, Annie was thankful for them, and their care for Mary and their expected grandchild, her baby.

Dolly's was one of many small licensed music halls that had sprung up in London since the war. While museums and galleries had closed, the hectic search for pleasure led many a serviceman on his all-too-brief leave to places like Dolly's in Lamp Street, just off Piccadilly, crowded to capacity night after night. Cinemas provided an escape from dreary reality with silent two-reeler films, and Londoners flocked to see Charlie Chaplin's antics – but it was the live shows like the ones at Dolly's that drew the men to see pretty, scantily dressed girls dancing, singing and posing in brilliant tableaux. The orchestra often consisted of only a piano, a violin and a clarinet, backed by a shirt-sleeved percussionist, banging a drum and clashing cymbals. The stage was small, but could be converted into three levels by the use of movable sections and a curving staircase down which the girls trooped in a line, one hand on hip and bestowing dazzling smiles on their audiences, many of whom sat through the two nightly performances while the bar did a good trade in spirits, wines and beers.

Grace Munday was in the chorus line, having been introduced by Madge Fraser to Mr George Dean, the owner-manager of Dolly's; he had nodded approval and passed her on to Mrs Moore the choreographer who trained the girls at rehearsals each morning, getting even the most unpromising of them to do high kicks. Grace soon established herself as a natural entertainer, and Mrs Moore put her into a quartet of girls who danced seductively to 'Clair de Lune', the dimmed lights and flimsy, floating dresses adding a dreamlike quality to their act; it met with tremendous applause. Mr Dean was frequently approached by eager patrons wanting introductions to one of the 'Dolly Girls', to take them out to one of the many supper clubs in the West End, hoping to enjoy a pretty girl's company for an hour or two, before having to return to the trenches. They soon discovered that he felt responsible for his girls, and was careful about which ones he chose to take up these invitations; he preferred to arrange foursomes rather than couples, and had an agreement with Madge Fraser to see that all three of her fellow lodgers at 17 Lamp Street, which included Grace Munday, were home by midnight.

Grace relished her new life and its mood of reckless gaiety which matched her own. She, who had been rejected by Lady Neville, Everham General Hospital and finally by her own parents, was now not only accepted but applauded; there was no reason to look back, only to enjoy the present, and not waste a single hour of it.

The Zeppelins having disappeared from the skies for several months, Londoners were dismayed when they returned at the end of September, dropping bombs that caused explosions and fires, indiscriminately killing and injuring civilians, and destroying their homes; but Britain was now better equipped and experienced at locating the airships in searchlight beams and then attacking with a newly developed explosive bullet that set fire to the great balloons on impact, illuminating the night sky with a blaze of white-hot flame as the airship fell to earth, an unearthly glow reflected in the Thames. People cheered in vengeful triumph at these awesome sights, but to the Rev. Richard Storey and his daughter-in-law it was like looking into the mouth of hell.

The bombs had brought terror and destruction to Bethnal Green and the parish of St Barnabas', slum districts being as vulnerable as more salubrious areas. Some houses were damaged beyond repair and Isabel saw fire-blackened rooms exposed to public gaze, and broken furniture half-buried in brick dust; banisters could be seen still curving upwards after the stairs had collapsed and the roof fallen in. Where the houses still stood, their shattered windows were replaced by sheets of cardboard, useless as soon as rain came and soaked it.

Isabel Storey stood before her looking glass in the room she had shared with Mark. It was morning, and time to get up. She pulled her nightgown up over her head, and before she dressed she appraised the reflection of her young naked body. Two years of marriage to an East End vicar had not changed her slim figure, but her face looked older than her twenty years. Anxiety for Mark, her brother Ernest and her sister Grace had brought shadows to her blue eyes, and there was a little droop to her mouth when in repose; but not at this moment, for she was smiling at the face which smiled back at her, rejoicing in the secret they shared – and which she did not want to share with anybody else but Mark, though as yet there was nothing definite to tell, because her period was only a few days overdue – and yet she *knew*, she was certain in her mind that Mark's last night of desperate love-making, when he had finally and completely entered her, had begun the process of a new life taking shape within her, her child and Mark's. She no longer saw his behaviour as brutal, but natural, a need to leave a child behind him as he faced death on the battlefield; it would be a part of him to love, nourish and care for, a reason to be courageous and resolute. She did not intend to tell her parents and father-in-law until three months had passed; until then she would hug her secret to herself, a treasure hidden deep within her body.

She smoothed her hands down over her flat belly and smiled again at her mirrored image.

Number 17 Lamp Street was one of a row of solid terraced houses built in the mid nineteenth century as respectable West

End residences for those making their way up in the world, but in the past two or three decades it had lost its former gentility and become shabby, verging on the disreputable, a dwelling place for second-rate actors, artists and musicians struggling to make a living. Since the turn of the century, however, it had begun to look up again: a public house known for its noise and rowdiness had now been closed, and an antique shop had opened, attracting bona fide collectors who welcomed the coffee shop next door. With the opening of Dolly's at the Piccadilly end of Lamp Street, it had become acceptable, if not exactly fashionable as an address, with a quasi-Bohemian attraction very different from anything North Camp or Everham had to offer. The ground floor was rented to a small grocery and hardware shop, and the first floor was home to stage-struck young ladies employed by Mr Dean of Dolly's. Madge Fraser occupied a good-sized room and Grace Munday a smaller one; another large room was shared by Iris and Audrey who did a high-wire act as well as being in the chorus, and another small one called Number Four was occasionally occupied by visiting artistes. It was kept locked, and Madge Fraser had the key.

For Grace it was an ideal place to live, perfect in every way, and she was indebted to Madge for recommending it and welcoming her both as an entertainer at Dolly's and a privileged lodger at number 17 Lamp Street, so conveniently near.

When Grace first found herself invited with Madge to a late supper after the show, by two young uniformed officers, she could hardly conceal her excitement. A taxi was booked to call at 17 Lamp Street at a quarter to eleven, giving the girls time to change into suitable dresses, and to reapply the face powder and lipstick which every smart young woman seemed to be using nowadays. The two officers were charming, and whether they were named Donald and Ronald, or John and James, or Simon and Peter, their names tended to be forgotten after they had gone back to the trenches, to be replaced by two other charming officers in need of a pretty girl's company for an all-too-brief hour. After a glass or two of wine, Grace entertained them with stories of her experiences at Stepaside with Mrs and Miss Brangton and Mrs Bentley-Foulkes, which they found highly amusing; Madge joined in the reminiscences of the Railway Hotel, and Grace could do a splendid imitation of CC, Tubby and Ratty – though her horrifying ordeal at the hands of Tupman was always avoided; she felt a certain vengeful glee in mimicking his surliness, making him into a figure of fun when the revelation of his treatment of Ratty earned him the sack.

Driving back in a taxicab with Donald's arm around Madge and Ronald's around hers, Grace's heart fluttered when she felt a gentle kiss on her cheek and then on her lips. He whispered, 'You're the sweetest girl, and it's been a wonderful evening. I'll think of you when I'm…oh, if only…'

Madge exchanged kisses and whispers with the other doomed youth, and when the taxicab reached 17 Lamp Street, both girls put their arms around the men's necks and gave them what Madge called 'a proper kiss and cuddle' before saying a last goodnight and hurrying up the dark stairs to their rooms in 17 Lamp Street.

So conveniently near...

Chapter Twelve

November, 1916

The platoon had been marching all afternoon on a road crisping with frost, and it was almost dark when they finally arrived at Famechon, once a pretty village with a stone church standing among farms, but now a wasteland, deserted and forlorn, with scarcely a sign of human or animal life, save for two thin cows grazing on withered brown grass between the shell holes; there were no horses, pigs or chickens to be seen. The farmhouse was without a roof, and the outbuildings were in ruins except for an ancient cow byre.

The ten men made for the battalion headquarters, the colonel's dugout at the side of the yard, where they were awaited by two of their number who had gone on ahead. It was deep and dry, warmed by an oil stove and the body heat of the men who now crowded into it, footsore, hungry and tired out. They could not take off their boots or their mud-stained puttees, their socks had not been off their feet for three weeks, and their underclothing was lice-ridden; with their gaunt, unshaven faces they were grotesque shadows of the eager young men who had enlisted to fight for their country. Now they gathered round the stove, setting aside their discomforts as they hungrily consumed scalding hot tea and slices of bread and jam; then they slept where they sat, arms and legs entwined, heads lolling on each other's chests or bellies for a few blessed hours of release from the horrors they had so far survived. An unearthly quiet wrapped around them; there were no exploding shells and whizz-bangs, no machine gun fire, no screams and groans of the injured and dying. Nobody noticed when two of them quietly got up and climbed out of the bunker.

'Come on, let's go to the byre, Ernest, just the two of us,' whispered Aaron. 'I noticed there was some straw in there, and a blanket we can use to cover ourselves.'

Above them the frosty night was full of stars as they settled down fully dressed upon the straw, wrapped in the rough horse blanket left by previous occupants. Aaron fell asleep instantly, and Ernest marvelled at the peace that surrounded them.

I'm *happy,* he reflected in astonishment; it's *happiness* I feel at this moment, lying beside him I love more than life. For months they'd campaigned together, faced death and every kind of misery – hunger, exhaustion, their bodies itching from lice and sore from scratching – yet they'd teased each other, quoted bits of poetry, shared their deepest thoughts, consoled by each other's company.

As Ernest drifted into sleep, Aaron stirred and briefly awoke. Soon we shall have to go back to the front line, he thought, the stinking mud of the trenches, the constant battering of shells flying over No Man's Land, the rotting bodies of men and horses, the ever-present fear of death. And yet it has taken this cruel war to make me understand at last how truly I love this dearest of friends, more than I could ever love a woman. Ah, Ernest, I'd rather be in the trenches with you, facing danger and death, than to be safe at home without you.

And so for a few hours they slept in deep peace with their arms around each other, closer than brothers.

Fog hung over London, and Mrs Mark Storey lit the gas mantle at three o'clock in the grey November afternoon; seated at her husband's desk, she began to write a careful letter to her parents, telling them of her news and emphasising how well she felt, now three months into her pregnancy.

'Please do not worry about me,' she wrote, knowing that they would want her to come home. 'I am convinced that the Lord wants me to stay here with the people I have grown to love and respect. They would miss me, and heaven knows I would miss them if I were to return to North Camp. Mark is not here to serve them, and his dear father needs my support in caring for the parish, especially those women and children whose menfolk are away fighting this hateful war. News from the front is rather vague, and I've had only one brief letter from Mark which took over a month to arrive. The men are not allowed to give details of times and places, for fear of giving information to the enemy. I have written to him to tell him about the baby which the midwife here says will be born in May. Dear Mum and Dad, I am so happy, and I thank the Lord for sending me this precious blessing.'

Isabel sat for a few moments before dipping her pen in the inkwell again. She knew that her parents worried about her, and that there was little she could say to reassure them. With the ending of the Zeppelin raids, London was now facing a new danger: enemy aeroplanes which came over to drop explosive bombs on the city, aiming with greater accuracy than the airships had. If aerial bombing were to take place on a large scale, as some predicted, Isabel had no fear for herself – but what about the baby, hers and Mark's? Would it be fair to stay in London, exposing the child to danger? She had prayed to be given the right guidance, and decided to wait for the time being, and see if the air raids increased. She had grown fond of her father-in-law who she considered worked too hard for a man of his age, and she knew that he depended on her support.

Picking up her pen again, she wrote, 'I am so sorry to hear that Grace has not re-appeared, and I can give you no news of her. She knows where I am, and surely knows that I would be overjoyed to see her if she came to me. I'm thankful at least that you have had a postcard from her. Have you had any news of Ernest? The Schelling and Pascoe families have received a letter from Aaron, they told me. They live in Tamarind Street in Whitechapel, and manage a small tailoring business there.'

She paused again. Her father-in-law had thought it strange that an Anglican vicar's wife should visit a Jewish family, but Isabel was sure that her brother Ernest would have appreciated it, and news of Aaron meant news of Ernest too. And soon there would be another recruit to the army: Aaron's younger brother Jonathan was now eighteen and so due to be called up. Isabel shivered; oh, when would all this fighting and killing come to an end?

She sighed, realising that she was tired, and brought her letter to an end. It was now time to tell her father-in-law and Mrs Clements, also the headmistress of Barnett Street School, for she would not be able to continue teaching after the February half-term, when her condition would have started to

show, and could be a secret no longer. She thought again of the
night when conception had taken place, and longed with all her
heart to see her husband again, and to hold him close against
her body and their child growing within her.

Tom Munday's thoughts were far from hopeful as he worked on
a new kitchen table for Hassett Manor, and he suspected that
Lady Neville had ordered it just to give him work. Carpentering
jobs were not easy to come by, and there was almost no outdoor
work at all: farmers mended their own fences and gates, and
Harry Hutchinson's team could replace roof tiles and repaint
door frames; the builder was quick to canvass work that should
rightly be Tom's or Eddie Cooper's.

Poor old Eddie, he was going through a fiery hoop, and no
mistake, thought Tom. Some people were so unkind about his
daughter being six months' gone, and although she never left
the farm, gossip could see through walls, and Mary's plight was
known in North and South Camp, with much head shaking
and reference to her mother, as if Joy Cooper's alcohol addiction
could affect her daughter's morals. Tom Munday was angry on
Eddie's behalf, and only wished that he could do something
for the friend who had always shared his own troubles. Violet
had been like all the rest of the women, condemning Mary
as a girl no better than she should be, and the identity of the
child's father was discussed with a certain relish; while anybody
might assume that Dick Yeomans had taken advantage of her
before he went away, there was always the possibility that his
name was used to cover up for some other man, now that Dick
was dead and unable to clear his name. When Tom Munday
rebuked his wife for repeating such idle speculation, she had
rounded on him and accused him of showing more sympathy

to Eddie Cooper and his wayward daughter than to herself, who dreaded every minute to hear that their own son had gone the same way as poor Dick Yeomans, whose death had made him a faultless hero.

The latest news from Eddie was that Sidney Goddard had come to him after dark to avoid being seen, and had told him that Mary was very unhappy and cried a lot. When Sidney had shyly asked her what was the matter, she'd burst into another gush of tears and said that the Yeomanses were only keeping her at the farm because of Dick's baby, and that when the child was born they would take it from her and bring it up as their own, because after all it was their grandchild, and Mary feared being sent away. Sidney had tried in his way to comfort her, but to no avail; and remembering Eddie's request that he should keep an eye on Mary and report anything upsetting her, he had duly come to her father.

'He didn't actually say she was being badly treated, Tom,' said Eddie, 'just that she was unhappy and afraid they'd dismiss her after the baby's born. I s'pose they'd keep her on as long as she was feedin' it, but they could turn her out as soon as it's weaned.' Eddie spoke contemptuously, and went on, 'Y'know, Tom, I never did think much o' them Yeomanses, and if she feels bad enough for *Sidney* to notice, she must be really upset and feelin' alone when it's just the time she ought to be calm an' easy in her mind. But what the devil can *I* do, Tom? Go an' see her an' tell her to come home to me and Annie? Y'know there's always been ill feelin' there, though not on Annie's part.'

Tom Munday listened in silence, frowning as he pondered over Eddie's dilemma; then he looked up and asked a question.

'What does young Goddard think, d'ye suppose? Does he like Mary?'

'Well, yeah – enough to come and tell me about her. Why?'

'How d'ye think he'd feel about marryin' her, Eddie?'

'Good God, no! A booby like young Goddard marryin' my girl? Not likely!'

Eddie looked quite offended, and Tom thought it wise not to continue along that train of thought; but the seed had been sown, and Eddie could think it over and perhaps change his mind. Stranger things had happened.

'At least you know where your daughter is, Eddie,' he said. 'We've only had two postcards from Grace, and no real news on either o' them, just that she's got a job and lodgings in London.'

Eddie looked apologetic. 'Sorry, Tom. I hope she'll see sense one o' these days. And – what about Isabel?'

Tom's mouth hardened into a straight line. 'We've just had a letter from her. She's expecting, too – after Mark Storey as good as promised me and his father that there'd be no children until the war was over, whenever *that'll* be. And now he's gone off to be an army chaplain over there, and she's on her own in a slum parish and says she's going to stay there. God knows whether he'll come back or catch a bullet like Dick Yeomans. And now Jerry's sending over aeroplanes to drop bloody bombs on London, so – these are bad times all round, Eddie.'

'Yeah, you're right. How old is she now, your Isabel?'

'Not quite twenty-one.'

'Old enough to have a kid, and she's the sort that'd look after it well. So, Tom, we're both goin' to be granddads, then.'

The two men looked at each other with a rueful smile; there just weren't any more words to say.

⁓

December, 1916

'She did, she took him upstairs, Grace – we saw 'er, didn't we, Audrey?'

'You mean – she took him up into her room?' asked Grace incredulously.

'No, they went into Number Four,' said Iris. 'We 'eard the key turn in the lock.'

'And...er, when did he leave?' Grace inquired.

'Dunno, but it must've been well after midnight, 'cause we was both fast asleep, wasn't we, Audrey?'

Grace considered this piece of information about Madge Fraser, the friend who had been so good to her, introducing her to Dolly's and thereby changing her life. Now that she came to think of it, there *had* been times lately when she had heard unfamiliar footsteps on the stairs of 17 Lamp Street, and the sound of a door opening and shutting after Iris and Audrey had gone to bed. And the last time that she and Madge had been taken out for supper by two servicemen, Madge and her escort had disappeared while Grace was still having a long goodnight kiss and cuddle in the back of the cab with hers; the driver didn't mind, it added to the fare and meant a good tip. When Grace had finally extricated herself from the arms of her admirer and run up the stairs to the first floor, there had been no sign of Madge, and Grace assumed that she had cut short the ritual goodnight kiss and gone to her room without waiting for her friend. But after hearing the high-wire girls' story, she began to wonder; had Madge really taken her fellow to her room? And was it a regular occurrence? Grace told herself that it was no business of hers, but she was troubled by it, and wondered if she should speak to her friend and find out for certain what was going on. Madge had become a self-assured woman of the world since their days at the Railway Hotel – but this was surely going too far, if it was true.

In fact, it was Madge who spoke first.

'Come on, lazybones, it's only three weeks to Chris'muss!' she cried, bouncing on Grace's bed. 'It's gorn ten o'clock, time yer was up an' doin'!'

Grace yawned and marvelled at her friend's exuberance. None of the girls were early risers, having been on stage the evening before at Dolly's. 'Shouldn't we be at rehearsal with Mrs Moore?' she murmured, sitting up and stretching her arms.

'Nah, it's Sat'day, an' Sybil Moore's gorn off Chris'muss shoppin', an' that's what *we're* goin' to do, soon as ye've shifted yer carcase out o' that bed an' put on some clo'es. C'mon, we'll parade oursel's down Piccadilly an' see what's on offer!'

'I…I haven't got a lot of spare cash, Madge,' Grace admitted, turning down the corners of her mouth. She quite often found herself short of ready cash, and wondered how Madge managed to look so smart; today she was wearing a dark-blue hobble skirt with a tight navy jacket with white piping that showed off her waist to perfection. Her blonde hair was pinned up, and two stray locks were carefully arranged to fall in front of her ears when her wide-brimmed hat was put in place.

'Don't worry, duck, I can lend yer a bob or two if yer see somethin' yer fancy. I got to get a present for me sister an' 'er two little darlin's – they're gettin' bigger, an' so's she, there'll be another of 'em soon!'

Grace got out of bed and went to the shared lavatory and

washroom. She quickly dressed, and applied bright-red lipstick, peering into the small mirror on the dressing table. She put on her hat and gloves and picked up her leather handbag.

'I'm ready,' she said.

'Cor! Ain't yer got a better one than that?' asked Madge, looking at the worn state of the leather. 'I'll treat yer to a new one at Selfridges.'

'Oh, no, I couldn't let you do that,' Grace replied, following her friend down the stairs and out into Lamp Street.

'Let's start 'ere in Piccadilly,' said Madge, linking arms with Grace. 'We'll find oursel's a nice little tea shop, somethin' like that posh one you worked at in Everham – what was it called, Stop an' Spend?'

'No, Stepaside,' laughed Grace, remembering Mrs Bentley-Foulkes.

Seated at a table by a window, Madge gave Grace a long, appraising look.

'Ye're a proper little beauty, Grace. Sybil Moore says so, and so do the fellers who come to Dolly's,' she remarked pointedly.

Grace flushed slightly and gave a modest shrug. 'Nice of you to say so.'

'Aw, come on, duck, don't try to make out ye're that innocent! Listen. Yer could earn three times as much as old George Dean doles out to us girls, *and* give the boys a treat before they go back to them bloody trenches. Ye're brilliant when we're out for supper with a couple o' fellers, an' ye're not so bad with the kissin' an' cuddlin' bit – an' it's only a short step from that to a bit of the other, d'yer see what I mean? Yer must do, ye're blushin' red as a beetroot!'

'Yes, Madge, I think I do, but I've never ever done it before.'

'Come orf it, yer must've done! Wasn't there some bloke

yer met at the Railway 'Otel? Yer used to meet 'im on yer way 'ome, same time as I was seein' Sergeant Samms. Look, Grace, there's an army captain got 'is eye on yer, ever so 'andsome, a proper gent, an' Sybil can arrange for yer to meet 'im an' bring 'im to number 17, an' I'll see that room Number Four's ready, unlocked with the key on the inside, easy as winkin'!'

'But Iris and Audrey will see!' said Grace, quite shocked. 'And hear! They've seen an' heard *you*!'

Madge laughed. 'Poor things, it gives 'em somethin' to talk about. Now, then, shall I tell Sybil that ye're on, so's she can make arrangements with this 'ere captain, and I'll let yer know what day, or rather night, an' see that Number Four's ready with a bottle o' bubbly on the table. Yer don't 'ave to ask for any money, he'll pay Sybil before'and, an' she'll pass it on through me to you. What d'yer think, little Gracie?'

'Oh, no, Madge, I couldn't, I just couldn't. I thought Mr Dean was so particular about us girls, accepting invitations to supper—'

'Christ Almighty, don't tell '*im* nothin'! Mrs Moore's in charge o' room Number Four, an' she lets the ol' fool go on thinkin' we're all as untouched as nuns.' Madge laughed heartily at Grace's embarrassment. 'Think o' the Chris'muss presents ye'd be able to buy, an' new clo'es an' 'andbag for yeself!'

Grace swallowed, and made herself look Madge in the eyes. 'You've been very kind to me, Madge, and I'm grateful, but wouldn't that mean…some people would call it…I mean, isn't it selling your body?'

'Good grief, 'ark at you! If ye're tryin' to say "prostitute", that's a different thing altogether,' replied Madge in mock horror. 'Prostitutes are them women who line up in Piccadilly an' Leicester Square, lookin' to pick up a man, any sort o' man, an' give 'em a good spend. Dolly's girls 'ave it all arranged before'and by Mrs Moore, and she sees that it's all fair an' above board. Now, if yer don't want to meet this captain, I won't try to persuade yer, just think about it, that's all. C'mon, let's go to Selfridges in Oxford Street, an' see all the nice things yer could buy if yer 'ad a spare fiver or two.'

Grace found herself being led to the various departments of the famous store, the counters full of gloves, scarves, brooches, belts and purses, and upstairs the dresses, blouses, skirts and petticoats – and the hats and shoes she would have loved to buy for herself. Madge spent extravagantly, and treated them both to scrambled eggs on toast in the restaurant, finishing with ice-cream. She made no attempt to try to change Grace's mind, and was not at all put out by her friend's rejection of a good offer. Give her time, she thought, just give her time.

Tom Munday's words went round and round in Eddie Cooper's head, and after a while they took root and became a possibility. Should he speak to Mary? No, he must first sound out Sidney Goddard, and if he refused, Mary need never be told.

So Eddie took the bull by the horns, as he later expressed it to Tom Munday, and went to Yeomans' farm one cold December morning, at the time he knew Sidney would be at the piggery.

'G'mornin', Sidney!'

''Morning, Mr Cooper!'

Eddie hesitated, bracing himself for what might be an acutely embarrassing exchange. There was no point in beating about the bush.

'About my daughter Mary, Sidney – is she any happier these days?'

Sidney stood up straight and pushed his cap back. 'Yes, I think she's looking a bit better now, Mr Cooper. I- I try to talk to her when we're on our own in the kitchen, but that doesn't happen very often.'

This sounded encouraging, thought Eddie. 'No I don't s'pose it does,' he said, 'but tell me somethin', Sidney, and I'll never repeat it to another soul. Y'know that my Mary's expectin' in February?'

'Y-yes, I do know that, Mr Cooper, and I'm very sorry.'

'*You're* sorry? Why, are you responsible?' asked Eddie, knowing full well that Dick Yeomans was the father.

Sidney flushed. 'Of course not, Mr Cooper, it happened before I came to work here. I meant that I'm sorry she's in such a...a situation, at the mercy of the Yeomanses.'

'Ah, Sidney, I'm glad to hear you say that. S'pose it was in your power to help her, would you do so?'

Sidney shifted his feet and looked self-conscious. 'How exactly do you mean, Mr Cooper?'

'By marryin' her, Sidney. She's not a bad girl, she's just been unlucky. She's a good cook and house cleaner, and would make any man a good wife. I'd help out with any expenses, and I'd pay the rent if you moved into that little white cottage by the Blackwater bridge. What d'you say?'

Sidney was clearly taken aback, but not offended. 'Oh, I don't know, Mr Cooper, it's very sudden to make a decision about something as important as that. I-I'd need time.'

'D'you like Mary?'

'Yes, yes, of course I do, but I don't know if she likes me, Mr Cooper. We've never spoken about anything like this.'

'Then it'll be up to her to accept or turn you down. Time's gettin' on for her, and if you agree to ask her before the week's out, I'll drop her a hint, so's she'll be prepared.'

'But what about my job here?' asked the bewildered Sidney, still unable to take in what was being put to him.

'You could carry on with it. Blackwater Bridge isn't far.'

'B-but what about the Yeomanses?'

'What about them? They can't stop you marryin' her, and her child will be a Goddard, and legitimate.'

'And what about my parents?' asked Sidney helplessly.

'What have they got to do with it? You're a grown man, aren't you? Look here, Sidney, I'll give you till the weekend. And the final decision will be Mary's. If she says yes, I'm on your side, and you can count on me to help in any way I can.'

There was a long pause, and Eddie was about to take his leave, but a change came over Sidney, who suddenly seemed to make up his mind. He stood up straight and tall, looking Eddie full in the face.

'All right, Mr Cooper, I'll ask her – and there's no need for you to speak to her first, because I'd rather she didn't know that we've talked about her. If Mary's willing to take me on, I'm prepared to marry her and look after her and the baby.'

Eddie's eyes were moist as he held out his hand. 'Thank you, Sidney. You won't regret it, I'm sure.'

The minister at South Camp Methodist Church was not won over by the offer of money from the bride's father. It was young Mr Goddard's urgent need to marry the listless, pregnant girl that persuaded him to agree to a quick, quiet wedding just before Christmas, the news of which rapidly spread. The fury of the Yeomanses provoked a second wave of gossip in North Camp, and opinions about the match were divided: there were those who thought that Goddard was actually the father of the unborn child, and those who believed that Eddie had offered him his life savings to make it worth his while to take on Dick Yeomans' child. Generally speaking, Sidney's image was enhanced, especially when it became known – and the story lost nothing in the telling – that he and old Yeomans had had a stand-up row in the farmhouse kitchen that had almost come to fisticuffs.

'Yeah, Tom, we got them Yeomanses over a barrel!' chortled Eddie with satisfaction. 'If they was to sack Sidney, he'd leave the farm, takin' Mary with him as his wife, carryin' the child who'll be registered a Goddard when it's born. Besides which, they can't manage without Sidney now, he's worked like a slave all hours, in all weathers, learnin' to be a stockman to be relied on. Short sight ain't a handicap when ye're workin' with cows and pigs, or sittin' up behind them two great shire horses ploughin' a field. Sidney's been up early on dark mornin's, freezin' cold, to dig turnips and mangolds for winter feed, chilblains on his hands and feet...'

'So, not such a booby after all,' grinned Tom Munday slyly.

'No, I never should've said that, Tom – and I owe you a lot, too, for bringin' it about. And not only that, but somethin' else – when Mrs Yeomans got huffy with Mary over it, Sidney told her she should make it up with my Annie, and brought her round to see us. Mary burst into tears, but I stood back and left it to Annie to comfort her, and she did. Meant everythin' to me, that did. Now they get on like a pair o' sisters, makin' up for lost time, and Annie's doin' a weddin' breakfast at our house.'

Tom smiled in acknowledgement, silently thanking his lucky stars that his scheming had paid off. He and Violet were privileged in being the only non-family guests invited to the wedding, the Yeomanses having declined to attend. Once married, the couple were to move into Eddie's and Annie's home temporarily, until the Blackwater cottage could be cleaned up and rented, and Sidney would continue to work at the farm, though Mary would not return there.

Sitting beside Tom in the Methodist church, Violet watched Mr and Mrs Goddard and their daughter Betty putting a brave face on their son's choice of a wife, for they had not been consulted or given a chance to object to it. Mary looked pale and serious in a loose-fitting grey coat and matching hat decorated with one blue silk rose; she trembled as her father put her hand into Sidney's, but looked up trustingly as he stood by her side, a proudly defiant expression on his face, and his responses clearly audible.

'It'll be a nine-day wonder, I dare say,' said Tom Munday when the ceremony was over, and they made their way on foot to the wedding breakfast at Eddie's. 'But it'll be the making o' Sidney, just you see.'

But the hasty wedding was forgotten in news of a very different kind that arrived by telegram to the Bird household on the following day, bringing utter desolation to them: their eldest son Tim had been badly injured and had died of his wounds in a field hospital, so now both their sons were lost, never to return. There was also news that William Hickory had been wounded, but was on his way home. It was Phyllis Bird's only consolation over that dark Christmas.

Chapter Thirteen

Christmas, 1916

Standing beside Violet in their usual place on Christmas morning, Tom Munday looked around the church, and could not remember a more sorrowful Christmas. The loss of the Birds' two sons brought a desolation that was beyond words or tears, and the Rev. Saville offered up prayers for all bereaved families in the parish, including the Yeomans family who did not attend church, but who mourned the loss of their only son, killed so soon after being forcibly conscripted. The vicar then went on to name all North Camp and Hassett families who had sons, brothers or other relatives serving in the war, and these included the Nevilles, the Mundays, the widowed Mrs Hickory and the Savilles themselves; he also mentioned Mrs Storey, formerly Miss Isabel Munday, whose husband was in the army as a chaplain.

Tom saw Lady Neville in her front pew, flanked by Mr Cedric who was on home leave, and Miss Letitia, pale and unsmiling as ever. Mr Bird occupied a pew near the back of the church with his daughter Phyllis beside him; they sat, knelt or stood at the appropriate times, and spoke to no one, except when the service was over, and Mr Bird replied briefly to the whispered enquiries about his wife with a polite 'She's much the same, thank you.'

'Which means she's breaking her heart over her two lost boys and wishing she was where they are,' commented Violet Munday, sadly shaking her head. 'I'm surprised at Bird leaving her alone in the house this morning.'

'She's not alone, she's got Mr Bird's sister over from Aldershot staying,' said Mrs Lansdowne, wanting to correct a wrong impression.

'But I thought the two sisters-in-law never got on – they fell out years ago, something to do with the boys' confirmation.'

'This is no time for bearing grudges, Mrs Munday,' came the sharp retort from Mrs Lansdowne. 'Bert and I went round there last night with a few bits and pieces for the larder, and Miss Bird – the elder Miss Bird, was most civil to us, and said she was doing her best in a very difficult situation.'

Violet Munday, suitably rebuked, joined the congregation filing out through the south door; Mr Saville shook hands with everyone, and instead of 'Happy Christmas', said 'Peace be upon you.'

Outside in the churchyard people spoke in hushed tones. Lady Neville exchanged a word or two with as many as she could, and enquired after Ernest.

'Wasn't it a happy chance that Cedric met your son and his friend at Gallipoli?' she said, adding that he had been most impressed by their bravery. Tom noticed that Cedric looked thin and war-weary, but smiled when he approached them.

'What about that jolly daughter of yours, the one who entertained us so well at Hassett Manor?' he asked, and Violet's face fell.

'Grace worked at Everham General Hospital for a few weeks,

and now she's in London,' Tom replied, trying to speak lightly. 'She doesn't tell us much, but we gather she's well and making new friends – doing her bit for the war effort, no doubt!'

'And your elder daughter, the one who married that clergyman – my mother mentioned that he's away at the front, too?'

'Yes, Mr Neville, he is, and Isabel still lives in Bethnal Green in East London, and does a lot of good work there, we hear,' said Tom with pride. 'Of course we worry about her, with these bombing raids going on, but...' he shrugged. 'Isabel always followed the path of duty – a good girl, she's been to us.'

'Though I can't understand why she couldn't leave that dreary vicarage, just for Christmas,' interposed Violet. 'We are her parents, after all, and with Mark away, I'd have thought we meant more to her than those rough East Enders – like that young widow she's taken up with – what's her name, Tom? Tanner!'

'Sally Tanner probably needs Isabel more than we do, to see her through Christmas,' said Tom gravely. 'As long as no harm comes to our girl and the baby—'

He stopped short, realising he'd said more than he'd intended. Violet flashed him a furious look that said, *Wait till I get you home*! Talking to a *man* about such intimate family matters, it was too bad of him; and other people may have overheard!

Cedric smiled and tactfully changed the subject. He told them that he would not be going straight back to the front after Christmas, but was to take a course at a place he could not mention, to learn about the use of a new form of transport on the battlefield, a heavily armoured vehicle that had no wheels but moved on a 'caterpillar' track and could plough through barbed wire and cross a ditch eight-feet wide, its occupants able to fire at the enemy whilst protected from German machine gun fire.

'And the sooner we get it up and running, the shorter the war's likely to be,' he said to Tom, 'before the Jerries get on to the idea.'

January, 1917

It took Grace Munday just two weeks to change her mind. Madge Fraser laughed and gave her a congratulatory kiss.

'Good gal, I knew ye'd come round to it once ye'd thought it over – easy money for doin' a valuable service to the nation, that's what Mrs Moore calls it! I'll let 'er know ye've seen the light, an' she'll pick yer out a nice young chap who needs cheerin' up. You'll be fine!'

Grace's nightmare memory of Tupman's attempted rape had lost much of its horror after more than two years had elapsed; the young men who had taken her out to supper in a 'foursome' with Madge or some other 'Dolly's girl' had all been good fun, and their kisses and cuddles pleasant rather than otherwise; it was the same with the wounded men she had met at Hassett Manor.

Madge lost no time in telling Mrs Moore, and the very next day she beckoned to Grace after their morning rehearsal.

'Sybil's found us a couple o' fellers, an' tomorrer night after the show we'll get into a taxi with 'em, so ol' Dean'll think we're goin' out on a foursome, but we'll go straight to 17 Lamp Street,' she said with businesslike authority. 'Yours is a poor boy goin' over there for the first time, an' mine's 'is pal who's arranged this little rendy-voo for 'im, an' a bit for 'imself as well. Yours is Derek, mine's Bob, an' I'll take 'im to me own room.'

The following evening the girls were duly introduced by Mrs Moore to their clients. Derek had said goodbye to his parents that morning, and they'd thought him on his way to Southampton and the ship to take him to Calais; it had been Bob's idea to find a couple of girls to enjoy before looking death in the face.

'There's the key to Number Four,' said Madge. 'Lock it be'ind yer when yer go in. There's clean sheets on the bed, an' a bottle o' bubbly on the table with glasses an' a corkscrew. Make sure yer knock back a couple o' glasses 'fore yer get down to business. Ye've got a decent-looking little feller there –'e may not want to do it, only talk – but make sure ye've got the doin's in.'

The 'doings' was a piece of bathroom sponge about the size of a plum, that had soaked in a jar of vinegar. Madge had expertly shown Grace how to push it up into the vagina – for which Madge had an extremely vulgar name – as a preventive measure.

'No need to be scared, kid, one man's much the same as another, an' they all look the same in the dark!'

So Grace found herself leading Derek up the stairs and into room Number Four. She locked the door and turned to him, her first client.

'We've got a b-bottle of champagne to share,' she said shyly. 'Er…are you any good at opening bottles?'

With cold hands that shook slightly, he drew the cork; there was a pop, and the glasses were filled with the sparkling, bubbling liquid. They clinked them together.

'What shall we drink to?' she asked.

'Victory!' he answered at once, and she replied, 'Death to the old kaiser!' She swallowed hers straight away, and he poured her another. Presently she felt herself relaxing under its influence, and her nervousness eased a little. His arms went round her waist, his face was near to hers, and she closed her eyes as his lips touched her cheek and then found her mouth. They stood together, swaying slightly, and it occurred to her that he was as nervous as herself. Madge had told her that a nervous client needed gentle encouragement, and should not be hurried; she should help him remove his clothes, and ask him to help remove hers, unbuttoning and unhooking as necessary, slowly and between kisses.

'Let 'im see yer tits, an' 'old 'em up for 'im to kiss,' her mentor had advised.

'Most of 'em don't need no second biddin', but it's up to you to bring 'em on. Get into a nice, steady rhythm, not too fast, not too slow. Once 'e's kissed yer tits, it's time to let yer 'and go wanderin' down to 'is trousers, an' see if e's risin' to the occasion.'

Grace was now definitely feeling the effect of the drink, and her body was soft and pliant in Derek's arms. Her clothing seemed to melt away, and she gave a little hiccup as they lay down on the bed. The room circled slowly round, and then to her surprise they were both naked, and he was lying on top of her.

'Oh, Grace – you dear girl – are you ready?' he asked thickly, knowing himself to be so. 'You don't mind?'

She gave a little laugh, and what happened next was so surprising, so different from what it had been like with Tupman; this was nice and warm and comfortable. Derek tried to be gentle as he entered her, and after a few thrusts he ejaculated, groaning incoherently. This was *very* different from Tupman!

'Good, good, that's so *good*, Grace – oh, Grace, oh, *Grace*!'

Grace's head was swimming, and she scarcely realised that it was over. She lay peacefully and contentedly until roused by the sound of weeping: it was Derek, trying to stifle his sobs. She sat up, pulled the sheet and blankets over them, and put her arms around him, hugging him to her bare breasts and stroking the top of his head.

'Sssh, sssh, Derek, it's all right, don't cry,' she whispered.

'It's *not* all right, Grace, I've got to go to *hell* tomorrow, and the chances are I won't be coming back,' he sobbed against her softness. 'I don't want to go – I'm afraid – I'm so afraid, Grace.'

She could only try to comfort him with her warmth and nearness, and gradually he became calmer. 'Want to stay here for ever,' he muttered. 'Wish there was an air raid, and a bomb to kill us both – we could die together.'

Grace had no such wish for death, and held him closer. 'Sssh!'

After a while he spoke more clearly. 'I'll remember you all the time I'm in those trenches, Grace. All the time. God bless you, Grace. I'll never forget you.'

Presently the drink and their love-making had its effect on them, and they both fell asleep, their limbs entwined, to be awakened by a knocking on their door at five o'clock. Grace unlocked the door and saw Madge and Bob; he was dressed and ready to go to Waterloo Station, and from there to Southampton and the troopship.

'Come on, come on, Derek! It's time we were up and away – hurry up!'

With a sinking heart Grace helped Derek, still half-asleep, to find and pull on his clothes; he gave her one last kiss before going off with his friend, and Grace was left to ponder on the experience. Her thoughts turned to Nick, probably dead, and to her brother Ernest and his friend Aaron. And her sister Isabel's husband. Surely, if what she had done had given comfort to one young soldier going off to war, it couldn't be entirely wrong – could it?

When Madge handed her the money in a sealed envelope, she was amazed. Even after Mrs Moore had taken her share, and Madge had generously waived hers, it was still equal to two weeks' pay at Dolly's. For some reason she did not want to spend it straight away, but put it into a post office savings account.

The cold January days passed mournfully by. The news from the front, what there was of it, was not encouraging. Casualty lists continued to lengthen, and under the new prime minister, Mr Lloyd George, regulations and restrictions seemed to proliferate, and shortages began to be felt.

'Lucky for us, growing our own spuds,' remarked Tom Munday to Eddie as they heaved a sack out of the coal shed where the potatoes were stored to keep them frost-free. In the towns shops were running out of vegetables and all kinds of goods; the public were asked to cut down on the amount of bread they ate, and flour became scarce. Yeomans' farm was a centre for meat and dairy produce in North Camp, and even at this winter season Sidney and the land girls were kept busy.

'We hardly ever see Sid,' said Eddie. 'He's up and out 'fore it's light, an' don't get back till after dark. Not much of a marriage for him and Mary, but—' He hastily checked himself, thinking of Tom's daughter Isabel who saw nothing at all of her husband, and who like Mary was expecting her first child. 'How's she doin', your Isabel?' he asked.

'She's the only one we hear from, and the poor girl tries her hardest to give us good news,' replied Tom heavily. 'We didn't get so much as a Christmas card from Grace, and Ernest's too busy just staying alive in those winter conditions over there. Have you heard anything about young Hickory since he came home?'

Eddie hesitated. 'Poor lad, he's in a bad way. He's stone deaf from shellfire, and his brain's been affected as well. His mother don't encourage visitors.'

'When did you hear this, Eddie? Who told you?'

'Well, to tell you the truth, I overheard Betty Goddard tellin' Mary when she came to visit her. They used to be friends at school, along wi' your Isabel and poor Phyllis Bird.'

'Phyllis Bird? Oh, yes, she and young Hickory were…er, sweethearts, weren't they? There was a time when she had her eye on Ernest, but he…well, he was never much interested in girls. She must have been counting on Will Hickory to bring a bit o' sunshine back into her life. So – did she go to see him?'

'She did, Tom, and that's what Betty Goddard was tellin' Mary about. It must've been terrible. Phyllis told Betty that Mrs Hickory wouldn't let her in at first, but Phyllis begged to see him, and at last Mrs Hickory took her into the kitchen where he was sittin' by the oven. She said he was so altered, and wasn't sure if he knew her at first. He kept his eyes on his mother who stayed in the room, callin' him her poor boy, and sayin' what he'd been through – and when Phyllis went to take hold of his hand, he drew back and turned to his mother, just like a kid. He said somethin' like "pretty girl", but he didn't actually speak to Phyllis at all, only his mother.'

'Good God, Eddie, what a terrible blow for the girl! Whatever did she do?'

'She told Betty she couldn't bear it, and got herself out of the house before she broke down an' cried – that's when she went round to the Goddards an' told Betty, seein' as she hadn't got anybody at home to talk to. Her mother's pinin' for the boys, and won't speak a word or eat a morsel. Bird keeps the shop goin', but it must be like a morgue round there.'

Tom was shocked, picturing Ernest or Mark Storey in such circumstances.

'Is there any chance o' young Hickory improving and getting his hearing back?' he asked. 'And his memory, maybe?'

'Dunno. How can anybody tell? His poor mother fusses over him as if he was a baby, and won't have him upset by anybody, not even Dr Stringer – not that *he'd* be much use in a case like that. I reckon we can only wait an' hope, but I can't see him marryin' Phyllis or any other girl, as he is now.'

Tom shook his head and when he spoke again it was to say to Eddie what he could never say to his wife.

'Y'know, Eddie, when you think about the Bird brothers and the Hickory boy, it makes you wonder how many homes there must be, up and down the country, waiting for telegrams to say that their boys are dead, or missing or wounded. I can't see that our lives are ever going to be the same again – how can they be? How much longer can it go on till some sort of an agreement has to be made with the Germans? And when you come to think of it, *they* must be getting a bit of a pasting, too – the women and kids left behind while the men march off to get killed, likely as not.' He sighed heavily. 'My son could be killed at any time, Isabel and her baby could be killed by a bomb, and God only knows about Grace. I might not ever see her again.'

Eddie Cooper stared at his friend and could think of nothing to reply. He could hardly say that the war had at least brought together his wife and daughter, so long estranged, and that the Goddards had decided reluctantly to accept Mary and her baby. The marriage had done Sidney no harm; on the contrary, it had made a man of him. The Yeomanses, however, could not forgive Mary for marrying their indispensable stockman whilst carrying Dick's child, and old Yeomans had told Sidney in his surliest tones that they wouldn't be visiting the young Goddards until after the baby was born – 'to see who it looked like'.

‷

Mrs Moore did not send Grace another client for Number Four in the next two weeks, though Madge Fraser entertained several while Grace went out with other 'Dolly girls' in foursomes to supper, gaining experience of a wide variety of men in the armed services. She was then introduced to Stanley, a sergeant who had served abroad and was about to return to the front; he had no illusions about life.

'Soon as I saw you, I thought what a pretty little kid, lucky for me to get such a – how old are you, sweetheart? Seventeen, and on this game? Does your mother know what you're up to?'

He didn't wait for answers to his questions, but went on talking non-stop, commenting on their surroundings, and much impressed by room Number Four, with its clean bedlinen and champagne.

'Blimey, this is posh! I haven't been to many places as swanky as this – in fact I haven't been to any places like this in England, only abroad, where you don't know *what* you're getting, and half the time they can't speak English. D'you want me to open the bottle? Whoosh, watch out for the cork! I'll have summat to tell the lads when I get back to…to…yer mustn't blame me for wanting this, Gracie – that *is* your name, isn't it? I reckon I've earned it after what I've seen and been through – terrible – couldn't tell anybody at home. Come on, give us a kiss, dear – what a little darling you are, you remind me of another girl I once knew, that was before all this bloody war started. Proper little beauty, she was.'

Grace forced a smile and poured herself another glass of champagne.

'That's right, darling, you drink up. I'd better not have any more. To tell you the truth I'm feeling a bit shy, which isn't like me, I'm usually as cheeky as a vicar's parrot!' He laughed, and seized her round the waist. 'It must be 'cause you're so pretty an' young an' sweet – come here, Gracie, let's get 'em off! Kiss me, dear, hold me tight, let me forget, Gracie, *make me forget!*'

Lying on the bed, Grace obediently held Sergeant Stanley in her arms and let him lie between her thighs until his talking turned to gasps and groans, and finally to heaving sobs. She wondered uneasily if it always ended like this; his weight flattened her uncomfortably, and made breathing difficult, let alone speaking, but she endured it without protest until he became calmer, and rolled off to lie beside her.

A valuable service to the nation. That was what Mrs Moore called it, according to Madge, and Grace thought she was learning how to do it, adapting her speech and manners to the kind of man she encountered, and giving him what he needed before facing death and danger in the trenches. *Surely* it couldn't be wrong!

February, 1917

The headmistress and staff were sorry to see young Mrs Storey leave Barnett Street School at half-term, the reason for which was 'beginning to show' as the women said among themselves, and there was much speculation about when the baby was due. Soon afterwards Mrs Clements had a fall while standing on a chair to reach a packet of sugar from a high shelf, and fractured her tibia, or as she said, broke her leg. She had to go into the London Hospital in Whitechapel, where Isabel visited her and found her blaming herself bitterly, wondering how young Mrs Storey would manage without her help in the vicarage; she was full of dire warnings.

'Don't go out after dark for any reason at all,' she said, 'specially on these cold winter nights. No respectable woman's safe round 'ere, so don't stop an' talk to a woman unless yer know her, 'cause she'll be a streetwalker, likely as not. Mind yer lock an' bolt the doors at night, an' close all the winders.'

'I'll carry out all your instructions, Mrs Clements,' said Isabel, smiling, torn as usual between gratitude and exasperation at the woman's anxiety over her.

'Well, mind yer do, 'cause I lay awake 'ere at night worryin' about yer. And don't let 'em ride over yer roughshod at that Mothers' Union,' continued the lady, sitting up in bed wearing the mud-coloured cardigan that did duty as a bedjacket. 'Some'ow or other ye'll 'ave to carry on without me while I'm laid up 'ere, and don't let that stuck-up schoolteacher worm 'er way in to bein' the leader – though I can't think of anybody who'd be best to do it. It's no good, I can't think straight. I'm sorry, Mrs Storey, I've let yer down!' Her eyes filled with tears.

'Don't upset yourself, my dear,' said Isabel patiently. 'There's no need at all for you to worry. As a matter of fact, *I* shall take over as leader until you're well enough to come back. The lady treasurer can be temporary secretary, and her work can be taken over by Mrs Tanner who's very good at figures.'

'*What?* D'yer mean that Sally Tanner? Yer can't put 'er in charge o' the money, she *drinks!*'

'Not any more, Mrs Clements. She's changed her ways, and is a very useful member of the Mothers' Union, and of the parish.'

'That's as maybe, Mrs Storey, but don't go lettin' 'er into the vicarage, whatever yer do. Take the money 'ome with yer, and put it in Mr Storey's safe, or ye'll rue the day, I'm tellin' yer!'

Isabel stifled a sigh. There were times when Mrs Clements' dedication could be extremely trying, but her concern was genuine, and Isabel leant over to kiss her when the visitors had to leave, and promised to come again soon.

Her spirits were low as she returned to the vicarage, dark and silent in the fading light of a February afternoon. There was no light on in the study, and the curtains were open, a sign that her father-in-law had fallen asleep in his chair. Poor old Pa, she thought, living apart from his wife in this cheerless place, endeavouring to cope with his son's parish; he was looking frailer these days, six months after his arrival, and Isabel secretly feared that he might not live to be reunited with his wife in their little country cottage. Heaven only knew when this hateful war would end. *Oh, Mark*, she thought, *when shall I see you again*?

She gave herself a mental shake, and put her key in the lock – and suddenly, as she stepped inside, a dark figure emerged from the shadows and pushed her forward, slamming the door shut. She was seized round the waist from behind, and a hand was clamped over her mouth. She was too terrified to struggle, and thought she was going to faint: she drooped in the grip of her captor who shook her roughly.

'Listen, missus, I need two things, grub an' cash, an' if yer know what's good for yer, do as ye're told,' he growled. 'Come on, missus, where's the larder?'

She pointed a shaking finger towards the passage that led to the kitchen, and he hustled her along it. When they got there, he banged the door shut behind them, and she thought of her father-in-law: surely the noise would wake him up. The intruder took his hand from her mouth, and gripping her right arm, made her lead him to the bread bin which stood on the stone floor of the larder; on a shelf above it was a bowl of beef dripping. He tore off a hunk of bread, rubbed it in the dripping and ate it ravenously, tugging at the crust with his teeth and grunting from the sheer relief of assuaging his hunger.

She heard the doorbell ring, and he looked up sharply.

'Don't answer it, an' they'll go away.' When it rang again, Isabel thought she heard her father-in-law's chair creak, followed by the faint sound of his slippered footsteps crossing the hall. Evidently the intruder didn't hear, gorging himself on bread and dripping, and drinking milk straight from the jug, but she made an effort to speak, to cover the sound of the front door opening. Oh, let it be a man or somebody to rescue her!

'W-where have you come from?' she asked.

'Out o' the army,' he muttered between mouthfuls, and Isabel guessed he must be a deserter.

'Why did you come here?'

'It's a church 'ouse, innit? I've begged 'ere before, an' got a dry crust an' a penny. Well, missus, I'm gettin' more 'n a penny orf yer today. Blimey, it's too dark to see. Can yer light the gas mantle?'

'We don't have gaslight in the kitchen,' she said. 'But I'll light the oil lamp.'

As with trembling fingers she put a match to the lamp and turned up the wick, she strained her ears to hear what was being said at the front door, and made out the old man's voice, speaking low and rapidly. She would have run out of the kitchen, but the man kept a grip on her right arm.

'Before yer scarper, missus, I need a bit o' the ready. Where'd yer keep it?'

The church funds were stored in a safe in the study, and the key was in a desk drawer; by now Isabel was finding her courage and ability to think quickly.

'There's very little money in the house,' she said. 'My, er, husband takes it to the bank regularly.'

'Ah, yeah, he would, I dare say. Nice easy job e's got, stayin' at 'ome while there's men out there who—'

'My husband's in France, an army chaplain, so he's got a

good idea of what it's like,' she said sharply.

'Yeah, an' so 'ave I, missus – that's why I can't go back to it – sooner be shot for cowardice.'

Isabel turned and looked at him full in the face, and saw the blank despair, the haggard eyes in his thin face; and as she looked, she felt her fear melting away, to be replaced by deep pity.

'I can let you have a little money,' she said, 'and you can take what food you can carry. There's the last of the Christmas cake in a tin.' She saw his eyes gleam, and realised that the man was truly starving.

'Yeah, I could eat a bit o' cake, missus.'

But before Isabel could reach for the cake tin on its shelf, the kitchen door was flung open, and Sally Tanner appeared, eyes wide with astonishment. Mr Storey, white-faced, stood behind her.

'Bloody 'ell, what's goin' on? What's 'e doin' 'ere? 'As he 'urt yer, Isabel?' demanded Sally, forgetting to say Mrs Storey.

'No, Sally, no,' answered Isabel quickly. 'He hasn't harmed me or anything. He's deserted from the army, and has nowhere to go, and starving.'

'Maybe so, but 'e can't stay 'ere, Mrs Storey. Poor ol' Mr Storey was frightened out of 'is wits – 'e woke up and 'eard this goin' on in the kitchen, an' when 'e opened the door to me, 'e said God 'ad sent me, but in fact it was Mrs Plumm who's 'ad a summons, an'…but what're yer goin' to do with 'im?'

'I'm going to send him on his way, and pray for him,' said Isabel quietly but firmly. 'It's not our place to condemn a man who can't face this dreadful war any longer.' Taking down a teapot from the shelf above the oven, she took out a half-crown piece. 'Here you are, then – and here's the cake tin, and I'll put the bread in with it, and some biscuits, but you must leave now. Goodbye, and God go with you.'

'Thanks, missus. Cheerio,' muttered the man as he left by the kitchen door, pointedly held open by Mrs Tanner who looked on in utter disbelief at such misplaced trust, but Mr Storey put a hand on Isabel's shoulder and said, 'Thank heaven for a good woman.'

After this incident, Mr Storey had a frank talk with his daughter-in-law, and said there would have to be changes.

'A clergy house is vulnerable at the best of times, and I'm an old man and you are expecting a child, my dear,' he reminded her. 'We must advertise for a reliable resident housekeeper who will also be a companion for yourself. I shall go to the office of the local newspaper tomorrow.'

But no advertisement was necessary. When Isabel asked Sally Tanner if she would care to give up her job and move into the vicarage on a very small wage, the answer was so emphatic that no further discussion was needed.

'Sybil Moore's got big 'opes for yer, Gracie! She's savin' yer for the posh ones!' laughed Madge, whose patrons far outnumbered Grace Munday's. Mr Dean frequently chose Grace for the supper foursomes, introducing new 'Dolly's girls' to the sort of light-hearted companionship expected of them, and to yield gracefully to the final kiss and cuddle in a taxi that ended the evening.

But for Mrs Moore's girls a good deal more had to be learnt. The Dereks and Stanleys were in search of solace before facing the jaws of death awaiting them at the front. Patience and sensitivity were needed, and the girl had to discern the needs of her client: sympathy, gaiety, laughter or whispered encouragement, and to adapt her response accordingly. Grace was fast learning the arts of a skilful courtesan, and when she was introduced to Captain X, his tall figure and handsome features promised an enjoyable encounter; he didn't look the type to break down and weep in her arms, and she smiled as she led him up the stairs of 17 Lamp Street and into room Number Four where a small fire burnt in the grate, the bed was freshly made up, and the usual bottle of champagne stood on the table with two glasses beside it.

Captain X's cold blue eyes looked round the room. 'Hm. This looks reasonably civilised – so it should, after what I had to pay that woman. I suppose you're an expert at opening champagne bottles. Well, go on, then – get a move on, girl.'

Grace gave him a little sideways smile as she twisted the cork up out of the bottle's neck, pulling on it with all her might. Up went a pillar of foaming liquid, spraying them both and raining down on the bed and floor. Grace began to laugh, but he turned on her furiously.

'You haven't got much idea, have you, you stupid creature,' he said irritably. 'Why didn't you ask me to do it? Is any of it left in the bottle, or did you lose the lot?'

Grace held up the bottle in dismay. 'There's a bit left in the bottle, sir. Do you want it?'

'Of course I do. That's what it's for, isn't it? Oh, give it here.'

He snatched the bottle and poured himself a full glass from the remainder. 'Well, don't just stand there gaping, get your clothes off!'

Turning his back on her, he quickly divested himself of his jacket, tie, shirt, vest, trousers, underpants and socks. Grace began to undress, but her fingers shook and she was slow. 'Can you, er, unhook these at the back for me?' she asked shyly, for this was a move that nearly always worked with a nervous client.

'Don't tell me you can't get it off yourself!' he sneered. 'It's no use trying out your whorish tricks on me, girl, I'm here for one thing and one thing only, and we both know what it is.

Christ Almighty, are you simple or something? I've paid a king's ransom for this, so get 'em all off and get on that bed.'

Grace felt herself shivering, as much from apprehension as cold. This man clearly expected to be obeyed instantly. He now lay naked on the bed, his penis hardening as he watched her efforts to unhook her corselet which at last fell off her; she awkwardly pulled down her drawers which got caught on one foot, so that she nearly toppled over. Hesitating, she lay down beside him, turned her face to him and attempted a smile. She raised a hand to touch his face, trailing a forefinger down his cheek, intending to circle his mouth.

'Do you want to kiss me?' she asked, forcing a come-hither look. 'Tell me what you want me to do, darling.'

For answer he pushed her hand away and slapped her across the mouth. 'You know what I've come for, so don't waste your tart's talk on me. Get on to your back, spread your legs – wider – come on!'

He flung himself on top of her, pushed her thighs apart with hard fingers, and thrust himself inside her. She gave a low cry of pain and fear, and he slapped her face again.

'Shut up! Just close your mouth and stay still.'

Grace was utterly terrified as he thrust his hardness back and forth inside her. She tried to heave herself up in an effort to shake him off, and got yet another vicious slap across her face.

'Take *that*, you little whore, damn you to hell! If you only knew how I despise myself for using the likes of you – I find your flesh disgusting, your – ah! Oh, God…oh, *God*…aaah!'

His stream of invective changed to the familiar grunts and groans of a man reaching an orgasmic climax, crushing and bruising her, and when at last he slithered off her, she was unable to move, overcome by the horror she'd felt when Tupman had assaulted her on the Everham Road. Except that this was a far worse humiliation. Tupman had attacked her without her foreknowledge or consent, but Captain X had paid good money for the service of a prostitute.

He got off the bed, pulled on his clothes, and left without another word, leaving her to ponder on what she had become.

Meanwhile...

Annie Cooper was sitting at her stepdaughter's bedside to give the midwife a rest, for it was now twelve hours since Mary's pains had begun that morning; now it was nearly eight o'clock in the evening. Annie wiped the girl's face with a damp towel, and held a cup of water to her dry lips.

Nine o'clock, and Eddie Cooper waited with Sidney Goddard in the kitchen. Both had done a full day's work, hoping that Mary would be delivered by the time they came home. Betty Goddard had called twice, and returned home to tell her parents that there was as yet no news.

Upstairs the midwife was thinking about sending for Dr Stringer, but to her great relief the child's head began to descend; the two women sat Mary upright, supporting her on either side, and encouraging her to push down with all her strength. And just after ten o'clock the child was born.

'It's a girl, Eddie!' Annie called down the stairs. 'Ye've got a granddaughter!'

Eddie Cooper and Sidney Goddard hugged each other, unable to speak, so great was their relief. The welcome sound of a newborn baby's cry filled the air, and the midwife triumphantly showed her to her mother.

Little Dora Goddard had arrived, born to a Cooper and fathered by a Yeomans.

Chapter Fourteen

March–May, 1917

'That baby's brought happiness all round, Tom,' said Eddie Cooper with satisfaction. 'The Goddards were a bit stand-offish at first, though Betty always stayed friends with Mary – but now that little Dora's born, the parents've come over to see her, though she's not their granddaughter in the same way as she's mine – but as soon as they set eyes on the pretty little thing layin' there in her cot, they was won over. And Mr Goddard's gastric ulcer's much better, they say, so I reckon that was all due to worry about Sidney bein' treated like a coward by half o' North Camp, and then marryin' my Mary when she was – well, you know how it was, Tom. But little Dora's changed everythin'.'

'Glad to hear it, Eddie. Violet's going round there tomorrow afternoon with a little jacket she's knitted. Er, how about the Yeomanses?'

'Not so easy there, though o' course old Yeomans always was a misery. I reckon they'll have to come over sooner or later, seein' as Dora's their granddaughter, and Mary's been like a daughter to them for years, ever since she left school. And what pleases me most is to see Annie and Mary gettin' on so well these days, just like a proper mother and daughter. I tell you, Tom, that baby's touched a lot o' hearts.'

Tom smiled, pleased for his friend, though his own thoughts were sombre. The deaths of Dick Yeomans and the Bird brothers had cast a deep shadow over the village, and who could say whether Ernest too would be massacred? Or Aaron Pascoe and his newly recruited brother Jonathan? Or Cedric Neville and Philip Saville? Such daily anxieties had set aside less important considerations, for families could not afford to bear ill will at such a time. There had been a postcard from Ernest since Christmas, and the Pascoes had received one from Aaron. Their messages were shared between the families, and Tom noted that both men had put 'we' instead of 'I' on the cards – 'Jerry's been throwing a lot of hardware across No Man's Land, but so far we've managed to dodge it,' and the brief messages had ended with 'Love from us both.' Isabel kept in regular touch with her parents by letter, and told them that she now had a resident housekeeper to help with the work, which was good news, except that her name was Sally Tanner.

'Sally Tanner? The woman who *drinks?*' exclaimed Violet in dismay. 'What can Isabel be thinking of? What she should do is come home to *us,* and be properly looked after. We are her parents, after all!'

Tom gave a non-committal grunt. He too worried about Isabel, but understood her loyalty to old Mr Storey – and Mrs Tanner sounded like a reformed character, thanks to Isabel's care and concern for her.

'Well, if she doesn't come home for her confinement, I shall have to go to *her,*' said Violet. 'I'm not leaving her to the tender mercies of Sally Tanner and some East End midwife!'

Tom's thoughts turned to his other daughter; there had been

a postcard from Grace at Christmas, in which she had sent her love but nothing else; Isabel too had not heard from her sister.

All in all, 1917 had come in with no good news other than the safe arrival of baby Dora Goddard; and when a few days later a jubilant Eddie told Tom that Mr and Mrs Yeomans had visited with little Billy, and how Mrs Yeomans had wept over the baby that was her son's daughter, Tom rejoiced with his friend and said nothing of his own worries.

From Hassett Manor came the news that Cedric had completed his course on the new heavily armoured vehicles, now ready to be tried out at secret locations in the front line. Lady Neville put a brave face on her son's departure, but Miss Letitia was said to be heartbroken, and had taken to her bed.

'*No*, Madge, absolutely *not*. I can't do it, so don't ask me. Tell Mrs Moore that I've changed my mind, and I'll never do it again.'

'But Grace, ye're throwin' good money away, an' ye've been doin' so well at cheerin' 'em up, the poor lads. It's just plain daft to let one bad 'un put yer off, though I must say I was surprised about that captain. 'E was so tall an' 'andsome, just like a film star, the sort who'd give yer a little extra tip for yer trouble!'

Grace shivered at the memory of the captain's contempt. 'Not from *him*, Madge, not unless you call bad names and slaps across your face an extra. Never again – no, don't bother asking me, my mind's made up. Dancing on the stage is all right, and so is going out to supper, as long as it's a foursome, but…but the *other* I'll never do again.'

Madge was nonplussed. 'I mean it ain't like streetwalkin', 'angin' around on corners, waitin' for a pickup who could be *anybody*. All our clients are 'and-picked for us by Sybil Moore, an' we don't even 'ave to take money off 'em, it's all been booked and paid for! Hey, where are yer off to?'

For Grace Munday had walked away, unable to listen any longer. Out of a sort of politeness to Madge, she did not add that the shameful episode with Captain X had opened her eyes to the truth of what she and Madge had been doing. It was called *prostitution*, and the captain had shown her what disgrace it brought to women who practised it. She now thought back on Sergeant Stanley and poor Derek, men looking for a woman to embrace before going to face death at the front. They might feel a brief affection for her – gratitude, even – but not respect. They might mention 'a jolly girl I met' to their comrades-in-arms, but never to their parents or – perhaps in the case of Stanley – a wife. Just suppose that her own parents…but Grace dared not even imagine the terrible scandal that would erupt if her recent lifestyle became known in North Camp. The very thought made her break out in a cold sweat.

The depleted C Company was in retreat from the ridge they had thought to take; the Germans had held on and had not run out of ammunition as the Allies had. They were being led by a competent, stony-faced sergeant, the officer in charge having been shot dead, and were heading for billets in one of the villages, where there was also an emergency clearing station. Clouds hung low and it was getting dark as they plodded over sodden ground, trying to avoid collapsed trenches filling up with water, covering the corpses of men who had lately stood there with their rifles, facing the enemy.

Ernest Munday stumbled on, longing to close his eyes and sleep; the distant rumble of artillery was muffled in his ears; he had not seen Aaron since the order to retreat had been given.

Suddenly there was a shout ahead: '*Gas!*' – and somehow or other the men struggled to put on their gas masks, and resume their crazy game of follow-my-leader, getting mixed up with another battalion, also in retreat.

Passing over a shell hole, Ernest felt a stinging pain in his left calf, from a flesh wound sustained earlier in the day. He staggered, held up his arms and dropped into the hole, calling out to the man behind him to go on, as he thought he could manage to crawl out unaided.

It was only when he tried to liberate himself that he understood what a deadly trap he was in; the hole had appeared to be fairly shallow, but in fact it had become a deep quagmire of mud and slime. Ernest's feet sank into it and were quickly covered; weighted by his kitbag, he sank lower, and the stinking mud was up to his knees, and then to his thighs. He had heard of men who had drowned in mud and rotting bodies, and his cries for help went unheeded, as the company had gone ahead, and every man had as much as he could do to look after himself in the fading light and on such treacherous ground. Ernest gave himself up for lost, and thought of Aaron.

And miraculously, like messengers from heaven, out of the dusk and drizzling rain came Aaron and a young cockney private they called Sparrer. Aaron had been frantically searching for Ernest, fearing him to be among the wounded and dying after the failed attempt to storm the ridge. Now he stood on the edge of the shell hole. 'Ernest! Is that you?' he shouted to the feebly waving arms beneath him.

'Go on, Aaron, I'm done for,' came the faint reply. 'For God's sake don't you fall in as well. Goodbye, my—'

'*No*! Not yet, Ernest – here, take hold of my rifle,' cried Aaron, extending the barrel to him, but it was too short for the purpose. Aaron whipped off his kitbag and took out a length of strong rope which he always carried. Holding the two ends, he threw the loop to Ernest who grasped it with both hands, but as Aaron started to pull on it, his own feet began to slither forward over the rim of the hole, and Ernest let go his hold on the rope, rather than be the cause of his friend's death.

''Ere, mate, let's get this bloody plank down, so's yer can stand on it,' said Sparrer, heaving up a half-submerged duckboard, one of the many used for laying over mud when walking on wet ground. 'Stand on this.'

Aaron did so, and threw the rope back to Ernest. 'Hang on, hang *on*, I shan't move away till you're out!' he shouted.

Sparrer also got on the board and took one of the ends of rope. 'Pull for all ye're bloody worf, mate! We're two against one!'

The mud seethed and sucked around Ernest's body, a hell-broth of stench and slime, seemingly unwilling to yield up its victim. It had reached his waist.

'Pull, Ernest, *pull* for the love of God!' pleaded Aaron, adding under his breath, *Give me Samson's strength, O Lord, for I will save him or sink with him.*

'Yeah, for the love o' Gawd – or the devil!' panted Sparrer, and they saw that Ernest had ceased to sink, but could not raise himself. His thoughts blurred into a muddle of confused sensations, suspended between life and death.

'We ain't gettin' nowhere,' muttered Sparrer, and Aaron grabbed the rope from his hands. 'Get behind me, put your arms round my waist and pull on me. If I sink down into this damned hole, just let go.'

'Not arf I will, mate! Blimey, what a way to go!'

For what seemed a timeless interval of wavering between

hope and defeat, Ernest pulled on the loop of rope, Aaron tugged at the two ends, one in each hand, and Sparrer pulled on Aaron, bent over with the effort.

'Talk abaht a bleedin' tug o' war!' gasped Sparrer, 'but 'e's startin' to move!'

'Keep going, keep it up, we're getting there,' urged Aaron as slowly, slowly, Ernest began to rise up out of the mire; inch by inch his body was dragged above the surface. When Aaron could lean forward from the duckboard and grasp his hands, the progress accelerated, and when his thighs were free, the rope was dropped and his arms were gripped by his rescuers.

'Nearly there, Ernest, nearly there...' puffed Aaron, his heartbeat singing in his ears, his lungs hardly able to draw breath.

When Ernest could raise his right knee and place it on the rim of the listing duckboard, he knew he was safe; he pulled his injured left leg up, and sat, a grotesque mud-covered creature wearing a hideous mask.

'Yer can get rid o' *that* bloody thing,' said Sparrer, pulling the gas mask over his head. 'There weren't no gas, it was just smoke an' mist from the firin'. Ye've been *saved*, mate, an' we'll get yer to the clearin' station to clean yer up.'

Ernest laid his head on Aaron's shoulder, and closed his eyes. Sparrer's reference to being 'saved' took him back to those Sunday afternoon Bible study groups at the Woodmans', and words from Psalm 40 came to his mind.

He brought me up out of an horrible pit, out of the miry clay, and set my feet upon a rock.

Well, upon the relative safety of a duckboard.

❧

Grace felt awkward, to say the least, when she next encountered Mrs Moore at a morning rehearsal, but she need not have worried, for the lady's manner towards her was quite unchanged; she had never spoken directly to Grace about arranging hand-picked clients for 17 Lamp Street, because all messages passed via Madge Fraser, who was paid a commission for selecting and supervising suitable girls for the purpose of 'comforting' men due to return to the trenches. Grace now realised that if any girl complained, Mrs Moore would deny all knowledge of the matter, and the blame would fall on Madge. After Grace's refusal to take on any more clients, Madge distinctly cooled towards her, and threatened that if she ever breathed a word, Madge would tell everybody that Grace had entertained men in her room on three separate occasions. Their friendship was over.

Mr Dean, however, still called upon Grace to join foursomes, for which the only payment was an evening in congenial company and a free supper. Madge seldom took part in these, having a far more lucrative sideline to her stage work at Dolly's, so Grace found herself in the company of other girls in foursomes, and it was tacitly agreed that she would instruct them in how they should behave: whether to smile and listen sympathetically to their male companions if required, or to indulge in light-hearted flirtation and look inviting – in short, to promise much and to yield nothing – except for a goodnight kiss and cuddle in the taxi at the end of the evening.

'Grace, my dear, I've got a couple of officers looking for two nice girls to take out to supper tonight,' said Mr Dean. 'Can you take young Trixie with you, and show her the ropes? She's a bit cheeky, and will need guidance, but she speaks well enough. Make sure she returns to Lamp Street and doesn't get persuaded to go off with one of 'em, there's a good girl!'

Grace knew what he meant about Trixie, and could foresee the girl being destined for room Number Four before long. She stifled a sigh, for she felt tired and her head ached; she would have preferred to go straight to bed after the show.

The curtain had come down, and the girls were chattering in their communal dressing room. Grace changed into a silk dress in a deep turquoise colour, and reapplied face powder and lipstick. Trixie was dressed and waiting impatiently for her. At the stage door Mr Dean nodded his approval, and gestured towards two uniformed army officers. Grace put on a winsome smile for Captain Garth and Captain – oh, God, what a calamity! – Captain Neville!

Captain Garth returned Trixie's saucy 'How d'you do, sir?' with a grin, and she smiled, anticipating a delightful, perhaps daring evening of exchanging banter with this handsome admirer. Garth took her arm, beckoning the other couple to follow them to a waiting taxi. Cedric's eyes were on Grace, in total amazement.

'Nurse Munday,' he said, remembering those evening entertainments at Hassett Manor. 'I didn't expect to find *you* here.'

Grace could foresee a tricky evening, to say the least. 'G-good evening, Captain Neville,' she said with a half-smile to cover her dismay. 'Yes, this is an unexpected pleasure, isn't it?'

Blushing, she took his arm; Captain Garth was helping Trixie into the back seat of the cab. 'We've got a table booked at Rotters in the Strand,' he said. 'Hurry up!'

Grace got in, her thoughts whirling. Was this an unfortunate accident, or had Neville come here deliberately to spy on her?

No, that was impossible; nobody in North Camp, her parents included, knew where she was in London. Trixie and Garth chatted happily, while Grace and Cedric sat in a strained silence, neither of them knowing what to say.

Rotters was below ground level, which meant that there need be no dimming of the lights, even if enemy planes were overhead. The two officers carefully escorted the girls down the steps, to be met by a smartly dressed commissionaire; he nodded in recognition to Captain Garth, and showed them to the cloakrooms. When they emerged they were led to a table in the crowded dining area, and a waiter hovered ready to take their orders.

'This is a bit of all right, isn't it, Gracie?' murmured Trixie. 'You can order mine, Captain Garth, and I'll have the same as what you're havin'!'

'Ah, but I'll be having the same as *he's* having,' teased Garth. 'What about your friend – Grace, isn't it? Would you like a mutton chop?'

Mutton chops with French fried potatoes were ordered for them all, and while the men drank keg beer, Trixie asked for port and lemon, and Grace chose soda water, knowing she would need a clear head if this evening was to be saved from disaster. Trixie and Garth were already indulging in cheerful repartee, and Grace braced herself to converse naturally with Cedric Neville who looked puzzled and unsmiling.

'I had no idea that I'd find you here, Miss Munday. Rotters was John Garth's choice, as was the visit to Dolly's, and I suspect he may have wished to meet your friend. The show was very good, and you were splendid on the stage. Have you been at Dolly's for long?'

'Quite a while now, Captain Neville,' she answered lightly,

forcing a smile. 'It's what I've always wanted to do.'

'Yes, I well remember how you used to entertain us at Hassett Manor, but I never expected to see you performing on a London stage. My mother will be interested – she always thought you were talented. What do Mr and Mrs Munday think about it?'

This was the question she had dreaded.

'Oh, I really don't know, Captain Neville, it seems such a long time since I was at North Camp,' she said with a little shrug.

'I gathered as much when I saw them at Christmas,' he answered seriously. 'Anyway, Mrs Storey must be glad to have you near at hand, especially with her husband away, and the, er, the happy event due to take place.'

Grace had been blushing as she spoke, but on hearing this, she felt the colour drain from her face. 'You mean…is Isabel expecting a b-baby?' she whispered.

'Yes. Don't say that you have no knowledge of it! Surely you go to see her when you have some time off?' When Grace stared down at the table, he added quite sternly, 'When was the last time you visited Bethnal Green?'

She could not answer, and Trixie, sensing the fraught silence, turned to her in mock reproof. 'What's up, Gracie, you look like a week o' wet Sundays! Has the captain been makin' improper suggestions?' She giggled, and said to both men, 'You mustn't think she's always as glum as this! On the contrary, she's a proper little firecracker, our Gracie. You should hear how the fellows go on about how she entertains the troops!'

The dead silence that followed this made even Trixie aware that something was amiss. Grace continued to sit still and speechless, and ignoring Trixie, Captain Neville spoke quietly to Grace.

'Please accept my apology, Miss Munday, if I've spoken out of turn. I seem to have touched on matters that are no concern of mine. I'm sorry if I've offended you.'

Grace still sat motionless, her eyes downcast. She did not see Cedric's quick glance in Garth's direction, finger on mouth to indicate that he should draw Trixie's attention away from Grace. Garth replied with an understanding wink.

'My mother much admires your father as a first-rate carpenter,' Cedric continued. 'She's always taken an interest in your family, as you know, and she was sorry when you had to leave Hassett Manor. She thinks you have great talent.'

Grace gave a choking sob, and covered her face with her hands.

'Are you not well, Miss Munday?' he asked in consternation. 'Would you like me to take you ho…to where you live?'

When she nodded silently, he rose from the table, excusing himself and Grace, saying that she was unwell and he was taking her away.

'I say, that's too bad!' exclaimed Garth, but Trixie hid a little smile, for she wasn't sorry to be rid of two such wet blankets; she now had the field to herself, and had her own plans for Captain Garth before the night was over.

When Neville and Grace had collected their cloaks, he hailed a taxicab and helped her into it. She whispered that she lived at 17 Lamp Street, and as the taxi started, she burst into uncontrollable sobs.

'My parents don't know, nor does my sister,' she confessed, her shoulders heaving.

'I'd rather gathered that, Miss Munday – Grace,' he replied. 'It's not my place to pass judgement, but I recommend that you visit your parents as soon as possible to put their minds at rest.

Since the death of the second Bird brother, and with Ernest and Isabel's husband facing constant danger, your father and mother have enough worries, without you adding to them.'

'I'll write to them, and I'll go to see Isabel, I really will!' she sobbed. 'I'll go tomorrow – I didn't know she was having a… oh, how selfish I've been!'

Cedric spoke more gently. 'Would you like me to call on Mrs Storey to prepare her, Grace? Our ship doesn't leave till Friday afternoon, and if it would ease the way for you, I'd be glad to call on her in the morning with my mother's good wishes, and say that I've met you and that you want to see her. Shall I do that?'

'Oh, yes, please, I'd be glad if you would, Mr…I mean Captain Neville,' said Grace thankfully, making an effort to calm herself, and when they reached Lamp Street she shook his hand in gratitude and wished him luck on his return to the war.

At least he doesn't know about – the *other*, she reminded herself, and shivered at the thought.

'Somebody at the door, Mrs Storey – d'ye want me to answer it? If it's that man come round beggin' again…'

'No, it's all right, Sally, I'll go. It might be Mrs Plumm.'

Rising from her desk where she was sorting through church accounts for the diocesan bishop, Isabel put on a welcoming smile as she opened the door. An army officer stood on the step, and her hand flew to her throat in dread.

'No,' she whispered, turning deathly pale. 'Oh, no, no, no…'

She swayed where she stood, and he stepped over the threshold in time to catch her as she fainted. Holding her in his arms, he called for help, hoping there was somebody else in the house, and Sally Tanner dashed out from the kitchen to behold Mrs Storey chalk-white and lifeless in a stranger's arms.

'Omigawd! What's up? Quick, bring 'er in 'ere and put 'er on the sofa! Oh, Isabel, me poor sweet, wake up!' She turned to the officer. 'What've yer been tellin' 'er? Is it 'er 'usband or 'er bruvver?'

'No, I've come with *good* news,' he told her while she chafed Isabel's hands and implored her to wake up. 'It's about her sister, and—'

'Look, she's comin' round,' interrupted Sally as Isabel's eyelids fluttered, and she opened them to see the officer.

'What's happened?' she moaned weakly. 'Is it about Mark?'

'No, no, Mrs Storey, I've come with a message from your sister, and I'm terribly sorry for upsetting you,' Neville apologised.

'I should damn well think so, frightenin' 'er like that!' muttered Sally, smoothing the hair back from Isabel's forehead. 'All right, me duck, nothin' to worry about, just somethin' to do with that blinkin' sister o' yours.'

'Grace?' said Isabel, sitting up and looking intently at their visitor. 'I-I seem to know you, don't I?'

'Yes, Mrs Storey, my name's Neville, and I live at Hassett Manor. I'm the younger son of—'

'Yes, yes, of course, Mr Neville. Have you seen Mark, or had any word from him? Or my brother Ernest Munday?' she asked eagerly.

'No, but silence is usually good news, Mrs Storey. My news is of your sister Grace, who wants to come and see you.'

'You mean she's been *found*? Oh, praise God for that, Mr Neville!' cried Isabel, not knowing his army rank. 'And coming to see me? Oh...' A cloud passed over her face. 'Is she...is she in any trouble?'

'I don't think so, Mrs Storey,' he answered, smiling and thinking to himself that whatever Grace had done, it couldn't be worse than what this poor young wife had feared. 'I offered to come and prepare you, seeing that...' He glanced briefly down at her loose-fitting smock. 'The fact is, a friend and I went to a music hall just off Leicester Square, and he took a fancy to one of the girls in the chorus. When he asked if he might take this girl out to supper, the manager said the girls were only allowed out in pairs – hence our second visit when he got his choice, and I found myself partnered with your sister, poor girl, she was clearly horrified at seeing me, for fear that I should tell her family.'

'How good of you, Mr Neville,' said Isabel Storey. 'It must have been *meant* that you should meet her – to give me a chance to hear her story first, before our poor parents find out. Yes, you can be sure that I'll send her back to North Camp, and forewarn them, as you have forewarned me.' Isabel's colour was returning, and she gave a wry little smile. 'Performing on the stage of a music hall – poor Grace, I can see why she kept it quiet. Meanwhile I can't thank you enough, Mr Neville. Will you be returning to Hassett Manor?'

'No, Mrs Storey, the troopship sails on Friday – and if I should meet your husband or brother out there, I'll remember you to them, and send your love.'

'God bless you, Mr Neville, may He watch over you, and keep you safe for your loved ones,' said Isabel, her voice breaking as she stood up and shook his hand.

ରେ

Grace arrived at the vicarage that same afternoon, and wept afresh at the sight of her sister, heavily pregnant and looking tired. Isabel held out her arms to the prodigal daughter, and for the next hour there was no talk of blame, only joy and relief.

'Mr Neville told me about you performing on a music hall stage, Grace, and I don't think that sounds *very* terrible – but you were wrong in disappearing from us all, sending an occasional postcard with no information about where you were.'

'I knew that Mum and Dad would worry if they knew I was on the stage,' said Grace, shaking her head and turning down the corners of her mouth.

'Not as much as they worried through *not* knowing where you were,' her sister reproached her. 'Think of their embarrassment when neighbours asked about you – and the sort of suspicions that some of them might have had, the whispering in North Camp that Mum and Dad have had to endure. Didn't you ever think about this, Grace? Didn't you realise how cruel you were, cutting yourself off from us all?'

Grace hung her head, unable to meet her sister's eyes.

'Anyway, Grace, you've been restored to us, thanks to Cedric Neville, and we won't waste time looking back. Mum and Dad will be overjoyed to see you, and you'll find there's plenty of work to be done by women, with so many men away. I'll pray that you'll be led to the work the Lord wants you to do.'

Her sister's kindness was like a sword thrust to Grace, making her all the more conscious of the deception she must practise on her family for the rest of her life, for she could never confess the awful truth about what she called *the other*. It was a burden that she must always bear, because it could never be shared.

છ

Tom Munday was waiting for her at Everham Station, and held out his arms.

'Thank God ye've come to your senses, girl, and don't ever do this to us again,' he said, hugging her. 'Whatever you do, wherever you go, keep in touch with us.'

Grace knew that he meant what he said, but doubted that he would be this tolerant if he knew that she had actually worked as a *prostitute* on three occasions.

Her mother's welcome was less warm. 'Well, my girl, you've certainly shown us up for a pair of fools, I must say! Your father ran out of excuses about you "doing your bit for the war effort" in London, which everybody knows is full of soldiers on leave. Of course there's been gossip about you, and we've had to bear the brunt of it, because we didn't know ourselves what you were up to!'

'I'm so sorry, Mum, I've been selfish and thoughtless, and I...please forgive me,' Grace pleaded, horrified that her mother's suspicions had been so near the mark.

'That's all very fine, but if young Neville hadn't found you in that...that *music hall,* we'd have gone on not knowing,' said Violet Munday bitterly. 'What with my son at the front, a daughter in London having a baby, looked after by a known drunkard, and in fear o' bombs night and day, it's no wonder neither of us are well!'

And to Grace's dismay, her mother burst into angry tears, and turned away from her daughter's attempt to hug her. Tom tried to make peace between them, and admitted privately to Grace that her mother was troubled by chronic indigestion, for which Dr Stringer had prescribed milk of magnesia and a diet of milk puddings and steamed fish; but she had no appetite.

'It's due to the constant worry, y'see, it's given her an ulcer, like old Mr Goddard had, only he's much better since Sidney married Mary Cooper and now they've got the baby,' he said.

Grace was having serious doubts about staying at her parents' home. She'd be better employed at Bethnal Green, she told her father.

'I could help out when Isabel has the baby, Dad, seeing that she refuses to leave old Mr Storey in London. Mum doesn't really want me here. She and I just don't...' She stopped speaking, and Tom Munday sighed, for he could not contradict her unfinished sentence. Lady Neville had visited Mrs Munday, and told Grace that her mother's symptoms seemed similar to those of her own daughter Letitia.

'She refuses to eat, and stays in her room at mealtimes; she hardly ever leaves the house, and is so dreadfully thin,' the lady had said with a sigh. 'Dr Stringer says it's a form of melancholia, and that I should be firmer, and *insist* that she eats, but I'm afraid I get exasperated with her, and then of course I'm sorry.'

The longer Grace stayed in North Camp, the more depressing she found it. Her mother continued to be low-spirited, and seemed to resent Grace for not being Ernest or Isabel. The only happy people she met were Sidney and Mary Goddard and their baby daughter, now living at Yeomans' farm, where Sidney worked long hours and Mary helped in the house as she had done before, stopping as necessary to feed little Dora who was cooed over by her grandparents as Billy's little sister.

'We'll have a home of our own one day after the war,' Mary told Grace, 'but for the time being this arrangement suits us well. When's Isabel's baby due?'

'About the middle o' May, so the midwife thinks. Our mother wants to come up to Bethnal Green to look after her when the time comes, but Dad thinks she's not well enough, with this gastric ulcer. Anyway, I'll be there to help Isabel all I can.'

'Oh, aren't you staying here, then?' asked Mary in some surprise.

'No. I can be more use at Bethnal Green,' replied Grace, privately thinking that one more month at Pretoria Road would send her quite mad.

Grace left North Camp in April, and needed to find employment in Bethnal Green; women were taking on many jobs formerly done only by men – driving vans for milk and bread deliveries, postmen's rounds, and as conductors on buses; when she answered an advertisement in a local butcher's shop, she was taken on by dour Mr Clark whose son was at the front. He dealt with the cuts of meat and offal, but needed help with serving and working the till. Grace was appalled at the shabbiness and tired faces of the customers who queued up long before the shop opened, eagerly accepting the cheapest offal, but the constant contact with raw meat and Mr Clark's striped, bloodstained apron made her feel nauseous, though she was glad of the money which paid her sister for her bed and board. And Isabel, who was happy to have her back, believed that seeing the hardships that the poor had to endure in a slum area would do Grace no harm.

Sally Tanner jealously guarded her position as housekeeper, insisting that Mrs Storey rested undisturbed every afternoon; the parish visiting was taken over by a delighted Mrs Clements, and the Reverend Mr Storey quite enjoyed being spoilt by the ladies of the vicarage.

જ

Isabel's pains began on a Wednesday morning in May, and continued all day.

The midwife Mrs Prebble was summoned, and confirmed that she was in early labour, but that the birth was not imminent, so she left the vicarage, to return in the afternoon. However, it proved to be a long day and an even longer night, not only of Isabel's seemingly endless painful contractions, but at around midnight the sinister sound of enemy aircraft was heard overhead, and the thud of bombs exploding not too far away, followed by the sirens of fire engines and ambulances hastening to the scenes of devastation. The raid did not last long, but the danger gave a bizarre extension to what was happening in St Barnabas' vicarage, a threat of death overshadowing the birth of a new life.

Sally and Grace took turns at keeping vigil, making tea and keeping a fire going in the kitchen to heat the water. At around five o'clock the midwife told them that she could just see the top of the baby's head, and that Isabel must push down hard to help it to be born. Two hours of pushing were then needed before a baby boy emerged, amidst tearful sighs of relief all round. He seemed pale and silent at first, but Mrs Prebble expertly held him upside down and blew her own breath onto his little face, which made him gasp: his face puckered up and he gave a weak cry. His arms and legs jerked, and as he gave a stronger cry, his skin turned from white to pink. Baby Paul Storey had arrived, and his exhausted mother held out her arms for him and whispered, 'Praise God, dearest Mark, we have a son!' Sally Tanner ran downstairs to tell the Reverend Storey that he had a fine grandson, and while he fell to his knees to give heartfelt thanks, she wiped away a tear at the memory of her own loss.

'Thank you all, every one of you dear people,' said the new mother, and turning to her sister, she smiled and asked, 'How does it feel to be an auntie, Grace?'

Grace managed to smile and murmur something about her 'dear little nephew,' but her thoughts were in turmoil. It had been a harrowing night for her, witnessing her sister's pain and hearing the explosions of bombs being dropped on London, but that wasn't all. During those long night hours, a suspicion that had been growing in her mind now turned into an undeniable certainty: she too was carrying a child. Three months had passed since the ordeal she had suffered at the hands of Captain X, and although it was possible that either Derek or Sergeant Stanley might have fathered the child, it was on that third occasion that she had not inserted the vinegar sponge.

Chapter Fifteen

1917

Padre Mark Storey feared that he was losing his sanity. He longed to give way to the overwhelming need for sleep, and had in fact almost dozed off while standing up, even when stumbling along in darkness while shells burst nearer and nearer, a firework display enough to confuse the most carefully contrived signals. He found himself pitying the Jerries, too; hatred of the enemy, deliberately fostered in training days, had now faded away like a vapour. Why were they fighting individuals like themselves, equally fed up and anxious to be done with it all? The presence of rats, great loathsome beasts gorged on dead flesh, inspired more revulsion in Mark than a battalion of Jerries.

And yet at dawn, after a relatively quiet night, there was a charge across No Man's Land, a direct frontal attack involving hand-to-hand fighting with knives and bayonets, cursing and brutality on both sides, showing the depths to which men can sink when it's a case of *your life or mine.* It was a filthy hell of mud and stench, unattended wounds, the screams and groans of the dying.

And at the end of that dawn battle Mark Storey suffered a spiritual loss as grievous as any bodily wound, for it robbed his life of meaning. A young soldier of his own section was suddenly struck by a shell fragment square between his eyes. He fell down, calling out, 'Lord, Lord, I'm blinded! Save me, I'm *blind*, O God!' He shrieked the words again and again, until he choked on his own blood, and the officer in charge ordered them to leave him where he lay, for he could not possibly survive. Mark ignored the order, and knelt down beside the whimpering boy, now sinking into merciful oblivion.

'May Almighty God, the Father, Son and Holy Ghost...' He made the sign of the cross, and gently laid a hand on the bloodied head, the blessing unfinished; and in a momentary flash of utter dismay he denied the meaning of the words. For it now seemed to him that there was no God protecting them, no divine intervention, no tender mercies; there was no such thing, it was all meaningless, a myth shown up for what it was in this glaring hell.

So when Storey rose from the dying soldier, he was no longer a priest in the Church of England, but an unbeliever, a born-again atheist.

Having finally faced up to her suspicions, Grace Munday was gripped by panic. What was she to do? Where could she go to get help? She couldn't tell Isabel, for she knew that the young mother would emphatically oppose what Grace was intending to do. Similarly she couldn't confide in either Mrs Tanner or Mrs Clements, both of whom cared only for Isabel and her baby, jealously protecting her from anything that might upset her and dry up her milk. In the end Grace decided to consult Mrs Prebble who lived in a terraced house in Turin Street, about three quarters of a mile from St Barnabas' vicarage. Leaving Mr Clark's shop at half past five as usual, on pretext of doing a little shopping, she called at the midwife's home and rang the bell twice. Nobody came, and Grace's heart sank. She tried a third time, and a woman appeared at the house next door.

'She ain't in, she's out on a case down Spitalfields!' the woman yelled. 'Dunno 'ow long she'll be. Gimme yer name an' I'll tell 'er yer called. Where'd yer live?' Grace shook her head, hoping for better luck the following afternoon.

Her luck held, for when she called again, Mrs Prebble came to the door, munching a sandwich. She raised her eyebrows on recognising Grace.

'Ye're from St Barnabas', aren't you? Is something the matter with Mrs Storey or the baby?'

'No, they're all right, thank you, Mrs Prebble, but I'd like to see you myself if it's not too inconvenient,' faltered Grace. 'If I might come in for a moment and have a word…'

Mrs Prebble opened the door to admit her, and led her to a back parlour.

'Sit yourself down, Miss…er…'

'Munday, Mrs Prebble.'

'Oh, ah, Munday. What's brought *you* here, then?'

Grace's trouble was soon told. A few brisk questions about the time of her last period, her last contact with her 'young man', and the nausea she had put down to the smell of the butcher's shop, established that Miss Munday was indeed three months' gone, and due to give birth in November. Mrs Prebble shook her head.

'Hm. I did wonder that night you sat up with Mrs Storey,' she said. 'Have you said anything to her about it?'

'Oh, no, Mrs Prebble,' answered Grace wretchedly. 'I was hoping I wouldn't need to, not if you – if you were able to do something about it.'

'Get rid of it, you mean?'

After a momentary hesitation, Grace nodded and replied, 'Ye-yes, Mrs Prebble. M-my young man's been k-killed in France.' Her voice trembled as she uttered the words, and the midwife shook her head.

'At three months? And your young man's gone off and got himself killed at the front? Hm, the usual story.' She spoke as if she doubted the truth of it, and Grace held her breath as she waited for an answer.

'Ye've left it too late, girl. I never touch a woman more'n two months' gone, so you'd better get ready to carry it through. Have you told your parents? It'd be best to go home and tell 'em before everybody can see for themselves. How old are you? Eighteen? You haven't showed much sense, have you?'

'I know I haven't, but what am I to *do*, Mrs Prebble?' asked Grace with such despair in her voice that the midwife relented a little.

'There are various places where you can go to have the baby and get it adopted. The better they are, the more money they want. There's a good place called the Women's Rescue in Battersea, and the Salvation Army place in Pentonville, all hymn-singin' and scrubbing brushes, though they're decent people – and of course there are the workhouses, but most girls'd throw 'emselves into the Thames first, and I can't see Mrs Storey letting you go to one o' them. And you'll need to book a doctor in case there's complications when it comes to the birth. That's the best I can advise, girl. Tell your sister, and then go back to where you came from, and be quick about it. Ye've made your bed, and now you must lie on it, you poor kid.'

℘

'Grace! Oh, *Grace*! Are you really *sure*? What a burden you've been bearing, my poor little sister!'

Isabel's reaction was certainly one of surprise, and Grace wept as she told the half-true tale of a brief relationship with a soldier on the eve of his departure to the war, where she said he'd been reported as missing only a week later. Isabel, now a mother herself, pitied her sister for the loss of the man she had presumably loved, and for the prospect of giving up the baby she would bear.

'You must stay here for the confinement, Grace,' she said firmly. 'I know Mr Storey will agree. We'll book Mrs Prebble and Dr Whitefield. It won't be easy to keep such a secret from Mum and Dad, but Mum isn't well, and we must spare her the extra worry if we possibly can. I'll help you to look the rest of the world in the face.'

Grace hid her face on her sister's shoulder. 'Oh, Isabel, you're so good to me,' she sobbed. 'I know I don't deserve it, but I don't know what I'd have done if you'd turned me away. Mrs Prebble told me that girls have drowned themselves...'

And Isabel, knowing something of the despair of women who *had* thrown themselves into the unforgiving waters of the Thames, hugged her sister closer still.

For Tom Munday a succession of bright summer days only brought back poignant memories of happier times when the family had all been together; when Ernest had been a solemn schoolboy, content to spend Sunday afternoons at Mr Woodman's Bible class, and Isabel and Grace were the prettiest girls at Miss Daniells' school. And Violet his wife, bustling around on Sunday mornings, getting the children ready for church and putting on her flowery hat, securing it with a long pin at the back, while telling him to get a move on and not to forget a clean handkerchief. Tom closed his eyes, remembering the years that he now saw as the happiest of his life.

Now Ernest was away and might never return; Isabel had given birth to a son who might never see his father; Grace, thank heaven, had come to her senses and was helping her sister, not ashamed to work in a butcher's shop to pay for her board. And Violet – his pretty, dark-eyed girl, loved from the moment he first saw her at Hassett Manor – was drifting into a deep melancholy, losing interest in everything that used to give her pleasure. Dr Stringer had said that she needed company, and should visit friends and neighbours, invite them to afternoon sewing sessions or evenings of whist. It was no use; Violet would only visit Mrs Bird whose grief over her lost boys had aged her ten years, and was similarly turning in upon herself. When Tom asked Dr Stringer if Violet should see a specialist, the GP had frowned, shrugged and said it would be a waste of money; many women were reacting in this way to the constant fear of the dreaded telegram.

Not for the first time Tom had to conceal his own fears and assume a positive attitude that he did not feel. Violet would not be cheered, and told him he had not the same care as herself for their only son. How wrong she was, he reflected sadly, for his son was seldom out of his thoughts, and he reproached himself bitterly for not showing Ernest greater understanding in the past.

At the beginning of September North Camp was agog with the news that young Philip Saville, having lost a leg, had been discharged from the army, and had come home. The congregation eagerly looked forward to seeing the boy they remembered as a golden-haired youth, and though without his left leg, he was now spared any further injury. The weeks went by, however, with no sign of Philip, either in church or out of it, and rumours began to circulate, such as that he had been hideously scarred, would never walk again, or that he had lost his reason. The tense faces of his parents neither confirmed nor denied any of these dire stories, but all enquiries were met with the reply that 'it would take time before he was better.'

Then Tom Munday was summoned to the rectory to make a number of additions and modifications to make life easier for Philip. There were handholds to be put along corridors, convenient hooks for hanging up clothes, crutches and walking sticks; Tom was asked to make a discreet commode chair for use in Philip's bedroom, and outside he was asked to make a garden bench against the south wall, protected by a small gabled shelter around it to keep out rain and wind. It was while he was engaged on these additions that Tom came face to face with the returned soldier, and his heart ached within him at the sight of a boy not yet twenty, a one-legged cripple walking unsteadily on crutches, apparently unable to speak, for when he opened his mouth, only a deep, rattling cough was heard, the result of inhaling poison gas. His hair was lank and lifeless, and the blue eyes were sunken into their bony orbits; he had the haunted face of one who had looked upon unspeakable horrors.

Tom managed to smile and greet Philip briefly, though he got no reply; in answer to neighbours' enquiries he simply repeated that the young man had lost a leg and would take some time to recover from his experiences. He said nothing to Violet, knowing that she would picture Ernest in the same state, echoing Tom's own fears. He hoped that he would show the same courage and steadfast faith as the Savilles if that were ever the case.

'It's such a bloody shame, Eddie, to see a good-looking

young chap turned into such a wreck,' he said to his friend, to which Eddie replied that at least his life had been spared – 'not like poor ol' Bird over there,' he said in a low tone, for Mr Bird had taken to dropping into the Tradesmen's Arms on a Friday evening to have a pint with Tom and Eddie. A dapper, somewhat formal man who found Christian names difficult to use, he confided to them that his wife had withdrawn into a shell of solitude in which she lived with her memories of Tim and Ted, kissing their photographs each night and seldom going out.

'It's not much of a life for Phyllis at home,' Bird admitted. 'And it's hard on her to see Billy Hickory as he is now. You may know that they were unofficially engaged when he went out there, but...' Tom and Eddie stared back at him in helpless sympathy. 'He's better now than he was,' remarked Eddie, 'I mean he just about manages to sell and deliver the orders – though it's his mother who runs the business, and God knows what'll happen when she's gone.'

'Your Phyllis is a handsome girl,' said Tom. 'I reckon there'll be another young chap for her sooner or later.'

'I'm not quite so sure about that,' replied Mr Bird, looking into his half-empty glass. 'There's been such a bloodletting since this war began, and no sign of it ending. I sometimes think my daughter and her friends may not have enough young men left in their generation.'

Neither Tom nor Eddie had an answer to that, and did not try to contradict him, a man who had lost not only his sons but his wife, too, in a sense – the woman whom he had loved and married. Tom Munday understood only too well, but could not say so.

❧

Grace Munday had need of all her resolution, as well as her sister's support, once her baby began to 'show'. Suddenly it seemed as if everybody knew of her plight, and whereas old Mr Storey refrained from mentioning it – she suspected more for Isabel's sake than her own – the women of St Barnabas' Church could talk of nothing else. Mrs Tanner and Mrs Clements clearly blamed her, not only for 'getting into trouble' as they called it, but for bringing that trouble to poor Mrs Storey's door at a time when she had just given birth to a son without the comfort of her husband's presence, and as she was adjusting to the new routine of feeding, changing and being woken up in the night by the new arrival, though everybody agreed that Paul was a beautiful baby, and that it was a crying shame that his poor daddy was away comforting the lads who were risking their lives in this wicked war.

Overhearing these remarks as she passed by the open kitchen door, Grace could not defend herself to them, for they were not the only voices raised against her. Mr Clark, although of course he said nothing to Grace, had obviously mentioned the matter to his wife, earning Grace disapproving stares from the customers whose whispers seemed to follow her down the street.

'Why can't she go 'ome to 'er parents, that's what I'd like to know,' said a woman standing in the queue for rationed mutton, and the next rumour that passed round was that Mrs Storey's wayward younger sister had been thrown out by her father, and that was why she'd come back to poor Mrs Storey. This particular tale was the one that brought tears to Grace's eyes in the privacy of her room: as if her dear old dad would ever do such a thing, however badly she behaved – though regarding her mother she was less sure. She was learning about the intolerance, the shame heaped upon girls like her, getting bigger every week. Her back ached and her legs were swollen from standing at the counter and till all day; yet no matter how tired she felt, or how uncomfortable, she was resolved never to complain or reply to personal criticisms, though she was touched when two weary expectant mothers commiserated with her in the butcher's shop. Even when Mrs Prebble, examining her at five and a half months, told her she should try to rest more, Grace was determined to carry on working for Mr Clark right up to the day of her delivery; she'd go on serving the customers until she dropped – and in fact she almost did. She woke up on a grey, foggy November day when her back ached so badly that she couldn't get out of bed. As she tried to sit up a sudden warm gush between her legs made her think that she had wet the bed, but Isabel came and reassured her that it was her waters breaking, a sure sign that she was in labour. Sally was sent to fetch Mrs Prebble who came and felt for the baby's head, which she said was not down yet.

'Does that mean it's the wrong way round, Mrs Prebble?' asked Grace, gasping as another pain seized her back.

'No, just that the head's got a long way to go down before you can start pushin',' the midwife replied. 'You ought to get up and walk around a bit if you can, 'cause this is goin' to be a long wait. I'll leave a couple o' doses o' "mother's mixture" to take when the pains really get started, and I'll come back about noon.'

Grace passed a wretched morning of growing discomfort. Isabel helped her to sit out of bed on the commode chair, and gave her the 'mother's mixture' that tasted so foul that she brought it up again immediately.

'Oh, poor Grace, that's the stuff I had, potassium bromide with a few drops of opium,' said Isabel. 'Look, dear, lay down on your side and I'll rub your back for you. That helps a bit.'

'Mrs Storey, Paul's cryin', so can yer come to 'im?' called Sally, and Grace was left alone again to cope with pain after endless pain. By now they were coming round to the front of her belly, which tightened up to a board-like hardness with each contraction, and her back felt as if it was about to break in two.

'Oh, God,' she whispered, 'help me, please! Forgive my sins and help me, O Lord – have mercy on me!'

'All right, Grace, all right, I'm here,' said Isabel, bringing a cup of weak tea and a boiled sweet for her to suck after swallowing the second dose of 'mother's mixture'.

'Am I going to die, Izzy?' asked Grace in her agony.

'No, dear, you're not going to die – I'm here to help you see it through. Put your trust in God. Pa's praying for you downstairs.'

Mrs Prebble returned as dusk was falling, and announced that the head was going down, but it would be several hours before the delivery. Grace groaned, and the midwife drank a cup of tea and shook her head over the news from the front.

'The British and French've recaptured that place called Passchendaele in Belgium,' she told Isabel. 'Terrible casualties, though.' She finished her tea, and put on her coat. 'Gettin' dark already, and it's only just gone four. I'll nip home to feed the cat and see if there are any new messages. Carry on as you're doin', and I'll be back around seven. Wouldn't surprise me if this goes on till the early hours.'

But Mrs Prebble had underestimated the strength of the

contractions, and at half past five Grace cried out that she was having her bowels opened.

'I'm sorry, I'm sorry, Izzy, but I can't get out o' bed – I can't stop it coming, I'm sorry – oh, my *God*!' She screamed and rolled on to her back. 'Help me!'

Isabel pulled back the sheet and saw a baby's head emerging between Grace's thighs.

'Sally! Sally, come at once!' she called, and as she and Sally watched, the head was born, the face upwards.

'Oh, look at its little face – oh, bless it!' Isabel was hardly able to control her voice. 'All right, Grace dear, your baby's nearly here, don't worry.'

She took the head gently between her hands, and as Grace gave another involuntary push, the child's body slithered out followed by a gush of blood.

'It's a girl, Grace! Oh, Grace, you've got a little girl!'

'Five minutes to six,' said Sally, glancing at Grace's alarm clock on the bedside table. 'Look, it's breathin' an' movin' its arms an' legs.'

'Is it – is it all right?' asked the new mother.

'Yes, she's fine, she's crying – listen to her!' said Isabel shakily. 'Sally, dear, can you run over to Mrs Clements and ask her to fetch Mrs Prebble? She'll have to come and cut the cord and whatever else she has to do. There's the afterbirth still to come – oh, thanks be to God!'

Carefully she wrapped the baby in a clean towel, and as Grace sat up to look, her sister placed the baby, still attached to the umbilical cord, in her mother's arms.

'She's perfect, Grace – a sweet little darling.'

On her way out, Sally called to Mr Storey that a baby girl had been born, and his eyes filled with tears as he prayed that the child would go to a good home where she would be loved.

Christmas, 1917

'Are you sure you'll be all right here, Grace, if I go to see Mum and Dad at Christmas?' asked Isabel anxiously. 'You'll have Pa here, of course, and Sally to cook and clean – and do the washing. I won't be away long, just the two nights of the twenty-fourth and twenty-fifth, only I really want to show them how well Paul's doing.'

'Oh, you go and give them my love, Izzy, I'll be all right here,' answered Grace, gazing down at baby Becky, eagerly sucking at her breast. Isabel felt a stab of pity as she looked on the rosy, innocent child soon to be taken from her mother and placed in a new home by a Church of England agency, never to know her real mother or the grandparents who were unaware of her existence. It seemed wrong to take part in the deception, thought Isabel, but it would surely be worse to tell Tom and Violet the truth, especially as her mother's health was not improving. She sighed; it would be a sad Christmas, except for the fact of her precious son, hers and Mark's. May it please God to send her husband home to them, safe and well!

Isabel left with Paul on Christmas Eve, a Monday, travelling down to North Camp by train. Less than two hours after her departure, a telegram from the War Office arrived at St Barnabas' vicarage. Sally Tanner received it from the telegraph boy, her hands shaking as she took it to Mr Richard Storey in his study. He too gasped at the sight of it, as if it were a poisonous snake. It was addressed to Mrs Isabel Storey, and would certainly contain no good news, he knew; it would say that his son was dead, or that he was missing, which usually came to the same thing; or it might bring news that he was wounded, and lying in some base hospital.

'What am I to do, Mrs Tanner?' he asked in distress. 'It's not addressed to me, and if...if I opened it and saw that my...my son has been killed, I could telephone the Reverend Mr Saville at North Camp, and he could let Isabel know while she's there with her parents. Or should I keep it for her to open, and let her enjoy this short time with her family and friends? It might be the last...' The old man's voice faltered, and Sally laid a hand on his arm.

'Open it an' see what it says, Mr Storey. If it's bad news, it can wait till she's 'ome, and yer can tell 'er then, or we both can. Don't spoil their Christmas.'

'That's exactly what I think, Mrs Tanner – thank you. Where's Miss, er, Grace? Perhaps we should ask her opinion, too.'

'She's busy with 'er baby, and wouldn't know any better 'n us. Yer should open it now, Mr Storey.'

'All right, my dear. Please stay with me while I do so.'

She watched as he slit the envelope in fear, and took out the fatal piece of paper it contained. He stared at the message as if he could scarcely understand it, but eventually looked up and stared at Sally, his face transformed.

'Praise be to God, M-Mrs Tanner, he's been wounded, it doesn't say how or where, but he's in hospital at a...a place called, er, Chateau Mondicourt, it says. Oh, Mrs Tanner, he's alive!'

'An' 'e'll be comin' 'ome, an' won't 'ave to go back again – comin' *'ome*!' cried Sally, clapping her hands together.

'Thanks be to God, Mrs Tanner, my son is saved – we'll all see him again!'

They hugged each other, the elderly clergyman and the reformed drinker, weeping and laughing in their relief.

എ

A good congregation filled St Peter's Church on Christmas morning, though the festive season was shadowed by the sorrows occasioned by the war. One of the happier sights was of little Paul Storey, now seven months old, with his mother and his proud grandparents, for Mrs Munday had made the effort to come to church, and stood between her husband and Isabel. Neighbours who had not seen her for a while were shocked at her gaunt appearance, for she had lost weight and her face had a yellowish pallor, in spite of her smiles for her little grandson.

Lady Neville sat in her usual pew, accompanied by Mrs Gann, a thing unheard of before the war, but in the absence of husband, sons and daughter, her ladyship was glad of the companionship of her faithful cook-housekeeper. People craned their heads to see Philip Saville with his mother in the pew just below the pulpit. His general health was slowly improving, and though he had to use the hated crutches for walking, his mother explained that he was to be fitted with a wooden leg.

Mr Bird and Phyllis came over to speak to the Mundays after the service, for Mrs Bird had not been to church since the death of her sons; Isabel's heart ached for the family.

Lady Neville also came to admire baby Paul, and to speak quietly to Isabel about her mother.

'I know your father's worried about her, Mrs Storey, and she's obviously not responding to Dr Stringer's treatment. In fact she's as bad as my daughter Letitia who simply refuses to eat – but whereas my daughter's just being silly, as if starving herself will bring Cedric home safely, I think Mrs Munday gives real cause for concern. Do please ask your father to request a second opinion, my dear.' She sighed, and made an effort to sound more positive. 'It's good news about your sister Grace, isn't it, taking charge of your husband's father and running the vicarage while you're away. Whoever would have thought it at one time? *My* daughter could be of such help to me, helping to run my little convalescent home at Hassett Manor, it's the only thing that stops *me* giving way to useless melancholy, with my husband and Arnold in India, and Cedric driving these frightening *tanks* or whatever they're called. He says they could bring the war to an end – but forgive me, Mrs Storey, your own husband's away, and here's this dear little boy who's never seen his daddy – I'm being thoroughly selfish. Tell me, do you get much news from the front?'

Concerned for her mother, Isabel told her father what Lady Neville had said about getting a second opinion. It only confirmed his own worst fears.

'I should've done so before, I know, Isabel,' he said heavily. 'You know what she's like, says it's all worry over Ernest, and she's got this idea in her head that she's never going to see her son again, and there's nothing Stringer can do about that, and neither can I. Still, you've made up my mind for me, and I'll go round and see Stringer first thing on Thursday.'

'Ask him for a referral to a specialist at Everham Hospital, Dad. If there's nothing physically wrong with Mum, at least you'll be reassured.'

Tom nodded, thankful as ever for his good elder daughter. Doctors' bills were mounting up, and specialists didn't come cheap, but he would override Violet on this issue, for nothing was more important to him than her health and happiness.

When the train drew into Waterloo Station on Boxing Day, Isabel let down the window in the door, and put her head out to see if Sally was there to meet her. When she saw not only

Sally but her father-in-law and Mrs Clements, she clutched her baby to her heart. Good God, they must be here to support me, she thought; they've had news – something's happened!

When the train stopped they came to help her step down to the platform, with her baby and suitcase. Her face was ashen.

'What's happened? Is it Mark?' she whispered, and then saw that all their faces were wreathed in smiles. 'What – oh, tell me, do!'

'My dear, he's wounded and in a French hospital,' said Mr Storey. 'Which means he'll be coming home to us.'

'Oh, Pa...' Holding baby Paul under her left arm, she hugged her father-in-law with her right, as Sally and Mrs Clements both put their arms around her. She could not have asked for a happier homecoming.

When the three of them and baby Paul were settled in a horse-drawn cab, cheaper than the motor-driven taxis, Isabel asked about Grace. Mrs Clements and Sally glanced at each other, and Mrs Clements answered.

'Very low at present, 'cause it's nearly time for the baby to be took off 'er. The woman from the adoption says the first week in January.'

'Oh, poor Grace! However shall we comfort her?' asked Isabel sadly.

'Best thing's to keep busy, an' she'll be back at Mr Clark's by this time next week,' said Sally. 'That'll keep 'er occupied, as well as bringin' in a bit o' money.' The last words were uttered with a significant nod, as if to indicate that Grace should pay her way instead of sponging on her sister. Isabel heard the unspoken disapproval, and was about to say that Grace had always paid for her board, including the time of her confinement and since, using up her post office savings account; but then they would have speculated on the origin of that account, which Isabel thought was entirely from Grace's time at Dolly's music hall (for she knew nothing of room Number Four and its traffic), and the very words *chorus girl* would be linked in their minds to baby Rebecca's conception. So Isabel said nothing, but dreaded the moment her sister must soon face. And furthermore, she would have to tell her sister about their mother's deteriorating health. Poor Grace! Isabel felt almost guilty for being so happy in the midst of such trouble.

Chapter Sixteen

January–February, 1918

Another new year dawned on a grey, war-weary nation, stunned by the horrific losses of its sons, the bright and hopeful boys cut down in their hundreds of thousands, and without bringing victory any nearer; in fact the end of the war seemed like a mirage, fading into the distance, again and again. At home there were serious shortages, long queues for meagre rations, and families went hungry, especially in poor areas like St Barnabas', where pale, undernourished children shivered in draughty rooms. There was a deep desire for peace, but no great hope of seeing it, and the stirring patriotic songs of 1914 now had a hollow ring.

At 47 Pretoria Road in North Camp, Tom Munday was having to come to terms with another deep anxiety, and this time it was not for Ernest or his daughters. He now bitterly reproached himself for not recognising his wife's declining health, and Dr Stringer's failure to diagnose anything more sinister than melancholy. Now the truth was staring him in the face, though he still feared to give it a name. An appointment had been made for a reluctant Violet Munday to see a specialist at Everham General Hospital on January the seventh, and until then he had to hide his fears under a false optimism, something that had become second nature to him over the last few years, and he confided in no one, not even his old friend Eddie Cooper, until the specialist's opinion and recommendations had been given.

At St Barnabas' vicarage there were mixed emotions. Isabel and her father-in-law waited daily for news of Mark, lying wounded in a requisitioned chateau near Béthune; and Grace clasped her baby to her breast as the time for parting drew near.

On the eleventh of January, a Friday, two letters arrived at the vicarage where the family sat at breakfast. One was addressed to the Reverend Richard Storey, and the other was from Tom Munday to his daughters. Isabel hastily slit this envelope open, anxious for news of their mother. It was not good. Isabel read aloud that Violet had seen a specialist, a surgeon who had looked grave after examining her. An X-ray had been ordered, and blood samples tested, and now an urgent operation on the stomach was recommended, something Mrs Munday had always dreaded, and had at first refused to agree to it.

The sisters stared at each other in alarm, and Isabel continued to read aloud.

'I've had to be firm with your poor mother,' Tom had written. 'I saw the look on that man's face, and I blame myself for not pressing Stringer earlier for a referral. She is going into Everham Hospital next week, and I have to tell you girls to be brave. She'll need looking after when she comes home, and I'm hoping that Grace will be able to help us out for a while, seeing that Isabel has Paul to look after.'

Isabel whispered the last few words because of the irony of the situation, for Grace also had a baby to care for, though not for much longer, as she was to see the representative of the adoption society in two days' time, when she would sign the papers agreeing to the adoption of Rebecca Munday.

'Grace, dear – perhaps this is providential,' said Isabel softly. 'If you go home to help Mum and Dad, you'll be doing good work, and away from here, which will be best for you.'

Grace swallowed and moistened her lips. 'Yes. I'll write and tell them I'm coming home, and they'll never know what I've left behind.'

'That's very good of you, Grace, and so brave,' said her sister. 'It's a terrible wrench for you, but you know that Becky will go to a Christian couple who really want a baby...'

'I know, I know, for once in my life I'll be doing some good.'

'Bless you, Grace dear,' said Isabel, kissing her. 'Now, I wonder what's in that letter to Pa. It had a foreign stamp and a word in blue letters across the envelope. It may be something important, and I'm going to ask him about it.'

As she rose to go to Mr Storey's study, he appeared at the door and beckoned to her. She followed him, her heart pounding.

'What is it, Pa? It's Mark, isn't it? Tell me what it says!'

'My dear Isabel, sit down here and I'll tell you. Mark's very ill, but expected to recover. The letter's from another chaplain who's been talking to him. He feels that you...that we ought to be warned of my son's condition before he's put on a Red Cross ship for home.'

'Oh, Pa, what is it? Give it to me – let me see!' she cried, putting out a hand to take the letter from him, but he held it away from her, and told her again to sit down and listen to what this padre had to say.

'He's written to me rather than to you, my dear, so that I can talk to you quietly, and you must listen. I'll let you read the letter yourself after I've given you the gist of it.'

'Yes, Pa, I'm listening, only tell me quickly! Has he lost a limb?'

'No, Isabel, he has not. He's wounded in the lower abdomen,' said the old clergyman, trying to find the right words. 'He's damaged in the…the genital area. He'll need a lot of care, and patience too, when he—'

'*Where* in the genital area, Pa? Do you mean his penis?'

He nodded, relieved at her directness which made it easier for him.

'Yes, my dear, it is the penis that's been, er, damaged. The shaft of it has been reduced to a mere stump, this padre says, and it's sufficiently healed for him to pass urine through it, though he has to sit down, like a woman, but he will be unable to have normal marital relations with you. That's what it says here, my dear Isabel, and that isn't all, because Mark has become embittered by his experiences, and has lost his faith. He actually told this padre that he fears meeting you again because of the wreck he's become.' The old man's voice shook as he added, 'That's the actual word he uses – a *wreck* – oh, my poor boy.'

He brushed away tears with the back of his hand, and looked at Isabel. She was smiling, and reached out to take that hand in her own.

'Thank you, dear Pa. It must have cost you a lot to tell me this. But we'll help him, Pa, we'll help him through it, we'll show him what love can do. We haven't lost *our* faith, and we'll lead him back again, don't you see?'

'But my dear, this terrible injury,' he quavered.

'That doesn't worry me at all on *my* account, only on his. I
don't need that sort of relationship, in fact he refrained from it
all the time we were married, except for that last time, and our
dear little Paul was the result of it, but I shan't need it again.'
She smiled into his face. 'There are other ways, Pa, and we'll
still be close and loving. All I want is to see him home again,
here where he belongs.'

'Bless you, my daughter,' he answered, getting up and
coming to her side, embracing her like a father. 'My son is
fortunate in having such a wife!'

'And such a lovely little son,' she added, as if she didn't mind
that Paul would be an only child.

When the day came for baby Rebecca to be taken from her
natural mother and given up for adoption, the atmosphere
in the vicarage was tense. Isabel showed the pleasant-faced,
grey-haired lady into the study where Mr Storey sat, and they
watched her open her briefcase and put the papers on the table.
Grace was called in, and on seeing the documents she began
to moan softly, a keening sound like a lament; it made the old
clergyman think of a cat whose newborn kittens have been
taken from her, or a cow parted from its calf.

What were Grace Munday's thoughts? She had been refused
an abortion, and had accepted that this unwanted child would
have to be adopted, right up to the moment of its birth when *it*
became *she*, the daughter she had fed and nursed for more than
six weeks. The shameful circumstances of the conception were
overruled in Grace's heart by the love she now felt for this child
of her flesh; and now they were to be parted for ever. She wept
for her baby, resisting all efforts to calm and comfort her.

'Now, Grace, we can't have this,' said the lady, not unkindly.

'You know that this is all for the best, especially for Rebecca.'

'You must be brave, my child, for the sake of *your* child,' said Mr Storey. 'You're soon going home to do your duty, looking after your mother and father. Put your trust in the Almighty, and do this other duty for the child.'

Suddenly Isabel spoke, having stood silently beside her sister up until now. 'This must stop!' she said firmly and clearly. 'I can't let it happen. *I'll* take Becky and bring her up as my own, and my husband's. She's not going to a stranger.'

There was a momentary silence, and Sally Tanner, hearing Isabel's upraised voice, left her washing of sheets and towels to come to the study door. Mr Storey breathed a long, deep sigh, and Grace swayed as if about to faint, but Isabel caught her and sat her down on a chair, keeping an arm around her. The lady with the briefcase, hearing the voice of authority, gathered up her papers and left, leaving an address where she could be contacted. Sally went to put the kettle on.

'Try not to be too upset, Grace, in front of your mother,' said Tom Munday on meeting her at Everham Station, and noticing how pale and wan she looked. 'She's coming home at the weekend, so we must get the house looking decent for her. I'll take her armchair up to the bedroom, and the little table, so's she can sit at the window if she feels like it.'

'Yes, Dad. I'll help you all I can.'

'It's a comfort to have you home, my girl. It's not going to be an easy time for any of us. If only Ernest could be here to say g—' He covered his face with his hands before continuing. 'I'm sorry, Grace, but I can't get used to it. You'll come with me to visit her tomorrow, and that'll make it a lot easier. And she'll be glad to see you.'

One look at her mother in the women's ward of Everham General, and Grace Munday knew that there was no hope of recovery; she also knew that she would have to nurse her mother and comfort her father in the days and weeks ahead. Her father told her what the surgeon had said after the operation.

'I'm very sorry, Munday, and I wish there was better news. It had started in the pancreas and spread to the liver by the time we opened her. There was nothing useful to be done except to close the incision and let her spend what time she has left in resting and seeing her loved ones around her.'

'How long d'you think it'll be, sir?' Tom had asked, his voice thin and unfamiliar to his own ears.

'Not too long, Munday. Once a patient has been opened up, it seems to send the cancer cells spreading quickly throughout the system, and shortens the time. You've got a son and two daughters, haven't you? I suppose your son's away at the war, but send for the daughters as soon as you can.'

'And our little grandson, eight months old,' added Tom.

Violet Munday, a shadow of her former self, came home in an ambulance and was carried upstairs to the bed she shared with Tom. Grace tended her, washing her and changing the bedlinen, helping her on and off the commode and trying to tempt her appetite with Benger's Food and calf's foot jelly sent up from Yeomans' farm.

'What've they done to my stomach, Tom?' Violet asked pathetically. 'What have they done to my poor stomach? Where's Ernest? Why isn't my son here?'

Tom sent a letter to the War Office, requesting that Lieutenant Munday be granted leave to visit his mother, but the message never got through to the front, from where the news was confusing and contradictory as fresh casualties arrived at Charing Cross Station and fresh drafts were sent out to take their place, marching in grim silence: no 'Tipperary' or 'Pack up Your Troubles' was to be heard now.

Isabel came to visit, bringing Paul with her, and leaving baby Becky in the charge of Sally Tanner. Grace begged for news of her, and was told that she was doing well, taking her bottle feeds and putting on weight.

'But we mustn't talk about her, Grace, or our parents will find out, and that's the last thing we want,' warned Isabel, who was determined that Becky was to be adopted by Mark and herself, and to grow up as their daughter, regarding Grace as her aunt. All this had to be kept from the Mundays, and Grace's sorrowful looks were put down to her mother's illness.

Annie Cooper came to visit the invalid with Freddie, and Mary Cooper with little Dora, as also did Mrs Bird, Mrs Saville and Lady Neville, though her ladyship had her own worries: her daughter Miss Letitia had lost so much weight that it was said she looked like a skeleton, though she still refused to eat and was too weak to leave her room. In vain did her mother and Dr Stringer threaten and harangue her, and tell her that she would die if she did not pull herself together, and that it would be nobody's fault but her own; she turned her face to the wall of her room, and there she was found by a housemaid on a chill February morning, a gaunt, open-eyed corpse. Lady Neville was thrown into an agony of remorse at seeing her own impatient words fulfilled so exactly, and she refused to speak to Dr Stringer when he came to visit the wounded in Hassett Manor. The news was given out that Miss Neville had died of a form of consumption, and her funeral was a sad, black-clad affair on a wet afternoon.

When word came from St Barnabas' vicarage that Mark Storey had arrived in England and was in Charing Cross Hospital, Isabel was almost beside herself with joy. She bid her parents an affectionate farewell, promised to write to them and, taking baby Paul, caught the next train to London.

It was old Mr Storey who suggested that he and she should visit Mark together, leaving the two babies in the care of Sally Tanner.

Mark was in a long ward with a row of twelve beds on either side. When Isabel saw him she almost ran to his side, where he sat propped up on three pillows.

'Mark! Oh, dearest Mark, God be thanked for bringing you home again!' She eagerly embraced him, putting her warm face against his cool cheek, while his father looked on, smiling. Mark seemed unmoved.

'Isabel,' he said in a dull, flat tone. 'Poor Isabel.'

'What d'you mean, Mark? I'm not poor! I'm the happiest of wives,' she said joyfully. 'I can't wait to have you home with us – to show you our beautiful son – oh, he really is the dearest baby boy – isn't he, Pa?'

'He is indeed, my dear. I can see a resemblance to his daddy in his eyes.'

'So, I gave you a child on that last night, Isabel – the night I raped you.'

'Mark! How can you say such a thing? You were upset that night, that's all.'

He gave a mirthless laugh. 'And you didn't like it, did you? Something I'd promised I'd never do.' He turned to his father. 'But I broke my promise, and got on top of her, and raped her – are you listening, father?'

Heads were turning in their direction, both patients and visitors.

'Be quiet, Mark!' said his father sharply. 'Show some respect for your wife, she's one in a million, and has never spoken ill of you, not once. Stop using that word, and be thankful for her – and your son.'

'The child of a rape,' persisted Mark in a surly tone.

'Then all I can say is thank God you *did*, because you've got a fine son by it!' retorted his father with uncharacteristic vehemence.

'And an *only* child, eh, father? Because there won't be any more, will there? Have they told you I'm a eunuch, Isabel?'

Isabel answered calmly. 'I know about your injury, Mark, and I'm sorry, but not for myself, because we can still love each other in the way we did. And Paul won't be our only child, because it so happens that we have a little adopted girl. My sister Grace bore her, and I've said that we'll have her as our own, a sister for Paul, and of my own blood.'

'Your sister Grace? *That* little trollop? You never could see through that girl. Who's the father?'

'Somebody who has since gone back to the war and been killed,' she answered seriously. 'Don't be so quick to condemn people, Mark. Little Rebecca – we call her Becky – is now two and a half months old, and a dear little thing. You'll be won over when you see her, I know you will. We'll be her legal guardians, to bring her up in a happy, loving home. And you'll be vicar of St Barnabas' Church again!'

'No, Isabel, I bloody well won't – sorry, father, but there's no God, or if there is, he's an uncaring sod.' Seeing his father's horrified look, he went on, 'D'you remember how we used to talk about Matthew Arnold, Dad, and how he described his loss of Christian faith in *Dover Beach*? Not only that, he foresaw all *this* – don't you see? *And we are here as on a darkling plain, swept with confused alarms of struggle and flight, where ignorant armies clash by night* – couldn't have put it better myself, and this from a man who died thirty years ago. I bet he upset *his* father, too.'

The words he spoke and the tone of voice that uttered them sent a shiver down Isabel's spine. She looked helplessly at her father-in-law, who rose from his chair.

'I think it's time for us to be going, Isabel. Paul will be needing you.' He spoke regretfully, but patted Isabel on her shoulder. 'Say goodbye to her, Mark.'

He turned away so that he did not see their parting, the chaste peck on the cheek that Mark gave his wife; she was thoughtful as they made their way out of the busy hospital where ambulances were arriving and departing. He hardly dared to ask her how she felt, but she anticipated him.

'It's going to be a challenge, Pa, but I've got every hope of success,' she said with quiet conviction, for she was resolved to lead this stony-faced atheist back to the man he had been – the idealistic young clergyman who had courted and won her.

March, 1918

When Isabel left North Camp with her baby, Grace Munday faced the biggest challenge of her life: to be strong for her father and to care for her mother by day and night, hiding her own deep sadness under a hopeful front, always encouraging, never flagging. Her throat might ache with silent sobs, and her eyes brim with unshed tears, and her only reward was her father's appreciation.

'You go and get your tea, Grace, and I'll sit with her for a bit. I've left today's paper for you to look at.'

'Is that you, Tom? What time is it?' asked Violet in bewilderment, waking up from a dream about Ernest. 'He was *here*, Tom, I saw him and spoke to him – I *know* he was here.' When the cobwebs of sleep vanished and she returned to full consciousness, she sighed and repeated her conviction that she would never see her son again. Tom grew weary with reassuring her that their son was alive and well, something he was beginning to doubt seriously. There had been no word of Ernest or Aaron since before Christmas, and Tom secretly feared that if one of them was killed, the other would lose the will to survive, and grow careless of his life. There were certain questions that Tom could not share with Eddie Cooper, who would probably not know what he was talking about. The close emotional friendship between the two young men was understandable in a time of war and danger, but if it persisted in civilian life to the exclusion of women, would it be considered normal? Consulting the dictionary, Tom looked up *Sodom*, 'a city destroyed by God for its depravity', and a Biblical reference was given. *Sodomy* was 'unnatural and unlawful intercourse, especially between male persons, a criminal offence'.

Tom closed the dictionary, remembering how Ernest had told him about the goings-on among some boys at Everham Council School, and how he, Ernest, had always avoided it. He was sure that Ernest would never practise sodomy – but might others suspect the relationship to be unnatural? After the war, if it ever ended, Tom felt fairly sure that Aaron would marry a girl of his own religion, but of Ernest he was less sure. But oh, for a sight of his son now, home to gladden their hearts and in time to say goodbye to his mother!

When a letter arrived from Isabel, Tom tore it open at once, eager for news of his son-in-law. It seemed that Mark had been very ill following a serious injury in the genital area, but was hoping to be discharged from hospital soon.

'He'll need feeding up and cheering up, Dad,' wrote Isabel. 'He's been suffering from what's called shell shock, but I have no doubt that with God's help I shall be able to cure him.'

Dear Isabel, what a treasure she was, Tom thought, and what courage she showed, when other women might have given way to self-pity.

But there was a second page to the letter. 'Unfortunately, because of the injury Mark has sustained, there can be no more children for us. However, we have the chance to adopt a dear little girl, now three months old, and quite surprisingly like Mum! We are so happy about this, and so grateful to Providence for such a precious gift at just the right time. I look forward to showing you Paul's little sister Rebecca as soon as is convenient.'

Now *this* was news to tell Violet, and Tom went straight upstairs with the letter. Grace was clearing away the breakfast tray, and straightening Violet's pillows.

'Listen to this, Violet – and you too, Grace – it's a letter from Isabel, and she's got wonderful news!' He read aloud the first part of the letter, concerning Mark's serious injury that had made him unable to father any more children.

Violet listened and sighed. 'I don't call *that* wonderful news, Tom. Poor Mark! What a tragedy to happen to a man.'

'But wait a minute, Violet, and listen to this: our Isabel isn't one to let the grass grow under her feet, and she's *adopting* a baby, a little girl who happened to be available through a Christian adoption agency. Her mother's one of these poor single girls who's had to give her up. Her name's Rebecca, or Becky, and Isabel says she looks like *you*, Violet! We must arrange for them all to come down and see us – Isabel and Mark, Paul and Becky!'

His wife gave a tired smile. 'Isabel's always been a good girl, and now she's proving to be a good wife and mother, a daughter to be proud of—'

Grace abruptly left the room. They heard her footsteps going downstairs, and a door slamming somewhere in the house.

'It's too bad of Grace,' said Mrs Munday with a frown. 'Always so selfish, and now can't even be glad for her sister's sake. How different they've always been.'

'I'll have a word with her later,' said Tom, who was not entirely convinced that it was just jealousy that had caused Grace's odd behaviour. He had seen the stricken look on her face as she fled the room. 'Come on, Violet my girl, let's have another smile from you!' he said as he pulled her up the bed.

'Yes, Tom, we must ask them all to come and see us again soon, as soon as Mark leaves hospital,' she said. 'But oh, for a sight of Ernest!'

April, 1918

A slow procession of vehicles crawled along what had been a well-worn track for farm carts from time immemorial: new guns going up to their positions, ammunition wagons full of shells, overloaded ambulances on their way to the clearing station, ration carts for the troops in the line. Now and then a cart would have to pull round a heap of wreckage that had once been men, horses and wagons, and all along the route stood the skeletons of shattered trees. Over and around them the guns boomed ceaselessly, a series of livid flashes. The procession had to pause when a shell dropped in front of them, and to speed up when one hurled down almost on top of them. Shell hole merged with shell hole, death traps for the walking wounded, of which Lieutenant Munday was one, tramping along with the others, his left elbow bleeding through a grubby bandage. He ignored the excruciating pain from it and from his blistered feet, he resisted the deathly fatigue and the pangs of hunger, and pressed forward towards the clearing station set up in a medieval church, for he had learnt that Lieutenant Pascoe was there among the badly wounded, awaiting transport to the base hospital at Cherbourg and the Channel ferry. Home!

After what seemed an interminable march, keeping pace with the slow-moving traffic, Ernest arrived at the church with a Red Cross flag flying from its tower. He took his place in a queue of men waiting for medical attention, and once inside the church he saw a sight he would never forget. All along the nave lay improvised stretchers leading right up to the choir and chancel, where half a dozen tired-looking surgeons in bloodstained overalls performed operations, many of them amputations, and orderlies carried away limbs in baskets. Men died before aid could get to them, and these were carried through to the sacristy; the all-pervading smell of chloroform and ether failed to mask the stench of bodies and blood.

An orderly beckoned Ernest out of the queue. 'Just yer arm, is it? 'Ere, take these dressin's and a clean bandage, and see to it yerself. There's no time 'ere for minor stuff – see that chap over there with the bad leg? Get 'im to do yer arm for yer, and you can do 'is leg for 'im. There'll be another ambulance soon, to take as many as they can to the 'ospital train, so get a move on!' As soon as the two reciprocal dressings were done, Ernest began to search the rows of wounded men groaning in mortal agony, calling on their mothers, begging for water and relief of pain. Lieutenant Pascoe was not among them.

'If 'e's a goner, 'e'll be through there in the sacristy,' said the orderly. 'Yer can 'ave a look if yer want.'

Ernest duly went through into the dimly lit, relatively quiet room, where sheeted figures lay closely packed on the stone floor. It was a mortuary, and Ernest began the task of lifting the sheets from the faces of the dead and replacing them when he did not find the face he sought. As he worked his way along the silent rows, the orderly called to him from the door.

'Hey, Lieutenant, there's another ambulance ready to go, and ye'd better get on it! Reckon yer pal's already gone on ahead, and ye'll find 'im waitin' for yer at the base 'ospital, I dare say!'

Ernest straightened himself up. It made sense, he ought to take the chance to get out of this hell and home to his mother who was seriously ill, according to the last letter from his father, and might not live to see him again. But there was one more row of corpses, and he had to know whether Aaron was among them or not. He shook his head, and the orderly shrugged and disappeared.

And as Ernest folded back the sheet of the last body but one, he gasped and gave a wordless cry; for it was Aaron's beloved face he saw, and Aaron's eyes looking at him, recognising him! Ernest realised that Aaron must have been deeply unconscious when he was mistaken for dead, but there was a spark of life left in him, his heart still beat weakly and his lungs took in shallow breaths of air. He could not speak, but his eyes said all Ernest needed to know.

'Aaron, my love.' That was all Ernest said as he gently raised his friend's head and shoulders to cradle in his arms. It seemed to him that Aaron had waited for him to come before taking his leave of the world.

It did not take long before the eyes dimmed and the last breath left the body. Aaron was dead, and Ernest laid him back on the floor and covered his face, giving thanks to whatever God looked down upon them, both Jew and Gentile, and for granting them this last farewell.

Ernest never got on the ambulance and did not board the hospital train. He left the church in the company of the sergeant whose leg wound he had dressed. Three others joined them as they began to walk back along the way they had come, hoping to join their platoon or any British military in the area. Here and there dead and dying horses and mules lay at the side of the road, a sight which never failed to move Ernest, outraged at the suffering of these innocent creatures; suddenly he was overcome by nausea, and fell to his knees.

'Go on, chaps, go on and good luck,' he muttered. 'Don't wait for me, my number's up.'

The other men hesitated, unwilling to leave him at the side of the road with the fallen horses, but not wanting to lose the chance of getting back to their battalions.

'There's a farmhouse further along,' said one of them. 'Let's take him there and let him rest till he's better.'

Two of them put Ernest's arms around their necks and made for the house, a ruin that had become a hiding place for enemy soldiers, as they realised too late when a tin-hatted German came running to meet them, followed by another. Both were carrying rifles, and challenged the group to stop and raise their arms above their heads. Ernest was forced to get up and march between his comrades to a section of railway line where open trucks awaited them. By now it was evening, and the prisoners faced a pitch-black night's journey into the heart of Germany.

Aaron had gone, and for Ernest too the war was over,

though he cared little now whether he lived or died; both of them were reported as 'missing' on the telegrams that were sent to the Mundays and the Pascoes.

Tom Munday opened the door to his daughter.

'Hallo, Dad. I came as soon as I could. Lady Neville sent old Mr Standish with her pony trap to meet me at Everham Station.'

'Isabel! Thank heaven, you're just in time. She's rallied all these weeks, but I think she's near the end now. She sleeps a lot o' the time, and Grace and I've been trying to give her sips of brandy and milk, but she can't swallow. Come and see her.'

Isabel took off her hat and jacket and followed her father upstairs to her parents' bedroom, where Violet Munday lay. Grace was sitting at her side, and rose.

'She may not know you, Isabel,' warned Tom. 'She's been wandering a lot lately.'

Isabel looked at her mother's closed eyes, her yellowish papery skin. One hand lay on top of the counterpane, and Isabel placed her own right hand over it.

'Mum – dear Mum, it's Isabel.' She saw her mother's eyelids flicker, and leant over to kiss her forehead. Grace left the room.

'Where's Tom?' whispered Violet, almost inaudibly.

'I'm here, Violet my love. Isabel's come to see you,' he said brokenly.

'And…is.., Ernest…too?'

'Yes, my love, he's on his way.' Isabel glanced quickly at her father, but he shook his head and put a finger to his lips.

'Ernest,' whispered Violet, and her mouth formed a half-smile before sinking back into sleep. Tom motioned Isabel to follow him out of the room.

'I'll send Grace up to her again,' he said. 'Oh, I'm that glad to see you, girl. It's a pity you've had to leave the babies behind.'

'Sally Tanner's looking after them. She's a wonderful help in every way. Life isn't easy, Dad, and old Mr Storey's staying on to look after the parish for the time being, because Mark isn't fit; in any case, he says he's giving up the church and looking for a post in a school as a teacher of English and Latin.'

'My poor girl,' said her father, shaking his head. 'And now you're losing your mother. You heard me telling her that Ernest was on his way home?'

'Yes – I take it you only said it to comfort her?' asked Isabel sadly.

'That's right. He's not coming. We got the telegram yesterday – he's missing.'

'Oh, Dad, what trouble! Good God, will the world ever be right again?' She flung her arms around his neck just as Grace came in with a tray of tea.

'There's some soup to heat up, and bread and cheese,' she said. 'Dad and I haven't felt like eating much.'

'I'm sorry I've hardly spoken to you, Grace,' her sister apologised. 'Thank goodness you're here for Mum and Dad.'

'Well, it stands to reason you can't be in two places at once,' said Grace with an edge of bitterness in her tone. Suddenly she burst out with, 'You've got two babies to look after, and I haven't got any!'

In the silence that followed this remark, Tom Munday understood. He wondered why he had been so slow to realise the truth. All he could feel now was relief that Violet would never know.

And she never did. Tom was by her side when she died in her sleep as dawn broke on the following day. Outside the birds had just begun to sing.

Chapter Seventeen

Spring, 1919

Tom Munday awaited his son's return with oddly mixed feelings. The wild rejoicings of the Armistice being over, a weary nation was settling into the new conditions of peace, the return of the survivors, including the prisoners of war, men who had so longed for 'England, home and beauty', only to find that the remembered England of their childhood had gone for ever. Many of them found that their families had no idea of the horrors they had come through, and their terrible memories could only be shared by their comrades-in-arms, too many of whom lay in unknown graves abroad, leaving behind a generation of women doomed to spinsterhood, women who had lost their husbands before they had even met them. Relief and rejoicing had largely given way to disillusionment, and Tom wondered how Ernest would adjust to a future without Aaron; he suspected that his son's life had probably been saved when he'd been taken prisoner, for without his beloved friend he might have become careless of his own safety and followed him into the dark.

Aaron's younger brother Jonathan was home from the war and living with his family in Whitechapel, for the Pascoes had returned to London after the Armistice. Tom had never shared his worries about the friendship between his son and Aaron, tolerated in the horrendous conditions of the war, but which could have been a very different story in civilian life: they might even have been prosecuted for committing a criminal offence. Now that would never happen, but Tom wondered what life would hold for Ernest, and felt powerless to advise him.

And there was Grace, his sad daughter who had come home to nurse her mother and now kept house for her father as any dutiful daughter should. Everybody remarked on the change in her; not yet twenty years old, she was no longer the bold, self-centred girl North Camp remembered; she had become quiet and thoughtful, and there was sometimes a wistfulness about her that made people wonder if she had lost a sweetheart in the war. When Tom was asked about this, he replied tersely that many a young woman had lost many a young man, and curiosity could bring them no comfort. Lady Neville made a genuine effort to interest Grace in good works such as she did herself, like parish visiting of the sick and housebound, but Grace had not Lady Neville's authority, and found it disheartening as often as not. Tom sometimes came upon her brushing away a tear, and ached with pity for her loss and loneliness, while respecting her secret, not revealing to her that he knew it.

And there was Isabel. His poor Isabel, too young to have to bear the burden she carried. At Easter 1919 there was a new incumbent in St Barnabas' vicarage, and the Storeys had moved to The Oaks, a boys' preparatory school in Surrey, where Mark taught English and Latin. His father had found the place and persuaded the headmaster to take Mark on; the post held the great advantage of a house adjacent to the school, where the

Storeys could live for a very low rent, in return for some extra-curricular duties towards the two-thirds of the boys who were boarders. Sally Tanner had begged to be allowed to move with the family, and had got a cleaning job in the school, where she worked very hard for a low wage, all of which she paid Isabel for her board. Old Mr Storey had returned to his Gloucestershire cottage with his wife, both of whom had aged ten years in the last four.

It had sounded like an ideal arrangement, but Tom Munday could read between the lines of his daughter's determinedly cheerful letters. She never once criticised her husband, but wrote that 'poor Mark sometimes finds the boys and other members of staff difficult; they have no idea of what he has been through,' and 'the dear children are a never-failing joy and comfort to me,' and 'Sally Tanner is a true friend, always ready to help me, even after a busy day at the school; fortunately the headmaster is most kind and understanding.'

And he'd better stay that way, thought Tom grimly, suspecting that Mark was only tolerated for the sake of his long-suffering young wife. He was careful about what he said to Grace, knowing that she would be upset at the thought of little Becky living in a tense and anxious atmosphere. Much as he missed his wife, Tom could only be thankful that she was spared the trials of their three grown-up children.

The only good news was that with the war over, there was a demand for handymen of all kinds, and carpenters and decorators like Tom and Eddie found themselves with more work than they could undertake. With the return of the surviving servicemen, Tom decided to take on two as apprentices, and advertised in the *Everham Weekly News*. He got several replies from which he chose a shell-shocked local boy,

Charlie Brown who lived with his parents, and one who lived in lodgings in Everham. Tom went to see Charlie, and took him on for a month's trial, then decided to drop in on the other at his lodgings, a Rob Nuttall who impressed Tom by his candour, admitting frankly that he had no home, having been brought up in the Everham Union, and missed the comradeship the army had given him. What did not impress Tom was the shabbiness of the lodgings, the smell of stale cooking fat and the suspicious attitude of the stout landlady.

"E ain't in no kind o' trouble, is 'e?' she asked Tom. "Cause if 'e 'is, 'e can beat it out o' here. There's plenty more respectable chaps lookin' for clean lodgin's.'

Tom told young Nuttall that he would be taken on for a month's trial, and that lodgings would be found for him in North Camp, to save him travelling four miles each way every day.

'Thank yer, Mr Munday, it's good o' yer, and I'll do me best for yer,' said the young man eagerly as they shook hands and agreed on an early starting date.

With the help of Lady Neville who usually exchanged a few words with Tom after the morning service at St Peter's, lodgings were found with a sad married couple whose son had been killed in the war, and young Nuttall presented himself at 47 Pretoria Road on the following Monday morning, with the other new apprentice.

Tom formally introduced them both to his daughter.

'Grace, this is Charlie Brown, somebody we all know in North Camp,' he said. 'He thinks he'd like to work with wood, now that he's home from the war. Charlie, this is my daughter, Miss Munday who keeps house for me.'

Grace nodded at the young man, who gave her a nervous smile.

'And this is Rob Nuttall who served in Flanders, and left the army as a corporal,' began Tom, but stopped when he saw his daughter staring in astonishment, a light of recognition dawning in her eyes.

'*Ratty*!' she exclaimed. 'Oh, Ratty, I mean Rob, how nice to meet you again! I've often wondered what happened to you after the Railway Hotel!' She stepped forward to shake his hand with genuine pleasure, while he stood wide-eyed and incredulous.

'Miss Munday! Miss Grace Munday! I've never forgotten—' He broke off, seeing Tom Munday's frown at her reference to the Railway Hotel, which had not been a happy episode in his younger daughter's life. Grace saw his look, and eagerly turned to face him.

'Don't worry, Dad, Ratty – sorry, I mean Rob – was the one good thing about that place, and it's wonderful news that he wants to be your apprentice. Oh, I'm really glad to see you, Rob – shall I put the kettle on for us all?'

'Yes, let's reminisce over a cup of tea,' said Tom Munday, having not seen his younger daughter so enthusiastic for a very long time.

Lieutenant Colonel Cedric Neville had returned to Hassett Manor in the new year, to find his mother closing the rooms that had been used as wards, and covering their furniture with dust sheets. Beds were returned to their donors, and the various modifications dismantled. It was a melancholy task, and her guilt over Letitia's death had taken its toll of Lady Neville. She told Cedric that Sir Arnold was asking her to come out and join him at the hill station in northern India.

'He says he doesn't think England would suit him, now that

he's been a district commissioner out there for so long,' she told Cedric. 'Besides which, your brother has met a girl he wants to marry, from among the ex-patriates there. Arnold thinks I'd enjoy life on the hill station; the weather's good, not too hot, and servants are plentiful.'

'It sounds like a good proposition, Mother. How do *you* feel about it?'

'I'm very attached to Hassett Manor and my life here,' she admitted. 'But since Letitia died, there isn't any real reason to stay – except for you, of course, Cedric. How do *you* feel? Do you think you'll marry?'

Cedric smiled and shrugged. 'I intend to farm the estate if possible, and of course I'd like you to stay, Mother, if that's what you wish. As to marrying, I haven't yet met a girl who's free to marry.'

'My dear Cedric, does that mean that you've been in love with a woman who's *not* free to marry?' asked his mother, searching his face. 'A *married* woman?'

'No, I'd never let that happen, Mother,' he replied seriously. 'I mean that the only girl who's ever moved me to that kind of admiration is very definitely married, so unless another one like her comes along, who's willing to take me on, I'll stay as I am!' He smiled as if at a joke, and Olivia Neville privately resolved to stay at Hassett Manor as long as Cedric remained there as a bachelor; if at some future time he married, perhaps *then* would be the right time to join her husband and elder son in their pleasant-sounding colonial life.

Ernest returned at Easter. He embraced his father and sister, both of whom were taken aback at how much older he looked; at twenty-five his hair was receding and his forehead deeply lined; he wore spectacles which partly hid the sadness in his eyes.

'Have you any plans as to the future, son?' asked Tom when the three of them were sitting at table after supper. 'You look as if you could do with a good long rest.'

'I'd like to return to Schelling and Pascoe's, Dad, if they've got a place for me,' Ernest replied, at which his father urged him to wait a while, thinking that his son probably needed to make a fresh start; the familiar office would surely awaken so many memories of Aaron. Nevertheless, Ernest cycled to Everham the very next day, and threw his arms around Mr and Mrs Schelling as lovingly as if they too were his parents. After the Pascoes had returned to London with Greta and Devora, Mr Schelling had managed the office alone with the aid of a female clerk who also acted as typist. Business had slumped.

Abel Schelling came straight to the point. 'Are you willing to come back to the firm, Ernest?'

'It's always been my hope, Mr Schelling, that Aaron and I would return and be as we were,' said Ernest, equally direct. 'And now that there's only me, and if you still want to take me on...'

'My dear boy, what a question! The Lord knows we want you back! You'll be junior partner in place of our dear nephew, and the firm's name will change to Schelling and Munday from now on.'

'Oh, Mr Schelling, how can I say what I...' began Ernest, but could not continue. Ruth Schelling came to his side and took his hand.

'We're so grateful to have you back, Ernest, and we'll be your uncle Abel and Aunt Ruth, as we were to Aaron. No more formality!'

'And all we need to know now is when you'll be ready to take up your position here,' said Abel Schelling.

Ernest looked from one to the other, and tentatively suggested, 'Tomorrow?'

Amid laughter and tears the date was agreed upon, and Ernest became one of the firm and the family. Within a month of his appointment he spoke seriously to his father and Grace about a suggestion made by the Schellings.

'Abel and Ruth want me to move into their home, Dad. I'd have Aaron's room and sleep in the bed that was his. And I'd like to do this, now that Aaron has…has gone, and I've been made a partner. Would you mind very much if I did?'

Tom Munday said he understood, though it hurt a little to know that his son now considered Aaron's relatives closer than his own. However, he concealed his feelings, and assured Ernest that whatever suited him best also suited his father; it was a relief to know that Ernest was looking forward and not back. He turned to Grace, and found her unexpectedly smiling.

'Think about it, Dad, we'll have Ernest's room, so why don't we ask Rob Nuttall to move in with us?' she asked. 'It'd be much more convenient for him, and homelier than lodgings – and we've got room enough. It'd be a convenient arrangement all round, don't you think so?'

Tom Munday saw the brightness of her face, and was willing to agree.

'You're quite right, Grace, it's a splendid idea, and I'll ask Rob how he feels about it, first thing tomorrow.'

Ernest flashed his sister a grateful look, though he addressed his father.

'Thank you, Dad, I'd have hated to seem ungrateful after all you've done,' he said, shaking his father's hand; and so the arrangement was settled to the satisfaction of all concerned. As for Rob Nuttall, when the idea was put to him, he took Grace's hand and pirouetted with her round the kitchen.

With Ernest settled at Schelling and Munday, and hearing Grace's peals of laughter at some of Rob's observations on their clients, witty but never malicious, Tom Munday began to feel that life held more hope and less anxiety. The coming of spring once again in all its vernal beauty seemed a sign of better times to come.

Until in May there came news of a calamity that plunged Tom into despair again. The Reverend Mr Saville, grave and deeply sympathetic, came knocking on the door one evening with a message he had received from the headmaster of The Oaks, to say that Mark Storey was dead, a victim of the virulent 'Spanish 'flu' that had ravaged Europe for the past year, finding easy victims among the undernourished, war-weary civilians. Just as it seemed to have burnt itself out, the infection suddenly struck at The Oaks at the start of the summer term, and boys and staff members had gone down with it in their dozens.

A hastily scribbled letter from Isabel followed with more details. 'I didn't tell you that the 'flu had broken out at the school, Dad, as I knew you'd worry,' she wrote, 'but circumstances have overtaken us. The epidemic became out of control, the sick-bay was full, and the headmaster advised parents to come and take their sons home, away from the infection. Poor Mark rather unwillingly agreed to sleep in a separate room so as not to bring it home to the children, but then he collapsed in front of a class he was teaching, and was brought to his room where he soon became feverish and delirious. I nursed him as well as I could, and Sally Tanner took complete charge of Paul and Becky – oh, Dad, I could never find words to praise her enough, she's been such a friend. In his weakened state, Mark couldn't fight off the infection, and he died within forty-eight hours. The Lord granted him the time and the lucidity to tell me he loved me, and to ask forgiveness for his changed character, and of course I told him that there was nothing to forgive, and soon after that he left us.'

Tears filled Tom Munday's eyes as he read on.

'And now he has gone, leaving me with the two dear children and my faithful Sally. The headmaster has told me that we can stay in the house until September, when a new occupant will arrive. I won't have a pension because I'm not considered a war widow, but dear Mark left me all his army pay, and his parents have sent me money which they say was due to me. But what will happen now, Dad? We can hardly land ourselves upon you or at the Storeys' cottage; I pray that a home, however humble, can be found for the three of us and Sally in the next three months.'

Of course I'll send her money, thought Tom, and of course she'll have to come here, it's her home. Rob will have to move out, and Grace will have to face living under the same roof as her child. Oh, God, we shall *have* to cope, and help my poor Isabel all we can.

Summer, 1919

Once the school summer holidays began, Devora Pascoe begged her parents to let her visit her Aunt and Uncle Schelling at Everham, because Ernest was living with them. Her mother asked fifteen-year-old Greta, who had just left school, to accompany her sister on the train down from Waterloo to stay for a week. The two girls set out excitedly, feeling very grown-up at travelling alone, and their Aunt Ruth was there to meet them at Everham station, smiling as Greta described the very different life they lived in London, and Devora was full of questions about Ernest.

When he heard of their coming visit, Ernest felt uncertain of the way he should behave to Devora, now that she was no longer a child, but at thirteen not yet grown up. Would she expect him to kiss her, or just shake hands? What would they talk about, if anything?

All his questions were answered in the moment that she ran towards him with outstretched arms. She so resembled her lost brother that Ernest's breath left him, and he could not speak, but held her in his arms; they stood together, their hearts overflowing, bound by their mutual love for Aaron.

'She is only a child as yet, Abel,' said Ruth Schelling, correctly reading her husband's thoughts. 'When she's older, she'll realise that he is much older than herself, and not of her religion.'

'That didn't make any difference to him and Aaron,' her husband answered, 'and neither did it stop Rachael from marrying a Methodist minister. Give them another four or five years to see how they feel about each other.'

'The Lord only knows where we shall all be by then,' she said with a shrug.

'Dear, dear Ernest!' whispered Devora in his ear, kissing his cheek. 'It's like having our brother with us again.'

Ernest still could not trust himself to speak, but kept her encircled in his arms as he would have held her brother. He knew that if he could ever love a woman, it would be this one, Aaron's sister Devora, when she had grown to maturity.

❧

Life went on at Hassett Manor, and Cedric's determination to farm the estate began to show rewards. He was up early each morning, and worked with a couple of farm labourers and a stockman, all three of whom had served in the war. He grew tanned under the summer sun, and easier in his mind as the terrible memories of the war years receded in the peace of the countryside. He bought himself a car, one of the latest Ford models so popular in the United States, and found it relatively easy to drive after manoeuvring a tank. His mother kept herself busy as usual with church activities and visiting the sick and bereaved in the parish of St Peter's.

'Poor Tom Munday, there's always something new to worry him,' she sighed on returning from church one Sunday. 'No sooner does Ernest come home than off he goes to live with that Jewish family at Everham where he works – and *now* what do you think, Tom's elder daughter has lost her husband with the 'flu, leaving her with two small children to bring up. I suppose they'll come to Tom for the time being, and their new apprentice will have to move out.'

Cedric looked up quickly. 'Do you mean Isabel Munday, the girl who married a vicar and went to live in an East London parish?'

'Yes, poor girl. She hasn't had an easy time. Tom told me some time ago that her husband had lost his faith, so couldn't continue as a vicar. He was teaching at some boys' school in Surrey when he caught the 'flu and died within two days. She's got a boy and a girl, both very young, poor little dears. You can imagine how Tom feels for his daughter, she was always a sweet, sensible girl. And they'll have no home, because the house went with Mr Storey's position as a master. Why, Cedric, why are you staring? Did you know her husband?'

'No, Mother,' said Cedric slowly, 'but we all know Isabel Munday. And we must help her and the children, of course we must. What about Hassett Lodge? Couldn't we get it refurbished and redecorated, and let them go there until they find somewhere permanent?'

Tom Munday was surprised to see Lady Neville standing on the doorstep that same Sunday afternoon, having spoken to her earlier after church. He pulled back the door for her to enter, and showed her into the parlour.

'I'll come straight to the point, Munday. You were telling me about your daughter Mrs Storey and her situation following her husband's death.'

'Er...yes, your ladyship,' said Tom awkwardly, wondering what was coming.

'It has occurred to me that I can offer her some practical help. The Hassett lodge has been empty since Sir Arnold's last bailiff left, and it shouldn't take long to have it made comfortable. It's not large, but perfectly adequate for one woman and her children. What do you think, Munday?'

'Why, I just don't know w-what to say,' stammered Tom, but his amazed delight showed in his eyes. 'I never expected you to...oh, that's wonderful news, your ladyship, and I-I'll write to Isabel today. It'll save her no end o' worry. But Lady Neville, why should you—?'

'Good, that's settled, then. I'm only too glad to be of help,' she said. 'Mrs Storey has always been a good, sensible girl, and this is something I can do for her.'

Tom could hardly take in this turn in his daughter's fortunes, and he also thought of Grace who would not now have to face the prospect of living under the same roof as her child, and having to control her maternal longing. And he spared a thought for Rob Nuttall, who would not have to leave 47 Pretoria Road and his growing friendship with Grace.

'I…I'll always be grateful, Lady Neville, for the interest you've taken in my family,' he said with real emotion.

'Don't mention it, Munday,' she said briskly. 'I should have thought about the lodge as soon as you told me this morning. I'd like to write to Mrs Storey, if you'll let me have her address.' Olivia Neville smiled a little guiltily, aware that the offer of the lodge had not been her own idea.

By the time Isabel Storey received the two letters, one from her father and one from Lady Neville, she already knew what they contained. Soon after five o'clock on that Sunday evening, she opened the door to Cedric Neville who handed her a bouquet of red and white roses, some of them still in bud.

'Mr Neville!'

'Good afternoon, Mrs Storey, I'm here to offer my sincere condolences on your loss. May I come in for a word with you?'

'Of course, yes, please come in,' she said, rather flustered, and showed him into the living room. Sally Tanner in the kitchen heard the arrival of a visitor, and put the kettle on. Cedric came face to face with two little children who looked up with interest at this tall man who was giving a bunch of flowers to their mummy.

'Please take a seat, Mr Neville. This is my son, Paul, who's two years old, and this is little Becky, just eighteen months. We adopted her. Say good afternoon to Mr Neville, Paul.'

'Good af'noon, mister,' said Paul, glancing up at his mother for her approval, and she patted him on the head.

'They're lovely children, Mrs Storey,' said Cedric Neville,

smiling at their solemn little faces. 'This is very different from our last meeting at Bethnal Green.'

'Oh, yes, what a shock you gave me, standing there in your uniform, and I thought you'd come to tell me that Mark was… and now, of course, it's too true.'

'I'm so very sorry, Mrs Storey, and that brings me to the reason for my visit. When my mother and I heard the news from your father, we immediately thought of the Hassett lodge, and wondered if you and the children could make use of it as a home until your circumstances are easier – that is to say, of course, that you could remain there as long as you care to, reasonably near to your father.'

He heard her quick in-drawing of breath, and continued, 'Would it solve a problem for the time being? Oh, Mrs Storey, please don't distress yourself.'

For Isabel had covered her face with her hands. He waited for a moment and gently asked, 'Will this be acceptable to you, Mrs Storey?'

At that moment Sally entered with a tray of tea, and set it down on a low table. Isabel looked up, and caught Sally's silent question, *Shall I stay?*

'Thank you, Sally. If you'd just take the children and give them their tea, I'd be most grateful.' Sally nodded and discreetly retired with Paul and Becky. Isabel began to pour out two cups of tea with trembling hands.

'Merely to say *thank you* to your mother must sound very inadequate, Mr Neville,' she said. 'I simply can't believe it, that she should make such an offer. It's an answer to a prayer I would never have dreamt of.'

'I'll pass on your answer to my mother, Mrs Storey, and I know she'll be very happy to have two such delightful children in the lodge. She'll be making excuses to call on you every day!'

There was a short silence, and then Isabel asked rather shyly, 'Mr Neville, there is one request I'd like to make, if I may.'

'Certainly, Mrs Storey, ask me anything you like.'

'You've just seen Mrs Tanner, the very good friend I've brought with me from Bethnal Green.'

'Yes, I remember her from when I saw you there – a very capable woman.'

'I wonder if your mother would allow me to bring her to… to Hassett Lodge with me. You see, she's—'

'Say no more, Mrs Storey, she would be more than welcome.'

'Thank you for that, too. Lady Neville has always taken a kind interest in my family, and this is the kindest offer of all. Please thank her so very much. And I must ask you to offer her my belated condolences on the death of her daughter, your sister Miss Letitia.'

'And I must offer mine on the death of your mother, Mrs Storey. It's been a time of many upheavals and bereavements, but now that horrible war is over at last, we can start looking forward again.'

She smiled, and a few more pleasantries were exchanged before he rose to his feet and said he had better be going. She saw him to the door, and watched as he got into the smart black Ford; he waved to her as he started up the engine.

'Goodbye, Mr Neville,' she called, waving back at him.

'Au revoir, Mrs Storey!'

When she returned to the living room, Sally was clearing away the tea tray.

'I 'eard that bit about me comin' to this lodgin' 'ouse, Mrs Isabel. It was good o' yer to ask, and good o' him to say yes.'

'I couldn't manage without you, Sally,' replied Isabel simply, and added, 'His mother has always been good to our family. She actually lent her carriage for me to ride to church with my father on my wedding day.'

'She sounds a great comfort to yer, Mrs Isabel,' replied Sally, adding silently to herself, 'Sounds more'n just a good turn to a war widder an' 'er kids. Reckon that feller's got plans of 'is own, or my name ain't Sally Tanner.'

And out of delicacy to poor Mrs Isabel, she kept these thoughts to herself.

August, 1919

Tom Munday sat on his usual bench in the Tradesmen's Arms with Eddie Cooper, reviewing their family fortunes since the end of the war.

'My three have all suffered as a result of it, but they've all come through,' said Tom. 'In fact it's made them stronger, and they're now in a fair way to making good lives for themselves. Violet would've been proud o' them!'

Eddie smiled, for he too had seen his only daughter married to a kind husband who loved her and looked upon her baby daughter as his own. 'Sidney'll get his reward soon, 'cause my Mary's expectin' again in October,' he said. 'Your Isabel's got two, hasn't she?'

'Yes, little Paul and Becky. I see them nearly every day now they're at Hassett Lodge.'

'Shame about her husband dyin' off suddenly like that, after comin' through the war,' said Eddie, echoing the thoughts of many in North Camp. 'What d'yer reckon she'll do now?'

'Well, Lady Neville says they can have the lodge to live in

until…until circumstances change,' said Tom cautiously. 'It gives her a bit o' breathing space.'

'They say young Cedric's become quite the gentleman farmer since he came back. Not my business, Tom, but d'yer think 'e's got 'is eye on your…er…?'

'Mustn't say anything, Eddie, seein' as poor Mark Storey's hardly been gone three months. And he wasn't the man he'd been before he went to the front, in fact my Isabel's had a hard time of it, though she's never complained. Keep it to yourself, Eddie, we don't want to start the gossips off yet.'

' 'Course I will, mum's the word,' said Eddie, concealing his amusement, for gossip was already rife in North Camp. 'And what about that new apprentice o' yours, the one you've taken in? Comin' along all right, is he?'

'Yeah, he's a good lad,' said Tom, 'doing well for a boy brought up in the Union.' He drank the last of his bitter, and set down the glass.

'Better be going,' he said. 'Got a job over at the Methodist church at South Camp tomorrow, and young Rob can come along and try a bit o' woodcarving. So long, Eddie. Hope it all goes well with your Mary.'

Walking home in the mild air of a late summer evening, Tom pondered on his three children. It looked as if life would turn out well for them, as it had for him and Violet. He thought back to his first meeting with her at Hassett Manor, he an apprentice carpenter and she a dark-eyed, rosy-cheeked housemaid.

'We didn't make a bad job o' bringing them up, Violet, my love,' he whispered to the red sky above Hassett Manor. 'Hah! We little knew then that our first daughter was goin' to be the lady o' that house. We've come full circle!'